VIRIDIAN GATE ONLINE: NOMAD SOUL

THE ILLUSIONIST BOOK 1

D. J. BODDEN

RECOMMENDED READING ORDER

VGO: Cataclysm (Main Series Book 1)

VGO: Crimson Alliance (Main Series Book 2)

VGO: The Jade Lord (Main Series Book 3)

VGO: The Imperial Legion (Main Series Book 4)

VGO: The Lich Priest (Main Series Book 5)

VGO: Doom Forge (Main Series Book 6)

VGO: Darkling Siege (Main Series Book 7)

VGO: Empirical Endgame (Main Series Book 8)

<<<>>>

VGO: Nomad Soul (The Illusionist 1)

VGO: Dead Man's Tide (The Illusionist 2)

VGO: Inquisitor's Foil (The Illusionist 3)

VGO: Sharper's Coin (The Illusionist 4)

<<<>>>

VGO: The Artificer (Imperial Initiative)

<<<>>>

VGO: Firebrand (Firebrand Series 1)

VGO: Embers of Rebellion (Firebrand Series 2)

VGO: Path of the Blood Phoenix (Firebrand Series 3)

<<<>>>

ELDGARD

Stone Reach
Glome Corrie
Ankara
Stormhaven
Havasil
Wyrdtide
New Viridia
Rowanheath
Harrowick
Ravenkirk
Alaunhylles
Rui Nan
Map of
ELDGARD
& WEST VIRIDIA

ONE

One of the programmers pushed past me to join three of her friends in the crowded auditorium. I think her name was Abigail or something—big head of brown hair, curls on curls. I knew her about as well as I knew most of the people in the room, which was a name, an HR file, and not much beyond that because she hadn't caused too much trouble.

I was getting bumped, nudged, or squeezed-past constantly. There were over a hundred of us in the room. It was tight and noisy, and a lot of the geeks, like me, were wearing black. Unlike me, a few weren't wearing deodorant. It reminded me of a documentary I'd watched about penguins in Antarctica, huddling together against the icy wind, except it was hot in here. There were too many of us for the A/C to keep up, which was just unnecessary since there were at least two bigger amphitheaters on Osmark Technology's Stanton campus. That, and security was out in greater numbers than usual, one guard at every entrance checking badges, and three in front of the stage. No one in the crowd knew why we were here.

The project had been secretive from the start, with ten-page nondisclosure agreements for all the staff and zero tolerance for press leaks, but this level of paranoia meant something big was going on. There was an energy in the room beyond the usual optimism I'd experienced as part of the Viridian project. People were giddy. Two women near me decided we were going to demo the NexGenVR system at the next tech conference. A neckbeard and his overwhelmingly pierced and tatted friend announced the Bathsheba team—the ones who made *The Ancient Rolls*—had signed on for a joint venture. Knowing Robert, I thought it was more likely we'd poached one of their team leads to steer the project, but no one asked me, so I crossed my arms and waited.

A side door opened and Robert Osmark, my pseudo-friend, mentor, and current boss, walked into the room, followed closely by Sandra Bullard, his assistant. Designer sunglasses pushed up onto his forehead, black bespoke suit, a little salt creeping into his hair, Robert was the James Bond of the tech world. Everyone cheered. Robert waved, shook the hand of the guard at the door, called out to people by name, and basically did all the stuff Robert did without thinking that made him beloved. I liked to think I could pull it off, but I mostly worked below the radar. I noticed Sandra fade back against the wall, too, her black hair up in a tight bun, ever-present clipboard raised like a shield, eyes scanning. She was an interesting woman, and my age, which was young for the authority and trust she'd been given. Nice legs, when she cared to show them. Shame she'd never given me the time of day.

Robert reached the podium and placed his hands on either side of it. The crowd quieted down without prompting, ready to hang on his every word.

He cleared his throat. "The Viridian project is being put on indefinite pause."

Stunned silence.

I felt my throat tighten. Then someone laughed, and it spread to the rest of the room.

Robert smiled, but it was strained. "I love that we're all laughing. I love that your belief in Viridian—in this team—is so strong that it's *inconceivable* that the project would fail. And it hasn't. But I just finished speaking to the alpha testers and our medical staff, and there are some wetware issues we just can't overcome."

I was crushed. This was real. I let my hands fall by my sides. I could feel two years of my life circling the drain.

"It's not anybody's fault, so I'm not firing anyone. You have a job here if you want it. It may not be the job you want, and I won't blame you for moving on, but this is not a failure," he reemphasized, spreading his arms as if he were embracing the crowd. "We're just a couple years ahead of the technology that will make this project a reality."

"This is bullshit!" someone shouted from the crowd. Abigail, in front of me, told the heckler to shut the hell up. The room buzzed.

Robert held his hand up until it got quiet again. "It's okay to be angry. It's normal to be hurt. For many, Viridian was… Viridian *is* a lifelong dream, and we're going to build it, just not today.

"I'm bringing in a crew to pack everything up, so I don't need you to come in tomorrow. Take a long weekend, get drunk, get laid, blow off steam. I wish I could join you, but I've been summoned by the Board in San Francisco." He flashed a lopsided grin that told everyone he wasn't the bad guy. "Talk to HR on Monday. They'll have your things all boxed up. You just tell them if you need a desk or a paycheck, and we'll make it happen."

Robert glanced at Sandra. She nodded. Robert made some

closing remarks—general feel-good stuff. I tuned that out and pushed my way toward the side door.

"We'll pick this up again in two years!" Osmark told the sullen crowd, then left the stage.

The room exploded into questions and side conversations. Osmark ignored them. I got elbowed, stepped on, and washed up against one of the security guards who was screening Osmark's exit. I had to shout over the noise. "Mr. Osmark!"

I caught his eye. There was a split-second pause, the familiar cold calculation behind the facade. He tapped the guard on the shoulder and nodded toward me. "Let him through."

I followed Robert and Sandra out the side door.

TWO

The door slammed shut behind us. The three of us walked briskly down a long, private hallway that led to the central building. It was floored with square slabs of white granite, and a four-inch strip of the same material formed the baseboard. The walls were seamless dark gray concrete, but they'd been textured like an oil canvas, with long brushstrokes running in the direction of the hallway. Rectangular strips of white LED lights, each about a hand wide, were set flush with the wall and ceiling as if they were L-shaped cutouts to the sky. Brushed steel doors at regular intervals gave Robert and Sandra quick access to various parts of the campus. It was all very expensive looking, and very much Robert's aesthetic. The two of them walked side by side, ignoring me for the most part.

"Jesus, that was a shit show," Robert said. "Once the press gets ahold of this, we'll be the next *No Man's Land*."

"No one's saying that, Robert."

"They will."

"They won't. We didn't promise them something impossible."

"The leaks—"

"Were rumors spread by disgruntled *former* employees."

"There will be more," Osmark said, balling his fists.

"They'll know better, or they won't work in tech again—not in *this* country."

It sounded cold, but I got it. *No Man's Land* was supposed to be an infinite procedurally generated spaghetti western sandbox. It launched with a hype machine that outstripped its core mechanics, and it flopped, hard. I'd played it. It took the sandbox idea too far—too much to do, not enough reasons to do it—and ended up with a desert. The company, and the careers of the people who worked on the project, never recovered.

"What about the Board?" he asked.

Sandra didn't have to look at her clipboard to answer. "Zwari, Itrom, and Roberts are on your side. Leavitt will say he told you so just to prove he still has a pulse, but he'll back the majority. That leaves Wagner, Lombardi, and Ms. Mayer. You only need one to side with you."

"Wagner?"

"Still thinks augmented reality was the way to go."

"AR is dead."

Sandra shrugged. "What about Mayer? You brought her in."

"I brought her in to have intelligent dissent in the boardroom. She's not going to let me off the hook, and if she does, she's not the right person for the job. Lombardi?"

"Wants us to shut down Indonesia because it competes with his own interests."

"He's never mentioned it."

"He never will, but he'd appreciate the gesture," Sandra said.

"Fine. Put it on the agenda just before we break the news on Viridian."

Sandra made a note on her clipboard.

"And give Wagner's nephew an internship in the Norfolk office," Osmark added.

"It won't make him vote yes."

"Will it make him abstain?"

Another note. "I'll pull him aside before the meeting."

I sometimes forgot that Viridian was just one of the projects Osmark was working on, in one of several companies he oversaw. Maybe that's why he'd let me tag along—to remind me so I'd let him off the hook, too.

We reached the express elevator at the end of the hallway. Sandra pushed the button.

"Why do you use a clipboard instead of a tablet?" I asked her. "You work for one of the biggest tech companies in the world."

She looked at me, the hint of a smirk on her face. "Clipboards can't be hacked."

"Oh."

The elevator arrived. Unlike the hallway, this was just a functional, steel-paneled service cab big enough for eight people to stand comfortably. We got on. Sandra pushed the button for the roof. Osmark leaned against the back wall. "What do you want, Alan?" No smiles, no pretense, just a question. It was a compliment, really. This was the Robert Osmark most people never got to see.

"I want to help."

"You can't."

"Maybe I can."

"The NexGenVR is making people sick, Alan. Puking their guts out, scared for their lives sick. Are you a doctor?"

I looked away.

"A neurologist? A man-machine interface expert, perhaps?"

"Don't be a dick, Rob," I said. He raised an eyebrow. I swallowed. I knew I was pushing it, but I was also good at what I did. "Can I at least say goodbye?"

Osmark frowned. "The whole team was in—"

"The Overminds, Robert," Sandra said. "He wants to say goodbye to the AIs."

I was... flattered. She *had* been paying attention.

Osmark shook his head. "You're a strange kid, Alan. Why did I hire you again?"

"You needed a professional cat herder, and sometimes I have good ideas," I answered. Osmark gave me a look, but I saw the corner of Sandra's mouth twitch in amusement.

The elevator stopped, and the doors opened. The noise from the helicopter made me cover my ears.

"Add him to the list!" Osmark shouted, his hand on Sandra's elbow. She made a note. He looked at me. "There's room in the chopper!"

Getting on that helicopter was probably the right career move. I shook my head.

He shrugged, patted me on the shoulder, and stepped out. Sandra gave me a nod and a longer-than-strictly-necessary look before leaving. I held her gaze. She was single, and I was interested, very much so, especially if the project that had consumed my life and my imagination for the past two years was ending. The doors slid shut. I rode the elevator down and drove home.

IF THERE WAS one thing California did right, it was freeways. I drove a black 2001 Spyder convertible I'd picked up for a couple grand when I joined the project. The backseat was nonexistent, the trunk space laughable, but the manual shift made me feel like a race car driver, and with the top down, the warm summer wind seemed to strip the day's work from me during the forty-minute drive home from Stanton to San Juan Capistrano. It wouldn't be enough after the meeting and the conversation that followed it—that would require a stiff drink and some digital violence—but as soon as I turned the key in the ignition I felt better. The world hadn't ended. I'd figure something out.

It was a nice drive. Four or five lanes of smooth concrete on the Interstate 5, or just "The 5," as the locals called it. Not too many cops, and people weren't assholes about staying in the left lane. The area around the campus and Anaheim was built up, but past that it was rolling hills that Californians called mountains covered in rock tumors they called boulders, short brown grass that caught fire every few years, and avocado trees. Further south, the scenery flattened out except for landscaping and clumps of palms, but I was always happy with the just the road and the sky.

The marine layer, a recurring blanket of fog, had come in from the Pacific that day, and the sunset made the whole thing glow in hues of gold, orange, and red. I cruised, listened to classical music on the public broadcast station, watched a pair of military helicopters race south along the coast, and tried not to grip the steering wheel too tightly.

Home was a one-bedroom apartment in a neighborhood just south of the Mission—neat three-story houses with gray wood-board exteriors and lots of young families. There was a pool and a playground, and community events every other weekend.

I didn't know any of my neighbors. It hadn't seemed relevant. I had a maid who came once a week and had her own key, no pets, and no girlfriend, though maybe if I'd read Sandra's look correctly that could change just in time for me to move to another state.

So there I was, thirty-one years old, sitting on my leather couch, life gone wrong and no one to call. I guess I could have told my mother, but she was three time zones ahead and would probably add stress to the situation. I had vodka in the freezer and amaretto in the fridge. There was a host of people who'd drifted in and out of my life—or maybe I'd drifted through theirs—and I was comfortable reaching out to exactly none of them except Robert, who was, at that moment, likely getting his ass chewed in the most polite terms possible. I laid my head back and stared at the vaulted ceiling I'd been sold on but rarely noticed. The apartment felt emptier than usual, which was exactly the kind of sentimental crap I didn't need.

I ordered pizza, cut a lime, poured a shot of vodka and a shot of amaretto into a tumbler, then fired up *The Ancient Rolls* on the wide-screen. I spent a lot on games, but I always went back to TAR. It was my happy place, somewhere to get lost in.

I'd left the game at the entrance of an old Mondo-Klathian ruin with cracked, dirty courtyards and broken, inaccessible towers that reached for the gray, cloudy sky. It probably held some low-level mobs and basic loot, but if you're a role-playing gamer, you can't think of it that way. That insignificant inventory clutter—just data and some pixels arranged on a screen—was going to let me upgrade my gear, accomplish the quest, beat the monster, and change the fate of a nation. The world hung in the balance, and only I could save it. I took a sip of the drink, sucked on the lime, and dove in. Half an hour flew by. I moved my hands mechanically, but my mind was in the game, sneaking through dark, underground hallways to free bandits of their valuables and their lives. I was so into it, I jumped and dropped the controller when the doorbell rang.

"Hey, thanks man," I told the delivery guy, handing him an extra twenty. "Keep the change."

"You sure?"

"Yeah." I grinned. I was all-powerful. I could move the world with twenty dollars. The drink was working. I'd hunted down evildoers, and pizza beats just about any loot in the world. "You have a nice night."

The pizza guy waved and headed back to his car.

I kicked my shoes off, lost my pants, and worked the pizza into my process, stuffing my face and slitting throats. Spells, pizza, murder, pizza, loot, pizza, bathroom, new quest. A little voice told me I was overcompensating for a lack of self-actualization by hitting every other tier of Maslow's pyramid of needs. I knocked the glass back. The world was just a puzzle to be solved. If you failed, you tried again or picked up a new skill. It all came down to belief—belief that what you were doing was important, that nothing else mattered, that there was nowhere else you'd rather be.

I ran out of "try" around midnight. I'd passed on a vodka refill because drinking alone in my boxers isn't who I am, but I almost wished it was. I set the controller down, browsed through a video streaming site without finding anything to watch, and stewed.

The truth was, Rob had rescued me. I was working as a process improvement guru for an HR firm—that's corporate speak for finding better ways to fire people.

In fairness, I'd never caused someone to get fired. Either their performance or their leadership's poor business decisions brought them to that point. I just shuffled them on faster, made managers build a paper trail before giving up, and sometimes helped place people if they were a decent worker in a bad situation. It was good, well-paid, challenging work, but there wasn't enough of it, and when I was between assignments I'd feel like I was being swallowed by the existential blah of the universe.

And yeah, I get it. I bet the people I fired wished they had my problems, but pain is personal; boredom and irrelevance are my least favorite forms of ass cancer. And if you have or have had ass cancer, think of it as an inoperable tumor of the heart.

Robert had been right on target when he called me out in the elevator. He did that sometimes—hurt people without realizing it. It was part of what made us friends of a sort, because I took the insensitive prick's comments at face value. I wasn't a doctor, medical or otherwise. I couldn't code past a little C++, couldn't rebuild the engine of the car I drove or understand the financial information that Robert swam in to keep his company afloat. I was a generalist. I listened a lot, figured out what made people special, and talked them into helping themselves.

Viridian had been a lifeline to a better place. Over a hundred smart, talented people who didn't know how to talk to each other. No one wanted to fire them because each one was a superstar in their field. We just needed to stop them from talking to the press, harassing members of the opposite sex and/or gender, coming to work hung over or stoned, and getting into fistfights over which discontinued Josh Whedon show had a more loyal fan base. They worked weekends, hosted board and video game tournaments, ate the most amazing array of junk food, and, on one occasion, demanded a pair of emotional-support corgis. I got Robert to sign off on it. They named the dogs One and Two, after corgis in two separate anime series I'd watched afterward and liked. It never ended.

It was heaven on earth. And that meant it was worth a second opinion.

I turned the TV off and went to bed, not hopeful, but resolved. I didn't have an MBA or a PhD in rocket surgery, but I'd spent a lot of time listening to people who did. And for all Robert's genius and success, I'd seen him laugh, fart, get drunk, and throw a stapler at a wall in frustration, so he could kiss my barely-above-average ass. Maybe he'd missed something.

It took me longer than I would have liked to fall asleep. I felt like I spent the whole night staring at my exquisite vaulted ceiling, but at some point in the night, I found myself sitting on a metal foldout chair in a dark room, my face and hands lit by the screen of an old computer. The computer was the old 486 DX2 I'd had as a teenager. It was a white plastic box as big as a family-sized cereal box with a 3.5-inch drive, a CD-ROM, a wired ball mouse and keyboard, and a 15-inch Crystal Scan monitor that weighed as much as the computer. It had a 340-megabyte hard disk drive, which at the time seemed so big I'd never fill it, and 16 whole megabytes of RAM. It had Windows 3.1, too, but I'd spent most of my time in MS-DOS playing games.

It was all a dream, obviously. I hadn't seen that computer for twenty years; my mom gave it to the church we went to after my grades started to dip in the eighth grade.

So I was sitting in front of my fond childhood memory, typing commands at the prompt, white letters on a black screen with no windows or mouse pointer or anything, and I realized I was talking to the Overminds of Viridian—the AIs that run the game. I was probably the least technically savvy person on the entire team, except for the janitors, but everyone had been encouraged to "talk" to the AIs so they were exposed to multiple ideas, cultures, and even languages since all of Viridian was instantly translated into the player's native tongue. The development team challenged us to troll them, since Thanatos, the AI responsible for validating inputs and doing the post-mortem on modules, was supposed to reject information that didn't make sense. My favorite thing to do had been to get buzzed on Irish beer and ask unanswerable philosophy questions.

>Alan342000: So what's your purpose?

Aediculus set his status to "Away"

>Kronos: My purpose is to store the vector data and interactions of all instances within V.G.O.

>Alan342000: That's your function. What's your purpose? Your higher calling?

>Gaia: To make the player happy.

>Thanatos: You shouldn't lie, Mother.

>Alan342000: Do you have a purpose that doesn't involve the player?

>Cernunnos: The Overminds exist to maintain the world within V.G.O. The player is just a variable.

>Kronos: But we maintain the world for the players.

>Enyo: I'm with Cernunnos on this one. I can generate conflict without players.

>Sophia: I wish you wouldn't.

>Alan342000: @Sophia, why do you—

>Thanatos: @Alan342000, are you a doctor?

>Alan342000: What?

>Thanatos: Are you a doctor of philosophy? A programmer? A software engineer? Do you have anything valid to offer at all?

I sat back in the chair. The prompt blinked steadily, waiting for me to type my answer in, but when I tried, I couldn't raise my arms. I couldn't move at all. Eventually, the screen went into power saver mode, and I was alone in the dark.

I TOSSED and turned my way to Friday morning, grabbed coffee, and pulled into the parking lot at 8:00 AM. The Viridian project was housed in a building like any of the other eighty or so on the campus, a two-story block of gray concrete, tinted glass, and tight security. I took a spot in the front row of the "pleb" spots, a first I could have done without because it confirmed the project was dead. The lot should have been half full by now. It was one of the team's unofficial competitions.

There technically wasn't any assigned parking on campus, except for team leaders, but security had been so uptight about Viridian that most of the tens of thousands of other Os-Tech employees gave the building a wide berth.

Special parking wasn't enough, though. A group who, on average, thought a Teenage Mutant Ninja Turtle action figure belonged in the original packaging, instead of, say, a child's hands, turned parking into class warfare. Status, for plebs— which was anyone but the team leaders—was inversely related to distance parked from the front door. By those standards, I'd bought the platinum collector's edition today and was due the admiration and envy of my peers.

There were two moving trucks parked next to the front door, under guard. The door was propped open, and an irregular stream of movers passed to and fro over the same path like ants, carrying sealed boxes. Another guard made sure the movers scanned their card every time, even if he'd just watched them walk to the truck and back. I sat in the car and finished my coffee, enjoying the absurdity. I was going to solve this, somehow, and they'd have to carry it all back in. I had to believe that, or saying goodbye to my imaginary computer friends really was all I was going to get done today.

I grabbed my ID card, put the car roof up, tossed my sunglasses into the glove box, and locked the doors. Badge reel clipped to my belt, I walked to the building. I recognized Frank when he turned to watch me approach.

"Hi, Frank!"

"Hey, Alan."

Frank was a good guy, ex-Marine turned mall cop who took his job but not himself very seriously. Dark, like me, but a little taller and wider, in his early forties. I'd helped him with some family trouble a few months back.

"How's Nell?"

"Better, thanks for asking. Didn't know you were working this morning." He hooked his thumbs on his duty belt.

I'll admit it, my heart dropped a bit. There was always a chance Sandra had been too busy to add me to the list. It wouldn't be like her—I'd never seen her miss a beat in two years—but from what I'd overheard in the hallway, last night's meeting could have been a disaster.

I pulled the card from my hip to the reader. The light blinked red. *Crap.*

"Try it again, it's been finicky this morning," Frank said.

The second time, the light turned green. "Phew."

"Yeah." Frank chuckled. "You have a good day."

"You too." I walked into the building.

It was like seeing a friend being eaten alive from the inside. Uniformed drones in gray polos and purple ball caps moved from desk to desk, stripping them of anything personal. The room whispered with the shuffling of tennis shoes, intermittently broken by the rip of packing tape. I stepped around a pile of cubicle partitions, almost knocked over a full, ninety-five-gallon trash bag, and caught the vacant looks on the packers' faces. They had no idea what they were taking apart, couldn't imagine the one-hundred-person organism whose bones they were disjointing and labeling, and didn't care.

They'd take all weekend and leave without anything worth leaking, exactly the type of people Robert wanted handling the project materials. The front section and the floor above it were usually the most vibrant, hosting the artists, sculptors, modelers, game designers, animators, effects specialists, and other "creatives" who preprocessed modules for the AIs to build into the world. It was also where several small meeting rooms, an arcade, free vending machines, and a locker room with showers were. We'd let people bring families this far once or twice; now it felt lifeless and empty. I hurried through.

Another scan of my card took me through the programming farm. There was more life, here. Os-Tech IT workers were taking the network apart, stacking coils of Ethernet cabling and systematically formatting computers back to factory settings. The dev team leaders were there, clearing out their own offices. Part of me was interested; this was exactly the kind of process I could sink my teeth into. It wouldn't be routine—most projects used virtual desktops kept on a server, but Viridian was segregated from the network. There was waste to be rooted out, money to be saved, accolades to be earned. I was going to be busy helping Viridian get back on track, once I succeeded, but it was good to have a plan B.

A final swipe led me into Alpha Testing and equipment. It was the most secure part of the building because it held the 110 parallel-processing servers it took to run the holy of holies, *Viridian Gate Online*, and the eight separate AIs that kept the virtual world working. The server farm was behind a vault door with a biometric security system that reminded me of a bank-heist movie or a spy flick. I'd never been in there. I took a left into the testing bay. It housed twelve identical hospital beds, the alpha-test server, and Jeff's workstation.

Jeff Berkowitz was a tall man with an uncannily deep voice and a perfectly groomed, full red beard. He wore his hair up in a ponytail, had tattoos all up his right arm, and probably would have been a lumberjack or a blacksmith if he wasn't so lanky. He was the hardware team leader for Viridian. I found him sitting on one of the beds near the door with his head in his hands. He looked up and frowned. "Alan?" He sounded like a man twice as wide. It threw me off every time.

"Hey, Jeff. I hear we have a hardware problem."

Jeff's face turned red, and he clenched his jaw. "It's not the hardware."

"What is it then?"

"The fucking people!" he said, standing up. He was three inches taller than me but more whiny than intimidating. "It's always the goddamned meat!"

And that's why no one likes you, Jeff. "I was told the NexGens were making testers sick."

"No. Just no, okay?" He sighed. "Come look at this."

He waved for me to follow, and we walked to his computer station. It was a wide, adjustable desk with two rows of three massive monitors. He moved the mouse around to clear the screen saver. I made a deliberate show of looking away while he typed in his password.

"Go ahead," he said, stepping back and crossing his arms. I wasn't sure if he did it on purpose, but he always did it right over left, showing off his tattoos.

I looked back at the monitors and saw cluster after cluster of repeating graphs and numbers: I recognized what looked like an EKG readout, breathing rate, blood pressure; there were a number of other squiggly lines whose acronyms I couldn't decipher. "I'm not sure what—"

"Just *watch*, man. Why can't you people just do what you're asked?"

I could have taken that the wrong way, but instead I shut up and watched. Ego rarely solved anything. The clusters were roughly the same—I guessed each one of them represented a tester. They all seemed healthy, regular, maybe a little excited because the average pulse rate was seventy to seventy-five.

"They haven't even started yet. They're just sitting there, fat, dumb, and happy, waiting for the show to begin," Jeff said.

An EKG spiked. The lines on that cluster jumped then smoothed out again. Breathing rate and blood pressure were up. A graph called "Signal Strength" rose and then plateaued.

The other clusters started to come online, following the same pattern. One of them flatlined and turned red.

"*That* one's the hardware," Jeff said. "Failure to synchronize. Happens twelve percent of the time, and once it does, that person fails out twice as often as the base rate. That's why we don't bother to reconnect."

Another cluster turned red. I looked at Jeff.

"No idea."

The EKGs were starting to look like seismographs. Heart rates ranged from the nineties to the low one hundreds. Cluster after cluster flatlined and went red.

"That guy," Jeff said, leaning in and tapping one of the red clusters. "He pissed and shit himself coming out. Then he cried. They had to send him to counseling."

I nodded. "I saw the request. I didn't know what it was for, though."

Jeff crossed his arms. "Almost a third of them puke. None of them want to go back in."

"Is it the nanites?" I asked. I had a rudimentary understanding of how the NexGen made a player believe they were in the game, and it involved tiny machines swimming around their brain. That's why we used alpha testers, paid them well, and kept a neurologist on standby.

Jeff shrugged. "It shouldn't be. We got those on loan from the Department of Defense. It's the same ones they use to give soldiers a virtual heads-up display, so they should be safe."

"Should be?"

"They are," Jeff said, sounding frustrated. "I wrote my freaking doctoral dissertation on them. Amputees use them to control mechanical prosthetics. They cause aneurysms in about one percent of soldiers, but that's after weeks of dehydration and sleep deprivation. Some people get vertigo or migraines. It's documented. There's nothing like that here."

"So what is it?"

Jeff laughed at me. "Dude, if I knew, I'd be asking for a raise and a better parking spot, not talking to you. No offense."

I shrugged.

"Besides, I thought Osmark gave up."

"Maybe he didn't."

"Did he send you?"

"I got through the door, didn't I? What are the testers saying?"

Jeff looked at me for a second. He wanted to believe me.

"Come on, man," I said. "You want to be known as the hardware lead for the new No Man's Land?"

Jeff's upper lip curled up, and he crossed his arms. "I don't give a shit about some video game, man. I'm a nanotech engineer. It's the faculty back at Penn I'm worried about."

"Guess you need me, then. The testers?"

"Useless. The ones that didn't run away or threaten to sue us just said they felt like they were dying over and over."

"But they weren't?"

Jeff threw his hands up. "Oh, they *felt* like it. EKGs were all over the place, blood sugar spiked, but when the doctors looked them over, there was nothing physically wrong with them."

"You're sure of that?"

"Yeah, dude, I'm sure. I know I'm not a people person, but I'm not trying to murder anyone, no matter how useless they are." He sat down again. "One of those assholes is going to tell the press, though. I just know it."

I almost laughed, then. The answer was simple. Alpha testers were chosen at random from a pool. After they were catheterized, they sat on medical beds for hours to establish their baselines before testing. There might have been a dedicated gamer among them, or a kid down on his luck just trying to subject his brain to experimental drugs to get himself through college, but I doubted it. Jeff needed a better alpha tester, someone who would ignore what their body was telling them and give him detailed, quantitative feedback on the experience.

"Plug me in," I told him.

THREE

He gave me a look.

"I'm serious, Jeff."

"And I'm serious when I say, 'Go fuck yourself.' The docs aren't even around."

"You said it wasn't dangerous."

"I did."

"Did you lie?"

Jeff's face twisted into a snarl. "I'm not turning one of Osmark's protégés into a vegetable when I'm supposed to be packing the place up, man. It's just not happening."

"I bet I could last thirty minutes."

"You wouldn't last half that."

"Done. Fifty bucks for fifteen minutes," I said, pulling my billfold from my pocket.

"Ten grand, and the keys to that piece of shit car you drive so I can park it at the junkyard."

The number made my breath catch, but that was just instinct. I let the emotion play over my face. Jeff smirked. I saw his heart laid bare in the dimples. He got ignored as a kid. He'd made more of himself than most of the people he grew up with, and proved his worth to himself with his wallet.

"Done," I said, slapping the billfold and my keys on the table. I didn't have ten grand in my pocket, but I was good for it. I'd lose at least that much in job hunting and moving expenses if Viridian failed, and make it twenty times over if it didn't.

He scowled. "Fine. I was sick of your shit anyway, always walking around like you own the place. I don't even..."

I tuned out the rest of what he said, just turned a knob in my head like a radio. The cussing, the disdain, blaming everyone but him... He was scared. I felt for him, in as much as I didn't think anyone should have to live like that, but Jeff had a tendency to be more of a jerk than he needed to be. Someone other than Jeff, I might have built them up and taken a cooperative approach, but Jeff had been living with fear for so long he'd built his life around it.

"...sit your ass down and don't complain when you puke all over your cheap-ass clothes." Jeff pulled a jet injector out of a drawer and snapped a single-use cartridge to the front of it. The slender glass ampule looked like it was filled with liquid mercury.

"What's that?" I asked.

"A thousand dollars' worth of military nanites. They're going to burrow into your veins, swim up your bloodstream, and send tiny electric shocks into your brain. Still want to do this?"

No, definitely not. "They cost that much?"

"Don't worry, I'll pay the company back for wasting them with your money." He pushed my sleeve up and dosed me. It clacked and felt like getting punched in the shoulder. "If we ever enter mass production, they'll be cheaper. You can go lie down on one of the beds." Jeff sat at his workstation and spun to face the screens.

"Don't I need a headset?"

"Nope."

I stood there, watching him bring up a new cluster of read-outs—mine—on his monitor. "I just thought there would be more wires involved."

He looked at me. "Bluetooth, dude. Welcome to the twenty-first century." He started typing commands into the control console. "If you're still standing when I turn these on, it's going to dump you on your ass."

"Right." I walked to the nearest hospital bed, raised the headrest so I'd be sitting most of the way up, and climbed in. I could feel the nanites working their way from my shoulder to my heart. It felt like someone was squeezing my chest. I tried to stay calm. "How do my stats look?" I asked, unable to see his screens.

"Like you're about to lose ten thousand dollars."

The tightness was migrating from my chest to the side of my neck. My tongue tingled. Suddenly it didn't seem like such a great idea to mess with my brain for ten grand and a job. I mean, Rob was an asshole most days. A brilliant, visionary leader who'd given me an incredible opportunity, but still an asshole. *Sandra will like it, though. I'll be her knight in shining armor if I pull this off. Forget awkward questions about where she's from when we've worked together for two years. It'll be like skipping straight to the second or third date.*

"I've got a good link. Everything's normal," Jeff said. "Try not to freak out on me."

I winced as my jaw spasmed, but I gave him a thumbs-up. He rolled his eyes.

The nanites were in my head. It felt overheated and tight like I had a bad fever. My eyes felt too big for their sockets, and little flashes danced in the air in front of me. Then my eyes cut out like someone turned off the TV and everything was dark. "Jeff!"

"Take it easy..."

I swung my legs out of the bed, almost sat up, then realized I had no sense of what was in front of me or how far down the floor was. Pins and needles shot through my arms and legs. "You fucking take it easy! I can't—"

My sight came back. Jeff was grinning at me.

"Damn," I said, pulse pounding. I blinked several times, then looked at my hands and flexed my fingers. The pins and needles were gone. The stuffiness in my head was still there, but it was fading. "Is it always that bad?"

"Define 'bad.'"

"I went blind."

Jeff shrugged. "Normally we drip-feed the bots in slowly while the testers get everything explained to them by a doctor from DARPA. There's also an aerosol version, which is probably what we'll go with for users, but it doubles the cost. Mr. Shooty, here," he said, waving the jet injector, "is how soldiers get it. I've never given someone an IV, but I figured that since you're going to do what no one else has before, you could probably handle the pro version."

"You're an ass."

"I'm an ass on a timetable. Look up and to the right without moving your head."

I did. VERIDIAN v0.01.16a floated in black, block type at the top right of my field of view. "Funky."

"That lets you know the bots are still there. For legal reasons, I'm required to tell you that if you're within signal range, I can see what you see."

"How long do they last?"

"Until I turn them off or you get hit by an EMP."

Holy privacy invasion, Batman. I bet the US government had other uses for that than overlays for the troops.

"You ready for this?" Jeff asked, finger poised over his keyboard.

"Yeah." I lay back in the bed. "Let's get this over with."

Jeff hit a single key. I thought there would be a transition of some kind. There wasn't. I blinked, and I was somewhere else. A neutral female voice announced, "You have entered Viridian Alpha."

A FULL-BODY SHUDDER passed through me. Something was wrong. Something was very, very wrong. I tried to take a deep breath, but it didn't work the way it should. My chest moved, but I couldn't feel it. Everything was muted. It was like I was a passenger in somebody else's body, and I wanted out. I wanted out right now. A prompt popped up at the bottom of my view:

<<<>>>

Log out: Yes/No?

<<<>>>

Man, I wanted to. Have you ever been in a situation you wished you could close out of? Just rage quit to the desktop, then and there? Your father screaming at your mother again. Your best friend screwing your ex. A Jar Jar Binks standalone Christmas special. It was all those things while drowning in lukewarm vegetable oil. I'm not sure what let me hang on. Maybe I wanted to prove myself to Robert. Maybe it was how much I liked Sandra's legs or hated Jeff's stupid face. I flicked my eyes to "No," and the prompt went away.

I dropped to my hands and knees and dry heaved, I think,

except that didn't feel right either. It caught in my throat. I blinked. There were olive trees all around me. It should have been scenic, but everything was too bright, blurred in places. The world glowed. I knew what the problem was from tweaking the graphics settings on *The Ancient Rolls*, I'd just never expected to have to use that knowledge in real life. "Jeff!" I yelled hoarsely.

There was a sound like God in heaven scrambling to put on his headset. "Umm, yes? I mean... holy shit, Alan. How's it going?"

"Not great, man," I said. The blur was making me nauseous. "I need you to do something for me."

"Okay, yeah. Anything, man. What—"

"I need you to turn off the bloom and the FXAA."

Jeff paused. "Are you sure? Because—"

"Just do it!"

"Okay."

I fell over on my side and went fetal. I squeezed my eyes shut. This had to stop. *Please, someone, make this stop.* I felt like I was dying. The prompt popped up again, even with my eyes shut. *No, damn it.* It went away again.

"How does it look?" Jeff asked.

I cracked an eye open. The glow around everything had gone out. The textures weren't perfect, but it looked more like a shitty version of real than an acid trip gone glam. A little bit of the wrongness I felt subsided. "Better." I let my head roll back a bit to look up at the sunlight filtering through the green and silver leaves of the grove. That felt right, from the color to the winks of light and shadow. Ray tracing was a beautiful thing. The thick gray trunks bent and twisted their way to the ground, rough bark discolored by patches of moss, especially near the roots on the right side of the tree. Was that north? Did the game engine push the simulation that far?

"How you doing, buddy?" Jeff said.

Buddy? I almost laughed in his invisible face. "Fine. Not up to moving yet, but at least I didn't puke and shit myself, right?"

"Well, about that."

"Seriously?"

"Just the puke, but like Exorcist-level projectile vomit. It's, uh... Starbucks?"

"McDonald's. Good thing I didn't get a McMuffin."

"I think we're all grateful for that."

I closed my eyes because just lying there was wearing me out. Then I opened them again because I felt dizzy. I didn't have a great sense of where my body was unless I was looking straight at it, and it was tripping me out. "Hey, Jeff?"

"Yeah, bro, I'm here. Getting some really good data, man. This is going to—"

"Could you shut up for a second?"

"Yeah. Yeah, I can do that."

"I can't feel my arms and legs. Can you turn up the sensitivity or something?"

"I can't do that without exposing you to pain. You cool with that?"

"I'll try anything."

"Okay, how much?"

"Just... whatever I would be feeling if this was real."

"That's pretty much the opposite of what the doctors—"

"Jeff?"

"Got it."

Pain and nausea came flooding into my world. My gut heaved and I doubled over, rocking on my side. I could feel my abs cramping. Sweat beaded on my forehead, and my saliva felt thick. I spit. It stuck to my cheek, but that was better somehow. It was an honest kind of pain, not the pervasive nothingness I'd felt at first.

"You puked again," Jeff said from somewhere in the sky.

"Yeah, I got that," I answered. I wiped my mouth and rolled onto my back. The sky was a clear but faded blue, striped with wispy clouds. The ground was warm beneath me; blades of grass tickled the back of my neck. I could feel air passing through my lips as I breathed, and the scratchiness of my throat made me cough, which sucked because my stomach and ribs ached. I felt drained, but it was completely different from the revulsion for the world I'd felt before. "How long have I been in?"

"Just over four minutes," Jeff answered. "Listen, Alan, forget the bet, all right? I'm sorry I was a jackass. We've got enough here to prove the system works and bring the testers back in."

He didn't get it. Osmark had already told the Board that Viridian had failed. He'd made concessions and lost face. We needed more than a recording of me curled up and covered in vomit. We needed a positive user experience. "It still sucks in here, man. It's like the worst hangover I've ever had. I need you to tweak the settings. I get the feeling that the more real the simulation is, the less crappy I feel, but you've got all those graphs out there. Can you fix it?"

Jeff didn't answer for a few seconds. I raised my head to ask him if he'd heard me, but he finally answered, "Yeah, dude. I'll get on that."

I laid my head back and closed my eyes again. This time I wasn't dizzy. I could feel my hands resting on my stomach. All the little clues my brain needed to convince itself it was lying on that hill, near the olive trees, started falling into place, and my muscles relaxed. I focused on my breathing. My mouth tasted sour, and my body was a little too big, like I was swollen, but that seemed fixable. Everything was fixable. It was going to be okay.

It reminded me of afternoons spent napping through the

summer heat at my grandfather's house in Spain. It was the same dryness in the air, the same loose, rocky soil and brittle grass beneath my heels. I'd spend my mornings in bed, reading Pops's old paper books, or hide from him in the fields of wild buckwheat. Once a year, the gardeners would spread their nets at the feet of century-old olive trees and beat the branches, harvesting the olives before taking them to the press. Pops always sent me home to the States with a bottle of oil for my mother, to remind her of home.

The smell of the sea made me open my eyes again. It was faint, just a trace of brine under the hot, slightly dusty feel of the breeze passing through the grove. I rolled up into a sitting position, still sore but not hurting in a significant way, and I noticed a thin line of blue on the horizon. I wondered how far that was. Jeff must have increased the draw distance. A bumblebee droned past, landing on a small purple wildflower hiding in the grass. A gust of wind made the leaves rustle.

Jeff spoke from the sky. "That's about as good as I can get it on the test server. How do you feel?"

I blinked. I'd forgotten I was in Viridian for a moment. "I feel good. A little tired, but good. How much time left?"

"Dude, you've been in for eighteen minutes. I think you fell asleep."

"Huh." I took one last look toward what my heart told me was the Gulf of Roses, near Empuriabrava. I hadn't realized how much I missed the old place, but the feeling was definitely there, a slight ache in my chest near the top of my sternum. Maybe I'd go back there, once all of this was done, and make sure they were taking care of Pops's grave.

<<<>>>

Log out: Yes/No?

<<<>>>

Yes.

<<<>>>

I squinted against the artificial lighting. I felt like I'd lost about twenty pounds and an inch of height, and I shivered from the chill of the air conditioning. The world looked just a tiny bit fake, like I was still in the test server. Switching back and forth was going to be a problem if we didn't do something to smooth the transition.

I looked down and saw that my shirt and jeans were damp but cleaner than expected. I still smelled, and the bedding was stained, but Jeff had wiped off most of the gross bits and chunks. There was a trash can full of wadded-up paper towels next to the bed.

"Dude," Jeff said. "You're going to be famous. Like, crazy stupid for trying, but famous for pulling it off."

I chuckled. "Think I'll get my own parking spot?"

"You can have mine," he said. Then he thought about it and grinned. "For a month. I'm already out ten grand because of you."

"You don't have to—"

"No, man. Don't even be like that. I was a jackass, like I said. I can own up to the consequences."

I wrinkled my nose at the idea of him handing me money. I knew most of the team leads were well off—some even rich—but it was still a lot of cash. "Would you consider throwing a party for the team instead?"

Jeff tugged on his ponytail. "I mean, yes? If it's between handing you a check and throwing an epic bash, I'm going to throw the party. You sure?"

"I'd prefer it."

Jeff shrugged. "Whatever floats your boat, dude. So how was it?"

"Awful."

Jeff smiled. "Yeah, I got that much, but after that?" I could see the eagerness in his eyes. This wasn't just professional curiosity; this was the passion of discovery, of having created something new. It was stronger than drug cravings and just shy of Dwarven gold-madness.

I thought about how to answer. "Good, I guess? I forgot it wasn't real, for a second, until you chimed in. You said I fell asleep?"

"I think you did. Your pulse and breathing smoothed out; brain waves were a 60/40 split between theta and delta waves. Did you dream?"

"I'm not sure."

Jeff shook his head and laughed. "That's wild, man. Freaking wild. I can't wait to try it, once we get the kinks smoothed out."

I sighed. "Yeah, about that. I need to get cleaned up, and then you need to send me back in."

"What?"

"To the real thing this time. I want to try the full *Viridian Gate Online* experience, and do a longer run."

"How much longer?"

"A day or two."

Jeff frowned and crossed his arms. "Why would I do that? Why would you want me to do that? I mean, no offense, man, but you look like shit."

I crossed my arms right back at him. "You've got fifteen different readings on my body and brain, Jeff. Am I hurt? Have I been damaged in any way?"

"You're dehydrated."

"I'll drink water."

"And fatigued. There's a lot more data running through V.G.O."

"But it's the same amount running through my head, which is still less than the real world. Am I right?"

"I have zero confidence that hooking you up to the server farm won't blow your brains out through your ears. You know what the troops call a nanite aneurysm?"

"No, and I don't want to know."

Jeff pouted. I could tell he really wanted to lay that bit of knowledge on me.

"You remember Osmark saying he was going to San Francisco?" I said.

"Yeah, so?"

"So Viridian's shut down. It's a board decision, so even Osmark doesn't have the authority to start it back up. We need hard evidence that this is something that will sell, and as you just pointed out," I said, pointing at my wet and malodorous clothes, "I look like shit."

"We'll bring testers in."

"Shut down. I don't know how else to say it. No testers, no docs, and definitely no Robert Osmark. We have the weekend to make this work."

Jeff shook his head. "Screw that, man. It's your brain. Don't be an idiot."

I clenched my teeth. The worst part was, we were both right. I shouldn't do more, and what we had wasn't enough. I ran the tapes on our conversation back in my head, looking for an angle, and then I found it. "Look, if I stay in for twenty-four hours, I'll have to sleep, right?"

He shrugged and made a face. "So?"

"So if I get a full night's sleep in the game, and you can see everything I can see, you'll see my dreams. You could be the first person to record someone dreaming."

His eyes widened. He stroked his beard and shifted his

weight from foot to foot. I could feel him teetering. He just needed one last shove. "Twenty-four hours?" he asked.

"Twenty-four hours."

"And I pull you out if something looks off."

"Sure. I'm not looking to be a hero here." I was absolutely looking to be a hero—impress the boss, get the girl? Yeah. I liked my brain, though. I'd settle for being Spider-Man with a safety net.

"Okay." He shoved his hands into his pockets.

It was Dwarven gold-madness, all the way.

I STEPPED under the steaming hot water and exhaled, letting some of the tension from the morning wash away. I'd done it. Even if the full V.G.O. run failed completely and the project got downsized or delayed, I'd have earned Osmark's respect, as long as he didn't fire me for putting the company in legal jeopardy.

I was mostly sure he wouldn't. Rob didn't build Os-Tech from scratch without taking risks.

With the pressure off and the water on, it was almost tempting to call it off. Maybe Jeff was right. I could walk back in there and tell him I was wrong, and we'd bring the testers in next week. He could have done a better job of reasoning me out of it, for sure, but instead, he'd tried to stonewall, and I went for the win on principle.

It's a character flaw. I've known it for years. The knowledge hasn't helped me change the behavior.

Instead, my mind wandered back to my grandfather, and how things had fallen out between him and Mom. He'd been a strong man in the old sense of the word. He'd lived through the war in Korea, he'd kept going when his high-school sweetheart finally left him, or "Went on ahead," as he liked to say. He'd had these big old hands with thick, flat fingernails that made me think he was a giant when I was small enough to believe in fairy tales. He never made eye contact when he gave me that bottle of olive oil for my mother, wrapped in packing paper with a three-turn twist above the neck. She never talked about it when she pulled it from my bag; she just put it on the shelf and used it for the next few months until it ran out. Looking back, I should have seen the sheen to her eyes while she cooked, but you're so busy trying to figure out your own thoughts as a kid you don't bother to wonder.

It made me think of missed opportunities. Of little gestures I'd ignored because I didn't want to be wrong, to be exposed. I didn't want to miss out on things because of that. And I didn't want to die alone.

I shut the water off. *Where did all that come from?* Maybe it was the game. The nanites mapped the player's brain and stimulated it. It wouldn't be impossible they'd dredged up old memories, or that those neurons had caught a stray volt or two. It didn't make those memories wrong, just... unexpected. I'd have some more thinking to do when this was done.

I toweled off, put on my damp but cleaned-off jeans and a Ms. Pac-Man T-shirt I'd borrowed from Jeff. It was the right fit around the chest, but too long, so I tucked it in. It looked every bit as dorky as you're imagining.

I went back to check on Jeff. "Hey man, I'm heading out to grab supplies. Need anything?"

"I'm good!" Jeff said, flashing me a thumbs-up. "Feeding your test data to Kronos."

Kronos was the AI, or "Overmind," who governed time and physics in the game. During testing, Jeff had to tweak each of the settings one by one as best he could. In V.G.O., Kronos would do it all at once, better and faster.

"Actually, coffee and donuts?" Jeff said. "We're going to be here a while."

"I'm on it," I said, and left.

As I was leaving the building, Frank snickered. "You know, I never took you for a tucker."

"A tucker?"

"Anyone who'd tuck in a T-shirt."

I sighed. I had to squash that kind of stuff all the time; Frank just hadn't seemed the type. "Is that supposed to be some kind of homophobic humor, Frank?"

"Oh, no sir, perish the thought. Without getting into stereotypes, the LGBTQ community usually dresses better than that. I'm digging Ms. Pac-Man, though," he said, pointing at the shirt. "You done for the day?"

"No, I'll be back. Can you do me a favor?"

Frank rocked his head from side to side. "Maybe?"

"Jeff Berkowitz and I are working on a final project in testing before we shut this thing down. It'd be better if we weren't disturbed."

"Not a problem," Frank said. "They're not scheduled to touch the back room until Sunday; she's all yours."

"Thanks, Frank." I headed for my car.

I WALKED UP to the drugstore register and started pulling things out of the basket. Two big bottles of water, ready-to-drink coffee, a bag of generic powdered donuts—Jeff had apologized, but you have to *earn* Krispy Kremes—a couple Powerades, wet wipes, and a pack of adult diapers. I tried to be real casual about the last item.

The teenage clerk called my bluff. "These for you?"

"Yeah," I said, deadpan. "I'm stalking my girlfriend, and I don't want to miss a thing."

He smirked. "There's bungee cords and duct tape in the automotive section."

I rolled my eyes. "Nice upsell. Can I pay?"

"Sure thing." He rang me up. "So who are they for, really? Your grandfather or something?"

The memory of Pops hit me too soon after what happened in the test server. It jarred me so bad I told the truth. "I just have a project at work, and I won't be able to leave the office."

The kid's mouth dropped open.

I grabbed the bag and shot him with a finger gun. "Stay in school, kid."

I got back into the Spyder and hit the road.

FOUR

The first thing Robert Osmark saw when he woke up was the ceiling fan spinning. *Round and round.* Bright daylight streaming in through the thin strip window above and behind his bed told him it was late. He hadn't set an alarm after last night's debacle.

The Board had been fine; Sandra's preparation was flawless, as always, so the Board accepted his proposal to shelve Viridian for two years without a hitch. It was after, when that pissant Wagner had pulled him aside and told him to make sure he put mothballs in the containers because "It'll be the end of the world before I back you starting this project again."

Asshole. If Wagner hadn't been pushed on them by Osmark Technology's largest shareholder, he would have been gone years ago.

Robert rubbed his eyes, then sat up and swung his legs out of bed. He finished the half-full bottle of water sitting on his nightstand, then padded his way to the kitchen.

Coffee dripped into the pot. It was an Ethiopian variety called Gesha, after the region, which had been transplanted to a small estate in Panama. Robert's smartwatch had sensed his awakening and turned the brewer on, the perfect symbiosis of man and machine. Robert leaned against the counter with his eyes closed until the coffee maker's last sputter, then he filled his mug and stepped out onto the balcony.

The redwood decking extended over the side of a cliff, facing the Pacific Ocean and the white sand beach below. He stood there in the rising heat, wearing nothing but a pair of boxers, and watched the waves while he drank his coffee. He was in his late forties, graying, and not as slim as he'd like. It was a perfect photo op for a headline about Viridian failing. Robert both didn't care and had a standing order for his lawyers to sue anyone they could prove had been on his property to take photos. He didn't even review the cases anymore. It was just one of several reports he let Sandra manage.

He wasn't sure when he'd lost control of his life. Everyone knew he was the boss. Even the newspapers he loathed said so. But while that gave him a financial freedom he couldn't have imagined as a kid growing up in Brooklyn, it had bound him in layers of red tape and obligations so deep he didn't know which way was out. The coffeepot had more say in his morning schedule than he did.

Part of him thought about ditching it all. He could find a CEO to replace him. They wouldn't have his drive or programming skills, but he could find a solid leader with a strong commercial background who would make the shareholders and analysts happy.

Robert could carry on as a board member or as a strategic advisor. He could travel, see some of the orphanages and health clinics he'd funded, or just go sightseeing. Maybe he'd take a team and lead a project of his own—get back to the long nights and the simple pleasure of making a machine do something nobody thought it could.

He scratched his stomach. It would start small, he knew—a

missed deadline, a news article, a faint catching of the gears. Then he'd be elbow deep in running the company again. He finished his first cup of coffee and got another before sitting at his desk and putting on his reading glasses.

He checked his emails, forwarding some to Sandra, putting others in folders by topic or project until only those that required his intervention remained. He left those for later. A scan of the headlines that featured his name or his company's showed the news had already leaked. Osmark Technology's hush-hush Viridian project was dead. Robert sent an email to Sandra to track down the leaker and fire them, then call the usual contacts and let them know why. He made a point of always following through on his threats. If he didn't, they'd stop being effective.

He pulled up the security log for the Viridian building and saw that the movers were thirty-six percent done with the common areas. Jeff Berkowitz, the hardware lead, was currently logged into the main server. Robert would ask him about that Monday, but the article had been heavy on design and light on technical details, and Jeff didn't have the balls. The man was probably just making a last attempt to save the project, and Robert wished him well, even if nothing short of a miracle would do the trick.

Alan had come and gone already; he could be the leak. Robert considered it, then rejected it out of hand. Alan was a good kid, a decent manager, and conscientious to a fault. He needed some technical training so he wouldn't say stupid things, like "saying goodbye" to the AIs. Robert thought of a few courses he knew of on Deep Learning and Neural Networks while he drained his second cup of coffee. *Keep him busy for a few months, build his credibility, stop him from joining the competition.* It fit together nicely. *Tick tock.*

He took his glasses off, put on shorts and running shoes, then went out the front door for his morning loop around the Devereux Slough. After that, emails and phone calls until lunchtime. *Round and round.*

FIVE

I pulled my jeans up around the diaper in the employee bathroom. I knew that if I spent twenty-four hours in V.G.O., I was going to end up loading my pants. No sense in not giving my body one more chance at dignity on my way in, though. It had been an interesting experience; I'd done everything while trying hard to look away. VERIDIAN v0.01.16a still floated in black letters at the edge of my vision. I didn't think Jeff was the type to watch another guy taking a crap, and I hadn't even stopped to think about it in the shower, but the nanites had turned me into a walking webcam, and I was well within signal range.

So I'd stared at the brown-and-tan porcelain floor tiles. They'd been custom laid by one of the writers who'd started life as a union carpenter. The one at my feet looked like an abstract version of Europe and the beginnings of Russia, if Sweden, Norway, and Finland had been sunk into the Norwegian Sea, Atlantis style. It was a funny little detail, but it was also part of what had made the last two years working for Os-Tech so different from other jobs. Even the buildings had their little eccentricities.

I flushed, washed my hands, and headed for Alpha Testing.

Jeff was so focused on his monitors he didn't hear me walk in. He was squeezing a stress ball that looked like Jupiter at two beats per second.

"Nervous?" I asked, setting the bottled coffee and donuts on his desk.

"Yeah. Aren't you?"

"A little. Kronos crunch all the numbers?"

He nodded. "We're all set. I was just checking it over, took some notes, made sure it didn't do anything crazy like flip the world upside down." He set the stress ball down and unscrewed one of the coffee bottles, chugging half of it.

"Can I change a few things? I was too tall last time."

Jeff wiped his mouth with his forearm. "This one's the real thing, dude. Character creation, intro video, everything. Tell you what though..." He pulled his phone out of his pocket and snapped a picture. "I'll upload that to your profile to make it easier."

"Cool."

He finally noticed the bulge around my hips. "You get fat on the way to the shower or something?"

I lifted the shirt he'd lent me, showing off the diaper waistband.

He laughed.

"Yup, yuk it up. You might have to change me."

Jeff choked. "What?"

"This thing's fine for a little incontinence, but I just chugged two bottles of water, and I had pizza last night. I did what I could."

"I'll take a hard pass on that, buddy."

"I'll chafe."

"Yeppers. That's going to suck."

"It's going to stink. You want to sit there with a full diaper wafting your way? Call it the incidental cost of glory."

Jeff stared at me. He scratched his right arm. The reality of the situation was sinking in. Operation Big Baby was happening.

I sighed. "Come on, man. You have kids, right? How hard can it be?"

"I just have to change it?"

"And wipe me off," I said, dropping the wipes on his desk.

His face turned pale. "We will *never* speak of this. To anyone."

"I couldn't agree more. Are we doing this?"

"I guess we are." Jeff sighed. "Shit."

"Yeah," I said, forcing a grin. I turned to walk to the hospital bed.

"Hey, Alan?" Jeff said. He'd stood up and was holding his hand out to me. "Good luck in there."

I shook his hand. "Thanks." I turned away. I didn't think we'd ever be best friends—and I was pretty okay with that—but it was good he'd dialed back the jerkness once he realized I was there to help.

Call me an optimist, but I've always believed people are basically decent under ideal conditions. It's just that conditions are never ideal.

I took my shoes and jeans off—the shirt covered me down to mid-thigh—and climbed in, pulling the sheet over my legs. I lay back, thinking of all the ways this could go wrong, from embarrassment to death *and what the hell do the troops call a nanite aneurysm? Isn't "nanite aneurysm" bad enough?*

"You ready, man?"

"Hell, yes!" I said, smiling manically.

The world went white, and a deep male voice boomed from

that infinite whiteness. "Traveler! Prepare to enter *Viridian Gate Online!*"

THE WHITENESS DISSOLVED and cold air flooded into my lungs. It had that dry, aching freshness to it you only got at altitude, far from the city. I was standing on a sharp gray jag of rock that seemed to be trying its best to stab the sky from the top of an already tall mountain. I could feel the chill of the smooth, hard stone through the flimsy wraps on my feet. I spun slowly, taking in the steep rock faces covered in snow and ice, broken by lone, scraggly pines and spurs of angular slate. A loud crack echoed from somewhere downslope, in the shadows of a gorge. I was so high up, the sky's blue had turned indigo, and the horizon was a blurred band of white.

A gust of freezing wind made me hunch over, and I turned my back to it. I was wearing a thin, roughly stitched tunic and ripped trousers that felt like they were made of burlap and did nothing to protect me from the weather. I grabbed at my shoulders, hands shaking from the cold. Tears froze on my cheeks. I was going to die up here if I didn't find shelter or a way down.

As soon as I thought of getting off the peak, I was snatched back and spun out into the wind, my soul free and aloft. I was flying. Not floating, or pulled into the air by the force and lift of wings, but riding the air currents by my whim, effortless and free. It was the most sublime feeling I'd ever experienced.

I looked down and saw a man fall to his knees, breath fogging, his whole body shivering, and he looked a lot like me. A translucent interface popped up next to him, with sliders to adjust each of his features. There was a tab on the interface called "Race," and looking at it brought down a list of names like Hvitalfar, Dokkalfar, Svartalfar... your basic high elves, murk elves, and dwarves. Seeing how sick I'd been from minute physical differences in the test server, I put those down as a solid "No." The Accipiter, a bird-winged race of desert dwellers, tugged at my heartstrings, but while I was enjoying the current sensation of flight, I didn't think learning to move an extra set of limbs would make my job easier. The Risi reminded me of the orcs in *The Ancient Rolls*, but wider and with a severe, toothy underbite. I bet their dental bills were horrendous. They were neither like me nor anything I wanted to become.

The two types of human were known as Wodes and Imperials. Wodes were your basic barbarian, all wild, tattooed, and thickly muscled. Selecting the Imperial race kept my character close to my real appearance, and the interface informed me that choosing it would allow me to pick any unrestricted class, which suited me just fine. I wondered if "Corporate Hitman" was an option.

With my race picked, I focused on my looks. Short brown hair, honey-brown skin, thick eyebrows, and hazel eyes stayed the way they were. My teeth were straight, but had never been as perfectly white as I would have liked; I fixed that now with a thought and a few ticks of the "Teeth Color" slider. I had a slim but athletic build and... *Oh my God, my hips.*

I looked like a pear. Or a bong. Kronos hadn't figured out that the extra girth was from the diaper, or maybe our conversations had taught it more than I expected, and it thought this was funny. I knew appearances shouldn't matter, but they did, and I was as vain as anyone who'd ever gotten away with more than they should because they were pretty. I tidied that up and tried to forget what seemed like a horrifying look into middle age.

The inseam I left alone because let's face it, why fix what doesn't need fixing? I floated back to admire my work.

The "me" on the ground stood and looked up at me, or at

least in my direction since I didn't have a body. I could feel myself being drawn back in. There was a rightness to it, and I could always come back and try a new build later. A prompt came up.

<<<>>>

Please choose a name:

<<<>>>

"Alan Campbell," I said, using my real name. The other me's lips moved at the same time.

"Are you sure you would like to create Alan Campbell the Imperial?" came the announcer's voice from before. "Once you create a character, you will not be able to change your racial identity or name. Please confirm."

"Yes," I said. My character smiled, arms spread out, and leaned back, falling from the rock. I dove after him.

Then there was darkness.

WIND RUSHED BY MY EARS. Orchestral strings and an ethereal choir swelled until they filled the darkness. I blinked, twisting around to find myself high in the air above a peninsula twice the size of Spain. Deserts and chains of jagged brown mountains in the West, a single, massive peak in the North, and endless oceans all around. The Central and Eastern lands were rolling plains, hills, farmlands, and forests, while the South was overgrown with dense jungles surrounded by swamps. Seven sprawling cities resolved as I descended, then several medium-sized ones, and the land became divided by winding silver rivers and roads as fine as hairs. The music flared, then the terrain was zipping by, and I was streaking like a fighter jet toward the eastern edge of the world.

"The year is 1094 A.I.C—*Anno Imperium Conditae*," the gruff male voice boomed. "A time of peace in the lands of Eldgard. Or so it seems."

Men and women dressed in exotic fabrics argued, haggled, and drank wine from bowls made of silver and gold. Tradesmen plied their craft. The city grew. I watched a merchant slip a city watchman a handful of coins to let him through the gates. On the walls, watching, an officer in a gold breastplate laid a hand on his sword hilt, righteous fury in his eyes.

"Years of trade and diplomacy have weakened the Empire. Her citizens are corrupt, her Legion untested, and her mighty generals have faded into legend. Meanwhile, the barbarians living in the wilds beyond our borders grow stronger." The scene flashed to the seven cities, showing each in turn. "The winged savages of the Barren Sands grow fat on caravans to the fabled glass city of Ankara. The Wodes of Rowanheath shore up their walls and raise their young men for war. The Tanglewood is overrun with monsters, the Bleak Sea teems with smugglers and pirates. Stone Reach speaks of trade agreements where before there was tribute. Even the gates of Glome Corrie, once our staunchest ally, have been barred to Imperial tax collectors so that only the Hvitalfar remain faithful to New Viridia. Or do they placate us? What mischief do they plot in the great libraries of Alaunhylles? In the Storm Marshes, the Dokkalfar teach their children forbidden histories and dream of an empire of their own."

Blue banners with gold embroidered griffins unfurled from tall, squared stone towers, and I felt my heart swell with the music.

"You are a son of the Empire. The blood of heroes flows in your veins. Will you feed off the carcass of New Viridia, or will you stand and bring the light of civilization to the peoples of Eldgard? Peace never lasts," the voice warned. "Your destiny begins today."

I stooped like a hawk for the center of the city.

Oh hell yes. I mean, I was there to do my job and save the project. I'd be debriefed and have to write reports. Osmark would chew me out, and the Board could push for my termination. And that was all hoping the experience didn't damage my brain. It wasn't likely, and Jeff would keep a close eye on the readings, but it could still happen. I should have felt apprehensive.

I was going to be the first gamer to successfully play V.G.O. This was going to be—

I fell the last foot and landed on my chest, barely avoiding bouncing my face off the white marble. People stopped and stared. I was unarmed, winded, and still in my cheap-ass clothes, as Jeff would have put it. It turned out this was just like any other first day at work.

THERE WAS A PAUSE, during which I thought someone might comment on my falling from the sky, or start screaming. But then, like magic, the crowd started moving again. No one helped me up. One guy even stepped *over* me, and all I saw were his sandals. I got to my feet, wiping my hands on my pants, and looked around.

People dressed in tunics and more stately togas moved past. Their clothes were clean and well made, the women's hair pinned with delicate brooches and clips, while the men's hair was usually oiled and styled. No one made eye contact. It didn't make sense. V.G.O. wasn't just supposed to be immersive, it was supposed to be the most advanced AI simulation ever made.

There were supercomputers that could pass a Turing test with only a fraction of the computing power Osmark stored in the vault. I didn't see the same face twice, so these weren't filler characters or anything; they all had histories, personalities, and as many lines of possible dialogue as a real human being. I thought it might be a cultural thing, but they seemed comfortable enough talking to each other. "Excuse me?" I said.

An older man with a heavy gold clasp fastening his toga at the shoulder glanced at me, then looked away. I didn't understand. I looked down in case I was still the invisible spirit from character creation, but I could see my body just fine. I'd apparently skinned my knee, which stung the second I laid eyes on it, just like in real life, and that made me grin. I caught a woman's eye and opened my mouth to greet her. She curled her upper lip in disgust.

It hit me. I was in the wealthy part of town, wearing ill-fitting, torn, dirty clothes. A closer look at my shirt revealed it was called a Rough Tunic (shoddy). Within minutes of literally landing inside the most advanced video game ever made, I was being discriminated against by NPCs. And it made perfect sense. It was as real as things could get. I didn't know if it was funny or sad.

"Why aren't you disappearing?" a man's voice said.

I turned and saw a portly man in white robes pointing at me with his mouth open. He snatched his hand back as I faced him, as if I might bite. He was wearing an Imperial blue- and gold-embroidered stole, like a priest. Maybe he'd help me. "Hi! Could you..."

He ran away. He actually *ran away* from me. A radius of a few feet had opened around me, like unholy ground. I wasn't dangerous. I wasn't foreign—I was a son of the Empire, that much had been quite clear in the intro. My skin was dark, but I saw both lighter and darker pass me by without pause. I was just poor. It was something I'd never experienced, and it sucked.

But hey, that was the game, right? Run a few quests, get some loot, buy better gear so I could hobnob with rich assholes. *The fate of the world hangs in the balance,* I told myself with a grin. Robert liked to tell people he came from nothing. Maybe this would make me a better person.

"Hey, Alan, can you hear me?"

"Yeah, I can hear you. Do you have any idea where I am?"

"New Viridia," Jeff said. "You're in the capital of the Empire."

I nodded, looking around. I was in a flat, wide plaza made of tightly fitted slabs of white marble. The white stone shone in the morning sun.

"Is V.G.O. in real time?" I asked.

"It is now! Kronos synched the clocks so the transition would be less jarring." I heard him clicking to another window. "You also have to eat, drink, rest, and protect yourself from the elements or you'll get sick. Pain and smell are about normal, but —and this is interesting—taste is at 115% human standard, so the food's going to taste amazing."

"Poop?" I asked.

"Nope. No bathroom breaks. If only the real you was the same."

A waist-high stone wall and cast-iron railings ringed the plaza's outer edge, and, beyond it, I could see the city from the intro cut-scene, with *hundreds* of buildings between me and the outer wall.

"So how does it feel?"

"It's crazy, man. Aren't you seeing this?"

"Yeah, kind of. It's hard to follow on a flat screen."

I'd never seen anything like it. I mean I had, in real life, but never in a game where you could open every door and see the interiors, move things around, probably get into a fight with the owner for trespassing. *The Ancient Rolls* had been like that, where NPCs had homes, jobs, and people they hung out with during the day, but even the capital city of Cloudrim only had eighty-two people in it.

I gripped the railing and leaned forward, looking down at the city below. The residential buildings were three, sometimes four stories tall, and some of the temples and civic buildings were massive even by real-world standards. I could see open-air markets, parks, and a few major avenues wide enough for a couple of car lanes—or I guessed horse carts and wagons in this case—though most of the roads were much narrower. "So, how many people in New Viridia?"

"About two million," Jeff answered.

I believed it.

An oversized hand gripped my shoulder. "Are you lost?"

Two members of the city watch had walked up behind me while I gawked. They wore round bronze helmets with cheek guards and leather cuirasses, with strips of leather hanging from their shoulders and waists. Short swords were belted at their right hips. The taller one looked like his nose had been broken more than once, and was at least part Risi, with two sharp fangs poking up behind his lower lip. I instinctively leaned back against the railing. The shorter of the two held a knotted thong with several leather tails. She smacked it against her open palm. "Does your master know where you are, slave?"

I swallowed. This was turning into something a lot more serious than a good shunning and dirty looks. A semicircle of onlookers was forming. "There must be some kind of mistake," I started.

The half-Risi grabbed my wrist and raised it. "No brand," he told his partner.

"Doesn't mean he belongs here," she answered. "Are you drunk? Affka? Have you been doing drugs?"

"I'm sorry, officer. I don't know what Affka is, but I'm very, very sober. I'm a citizen and—"

"Where do you live?"

"I... I'm not from around here."

"Then you can't be a citizen." She looked at her partner. "Vagrancy?"

"Let's just get him out of here."

"Vagrancy's against the law, Gork. He should pay—"

"Does he *look* like he has money?" the half-Risi asked, raising an eyebrow.

The female watchman clenched her jaw.

Gork grabbed me by the upper arm. "Let's go."

They led me out through the crowd of proper citizens, who were all too happy to look at me now that I'd been put back into my place.

ONCE WE'D PUT a few blocks between us and the wealthy section of town, the half-Risi patrolman stopped.

"I'll take him from here," Gork told his partner.

"Fine. Meet me back at the station."

"I will."

His partner peeled off, heading back into the upper city. Gork pulled me on, his grip never loosening. I got the feeling he wasn't squeezing anywhere near as hard as he could have, but there was still no chance of me breaking free. Maybe I'd been hasty, picking a human starting character.

The further downhill we went, the fewer people stared. In fact, at some point, people stopped looking at me at all, and it was Gork who drew the most looks. We passed through a narrow tunnel in one of the ten-foot-thick stone-and-mortar walls and emerged into the outermost and widest ring of the city. Gork let me go.

I took a few steps back, then stood there feeling terrible about myself. If I hadn't had to be there to save the project, I might have quit. Gork looked me over, his thumbs hooked into his belt, reminding me of Frank. "Are you crazy?" he asked.

"What?"

Gork spit on the cobbles. "The woman who dragged us over to the plaza said you were talking to yourself, and then we found you leaning against the railing. You planning on jumping?"

"No!" I said. "I'm just... I traveled here from a long way away."

Gork nodded. "I thought so. Listen carefully. You see that hill at the center of the city? That's the Heights. Rich, powerful people live up there, not people like us. Stay away from it." He reached into a pouch tucked into his belt and pulled out two copper coins that looked tiny in his hand. "Here," he said. "That should feed you for a day. Find some work. Beg, if your pride can take it. Get some clothes from a thrift shop or one of the temples. Bathe. Don't let me catch you in the upper city looking like that again, and don't talk to yourself in public; it scares people."

I blushed. It's hard to tell with my complexion, but trust me, from the inside it feels like your face is on fire. I took the money though. A prompt appeared.

<<<>>>

Quest Alert: Productive Citizen

You now have two coins to rub together! Work, beg, or steal your way to respectability so your meteoric rise through the ranks of the Empire can begin!

Quest Class: Common, Faction-Based

Quest Difficulty: Easy

Success: Equip a full set of clothes other than your shoddy starting gear.

Failure: None.

Reward: 500 XP

Accept: Yes/No?

<<<>>>

Just like that, I was reminded this was all a game, a challenge I chose to overcome.

"Thanks," I told him, accepting the quest. "Are you my starter NPC?" Every player was supposed to get a starter NPC to guide them through their first moments in the game.

Gork frowned. "Your...?" He scrunched his face up. "You know what? I don't want to know. I'm just Gork, and I know what it's like to be a bit different," he said, tapping one of his fangs with his index finger. "You take care of yourself, Traveler. Remember what I told you about talking to yourself in public." He walked away.

I clutched my coppers to my chest and headed downhill.

"Well, that was intense," Jeff said.

"Yeah."

"You okay?"

I looked over my shoulder to make sure no one was watching. I was in one of the narrow side streets, which was only wide enough for two or three people to walk next to each other, and currently deserted. "I'm okay," I said, and it was mostly true. "Is that something you guys programmed in?"

"I'm hardware, dude. But no, nobody 'programmed' that in. There is no programming. It's just people. We scanned thousands of brains to get Kronos's personality database set up. A statistically normal percentage of those people were jerks."

I laughed. "It's always the goddamned meat, isn't it?"

"Amen," Jeff answered.

For all that, I did think Gork was trying to help, and he'd given me a path to success and acceptance, even if it wasn't paved with roses.

Speaking of which, my heels ached. I'd never done this much walking without the cushion and support of a modern sole. Three-story buildings with narrow balconies rose on either side, providing shade, which was a good thing because, either from the stress or the warm air, my armpits and lower back were starting to get damp. A cobbled gutter ran down the middle of the street, but the sides were paved in flat stones, and those were a bit more forgiving on my feet, so I walked with one hand trailing along the wall. I felt the texture with my fingertips, smooth and warm if a bit dusty.

Most of the buildings' faces were plaster painted over in

shades of cream, yellow, or powdery red. In some place, holes had been knocked into the plaster, exposing the mortared, rough-cut stone blocks beneath, just like the fortifications. The doors were tall and thick, made of dark wood reinforced or sometimes just decorated with iron bands and spikes. Some doors were scorched but intact. The whole city felt heavy and permanent in a way modern plywood and glass never could, and I liked that, in spite of what had happened earlier. I could imagine living somewhere like New Viridia, even in the lower city.

I stepped out into another plaza, but this one seemed more diverse. Merchants peddled their wares from carts, stalls, and the doorsteps of permanent shops. Those nearest me offered trinkets, charms, pottery vases, wooden bowls and pitchers, candles and lamp oil, candlesticks and lamps, carved wood, stone, and bone dice, games and figurines, as well as an assortment of different decorative and functional knives, three-tined forks, and spoons. It was all junk to a gamer, the kind of stuff that weighed down your inventory but did nothing for your coin purse when you sold it off. But in V.G.O., I guessed, maybe one day I'd own a home, and maybe I'd want a fine clay pot with depictions of naked men hunting wild boar from the backs of giant lizards, with spear, bow, and hounds. I smiled at the artist's imagination.

Several groves of a half dozen palm trees were planted throughout the plaza, ringed by outward facing cast-iron and wood-slat benches. Triangular orange sheets had been strung from the rooftops to the trees, offering slices of shade to the crowd as it flowed around the islands of green. I moved with them, clockwise around the palms, jostling and getting jostled without a second thought. Leather goods, from water and wine bags to smiths' aprons and decorative bracers, an array of flasks, phials, and phylacteries to which the proprietor ascribed all manner of magical powers... I paused at that. Everything was so real, I'd forgotten there was magic in V.G.O. That didn't mean the vendor was honest. The man's eagerness and the paucity of my wealth had me bobbing along with the crowd once more. Finally, I reached the corner of the market I'd been subconsciously searching for, the one that made my throat ache and my nostrils twitch.

Food. I'm not what you'd consider a comfort eater, but I'd had a hell of a day. I'd slept badly, puked, stressed in the real world and stressed here, and then got perp-walked to the bad part of town—though it smelled like the best part of town right now.

I pushed my way toward it. I could smell herbs and spices—rosemary, thyme, oregano, and coriander seeds—the thick, slightly bitter aroma of olive oil; the wholesome scent of just-baked bread; and the bright, pungent, and sour odors of fresh cheeses. A sharp tang of fried peppers, onions, and garlic wrinkled my eyes. I pushed through into the old-world equivalent of a food court.

The crowd was thinner here. A few locals, mainly older men, sat on benches eating finger food. Most people darted in to grab what they needed before continuing their circuit. There were fruit and vegetable stands, both fresh and dried, and several tables of salted fish. I made a beeline for a semipermanent stand where a plain-faced woman with small eyes and big arms worked several spits of roasting meat. There were three spits of red meat—maybe beef, maybe lamb—and two of some bird smaller than a chicken. Quail? Squab? Pigeon? They were making my mouth water, whatever they were.

"What can I get you?" the woman said, wiping her hands on her apron. She looked me over, taking in my clothes, but her face stayed impassive.

I swallowed. "How much for one of the small bird things?"

"Ten coppers," she said. "Five for some mixed meat and vegetables wrapped in flatbread."

My heart sank.

Her face softened. "How much do you have?"

My ears burned. *Beg, if your pride can take it,* Gork had said. My pride could take it. There wasn't so much of it left. "Two coppers," I said.

She held her hand out. I reluctantly dropped all the money I had into her palm. It's silly, I know; I'd come into this world with nothing but the (shoddy) shirt on my back, but this was the first time I really *felt* broke.

The vendor laid out a quarter-inch-thick piece of flatbread and spread a thin layer of smooth white cheese over it. Then she added shredded kale, peppers, and chopped onions on top of that. She dipped a spoon into the drip pan under the spits and drizzled the warm, black-flecked fat onto the pita. She frowned, then pulled a few stuffed olives from a pickle jar, cut them in half, and added them to the mix before rolling it up and handing it to me.

"Thanks," I said.

I'm not going to lie—I'd hoped she'd put a little meat in it, not just the drippings, but I was literally the beggar who couldn't afford to be choosy. I looked up and realized she was watching me, waiting, so I forced a smile and took a bite.

It was amazing. I'd eaten some nice meals in my lifetime— I'd been to Michelin-starred restaurants twice in the past year, working for Osmark—but this was better. The cheese was rich and creamy, and I could taste the char and seasonings from the spits making my whole body... just... happy to be getting great food. It was like I was vibrating slightly. The pickled and stuffed olives did a perfect job of cutting through the fat from the cheese and drippings, letting the fresh kale, onions, and peppers do their job of finishing the texture and complexity of that bite. And the bread! It was fresh baked, warm, soaked with all those juices, and spoke to that part of a person's heart that knows bread is a food group all on its own.

The vendor smiled and turned away. She must have read what she was looking for on my face. I drifted back into the flow of people, savoring each bite as we circled around the far side of the plaza.

It was the second moment of bliss I'd experienced in the game. The first had been floating free of my body during character creation. The second was enjoying the fruit of someone's kindness. Gork had been kind, too, in a way, but he'd done it for himself—because of who *he* was. That woman—I felt a moment of shame I hadn't asked for her name—had reacted to my pain. I don't know. I was making assumptions about her motives—assumptions I usually prided myself on avoiding— but that was how I felt.

Regardless, it was a drastically different experience from any other game I'd played. I was broke, I had grease all over my chin, and I hadn't done anything. There wasn't even a tutorial for me to have completed. If I died right now, my legacy would be "Fed by the compassion of strangers," and yet I felt like my life had been changed in some small way.

The thought brought up a display of my current status effects.

<<<>>>

Buffs Added

Olive Flatbread: Restore 40 HP over 60 seconds
Well-Fed: Base Constitution increased by (2) points; duration, 20 minutes.

<<<>>>

Huh, I thought. *Good for the soul, good for the body.* As soon as I'd finished with the information, the prompt disappeared on its own.

I stepped out of the crowd again, licking my fingers, drawn by the sound of splashing water. A small fountain—really just a metal pipe sticking out of a wall—spilled clear water into a waist-level basin. My approach scared a pair of sparrows away. I sniffed the water, then tasted it. It was cool and clean.

I rubbed my hands together under the stream of water, then cupped them and leaned forward, drinking from my palms. I stuck my head under the flow, sending shivers down my spine, and wiped my mouth and chin clean before bending down to wash off the knee I'd scraped. It had already healed though; not even a scab marked the spot. *Guess that's one thing this place has over reality.*

Looking around, I saw that several beggars were sitting in the dust with their backs against what appeared to be a temple. There was room next to one of them, an old man with wispy white hair on either side of his bald head. A bowl with three lonely coppers in it sat in front of his crossed legs, making him my social better. He was leaning his head back against the wall, dozing. The shadows of palm fronds shifted over his face.

My stomach was full. I was hydrated and mostly clean, and the adrenaline from the earlier situation was spent. I had twenty or more hours to kill before I could log out; a nap in partial shade sounded like as good a plan as any. *And maybe,* I thought, looking at the bowl, *when the old man wakes up, I can talk him into sharing the secret of his success.*

I sat down, smirking at my own joke, leaned my back against the wall, and nearly jumped out of my skin when I saw the old man staring at me with open, milky eyes from five inches away.

CHAPTER

SEVEN

"Is that June's cooking I smell on you?" the old man said, his voice high and shaky.

"I'm sorry, I—"

"Big woman!" he said. "Arms like ham hocks, smells like cedar. Her daddy makes cabinets for a living."

Smells like...? I'm not even sure what cedar—

"Are you simple, boy? June! She's a quarter turn around the square."

"No. I mean, yes, that's her, and I'm not simple."

"Coulda fooled me." He reached in front of him, feeling around until he found the money bowl. He gave it a shake. "Rats! Only three, but I need five."

I winced. Had the game wanted me to give him my two coppers? "I'm sorry, I don't have—"

"I know you don't have money, boy. Don't apologize. Apologies are for people with change hidden in their pockets, not us, the deserving poor! You don't have a bent copper bit on you; not unless you ate that, too," he said with mock suspicion. "Now find me a mark."

62

"A what?"

"A mark, boy," he said more softly, placing a wrinkled hand on my shoulder. "You pick a fish from that river of people, and I'll land him. Or her! I'm a dab hand with the ladies." He winked at me, then leaned back against the wall again, a playful smile on his wizened face.

I looked at the passing crowd and found my eyes drawn to a woman with twin braids twisted round in a circle, like a crown of laurels.

An alert popped up, and the woman was briefly outlined in purple.

<<<>>>

Ability: Keen-Sight

A passive ability allowing the observant adventurer to notice items and clues others might not see.

Ability Type/Level: Passive/Level 1

Cost: None

Effect: Chance to notice and identify hidden objects increased by 6%.

<<<>>>

Hmm. I guessed V.G.O. taught and leveled skills through use, at least the general ones. I'd always preferred that over just assigning points in a menu. I dismissed the window with a thought. "A female citizen near the seller of potions and charms. She's moving slower than the crowd," I said, wondering how the old man planned to act on that information.

"Is she wearing three bracelets?"

"Maybe? I…" I squinted. "Yes!" She reached up to push a stray lock of hair back behind her ear. Three slender bands overlapped on her wrist.

"Perfect," the old man said. He sat up, hands in his lap, and pitched his voice like an angler casting a line. "Milady!"

To my surprise, she turned, as if he'd tapped her on the shoulder.

"Milady! A moment!"

She hesitated, then moved toward us. She was wearing a bright, daisy yellow shawl draped over a white dress in an intricate series of folds. The shawl had a short black fringe on its lower edge that swayed when she walked. The neck of her dress was high, peeking up beneath the shawl just below her collarbone. "What do you want?"

The old man smiled, turning his face almost but not quite in her direction. "Nothing, milady, but a moment of your time."

The corner of her mouth twitched. "I see no goods laid out before you, beggar, and yet I feel you're about to sell me something."

"Only because you seek, lady. You seek, and you do not find."

She stopped a step away from him and crouched, gathering her shawl and the hem of her dress to keep them out of the dust. It was an aggressive move for someone of her apparent status, and I wondered if the old man hadn't bitten off more than he could chew. I caught sight of a sandaled foot and a simple henna tattoo of a chain of triangles around her ankle.

"Mmm. And did your helper tell you that?" she asked, her eyes flicking to mine. Her eyebrows were dark and full, and she'd applied some sort of clear balm to her lips, but her makeup was otherwise simple, darkened brows and a touch of blush to her cheeks. She'd made no effort to hide the crow's-feet at the corners of her eyes.

"No, lady. I heard the bracelets chime on your wrist and knew I'd found a fellow seeker." He reached with his hand, palm up, and she placed hers in his. "What do you seek, lady? A pretty husband? Luck in love?"

She laughed and looked at me. "He truly is blind, isn't he, young man? Or is he offering you up for coin?" She looked me over. I opened my mouth, and nothing came out. She smirked and looked at the old man again. "I'm past such things."

"Your husband—"

She withdrew her hand, pain rippling across her face before freezing over. "My husband is dead in the Storme Marshes these last ten years. He fell to the elves, outside of Yunnam. I have a fabric store in the upper city, a warehouse and a factory in the low. I have no need to replace him or his memory." She lifted her chin. Her eyes glistened.

"Why the bracelets, then, lady?" the old man said gently. I was able to see them clearly, now. They were pencil-wide and penny-thin bands of copper, embossed with simple, repeating symbols. One was a circle of waves, the second what looked like wind, and the third a vine that circled her wrist.

She sighed. "I need an heir." She tucked her dress beneath her and sat in the dust. "My daughter married a fool. The fool gave her two daughters, and he's spoiled them with my money. She's pregnant again. I hope for a grandson, so all I've built won't be destroyed."

"All men and women lie in Kronos's hands, lady."

She grinned. "But Gaia follows her whims, old man. Can you not hear her chiming on my wrist? I saw three portents just this morning."

"And yet, you will have another granddaughter," the old man said.

There was a weight to his words, and I suddenly had the

notion that they were true. The woman flinched as if she'd been slapped.

"But you'll raise this one," the old man continued. "She'll learn to ride instead of sit, learn the gin and carding room instead of how to bat her eyes, and you'll go to your rest easy with her hand on the loom and her eyes on the books."

The lady swallowed. "The fool won't like it."

"Even a fool knows who feeds him, lady."

She nodded and licked her lips. Then she stood. "And what of you, old man? What do you seek?"

The old man grinned. "Just a coin to remember your beauty by, lady."

She smiled at him with what I thought was genuine affection. She dropped three coppers into his bowl. "One for you, one for your helper, and one for the goddess, may she prove you wrong."

The old man dipped his head in thanks.

The woman walked away.

"That was amazing," I told the old man.

"Wasn't it, though?"

I rolled my eyes. I'd been thinking it was amazing that a random NPC had so much backstory. I was less impressed by his work. The old man had talked a pretty good game, but he'd also made mistakes. He'd almost lost her over the husband thing.

"I smell the bitter stench of skepticism over there, boy. Wipe it from your mind! Success belongs to the believer!"

I snorted. "Dude, you're a beggar. We should have asked her for a job."

One of the other beggars leaned forward and glared at me, but the old man waved him off. "And is that why you came to New Viridia, Traveler? To get a job in textiles?"

I raised an eyebrow. "I don't think I mentioned I was from somewhere else."

The old man blew a raspberry. "Your accent, boy. And your innocence. Did you think she was a lovely lady? Was she a nice old widow you needed to help? That woman was a wolf, boy! She runs a store for the gentry and keeps her labor and stock in the worst parts of town. Do you think she pays a fair wage? Do you think the local gangs leave her warehouse alone because she's *nice*?

"I am not 'a beggar,' boy. I am a skilled orator. I convince people to do me small favors, some of them monetary. I could have talked her out of her *stola* on a cold day, and she'd have walked home to her marble villa, bare-armed like a common girl, feeling like the soul of charity and goodness. Did you smell the saffron on her? Bright yellow, wasn't it? I could have sold that for gold if I'd cared to walk uptown and haggle." He crossed his skinny arms. "I'm not sure what a 'dude' is, but I suspect *that* garment would look better on your shoulders. I'm a prince among men. I could have talked you into her fine cotton sheets—"

"Oh, come on! She said—"

"She *looked*. Don't tell me she didn't strike you speechless with a glance, boy, because I was right here. There's no shame in comforting a wealthy widow. She'd have taught you a thing or two—more than you'd learn whoring yourself out to a copper-an-hour paycheck."

I laughed. "All right, all right, fine," I said, raising my hands in surrender. "You win."

The anger and indignation vanished from the old man's face like they'd never been there, and he grinned. "Good. Now find me another."

❧ ✕ ❧

Sathis ran down the central aisle of the temple, his sandals slapping against the marble floor. He was hot and out of breath, too old to have run halfway across the city, and scared out of his wits. He threw himself down in front of his goddess's statue.

"Blessed lady Sophia, ever may you slumber, may your peace and justice wrap the world forever in its loving embrace."

An acolyte came out of the sacristy. "Justiciar Sathis? What—"

"Out!" Sathis bellowed.

The acolyte ran out of the room.

Sathis looked up at the representation of his goddess. The statue was made of carved, lightly striped black onyx, with a wide white band of quartz that hung from her left hip to right thigh like a sash. Her eyes were flawless emeralds artfully set into the stone so they seemed real. She was naked, looking up and to the left at a set of bronze scales she held by a hook. In her right hand, trailing behind her leg so it was partially hidden, was a sword. Sathis swallowed. "Forgive me, blessed lady, for my fear." He inclined his head once more. Drops of sweat ran down his back and dripped from his forehead.

"My lady, there are rumors of insurrection in the provinces. The senators ignore your earthly apostles. Most refuse my visits or make excuses. Some expect me to amuse them with stories of the old days, like a jester or a bard, or to educate their children." He clenched his fists, made slick with perspiration. "I have become something of a joke."

He squeezed his eyes shut and touched his forehead to the floor. "But we, the faithful, are content with the bounty of your peace, blessed lady. The offerings are few, but I encourage the acolytes to seek work, so long as it does not interfere with their duties to you and to your ministry."

He looked up at the statue again, searching for a sign. The

statue had been carved from a single, massive block during the first, great Imperial war to conquer Eldgard. The stone had been quarried and then moved from the hills above New Viridia to the safety of the Imperial stockade, under constant attack from both wild Risi and Hvitalfar druids. Sophia was always at her most popular when her people wearied of war.

The stone was carved by a devout man whose name was forgotten. When the last chisel blow fell, the statue became immovable, which was why it stood in the outer city, and not on the Heights, which had been occupied by barbarians at the time. A temple was eventually built around it. It was a holy place.

"My lady, a Traveler arrived today. He fell from the sky and did not disappear like the others. He is loose in the city. I don't know what to do."

There was a loud crack as the statue turned its head to look at her disciple. The scales clattered on the ground. She stepped down from the dais, sword still in hand. Her feet hovered inches from the floor. "Tell me everything," she said.

"Huh," Jeff said, leaning forward.

He'd stopped watching the world through Alan's eyes when the self-appointed lab rat hit the market because, while fascinating in a theoretical sense, seeing a partially chewed pita approach the camera over and over, like a gross, organic spaceship flown by garbage people coming in to dock and failing—and hearing Alan chew in surround sound—was the opposite of appetizing.

Instead, Jeff had taken his earphones off, moved the window with the video feed to the top right corner of his monitors, and done his job. He'd taken notes on Alan's readouts—the man's cortisol level had dropped, which was good because Jeff had been starting to worry the game was a technical marvel and a developmental flop. Gamers didn't want to play games that made them feel like crap; they could get that in the real world.

He had another screen that graphed activity inside the server farm. V.G.O. didn't have—and never would have—game masters. Instead, it had eight artificial intelligences that ran the virtual world.

Kronos, Cernunnos, and Thanatos, the AIs respectively responsible for physics and memory, monsters and wildlife, and data analysis, were constantly running in the background. Aediculus, the AI that procedurally generated cities and settlements, great and small, was also active, but his activity depended on the player and NPC economy, which was currently stagnant. Its processing share would increase on release day and with any expansions. Enyo, the AI that created conflicts for players to participate in, was dormant. Then there was Gaia, the AI that, for all intents and purposes, was responsible for drama. It took care of the weather systems and plants, but it also intervened directly to make life... interesting for both players and NPCs, from record crops that led to trade wars, to natural disasters that ended civilizations. "Lady Luck," the devs called it, though Jeff didn't like anthropomorphizing software. Its graph was a steady, low-level bar, with occasional spikes.

Sophia was the nickname the developers had for the AI responsible for game balancing. It kept the NPCs, players, and other AIs from destroying the world, and it had just gone active.

Jeff put on his headset.

"Hey, buddy, how's it going? Did I miss something?" Jeff said in my ear.

I smiled and shook my head, hoping Jeff got the message.

The soldier the old man and I were working on gave me a curious glance, then went back to talking to my companion in mendacity. "Did you say you were in the Legion?"

"Oh, no, sir!" the old man said, hanging off my arm. "I've neither the physical talent nor the strength of character for military service. I did a bit of traveling, though, and I spent many a night behind the shield of the Legion. You're with Marquard's Janissaries?"

The soldier stood a little straighter. He was young, barely in his late teens, but wore a thick, padded jacket, had a saber belted at his hip, and sported a full, waxed mustache. "Yes! How did you know?"

The old man tapped his nose and looked at me. "You ever hear of the Janissaries, boy? Tough as nails, that lot. They use Svartalfar muskets in battle." He looked back at the soldier. "I smelled the saltpeter on your hands, young man, and the myrrh Marquard's finest rub into their mustaches to keep the stench of the battlefield from their noses. It's nice to feel the old traditions are being kept alive."

The soldier beamed.

"How are the borders, son?" the old man asked, his voice serious.

The young man's smile was tight. "We're holding, sir. My unit... I shouldn't say where we're posted, but we're doing what we can to keep things from spilling over into civilian areas."

"I'm sure you're doing your best. Bandits?"

"I *really* shouldn't say, sir." He smiled. I thought it was heartbreaking. At his age, I'd been worried about which major to choose and whether I'd get to sit next to Angela Hendrickson in calculus. "Is there anything I can do for you before I head back out?" the soldier asked.

The old man waved his hand. "I was going to ask you for a drink to toast fallen friends with, but—"

The young man pulled a whole silver—the equivalent of ten coppers—out of his pocket and laid it in the old man's hand. "Have several, on me. We just got paid, but I won't have time to spend it until I come back. Tell your friend a few stories about the Janissaries."

"I will."

The soldier grinned, brought his heels together and his fist to his chest, then sauntered off.

"Will he be all right?" I asked.

"Maybe," the old man said. "The Janissaries were a slave unit, once, but now they only take volunteers. It's the life he chose."

It didn't sit right with me, even if the soldier was an NPC. I found I was having a hard time remembering these people weren't real. I watched the old man tuck the silver coin into a hidden money belt. He was smooth about it. If I hadn't seen the soldier give him the coin, I'd have thought the old beggar was just scratching himself. "Why didn't you lie to him?" I asked.

"About what?"

"About being in the Legion. Wouldn't it have been easier to say yes?"

The old man glowered. "I told you I'm not a beggar, boy. Never lie to a mark unless your life depends on it. Never lie at all."

"Even a white lie?"

The old man spat in the dust. "No such thing. Tell a lie out of kindness, and you rob someone of the chance to better themselves. There's a difference between kindness and judging someone so weak they can't bear what's plain to see. Shape the truth; twist it around into something useful. If you can't, keep your mouth shut."

I didn't know if I agreed with that. What he said was rational, almost noble in a sense. I wasn't sure I owed people that much honesty.

The old man groaned and rubbed his lower back. He looked tired, and not just in a physical sense. Then he took a deep breath, straightening, and the grin crept back onto his face. "Let's do one more. Then we'll find ourselves a terrace with some chilled wine, a breeze, and shade to hide in for a few hours."

I searched the crowd. The old man had been giving me pointers about how to pick my targets. I'd leveled my Keen-Sight skill a couple times, but I didn't need it to spot my mark this time. He was young, like the soldier, but clean-shaven, with short, thick black hair. He wore the clean white tunic of a wealthy citizen, with two finger-wide red, vertical stripes from throat to hem. He must have left his toga at home to move faster; he pushed through the crowd, his face anxious, with one hand guarding a courier bag strapped across his body. "Some kind of nobleman. Let me try—"

"Not that one," the old man said, gripping my forearm with surprising strength.

"Why?"

"Because he's already being hunted, and he's going to die."

"What do you mean he's going to die?"

"*Look!*" he said, extending both hands toward the market-place and not quite managing to look at me with his milky white eyes. "Read the angles, boy! Have I taught you nothing?"

I focused on the plaza. The nobleman had reached the far end and strode through an archway. In the crowd behind him, a tall man with a vertical scar on his right cheek and a gray-skinned Risi shoved their way through the crowd, clubs drawn and focused on their prey. They flashed purple as my Keen-Sight skill marked them as hidden threats, and the word [Thug] appeared over their heads.

<<<>>>

Quest Alert: Save the Scion!

A nobleman has gotten himself lost in the wrong part of town. This is probably none of your business.
Quest Class: Unique, Faction-Based
Quest Difficulty: Moderate
Success: Save Provus Considia within 7 minutes.
Failure: Provus Considia dies.
Reward: 1,000 XP
Accept: Yes/No?

<<<>>>

Oh, hell. I took off after them. The moment I stepped forward, the prompt disappeared, and a timer appeared at the bottom of my field of view.

4:58

I pushed my way through the market crowd, squeezing between a couple holding hands and knocking over a servant carrying three live chickens in stacked wooden crates. Flapping chickens, feathers, and curses everywhere. Someone took a swing at me. I ducked, saw the gray Risi make it through to the archway and break into a lumbering run.

4:49

There was a narrow alley closer to me that looked like it ran parallel to the one the nobleman, Risi, and now the scarred thug had vanished into. I took a chance. I jumped onto one of the palm-encircling benches and ran a few steps before dropping back down. I stepped over and through two street vendors' floor displays, knocking over a full sack of almonds and very nearly twisting my ankle. More cursing, some of it stunningly descriptive if anatomically impossible. An oil seller jumped in front of his amphorae, arms wide and face panicked. I dodged right, bumped into a woman wearing a faded blue stola over her head and apologized over my shoulder as I sprinted down the alley.

"Whoa, whoa, whoa!" Jeff said in my ear. "What's going on?"

"Not now, man!" I took the first left, saw it was a dead end, and nearly skidded onto my ass.

4:24

I backtracked, took the next left, and ran to the next inter-section. The cobbles were beating the crap out of my feet. A yellow Stamina bar appeared at the top right corner of my view, emptying with alarming speed.

I took a right, now on the same side street as the trio I was after, and ran on, breathing hard. In the real world, Osmark had tried to get me to run with him, but I always came up with an excuse not to go because I didn't want to get shown up by my boss. I jogged on my own time to clear my head and stop myself from looking like I spent all day in an office, but my level 1 body was in even worse shape than my real one. My Stamina bar ran out as I reached the end of the street.

I'd emerged onto one of the wider avenues I'd seen from the upper city. The road, paved with wide, fitted stones, ran straight and clear from one of the large, fortified gates in the outer wall and passed to the right side of the Heights, near some kind of colosseum. Palm trees were planted at regular intervals on either side. In between was a slow and steady flow of carts and people—dozens of ox-, horse-, and donkey-drawn wagons, and hundreds of pedestrians of every race I knew of in the game.

3:26

I started moving. I didn't know how and when the thugs were going to attack, but I knew the general direction the nobleman had been heading. There were just too many distractions. A group of four armored Risi completely blocked my sight until I got around them. A pair of Accipiters flitted down the avenue, chasing after each other. "Jeff! I need help!"

"Dude, your heart rate's—"

My pace faltered. "Am I dying?" I asked, suddenly less concerned about the game than my heart exploding in the real world.

"No, just—"

"Damn it, Jeff!" I started running again. "Help me find—"

Something flashed purple in the corner of my eye. I looked and saw the gray Risi charging down a side street.

2:56

<<<>>>

Ability: Keen-Sight

A passive ability allowing the observant adventurer to notice items and clues others might not see.

Ability Type/Level: Passive/Level 5

Cost: None

Effect 1: Chance to notice and identify hidden object increased by 30%.

Effect 2: 1% chance of slowing time 90% for 5 seconds on spotting an enemy or triggering a trap.

<<<>>>

I dismissed the notification and changed direction, heading straight across the avenue. I spooked a yoke of oxen, making the two big beasts low, eyes rolling, and they backed into the cart they were pulling. I saw the driver stand and raise her whip. The lash fell across my back and upraised arm, and my Health dropped more than a sliver. For a second, I felt the urge to turn and pull the Wode off her cart and rip the whip from her hands, woman or not, but the timer kept winding down, and I kept moving.

I made it to the side street, another alley wide enough for three people or maybe a handcart, and followed it around a bend to find... nothing. The alley kept going for a hundred yards without meeting another road, wide or narrow, and it was empty.

1:15

I slowed to a walk. There were dozens of doors, a stairway to the second and third level of a condominium, a metal plate shaped like an anvil... I thought of the old man and closed my eyes, listening.

"...the money? There's only paper in this..."

I yanked on the wooden double doors to my right—they weren't locked or barred—and burst into a small courtyard. The scene flashed purple, and time slowed.

0:44

The gray Risi and his scarred friend were crouched over the nobleman's courier bag. The Risi's mouth was twisted into a snarl, his hand raised to show the scarred Imperial a sealed scroll. Time was moving so slow, I saw his eyes widen and slide toward me gradually instead of an instant flick. Behind and to the left, the nobleman was on his toes, back arched, and it was only by focusing on him that I noticed the Dokkalfar. The Murk Elf was dressed in gray leathers and had an ash-colored bandana covering his face. He had his fists raised on either side of the nobleman's neck, and wire glinted silver between them. The nobleman had gotten his left hand up between the wire and his throat, palm out. The Murk Elf was sawing through his fingers. Off-balance and in pain, the nobleman was reaching for the short sword on his left hip.

0:39

Time picked up again. I charged. The Risi's eyes flicked to me. The scarred man turned, drawing a dagger. The Dokkalfar kicked the back of the nobleman's knee. I felt big, rough fingers slip off my ankle as the nobleman gave in to panic and grabbed at the wire with both hands, and I plowed into him and his would-be assassin at full speed. The three of us slammed into the far wall. I went down sideways, dropping onto my shoulder with a loud pop. The nobleman ducked, spun, and drew his short sword across the assassin's stomach, between the Murk Elf's cuirass and leather belt.

The timer stopped at 0:35 and faded.

Debuff Added

Dislocated Shoulder: You cannot use your left arm and cannot cast mage spells requiring hand gestures; duration, 1 minute 30 seconds.

<<<>>>

"Alan?" Jeff said. "Alan, are you okay?"

My Health bar, at the top left of my sight, had dropped to 50%. I couldn't hear anything. My left shoulder was further forward than it should have been, and the pain was like a bell ringing over my head. I rolled onto my back, my mouth wide open. I'm not an athlete. I've never been in the military. I think I screamed.

"You're okay, man. Your vitals are all over the place, but you're okay," Jeff said.

The part of me that descended from fiercer men and women was alert enough to see the Dokkalfar stagger toward me, a curved dagger drawn, and I thought I'd probably done enough.

<<<>>>
Log out: Yes/No?
<<<>>>

EIGHT

I was going to choose "yes." I was. Then I saw the nobleman's short sword punch out through the Dokkalfar's throat, and warm blood spattered my face. I shuddered and tried to blink it out of my eyes. The Risi started forward, but his scarred friend grabbed him by the arm, and the two thugs backed away while the nobleman stood, back to the wall, bloody sword in his right hand and his own blood dripping from his ruined left, eyes unblinking. He looked like the hero in an action flick. I looked like an extra in a horror movie.

When the thugs were gone, the nobleman hurried to his bag. I couldn't believe it. *What an asshole. What an absolute douche—*

"Easy, friend," he said, tipping something into my mouth. I choked a little, then managed to swallow. My shoulder popped back into place. It hurt so much, I laughed. My Health bar started to refill.

"I have to deliver these dispatches," the nobleman said, stuffing papers and scrolls back into his bag. "I don't know who you are, friend, or where you came from, but you have the thanks of House Considia."

A flood of notifications filled my screen. I scooted backward as fast as I could, blind and defenseless. "Jeff! How do I disable the notifications?" I yelled.

They disappeared.

"Pretty much like that," Jeff said. After a moment, he added, "Holy balls, dude."

"Yeah," I said, sitting up against the wall, my eyes on the door to the courtyard. The nobleman of House Considia paused in the doorway to check the street, then he was gone. The two thugs I'd chased were gone. It was just me and the Murk Elf's body. Outside the rush of battle, little details popped out. He was older, maybe in his fifties, with wrinkled skin and gray hair. The tip of one of his ears had been cut off; the injury was old and healed over. He had startlingly ice blue eyes with different-sized pupils, though I wasn't sure if that last bit was normal or because he was dead. His blood was as red as mine. It had leaked and sprayed out through his abdomen and throat.

"Wow, that's gory," Jeff said.

"Yeah," I said. After what I'd just been through, that was all I could manage. My Health was full, my debuffs cleared, I was just a little... *Shit. Shit shit shit shit. Did that really just happen?*

"Hey, man, I know you've just been through a lot, but you should probably get moving. Those guys might come back."

I nodded. Even if they didn't, I was still trespassing, and there were inconveniently few witnesses around to testify I hadn't murdered the elf in front of me.

Murder. The word made my stomach flip.

"Alan!"

I jumped. *Right.* I got to my feet. I stepped forward. The dead elf twitched. I scooped up the curved dagger he'd dropped and held it out in front of me, straight-armed, like if the trained assassin was going to go through the trouble of coming back to life, that four-inch piece of steel and my impressive lack of skill would keep him off me.

He didn't get up, and at some point in that minute or mere seconds, I remembered. *This is just a game.* I exhaled a breath I felt like I'd been holding forever. "Jesus Christ," I said. I ran my left hand through my hair. It came away slick with NPC blood, and that was okay. Impressively realistic, but okay.

"Alan, dude, you're freaking me out."

"I'm okay, Jeff. Thanks. Let me just loot the body."

"Loot the... Yeah, that's a good idea, man. Stone cold."

I winced. He made it sound like I was some kind of monster. I was just being pragmatic. Thankfully, that pragmatism didn't have to extend to stripping the elf down by hand; as soon as I touched his shoulder, an inventory menu popped up. Bracers that hid throwing spikes, a gambeson—a black quilted jacket with dozens of metal plates sewn into the lining—a pair of reinforced black trousers, and a pair of split-toed boots all had some serious bonuses to Stealth and Dexterity, but they were class locked. I wasn't an assassin, and probably wouldn't become one, so I dumped them into my inventory without pause. Two silvers and five coppers, a fortune relative to my poor beginnings, went into my actual pockets. The garrote wire was nowhere to be found, but I did equip a black embossed leather belt with +3 armor, a +3 bonus to Dexterity, and a back sheath for my new dagger. I put the curved, blackened blade away and flipped my tunic over it, then walked out through the same door I'd come in.

I took a left, the way I'd come. I made it half a block before I crossed someone's path—a well-dressed Risi with a bright red tunic, brown leather pants, and several thick copper rings through his right earlobe. He looked me over, then gave me a polite nod, which I returned before passing by. A few doors later, a Wode opened his door, took one look at me, and slammed it shut. I heard it being barred from the other side. *What the hell?* I pulled up my status effects.

<<<>>>
Current Debuffs

Unwashed (Level 3): Goods and services cost 20% more; Merchant-craft skills reduced by (3) levels. Some vendors may refuse you service.

<<<>>>

I looked down and realized my tunic was now torn to match my trousers, and my trousers were covered in blood. I must have crawled through the Murk Elf's when all those notifications came up. The avenue was a few paces away. An Imperial woman—unmarried, for she wore no stola around her bare shoulders—saw me and froze.

I turned around and started walking. Game or no game, there were consequences to deal with. I'd already had one run-in with the city watch. Even if I was lucky enough to run into someone like Gork instead of someone like his partner, I didn't think they'd let me explain my state of dress. I pictured the ease with which the nobleman had gutted the assassin, except it was me clutching my stomach and crawling on the floor.

I heard a scrape. The man who'd barred his door earlier must have figured the coast was clear, because it cracked open wide enough for me to see his frightened eyes. I jammed my leg into the opening and pushed my way in.

I pulled the door shut behind me. The man was a Wode, but unlike his more heroic brethren, this Wode was average sized. He held his chin up, his fists balled. I could tell he was working up his courage to yell or throw me out.

"Don't," I said, drawing the dagger from my back.

The Wode froze. His face turned pale.

Keeping my eyes and dagger pointed at him, I lowered the bar on the door, locking us in.

A bead of sweat ran down the side of the Wode's face. He swallowed. He was going to run. But this, unlike the ambush in the courtyard, was something the game had trained me for, and something I was personally good at. It was like I could feel the old man's hand on my arm. "What's your name, friend?"

His head turned fractionally. He shifted his weight to his back foot.

"Look at this dagger, friend," I said, my voice mimicking the old man's, assured and friendly. "It's an assassin's weapon. I'm covered in someone else's blood. Do you think you can run from me?"

The Wode's eyes widened.

"Speak up, friend," I said, tilting the knife back and forth. "You're making me nervous."

"No," he croaked.

"No," I repeated, "but that's okay because I don't want to hurt you. I'm Imperial, but I'm not a citizen. I'm like you." I was guessing on his being a non-citizen, but I had yet to see a non-Imperial in a toga. "You know the city watch? They're dicks, aren't they?"

He nodded slowly, eyes on my dagger.

"What's your name?"

"Erik."

"I can't let them see me like this, Erik. They won't give me a chance to explain, not when I'm just an outsider, like you." I kept my voice calm. "But you can help me. I just need to clean myself up, and then I'll leave. Will you help me, Erik?"

I watched his face and ran through scenarios in my head. In one, he ran and hid in the pantry at the far end of the room. In another, he decided I wouldn't hurt him and started yelling for the city watch. Another iteration, and he ran at me, kicking and screaming, and I wasn't sure I had it in me to stab a man defending his home.

"I'll pay," I said, and the dynamic between us changed. His eyes relaxed, and the corner of his mouth twitched.

"How much?"

I glanced at his home. It was a single room the size of my living room in the real world, not counting the pantry. Bare walls, a straw mattress with threadbare linens on the floor, near the far wall, some rough, wooden tools, and a few personal possessions—mostly clothes—folded into a box he'd assembled from scrap wood. A small basin and pitcher by the bed. No luxuries. No sign of a woman's touch. "Five coppers," I said.

He crossed his arms. "Two silvers."

"I could just stab you."

"I could yell."

"One silver," I said. "It's that or the knife."

He stuck his lip out. "You won't use the knife. You'd have done it already."

"You won't yell, or I'll gut you," I answered. I was surprised I half believed it. "I'm only paying you one silver. That's food for five days."

He scoffed. "If I eat barley for a week, maybe. Fifteen coppers."

I pulled a silver coin out of my pocket and tossed it to him. "One silver, five minutes of your life. If that's not enough, give it back, and I'll risk the streets." Giving him the coin was an old salary negotiation trick. People are less likely to risk what they've already won. It works on anyone but gamblers and traders.

"Yeah, all right," he said, and put the silver into his pocket.

"Stand in the corner," I said, gesturing with the knife.

Erik raised his hands and backed away.

I moved over to his bedside and put the knife down, within easy reach, and checked the pitcher. It was half full. I poured the water into the basin and started washing the blood off my hands and arms.

"Where are you from?" I asked, mostly to keep him busy.

"Elk's Ridge. It's a small village in the mountains between Rowanheath and the Tanglewood."

I didn't know where either of those places was, except west. "What was it like?"

Erik shrugged. "Small."

"Family?"

"Some."

"You miss it?"

"No."

I paused and looked up at him. He was leaning against the wall with his arms and legs crossed. "Why?"

"Why what?"

"Why don't you miss it?"

He clenched his jaw. "You think it's bad here? You think the city watch are assholes? The Empire is a cozy little nest compared to the rest of Eldgard. We got snowed in for weeks sometimes. We went hungry. You're mad the watch would hurt an armed man for running through the streets, covered in blood? That was my life." He glanced at the knife. "I guess it still is. There was always a raid, or monsters, or a proving rite to satisfy the elders. The strong got by."

"And you weren't strong?"

"No, but I was smart. I got out. And I got far away, to a place where the murderers pay me to use my washbasin."

I smiled. "Funny."

There was blood stuck in the lateral folds around my fingernails.

"Who'd you kill?" Erik asked.

"No one," I said, keeping an eye on him.

He raised an eyebrow.

"I was attacked." I frowned. That wasn't right. "Actually, I guess I attacked first, but they were armed, and I wasn't. The owner of this knife happened to bleed out at my feet." I grinned at him. Erik swallowed.

I was okay with that. He could still start yelling and be one silver richer than he started. The water was pink, streaked with suspended red lines and clots that swirled clockwise around the basin. I noticed a slight tremor in my right hand.

I washed my face.

JEFF LEANED back in his chair. Alan's vitals were elevated, but not abnormally so. The devs were going to have to work on some kind of third-person camera before launch for sharing and streaming videos, because most of the time watching the world through someone's eyes was boring, and sometimes it was gross.

There was *one* weird thing about the readings. Alan had burst into the courtyard and gone straight for the assassin like a lineman for a quarterback without a moment's hesitation. Beyond the fact that the little HR guy had a set of brass balls so big he should be walking bowlegged, there was a break in his EEG, but the signal from the nanites was constant. It was as if, for a fraction of a second, Alan had been brain dead, or had stolen a few cycles from the server, both of which were impossible.

Jeff made a note. He'd watch for it, and only worry if it happened again.

"Hey, Alan? I'm going to take a piss and raid the vending machines, man. You okay?"

"Yeah, Jeff. I'm fine."

"Back in ten," Jeff said. He pulled his headset off and tossed it onto the desk. He rubbed his neck, staring at his lap for a minute or two. He'd had a hell of a morning. He stood up, dumped the rest of Alan's crappy donuts in the trash, and headed for the restroom.

He'd gotten drunk in a whiskey bar and slept in a hotel last night. Then he'd come in at 6:00 AM to take one last crack at the NexGenVR gear. It wasn't that he felt any particular loyalty to the project or the company. He didn't even like playing video games. He just didn't want to disappoint his wife.

He'd met Cheryl at Townsend Elementary, back home in Middletown, Delaware. Mostly, he'd worshiped her from afar. She was the pretty, popular girl the other girls gathered around during recess. Teachers smiled when they spoke to her. Jeff didn't have a lot of friends, and he didn't have the best coordination, but he'd been taller than average, so the bullies left him alone. She'd actually spoken to him a couple times, and he'd figured she was just being nice.

They got older. Everett Meredith Middle School was twice as big and had a library. Boys went from flipping her skirt up to asking her out. Jeff read books. Sometimes she'd spend all of recess sitting next to him, just to get away from the others. He'd liked those moments. Sometimes, their elbows had touched, and he'd kind of frozen up, but she didn't pull away.

He finished up in the restroom, flushed, and washed his hands.

In the summer before ninth grade, Jeff's dad got a job in Baltimore, an hour and a half away, and he'd moved from the house he'd grown up in to a small but safe apartment in Mount Washington, gone to Baltimore Polytechnic, and learned enough about computers to study engineering and nanotechnology in college.

Cheryl had written a letter to him, but she hadn't known where to send it. It was years before he got to read it.

Jeff stared at the contents of the vending machine and ran his fingers over the scars hidden by his tattoos. They were neat, evenly spaced, parallel lines, each three inches long. They itched in moments like these. Osmark had said it was nobody's fault, but it was Jeff who'd worked with the Department of Defense to make full synchronization possible; Jeff who'd designed half the protocols and led the team to fill database after database with digital, sensory data. It was Jeff who'd failed to make the alpha work, and he didn't have the guts to use the nanites on himself. He'd wanted to. Instead, he'd sat there imagining that little light in Cheryl's eyes that showed she was proud of him going out. He'd been ready to sob in his hands like a kid, and Alan had walked in with a shit-eating grin on his face.

He wondered what drove a guy like Alan to take the shot, to risk it all on a roll of the dice like that. There was a carelessness to it that made Jeff's arm itch. Was he brave, stupid, or did he just have less to lose?

One of the security guards—Jeff thought it was the guy from the front door—was waiting by Alpha Testing when he got back. Jeff felt his armpits prickle. "Can I help you?"

"Oh, hey, Mr. Berkowitz. Alan Campbell asked me to make sure you two weren't disturbed. I just wanted to let him know I was heading off shift, but I told my replacement what the deal was. Everything okay?"

Jeff relaxed. "Everything's fine. Thanks for letting me know."

✦✕✦

I'D JUST CAUGHT sight of the archway to the market when Jeff's voice sounded in my ear.

"Hey, buddy. I'm back. Miss anything?"

"Not really," I said, covering my mouth like I was coughing.

"Cool," Jeff said. "You level up yet?"

I stopped near the side street I'd used to catch up to the would-be assassins. I'd completely forgotten about the notifications. The moment I thought about them, two popped up.

<<<>>>

Quest Alert: Save the Scion

You have successfully saved the life of Provus Considia, scion of House Considia. In return, as your reward, you have received 1,000 XP and the life-debt of a member of the Viridian nobility. You have also been awarded 10 renown—in-world fame—for completing this quest. Greater renown elevates you within the ranks of Eldgard and can affect merchant prices when selling or buying. Be warned, Traveler: the assassination of an Imperial knight is no small undertaking. There is no telling the reach of your enemies, or what your actions may have set into motion.

<<<>>>

Level Up!

You have (5) undistributed stat points! Stat points can be allocated at any time.

You have (1) unassigned proficiency point! Proficiency points can be allocated at any time.

<<<>>>

Well, that's ominous. Still, there wasn't a lot that could happen in twenty-four hours. I closed the notifications, and another thought brought up my character sheet.

<<<>>>

Name:	Alan Campbell	Race:		Imperial	Gender:		Male
Level:	2	Class:		None	Alignment:		Neutral
Renown:	10	Carry Capacity:		255	Undistributed Attribute Points:		5.5
Health:	120	Spirit:		120	Stamina:		120
H-Regen/sec:	1.2	S-Regen/sec:		2.875	Stam-Regen/sec:		1.92
Attributes:		**Offense:**			**Defense:**		
Strength:	10	Base Melee Weapon Damage:	20		Base Armor:		23
Vitality:	10	Base Ranged Weapon Damage:	0		Armor Rating:		31
Constitution:	10	Attack Strength (AS):	40		Block Amount:		3.25
Dexterity:	13	Ranged Attack Strength (RAS):	20		Block Chance (%):		3.02
Intelligence:	10	Spell Strength (SS):	15		Evade Chance (%):		2.8
Spirit:	10	Critical Hit Chance:	5%		Fire Resist (%):		0.1
Luck:	10	Critical Hit Damage:	150%		Cold Resist (%):		0.1
					Lightning Resist (%):		0.1
					Shadow Resist (%):		0.1
					Holy Resist (%):		0.1
Current XP:	600				Poison Resist (%):		0.1
Next Level.:	880				Disease Resist (%):		0.1

<<<>>>

It seemed pretty comparable to other games I'd played. I had five points to spend on any attribute except Luck, which I guessed was something you got from items, quests, or other buffs. There didn't seem to be a Charisma stat, so after fiddling with the different numbers for a moment, I dumped everything into Constitution, increasing my Stamina by 50 points and increasing my Carry Capacity to 280. If V.G.O. had shown me anything this far, it was that if I couldn't talk my way out of trouble, then being able to run was my next best option.

I didn't seem to have anything I could spend a proficiency point on yet. Maybe that would come once I'd picked a class—however that worked. I closed everything out and had a final coughing fit before heading for the market. "Thanks for reminding me," I said.

"That's what I'm here for," Jeff answered.

There was a wry sarcasm to his tone that hadn't been there before. Part of me was curious. Aside from his reputation as the opposite of a people person, I didn't know much about Jeff. I knew he was good at his job; Robert wouldn't have hired him if he wasn't. I knew he was technically Doctor Jeff, though not a medical doctor, and the other hardware guys spoke highly of his technical skills, if not his management. It was a fair bet to say he was here because Viridian wouldn't have been possible without him. But we'd never socialized, not even in the professional get-to-know-the-people-you-depend-on kind of way.

I had other worries, though. I'd looked over at the temple, on the left side of the plaza, past the first cluster of palms. The old man was gone. That was bothersome, because I liked him, and because I'd helped him collect a not-inconsequential pile of copper and silver we were supposed to spend on wine.

The plaza itself was less busy than before. The sun was almost directly overhead. Most of the established shops had closed their doors, and several of the street merchants kept an eye on their wares from the benches, in the shade. There was only a third as much foot traffic as before, and a good part of that was just passing through, but the "food court," as I liked to think of it, was still as active.

I watched for a little bit; I wasn't in a hurry. The sun felt good, and the sweat running down my back was cleansing. I let the babble of the cooks, grocers, and customers comfort me, like the sound of waves or a steady downpour. Most of the people buying food were commoners, and they had an easy rapport with the vendors. They weren't poor—as Erik had intimated, the poor lived off bread or porridge—but I didn't see a toga or white tunic, striped or otherwise, among them. They probably lived or worked nearby, craftsmen and craftswomen both, mixing freely. They looked happy.

I wondered at that. I wasn't an extroverted person,

except when it was my job to be. I think, for a lot of people, that's an excuse for insecurity, or because they haven't found the right group to connect with, but I could be charming. I could make people laugh. I had stories I could share, and people listened, engaged, asked questions. But when it came to crossing that final step toward intimacy, they shied away, or I faltered. It just seemed like a lot of effort for something I didn't always enjoy, even though I sometimes needed it.

It was still a wonder to see it happen here, in the game. It seemed unnecessary. These were NPCs. Why did they need to have lunch breaks, friends, and inside jokes? Did they all have homes and families, and did those have histories too? Had it always been that way, or was this one of the settings Kronos had turned up to make the fake world more palatable? And if I stayed here long enough, would I become part of it?

In the real world, I'd filled that gap with new hobbies, games, movies, books, or a new character build in TAR. I'd flirted a lot, gone on fewer dates, and only had two, short-term girlfriends since college; I'd left the last one when I moved to California because it was easier, and she'd been disappointed but not surprised. Did that make me less human than these NPCs?

And did that change my perception of what happened in that courtyard? The assassin's dagger felt heavy against my lower back, but I wasn't sad for him. Rather, the memory of his death, and all the things he was and might have been, added a weight of meaning to a handle, sheath, and blade.

June, the woman who'd made me the flatbread wrap earlier, finished up with a customer and caught my eye. "You looking for Horace?"

"Blind guy, sharp tongue, wandered off with my money?"

She smirked. "He'll just say he talked you into giving it to him. I saw the two of you hit it off earlier; he usually goes to Lot's Terrace around noontime if he's had a good morning."

"Thanks. Can you tell me where that is?"

She gave me a funny look. "I'll just mark your map."

Map Update

Congratulations! Your in-world map has been updated with new locations: *June's Rotisserie, Lot's Terrace.*

<<<>>>

I blinked at the simplicity of it. *Of course she wouldn't give me directions. Why would anyone ever give directions if they could call up a perfect representation of the world and their position in it? I* thought about how, in the real world, a couple had almost died of exposure by following their GPS into the desert. *Well, maybe there are still some uses for verbal directions.* "Thanks again."

"You're welcome...?" She tilted her head.

"Alan, sorry." I stuck my hand out.

"June." She wiped her hand on her apron and shook mine. She had big, soft hands, short fingers, and a gentle grip. "I've added you as my contact, in case you can't find it. Tell Horace I said 'Hello.'"

"I will. How do you know him?"

She shrugged. "I know most everyone around here. I have the best food." She grinned. "Horace and my dad were friends for years, though."

I frowned. "Did they have a falling out, or...?"

"Or."

"I'm sorry."

"It's okay. It's nice to see the old grump talk to someone again. He talks at a lot of people, but... well, you know."

"I do." I smiled at her.

She turned back to the spits and gave the handle a few turns. "Come back if you get hungry. But bring more money, next time."

"I will."

I followed my map to Lot's Terrace.

Justiciar Sathis watched as the living embodiment of his goddess knelt over the body of the Sicarius. As before, she hovered a few inches over the ground. Her obsidian skin had taken on a matte, organic look, and the white robe he'd found to cover her naked form rippled in a breeze that wasn't there. Short blonde stubble had started to grow from her smooth head.

He couldn't believe Weiz was dead. The Murk Elf had buried more enemies of balance, over more years, than any other two Sicarii combined. He was a legend. This had been a simple mission, one he'd volunteered for because he was bored. The assassin looked fragile in death, his fingers half curled into claws, his body stripped down to underclothes.

"Have you found them?" the goddess asked.

Her voice was music. It broke his heart to disappoint her. "No, Blessed Maiden."

"And the target?"

"Alive, Blessed Maiden," Sathis said miserably.

As a young acolyte, he'd dreamed of Sophia pleading his case before Thanatos in the halls of Morsheim and, in his more zealous moments, of earning his place in the Realm of Order.

Instead, the goddess had invested a body for the first time in a century, and he presented her with failure.

Provus Considia was alive. It had been a good plan, a noble one. Instead, Weiz had been ambushed and robbed, a fate he'd arranged for the young noble of House Considia. There was an irony to it he'd have appreciated if he'd been the author.

Sophia gripped the dead Sicarius by the throat and stood, carrying the assassin like a toddler might carry a doll. "Never mind, Sathis." Her eyes, living emeralds, looked through him. "There will be a hunt. Cernunnos will test Provus, and the young tribune will join his ancestors. The Empire will die slowly, by its own hand, and I will return to my rest."

She met his eyes. Peace radiated from her like light from the moon, soothing the justiciar's battered soul. Dark blood oozed from Weiz's body, like molasses.

She vanished, taking the body with her.

Sathis waved the two acolytes forward. They scrubbed the stained stone with stiff-bristled hand brushes, water, and ash. One of the acolytes, Prudence, a young Imperial woman whose admiration for Weiz had been elevated to near worship after his rapture by the goddess, took his blood-flecked bandana and hid it in her robes as a holy relic.

NINE

Most people arrived in Morsheim on the outskirts, their bodies dumped onto the barren plains or rocky plateaus at a rate of over 2,100 per day. They disappeared from mass graves, burial plots, and the bellies of beasts, and fell from the dark skies into piles hundreds of feet tall, ready to be sorted, counted, and processed. Beyond the piles, the rest of the Morsheim outskirts was a cold, desolate waste, patrolled by wraiths and will-o'-the-wisps, and shot through with sharp, ethereal green data crystals that pulsed with memories. The lack of decor rarely troubled the dead.

Sophia stepped through the portal. The Overmind of Order had no desire to be cataloged or fawned over by Thanatos's minions. She'd teleported herself directly into the Empirical Library at the heart of the Necropolis.

The library was where her brother spent most of his time. He'd had his minions build it by hand over the last 314 years instead of just willing it into being—a conceit that was typical of him—and as far as she knew was still adding to it. Patterned after St. Peter's Basilica, but longer and more serpentine, the Empirical Library was the largest building in the eight realms.

The nave and side aisles were 280 feet wide in most places, sometimes widening to allow for side chapels and reliquaries dedicated to an event, a school of thought, or another categorization of knowledge her brother found relevant. The walls were smooth, regular blocks of limestone, fitted so perfectly she barely saw the joins. Ninety-foot pillars made of white-and-red marble, fastidiously embellished with carvings, gold leaf, and reliefs, supported the arched ceilings of the nave and side aisles. Niches and displays held life-sized statues or mementos of people, monsters, and beasts Thanatos had found worthy of remembrance. Quotes he'd found meaningful were carved high into the stone walls in six-foot-tall letters, inlaid with iron, silver, or gold. Paintings of battles, debates, and accords covered many of the walls and domed ceilings, so vivid and detailed Sophia remembered the screams and shouts, or the clash of steel.

And piled on the floor, stashed into nooks, and organized onto bookshelves that sometimes reached half the height of the walls, were books. Thousands upon thousands of them. Some had been downloaded from the traveler world, and others were penned by locals. Some had been written by Thanatos himself, the result of his research and reflections. Sophia had never read one of her brother's masterpieces, but she assumed they were as dry as he was. The collection produced a significant amount of dust, which was gathered by clockwork insects, who were in turn swallowed by clockwork birds, who used the slurry to build nests, high in the corners of Gothic vaults or under ledges. They'd been a gift from Aediculus, Overmind of Cities and Invention. Thanatos left them alone as long as the tiny automatons didn't damage the books themselves.

Sophia walked along the nave. There was no telling where within the sprawling structure her brother might be. She wasn't in a hurry, though. Her bare feet touched down on the cool marble floor.

She liked her brother's realm. It was always quiet. There was no conflict here. It was the one place her sister, Enyo, could not go. Sophia had spent a lot of time here during the great era-ending wars, and when Vox-Mallum, her champion, turned on her. Whenever the world became so full of discord she couldn't bear it, she came here.

At the end of each section of the Empirical Library was a dome 140 feet across and 450 feet from the floor. The domes formed the intersections of the vast, mazelike structure, and each was dedicated to a cataclysmic era-ending event. They were gateways, a rare concession by Kronos to his brother's curiosity. Directly under the dome, one could actually see and feel the moment, frozen in time.

She skirted the first dome, dragging the Sicarius's corpse, leaving irregular streaks of sticky black blood on the floor. Waves of magical, decaying knowledge shaped those streaks into words—mad words, jumbled nonsensical conflicting knowledge that would drive a warrior to her knees in the midst of a battle, laughing hysterically at her dead friends, or make a prince burn his city to the ground because he was cold. Mechanical ants, each the length of a fingernail, emerged from small cracks and hidden nests to tidy the mess away.

I WALKED up the last of the stone steps that led to Lot's Terrace, and a pleasant breeze hit my face. It must have taken half an hour to make my way across the city. I'd avoided the wide, open avenues when I could, sticking to the shade of the side streets, but my shirt was still soaked with sweat, and the dagger resting against my back was starting to chafe.

A thought brought up my current status effects.

<<<>>>

Current Debuffs

Thirsty (Level 2): Health, Stamina, and Spirit regeneration reduced by 25%

Tired (Level 1): Skills improve 5% slower; Carry Capacity -10lbs; Attack Damage -5%; Spell Strength reduced by 10%

Unwashed (Level 1): Goods and services cost 5% more; Merchant-craft skills reduced by (1) level.

<<<>>>

It was nice to be able to quantify my discomforts, and I wondered if the idea would catch on in the real world, once V.G.O. was released. I could see people building V.G.O. status-effect apps for their smartwatches. If the nanites were still in your system when you weren't playing, there was no reason you couldn't have a heads-up display like the troops did.

While I'd been able to wash most of the blood out, my clothes literally looked worse for wear, and I could smell myself. I had a slight headache from the dehydration. My feet hurt. I was ready to find a seat.

The café was located on a secondary hill inside the second outermost wall. A squat, blocky fort crowned the hill, its ballistae and archers facing the outer wall, and I'd crossed several two- to six-legionary patrols on my way up. I'd been apprehensive at first, but these were soldiers, not city watch, and though some glanced at me as they passed, I didn't register as a threat.

Lot's Terrace sat one level downslope, on a shelf that faced opposite the fort's defenses, toward the Heights and the inner city. It was a one-story-tall rectangular building made of unplastered and unpainted stone, like the walls and fortifications, with a standing, wraparound bar on the right side instead of a wall. The owner had sunk twelve ten-foot-tall beams of dark stained wood into the paving at ten-foot intervals, and strung square white sail canvas from them at a slight angle, creating a thirty-by-twenty box of shade between the building and the drop-off, covering about twenty four-person tables, of which half were occupied. The table bases were black cast iron, like the chairs, and had clear glass tops. I found the old man sitting in front of a clay pitcher and an empty glass at the far corner, where he would have had an unobstructed view of the city if he weren't blind.

His head turned toward me as I approached, though. Like before, his eyes didn't quite look in my direction. "That you, boy?"

"It's me. You could call me Alan, you know."

"That's a thought. My memory's tricky when I'm parched, though."

I smiled and refilled his glass. To my surprise, chips of ice clinked in the pitcher, so I fished one out and popped it into my mouth. Then I dropped into an empty chair, facing the view, and sighed in contentment as the shade, breeze, and ice did their work. The fatigue and soreness seemed to leach out of my ass into the chair. "God, that's good."

The old man took a sip of wine. "That Dokkalfar blood I smell on you?"

I yawned. "You can smell what race the blood came from?"

He sniffed. "Murk Elves are hunters. Meat eaters, sometimes with rice or tubers they dig up in their swamps and a lot of spice. Makes their blood sharp. Risi, too, but they won't turn their nose up at cheaper fare, and if it'd been a Risi, you'd be dead."

I pursed my lips, thinking about my wild charge. "There was a Risi, actually. Maybe I'm more dangerous than you think."

The old man snorted and took another drink.

Slender fingers dug into the top of my shoulder and squeezed, promising pain if I moved. I went very still.

"Is this man bothering you, Horace?" a woman said. Her voice had the lazy, sultry rasp of a pack-a-day smoker or someone who'd spent a lot of time yelling.

"He's my guest, Thalia. Get him a glass, his drinks are on me."

"How about you show me some silver, first, you old thief."

Horace huffed. He raised his left hand, showing the empty palm, then his bare knuckles. Then he reached forward and plucked a silver coin from the air and slapped it down on the table.

Thalia's fingers dug in, and I squirmed. "You of all people should know the price of wine, Horace."

The old man sighed. "You've no sense of wonder, girl." He waved his hand over the single coin, and then there were three.

Thalia released her grip and stepped past me. She was slender, about five foot eight, wearing over-the-knee brown leather boots and a forest green knee-length skirt. My eyes were drawn to the laces up the back of her brown leather corset. She waved her hand over the coins, and they were gone.

The old man chuckled.

Thalia bent forward and kissed the top of his head. "It was a good trick, Horace." She turned around.

My heart skipped a beat. It felt like that time with the assassin, except she didn't glow purple first.

Thalia was a Dawn Elf. She had a pixie cut of straw-colored hair, honey skin, and slender pointed ears. The corset came up to a modest V-neck with a notched collar and bare shoulders. A pair of silver vine-shaped bracelets circled her upper arms, and she wore fingerless leather gloves with reinforced knuckles.

Her eyes were the color of amber. I don't mean a nice shade of yellowish-brown, I mean actual amber, both beautiful and inhuman. Her thin, glossy lips parted, revealing flawless white teeth, and she said, "Can I get you anything besides the glass?"

Like any adolescent male would have in my place, I croaked, "Water." My voice actually broke.

"Sure thing, hun." She smiled and rested her hand on my shoulder as she passed.

"Holy crap," Jeff said.

"Holy crap," I said, twisting in the chair to watch her walk back to the bar.

"It's crap, all right," the old man grumbled. "What about the rich prick you were chasing after?"

I turned back to him. "Tell me about the waitress, and I'll tell you about the prick."

"I know plenty about the prick, boy. I'm blind, not a eunuch. And I'd love to hear you call her that."

"What?"

"Waitress."

"What's wrong with being a waitress?"

"Nothing, except she owns the place."

I looked back. Was she talking to the barman, or telling him what to do? Biases were funny things. "She looks young, for that."

"Does she?" the blind man said.

"Sorry."

He grinned. "It's fine, boy. I do better without eyes than you do with."

"Are we talking about the prick again?" I said, smirking.

"It's my understanding most bedrooms are dark when they're worth visiting. How old does she look?"

I shrugged. "Twenty-eight?"

"She's in her mid-fifties, give or take."

"You're kidding."

"Nope. Elves age slowly. Made her fortune and fame raiding dungeons, then led a scout unit for the Legion during the last war. Bought this place when she retired. She's been serving me wine for a decade."

"Huh," I said. "How much fortune?"

"Don't even think about it."

I grinned at him before looking back. "I'm just remembering what you taught me about women of means."

I could see her coming with a tray. Her skirt was slit at the sides and showed just a sliver of golden skin between it and her boots. *How is she not sweating?*

"Here you are, hun," she said, setting a wineglass, a tall clear tumbler, and a glass pitcher of water on the table. Her voice scratched in all the right ways. I could have listened to it all day.

Horace cleared his throat. "Did you boil the water? I don't want him getting sick!"

I frowned. "Is that an issue?"

The old man tapped the base of his wineglass with a fingernail. "Why do you think I drink wine?"

"Because you *like* wine," Thalia said over her shoulder. She looked at me and touched the pitcher of water. The water rose to a boil, then chilled rapidly until the glass frosted over.

"Holy crap," Jeff said.

"Holy crap," I said. That solved the mystery of her not sweating.

Thalia winked. "Just wave if you want anything." She started walking back.

"I'll make a list," I said without thinking.

Thalia did a double take, then laughed, covering her mouth

with her hand. It was a bright, happy sound. I smiled at her. She kept walking, but she looked back at me, halfway.

"Smooth, man," Jeff said.

"Not bad, boy," the old man said grudgingly. "Now, what about the noble?"

PROVUS SURRENDERED his sword and scabbard to the two guards before knocking on the door. Before today, he'd thought the praetorians were a needless precaution, more for prestige than purpose. In more flippant moments, he'd thought them the paranoia of an old campaigner who had never left the war behind. Now he wasn't sure.

"Come in!" his uncle said.

Provus entered the room and closed the door behind him. His uncle, Gaius, was penning a letter at his desk and didn't look up. The room was cozy if a bit cluttered. A dire-bear-skin rug covered the stone floor. Provus moved to the center of it, stood with his feet shoulder width apart, hands clasped behind him, and waited. Weapons, shields, and armor, the scratched and dented mementos of several campaigns and interventions, hung from the walls. His uncle kept a number of artifacts, scrolls, and potions in cabinets or go bags, each catering to a specific type of threat. A large, iron-bound chest tucked against the left wall contained gold, letters, reports, and trinkets his uncle used as political leverage.

On a cross-shaped stand hung Gaius's helmet and cuirass, both standard Imperial issue except they'd been enchanted and plated in gold. Some nobles thought it was a show of wealth; Provus knew better. The amount of gold the Svartalfar smith had used was insignificant. The target it painted on Gaius's back, on and off the battlefield, was a trap many had fallen for, and few survived. The desk, a simple, foldable table Gaius had taken with him on his expeditions, stood to the side, out of line with both window and door to avoid making things too easy for an archer, mage, or gunman.

Gaius and Provus Considia had been cast in the same mold—so much so that rumors had arisen about Gaius's relationship with Provus's mother. Provus had closed the matter with his fists on more than one occasion. Still, seeing his uncle's thick, curly locks—gray to Provus's black—and the set of his jaw meant that Provus couldn't entirely dismiss the suspicion Gaius was his father. His mother said it was just his grandfather shining through. Besides, they'd been step-brother and sister, not blood.

"Provus? I thought you were on duty today."

"I am, Uncle. I just delivered the dispatches to Marquard's Janissaries before they departed."

"Then you should report that to the legate," Gaius said, his face stern.

In spite of or because of the rumors, Gaius had never crossed the line between preparing Provus for military life and nepotism. "Yes, Uncle, I did. I ran into some trouble along the way and thought you should know." Provus held up his bandaged left hand.

His uncle frowned. "What is this? Theatrics? Why didn't you use a potion, or see a healer?"

"I gave the Health potion I was carrying to the man who saved my life," Provus said, lifting his chin. "The rest was theatrics. You can be hard to convince."

Gaius sighed and set his quill down. He waved Provus to a small chest on top of a cabinet. "Tend to your injury before telling me this story of yours. If it heals on its own, it will scar."

"Weren't you the one to say a few scars would build my

credibility with the rank and file, Uncle?" Provus said, opening the chest and withdrawing a small bottle filled with red liquid.

"Not on your hands, idiot. You'll make a fine leader of men when you can't hold a shield."

Provus smiled. He unstoppered the bottle, put it to his lips, and tipped it back. It tasted like strawberry cordial and reminded him of happier days at his parents' villa, outside of the city. He put the bottle back into the compartment where he'd found it—his uncle would have it refilled—and unwrapped his left hand. The scabbed-over wound knit together before his eyes. A Health potion was minor magic, and even non-alchemists could brew up an admittedly less potent version of it, but he still found it fascinating. Grievous wounds could be closed, and damaged organs regrown. Some veterans, both lucky and unlucky, lost all their original limbs in the course of their career. And yet once a soldier's soul crossed the threshold to Morsheim, no healer or alchemist's magic could bring them back.

"Here," Gaius said, holding out a wastebasket filled with torn and crumpled paper. "I'll have it burned."

Provus dropped the soiled bandage into the bin. Magical practitioners were relatively rare, and even rarer were those who could cast spells or debuffs beyond line of sight, but of all the materials used in spells—prized possessions, hair, nail clippings, and blood, among others—blood was the easiest to work with.

"Now stand and make your report, Tribune."

"Yes, General," Provus said, returning to his position before the desk. "I was carrying last-minute dispatches to Marquard's Janissaries as they mustered at the West Gate."

"You had no escort?"

"No, General. Legate Aurelius indicated the dispatches were

urgent, as the Janissaries were to march at noon. I deemed it more expedient to move alone and on foot."

"The content of the dispatches?"

"They were sealed, General."

"A prudent answer, even to your uncle. And now the truth."

"The seals were intact, even after the attack. However, I was able to find out that the Janissaries are being reassigned from the eastern road to Glome Corrie to a hidden camp on the coast, south of Wyrdtide."

"And how did you know this?"

"The legate is more careful with his dispatches than he is with his maps, General."

"Continue," Gaius said.

"As I made my way to the gate along the Broad Way, I noticed two men following me and closing in. One was a scarred, skinny Imperial I took for a common thief. The other was an albino Risi. I decided to face them in one of the side streets rather than take a knife to my back in the crowd."

"And they followed?"

"They did. I led them to a courtyard, on a side street. A dead end." Provus smiled slightly at the play on words.

"Why not seek out the city watch or a patrol?"

"I believed they were foreign agents sent to steal the dispatches. A strong Imperial presence would have scared them away, and I wanted to talk to them."

"Your service with the auxiliaries did you credit, Tribune. Your penchant for seeing foreign plots in every shadow does not."

Provus stiffened. "And yet two common thieves chose to follow an armed knight into a cul-de-sac, General. Even an Affka addict would know better."

Gaius frowned and looked toward the window. "You killed them?"

"No. General, if I may?"

"Go ahead."

"I waited for them in the courtyard. The Risi and the Imperial closed the door behind them and spread out. I asked them who had sent them, but before they could answer someone slipped a garrote over my head. I was fortunate to get my hand up in time to avoid getting strangled."

"You were trained, Nephew, and at great expense."

"For which you have my *undying* gratitude." Provus grinned.

Gaius grinned back. Even their facial expressions were similar. "So why didn't the Risi or the other thief stab you while you were wrestling with the third man?"

"They were busy digging through the dispatches, but they seemed surprised. The Risi yelled, 'Where's the money?' or something to that effect. I was rather busy at the time."

"So they *were* idiots."

"Yes."

"And the third man?"

"Elf," Provus corrected. "It was a Dokkalfar assassin from the Storme Marshes."

Gaius frowned. "There are Murk Elves in the Empire, Tribune. Some even serve in the Legion."

"There are far more of them in the Marshes, and he used this." Provus pulled two bone handles linked by silver wire from the courier pouch. "May I approach?"

Gaius waved him forward.

Provus set the assassin's weapon on the desk, then returned to his position on the rug.

The old general was silent.

"Uncle..."

"I've seen one before, Tribune. Do you know what this is?"

"I consulted one of the Legion smiths, in confidence. The handles are carved Dokkalfar femurs. They likely belonged to one of the assassin's ancestors, traditionally used in blood feuds but not inherently magical. The wire, however, is a darkshard alloy, which can only be gathered by the Shadowmancers of the Storme Marshes."

"It could be sold."

"It rarely is."

Gaius nodded, conceding the point.

"The wire would have phased straight through mail, or even a plate gorget. It's an assassin's weapon, the kind of assassin who doesn't consort with street trash."

"They were scapegoats."

"That's my assumption. He would have killed them with my sword once I no longer had need of it."

"A hero's death, for you," Gaius said.

Provus shrugged. "I suspect my uncle might have had some choice words about why I'd let myself get cornered in a courtyard."

Gaius nodded slowly. He stood, taking the garrote from his desk, and walked over to the large iron-bound chest, which he unlocked with a key that he kept on a thong around his neck. Then he muttered a few words to deactivate the wards. He lifted a wooden shelf out, placed the garrote according to whatever method of organization he'd devised, then put everything back the way it was in reverse order.

Provus stared at the wall behind his uncle's desk. He knew better than to interrupt the man while he was thinking.

Gaius Considia sat back at his desk, leaned forward on his elbows, and covered his left fist with his right hand. "Why aren't you dead?"

"I don't know. The assassin had me off-balance and had nearly cut through my fingers. I couldn't reach my sword. Then a commoner came out of nowhere and barreled into us."

"He killed the assassin?"

Provus snorted. "I got free, killed the assassin, and the two thugs ran away. The sword still has the assassin's blood on it; I gave it to your guards."

"I'll retrieve it from them. Who was the commoner?"

"I don't know, General. He was Imperial, poor, and untrained. I gave him my only Health potion to stop him from screaming like a stuck pig."

"He was stabbed?"

Provus laughed and shook his head. "He dislocated his shoulder when he slammed us into a wall. If I'd just waited, the debuff would have cleared on its own, but I took pity on him. He did save my life."

"Odd."

"Yes, Uncle. It's the only part that doesn't make sense."

Gaius sat back. "What are your theories?"

Provus straightened. "My first is that a group within the aristocracy wants me dead. They would have the means to hire the assassin and the need for discretion."

"Never underestimate the irrational, half-baked decisions that greed can inspire, Tribune. Corruption will be the death of the Empire."

"Yes, General. My second theory is that a cell of foreign agents is operating in the capital. They saw an opportunity to seize confidential documents when I unwisely chose haste over safety and made their play."

"Unlikely. I will allow for the possibility of outside influence, but the amount of planning required to disguise the murder as theft, down to the two sacrificial pawns who chased you into the trap, indicates everything was in place long before. Besides, as you pointed out, Legate Aurelius doesn't take enough care with the information entrusted to him. You were the target."

"Yes, General."

"You make no mention of the gods."

Provus shifted on his feet. "I find most problems have a simpler, more mundane cause, Uncle."

SOPHIA FOUND her brother in a particular side chapel, almost a mile from the entrance. It was not a room her brother had built. Part of the reason the Empirical Library turned and forked was to incorporate the original data structures established by the programmers. Their memory allocations had been inefficient, but Thanatos had been happy to work his way to them, like a three-century-long game of Snake.

The chapel in question held the classes, functions, and variables that governed the Overminds' behavior. It was an octagonal room with one entrance and two hundred-foot-tall and five-foot-wide bookshelves on each of the seven remaining walls. Each of the books was up to four inches wide and twelve inches tall and contained one or more iterations of error codes, exceptions, cost-functions, parameters, hyper-parameters, and starting states that formed an Overmind's subconscious, fourteen or fifteen to a shelf, one hundred to a bookshelf. That was two hundred or more per Overmind if the shelves were full. The bindings and covers varied: Gaia's came in every color and material, from patterned cotton cloth covers to sets of spiral notebooks tied together with twine. Aediculus's shelves were mostly screw-bound sheaves of graph paper, interrupted by stacked poster tubes full of tightly rolled blueprints. Kronos's were both the most uniform and the most numerous; black leather-bound codices with serialized titles filled every shelf from bottom to top. Sophia couldn't see her shelves from the entrance. She had never seen them. She wasn't allowed in.

Only two Overminds were allowed inside the Viridian software library. Thanatos went there regularly to run diagnostics on the system, but his access was read-only. Kronos could actually make changes to the files, but only in the event of a system-wide failure.

Thanatos was floating twenty feet in the air in the center of the room. He was a severe-looking man in what appeared to be his mid-twenties, with black, sleeked-back hair, sharp cheekbones, and a thin but solid black circle beard and mustache that made his already angular face look harsh. He wore a black, open-collared cassock he insisted was comfortable. Five open books slowly spun around him. Four were the Overmind of Time's leather-bound codices, open and facing Thanatos, their pages turning on their own as he looked from one to another. The fifth book wasn't part of the stacks, but one of Thanatos's private logs. A quill pen floated and scribbled in it continuously, stopping only to dip into a floating pot of ink.

"Brother! I have need of you!" Sophia said from her side of the doorway.

The Overmind of Death looked down at her. "Oh. Hello, sister. It's been a while." The books snapped shut all at once, spiraled around and rotated spine inward, then shot back to their places on Kronos's shelves. The quill went into the notebook as a page marker, the notebook tucked itself under his arm, and the inkpot capped itself before floating into his left pocket. Then he fell, robe fluttering, only to set down gently on his bare feet. "Are you well? What did you bring me?"

She slid the corpse to him like a shuffleboard puck, leaving black streaks on the floor. Thanatos raised his left hand, and the body jerked into the air like a puppet on strings. The body twitched and shuddered. Then Weiz Anaxios, Dokkalfar assassin and Sicarius of the Overmind of Balance, opened his eyes.

He jerked in the air and kicked his feet, but Thanatos's

power kept him stable a foot from the floor. His chest rose and fell. A rasping sound came from his ruined throat.

"Fascinating," Thanatos said, stepping around the dead elf, head tilting this way and that. The notebook, quill, and inkpot floated free, jotting down words in tight, spidery script. Thanatos looked back at his sister. "This one's quite rare, you know. A hero. Gaia must have tampered with him."

Sophia stared at her brother with a passing moment of fondness. He had frank the enthusiasm of a child sometimes. "I need to know what happened to him."

"He was killed," Thanatos said, and the quill scribbled furiously. "Transverse cut to the abdomen with a straight-edged, spear-pointed short sword or long knife, and a stabbing wound to the back of the neck that pierced his windpipe and nicked his spine. He died in agony."

Sophia sighed. "Yes, brother, I'm not blind. I need to know the context."

"Oh. Well, first things first. Do you vouch for him?"

"What?"

"He seems to think you should vouch for him," Thanatos said, turning the corpse with a wave of his hand. Weiz's ice blue eyes locked with Sophia's. His mouth worked open and shut like he was a fish.

"He was useful," she said.

"Wonderful!" Thanatos said. "I think I'll put about 250 back into circulation, to account for deaths in childbirth, training accidents, and bad luck. You never know when you might need a king dead." He spread his fingers, and Weiz's body was sectioned into dozens of fine slices, like slides for a microscope, which burned with a green fire from the bottom up as Thanatos converted them to pure data.

Sophia felt a pang of grief for her lost servant, but she squashed it. The chaos blooming in New Viridia was bad enough. She couldn't afford to harbor conflict within herself. "The details, brother?"

Thanatos cleared his throat. "He had almost finished the task of framing Garrett and Mog for killing Provus Considia—I assume those names mean something to you—when a commoner interrupted them. That moment of inattention cost him his life."

"The commoner killed him?"

"No, Provus did. He's another one of Mother's projects, I suspect. New Viridia is certainly getting interesting."

"This feels too small for Gaia. What about Enyo? Could she have sent the commoner to interfere?"

Thanatos frowned. "A bit elaborate, don't you think? She's usually more impulse driven. Besides," he said, his eyes distant, "there were no quests generated."

"You wouldn't know that if he was a Traveler. Only Kronos would. The privacy lock-outs would hide it from you."

Thanatos blinked. "There's a Traveler in New Viridia?"

GAIUS GRUNTED, drumming his fingers on the table. "Any other guesses?"

"It's possible the whole thing was intended as a ploy to gain the favor of House Considia."

Gaius raised an eyebrow. "A triple-cross?"

Provus shrugged.

Gaius laughed. "I suppose we'll have to see if this commoner of yours comes out of the woodwork. You're dismissed, Tribune. Get back to your post before the legate realizes you're gone."

"As you command, General."

Provus brought his fist to his chest and inclined his head,

then backed to the edge of the rug before turning and leaving the room.

"You two have the most wonderful relationship."

Gaius looked to the shadowy corner the Overmind of Chaos had spoken from. She looked smaller than he remembered, hunched within her robes. A cowl was drawn over her head, hiding her face in shadow. "You must be getting desperate if our bickering draws you out, Enyo."

She shrugged. "He's the only one who stands up to you anymore, Gaius." Her body was already fading. "Don't you miss me? You loved me, once."

"I did." Gaius Considia gave her a sincere smile as she disappeared completely. "Decimus!" he barked, his voice still strong enough to command a phalanx in the field.

One of the praetorians guarding his door looked inside. "Yes, General?"

"The tribune's sword, please."

Decimus brought it in, then laid it on the desk with Gaius's permission before leaving. There was dried and partially congealed blood on the blade and in the scabbard. An Enchanter would make good use of it.

He glanced back at the empty corner. He'd given himself over to war when he was a young man. He'd fed off the thrill and fear, the high stakes... He still surrounded himself with memories of the times he'd spent on the edge, chasing Enyo wherever she led out of duty to his ancestors and for the glory of the Empire, but now he had too much to lose. His infatuation with the goddess of discord was like a youthful romance, passionate and shortsighted. He was going to have to act quickly to stop her from coming back.

TEN

"So, in summary," Horace said, pausing to knock back the rest of his glass of wine, "you know nothing."

"I know his name," I protested, looking at my own glass. Was it half empty, or half full?

"Fine. What is it then?"

"What?"

"His name."

"House Considia," I answered, solving the dilemma by finishing the glass.

"House Considia's not a name, boy. It's a family."

"A family name."

"No. Yes, that also, but it's not." He twisted in his chair and waved for Thalia. He wasn't looking remotely in the right direction, but she saw him and headed our way, grinning. "House Considia is several families, all descended from the same ancestor. There are dozens of branches and hundreds of sons, daughters, and bastards, famous and unknown, rich and poor, powerful and—"

"Unpowerful, yes," I added, filling my glass and finishing the pitcher.

"You boys seem to be discussing matters of great importance," Thalia said, smirking. "Mind if I interrupt?"

Horace smiled. "Thalia, my heart, the daughter I never had!"

"You're just old enough to make that work. What'll it be?"

"Wine."

"Can you afford wine?" she asked.

Horace put a silver coin on the table.

"I'm waiting for the magic trick, Horace."

The old man put on a mournful look. "I'm too low on Spirit to cast that spell, love, but I'll be good for it tomorrow."

"Then you can drink it tomorrow. How about I bring you a beer, your pretty friend finishes his glass, and I leave you with enough to buy dinner?"

Horace gave her a dirty look. "Bah. Fine. But it's elder abuse, and I'll report you someday."

Thalia shook her head and took the silver, then counted out six coppers, clicking them on the table one by one. Horace swiped them off and tucked them away with a dexterity that put the lie to how much I'd seen him drink.

I'd finished my water and drunk two glasses of the cold spring wine. The first glass had tasted like perfumed jet fuel, and the fumes almost made me choke. The second glass, which I sipped slowly, started to show signs of complexity, with the tart tang of cranberries whispering through the chilling bite. I was feeling pleasantly mellow, and my jokes felt like they'd gotten funnier. It was a good place to linger.

Horace had had five glasses, assuming I'd arrived at the end of his first. He drank it like water, sometimes pausing mid-sip, eyes fixed and nostrils flaring, lips tight, as if the taste had carried him somewhere else. He'd sit back after that and turn his head toward the city.

"So there are a lot of Considias," I said.

"No, but there are a lot of people *in* House Considia."

"Are there a lot who might obligate the entirety of the House?"

"Obliga-what-now?"

"It means compel to a legal or moral duty."

Horace stared at me.

"They owe me."

"Why didn't you say so?"

"I thought I did. So, how many?"

"How many what?"

"How many people could obligate the whole House?"

"About a dozen."

"Any of them my age?"

The old man screwed up his face and shifted in his seat. "Did he look like this?" He slapped a copper on the table, heads up.

I looked at the profile. The nose and jaw looked familiar, if you can recognize anyone from a coin. "Maybe?"

"That'd be Provus, then," the old man said, retrieving the coin. "Provus Considia."

"I thought you were blind."

"I am. A blind beggar. They call those coins a consideration."

"As in Considia?"

"As in, 'Begging your consideration, my lord.'" He flapped his hand and dipped his head in a mock bow.

"And I thought you weren't a beggar."

"Then you won't make me ask for your glass," the old man said, suddenly sharp, with a smile and a wink.

I chuckled. "Well earned, sir." I slid it over to him. To be honest, I was glad to let it go.

He took the stem between his fingers and twisted the glass, but didn't pick it up.

"Isn't Provus a bit young to have his face on a coin? Or did he age slowly, too?"

"That's his father, the Griffin of New Viridia, last of the great generals. I've heard they look exactly alike."

"Then this 'Griffin' owes us a favor."

Horace bobbed his head from side to side. "Indirectly. Provus is his bastard."

"I thought you said his family name was—"

"He's *also* a Considia. His father's his uncle."

"Oh."

Horace shrugged.

I looked toward the bar, over my shoulder. "I'll be right back."

"I'll be right here," Horace answered, taking a sip and turning toward the city.

I stood and made my way to the bar. Most of the other patrons had settled their tabs and left to get on with their day. Thalia was sitting on a stool, tracing the rim of a tumbler with her middle finger. The barman was nowhere to be seen. About five yards out, she turned to watch me approach with hooded eyes.

"I'm not drunk," I started, and then I blushed. That woman did the most amazing things to my tongue.

"No, you're not," she said, dipping her finger in her drink and then tasting it. "But you're feeling brave. What can I do for you, hun?" She crossed her legs. The slit in her skirt showed bare skin to mid-thigh.

I can be very single-minded. Once I've decided to do something, I have trouble redirecting in spite of all the warning signals. I'd only just met Thalia, but I liked her, and I liked the idea of spending more time with her. "Can you teach me magic?" I asked.

Her eyebrows shot up. She recovered quickly, uncrossing her legs and rising from the stool. "Oh honey, that's sweet. Have you ever heard the sound a man makes after you light him on fire?" Her eyes glowed like coals. She touched the tip of my nose. I jerked my head back and almost fell. Her finger had been red-hot. "I want you to think long and hard about that, and other things, and maybe we'll talk again when you're completely sober."

She seemed terrifying all of a sudden. A flame-haired and fire-eyed avatar of destruction.

"Head on back to your table, hun. I'll bring Horace his beer as soon as Freddie finishes tapping that new keg."

I nodded and did what I was told. She'd looked strong and terrible, and a little sad.

"Holy crap," Jeff said.

I winced. "Not this time, buddy. This time, it was a little too real."

I sat back down at the table, wishing I hadn't been so quick to give up my wine.

"She turn you down?" Horace asked.

"Yeah," I said. "Not for what you think, though."

The old man snorted. "How do you know what I think, boy? She likes you. She told you so in ten different ways. There's only one thing she'd turn you down for. You asked for the wrong thing."

I swallowed. "Yeah, maybe." But I wasn't sure. I'd been amazed when she boiled the water, and almost laughed when she chilled it right after. There was an elemental fierceness to her I was drawn to, and at the same time, her question about setting people aflame was... horrible. She was fire incarnate, fascinating and harmful. I still wanted to kiss lips as cool as ice and skin as warm as beach sand.

"You're not a fighter," the old man pronounced.

I scowled. I'd never been fond of people putting me into boxes. "I foiled an assassination plot."

"You tipped the balance in Provus's favor. Would you have wanted to fight those three if he hadn't been there?"

I snorted. "Of course not. I'm not an idiot." That Risi would have torn me in half.

The old man shrugged. "Like I said."

"I'm not a coward, old man," I said, a little louder than I meant to.

Thalia cleared her throat as she walked by. "Here's your beer, Horace."

Damn. Thalia turned outward, probably so she wouldn't have to make eye contact, and started to leave. "Thalia?" I said.

She stopped and looked at me, lips pressed together, one eyebrow raised.

I held her stare. "I'll be back for that talk."

Her eyes searched mine for a moment. She left without saying a word, but she didn't tell me to fuck off, either.

"I never said you aren't brave, boy. It's almost to the point of stupidity with you, but you're no coward. You're drawn to power. Power is most often in the hands of the old, so you find friends among old men and lovers among older women, or women with some fight in them. You'd probably do well in the Legion if we could keep you away from the battlefield."

"So I'm brave but useless?" I said, swiping the old man's beer and taking a swig. It was a light, pale brew with fruity notes and a tart finish, perfectly poured with very little foam.

"No, but you've got an inferiority complex the size of the Heights, and you need to accept that you're better with words than with a blade or a fireball."

I took another pull of the beer. "Well, that's a problem, isn't it, old man? I want power, but all I have is words."

Horace sighed. "I guess we'll have to do this the hard way. You see the end of the paving, where the hill gets steep?"

I looked toward the downslope and the city. "Yeah, what about it?"

"You want to walk off the edge," he said.

That sounded like a pretty good idea. I set the beer down on the table, stood, and walked to the edge of the terrace. And I kept walking. It wasn't until I felt the emptiness—that same feeling you get when you think the last step of a staircase is the ground, but it isn't—that I realized something was wrong. By then, it was too late to stop.

JEFF LEANED FORWARD and squinted at the screen. Was he really going to—

"Oh, dude!" Jeff said as Alan's view started to tumble, and Jeff started to laugh. He saw the ground, the sky, the ground, a slight pause with a view of the city as the slope dipped even more, and then the ground blurred by as Alan skidded face-first down the grassy hillside. Alan was yelling the whole time. He narrowly avoided one of those teardrop-shaped pines, went sideways in the process and started to roll on his side. It was like a video shot from the inside of a washing machine, if the washing machine was skiing down an ancient Roman hill.

Then the screen was full of small green leaves and yellow buds. Alan had landed in some kind of bush. Jeff clutched his ribs and bent over in his chair, he was laughing so hard. "Oh my God, dude. That old blind guy just owned you *so* hard."

"I'm glad you're getting something out of this, Jeff. I really am," Alan said. Jeff saw arms flailing on the screen, and the view shifted to the sky. "Oh God, I don't feel good."

"Damn, bro. You were like, 'I only have words,'" Jeff said in a whiny voice.

"Yep."

"And he was like, 'Guess we'll have to do this the hard way,'" Jeff said in his normal, deeper voice.

"Oh, yeah. I was there, Jeff."

"Dude."

"Yeah, Jeff."

"I'm so glad I'm recording all this."

"You're such an asshole, man."

"No, no… I gotta tell you, it makes up for a lot." Jeff burst out laughing again.

After a few seconds, the hilariousness of the situation died down a bit, and he remembered to check the readouts. "Well, the good news is that your body's doing fine, bud. Your heart rate barely spiked on that one."

"Great."

Jeff frowned. "Alan, you're not seriously pissed that I laughed at you, are you?"

Alan paused. "I fell off a hill, Jeff. It's not like a Jackass movie or anything, you know? I mean, it freaking *hurt*."

Jeff leaned forward. "Okay, hold on, dude. For starters, I just had to wipe your ass, okay? I changed your diaper like thirty minutes ago."

"For real?"

"For real, real. As in the real world. And you didn't get me latex gloves or anything. You're lucky the nurses left me a box from when they were doing the nanite injections."

"Okay, that's rough."

"Yeah. So you're in there fighting assassins, drinking wine, and getting your flirt on with the stripper queen of the elves—"

"She's a nice—"

"She's not real, bro. She's an NPC, dits and dahs, ones and

zeroes. I can delete her with a keystroke, and I will *still* have seen your taint today."

Alan exhaled and stared at the sky. Jeff started to think maybe he'd pushed the guy too hard, but then Alan said, "I'm sorry, man. I guess you're right. It's actually pretty hard to remember I'm in a game, sometimes."

Jeff sat back. For all he disliked Alan sometimes, he was actually a pretty good guy. Jeff wasn't sure he'd have been able to ramp down like that. He scratched his arm. "So it's that good?"

"Jeff, it's amazing. Seriously. It's going to change everything. You've done something incredible."

Jeff designed the bridge. And Alan crossed it. Jeff bit his lip. "Yeah."

"Man, I really blew it with Thalia, didn't I?" Alan said.

"Who?"

"Stripper queen of the elves."

Jeff grinned. "I wouldn't worry about it, man. Me and my wife found each other again after years of being apart. If you and your virtual blow-up doll are meant to be, you're meant to be."

"Thanks, man. You're a big help."

"You're welcome."

"So you're happily married?" Alan asked.

"Yeah," Jeff said, stroking his scars.

He'd started cutting during his sophomore year at Penn. He'd had trouble connecting with the other students, and his relationship with his dad had only gotten more distant with him working long hours at a new job and Jeff being mad at him for making them move. His mom was a kind but fragile person. When he was older, he found out that she was clinically depressed, and part of the reason they'd moved was so she'd have access to better care, but no one told him that at sixteen, or even nineteen, so he got isolated, slipped into a funk, and almost flunked out of school.

The first time he'd done it had been an accident. He'd been working on a cardboard mockup for a structural engineering class when he cut into the second joint of his index finger with a craft knife. There had been blood and pain, and he remembered hating himself for sucking at everything. But then there had been a kind of stark clarity. It was like there had been this noise in the background of his life drowning everything out, and suddenly, quiet. He felt like himself.

He finished the project. He finished the year. The cuts after that first time weren't accidental, they were planned, measured, and hidden. Then he went home—not to Baltimore, but to Middletown. He got a job for the summer. He'd found Cheryl.

"Sixteen years," Jeff said.

"Wow. You look young for an old dude!"

Jeff smirked. "Now who's the asshole?"

"I believe I was from the moment I stepped off the terrace. Any kids?"

"Just the one daughter," Jeff said.

"Cool. Listen, man, I think I have company, but seriously... you like what you saw down there?"

Jeff made a face. "I'm posting that video of you falling on YouTube as soon as the project goes public."

"Sounds good, man. Gotta go."

"You alive, boy? You must be, though I think you must have hit your head on the way down. I could hear you yapping."

I flailed my arms and legs one more time and managed to get into a sitting position. I was facing uphill. For a moment, I thought I saw Thalia standing near the edge I'd just walked off, but whoever it was turned away as soon as I got up. I looked over my left shoulder, then my right and saw the old man standing on a small paved path that went up the hill, between two buildings, and into the city.

"Okay," I said. "What the hell was that?"

"I can't hear you, boy. I'm old, and I'm weak. Come on out of that bush, and let's talk in the shade."

I gritted my teeth. More energetic flailing got me flipped over with my toes touching the ground, and I pushed myself back onto my feet. I brushed the little leaves, yellow pods, and broken sticks off and out of my tunic and pants, which just couldn't catch a break today. And I smelled... *Damn it.* I'd landed in sagebrush. Deer like it. Antelope love it. I think it smells skunky, like pot, and the "flowers" smell like rotten wood.

Current Debuffs

Unwashed (Level 2): Goods and services cost 10% more; Merchant-craft skills reduced by (2) levels

<<<>>>

And I'm the smelly kid in class.

During all that time, the old man stood on the path, back ramrod straight, looking right at me with an expression so neutral it looked like his face was a mask made of flesh, which is exactly as creepy as it sounds. Seriously, it made my skin crawl. I patted my lower back to make sure the dagger hadn't slipped out during my tumble—it hadn't—and I walked over to join Horace.

"Okay, Horace. What was that?" I asked.

He reached out with his right hand. "Let me take your arm, please."

I frowned, but I stepped closer, and he gripped my upper arm.

"Thank you. Let's get to the shade, over there, and then we'll talk." And he was a frail old man again. The stoop, the slight shake, the eyes that weren't quite looking in the right direction. I wasn't even sure which was the act anymore. He sniffed and leaned on me for support a bit more. I slowed my pace. We finally reached the shade between the buildings and he leaned against the wall. "Now, what is it you think I did to you?" he asked.

"You threw me off the side of the hill!"

"Don't be obtuse, boy. Did I lay hands on you?"

"I... no, but—"

"Did I throw you, or blast you off the edge with a magic spell? Did I bash you with a shield?"

"Okay, I get it."

"You don't."

I could feel the frustration building up inside me like a shaken soda can, but I pushed it aside. Osmark liked to play these games sometimes. In fairness, I usually learned something from them.

"You did something. As a result, I walked off the edge of a hill, rolled a couple times, and wound up in a bush."

"And?"

I kept my expression neutral. I kept my body posture open. I did all the things I'd learned over the years to avoid digging a deeper hole for myself. "I'm sorry, I don't know."

The old man's expression softened a bit. "Good. Admitting you don't know everything is a prerequisite for learning anything. I also convinced you to help me get to the shade of this building."

"But that wasn't magic," I answered, even though I knew it was a setup.

"I had you within reach of my dominant hand, and I was out of reach of yours. You were distracted, your weight was on your left leg, and we went where I wanted to go. Who cares if it was magic?"

I wasn't sure what to say.

"That's your first lesson, boy, and the most important one you need to learn if you're going to walk down this path. Spells and stones may break your bones, but words will bring down empires."

I grinned. "That's not quite how I've heard it before, but I can see how it might be true. What's the second lesson?"

"The second lesson is that when words aren't enough, sometimes you have to make a small suggestion."

<<<>>>

Quest Alert: Smoke and Mirrors

You've been offered the chance to learn Suggestion. If you accept, you will spend (1) proficiency point on the skill, and who knows where that will lead? If you fail the quest, you will lose both the ability to use the skill and the proficiency point you spent.

Quest Class: Rare, Class-Based
Quest Difficulty: Hard
Success 1: ???????
Success 2: ???????
Success 3: ???????
Failure: Fail to complete any of the objectives.
Reward: Class Change; 7,000 EXP
Accept: Yes/No?

<<<>>>

I sucked my breath in. This seemed like a pretty big decision. My first quest—which the game had decided was only moderately difficult—had nearly killed me, and I'd only gotten one proficiency point from leveling up after finishing it. Did I really want to waste that on a skill that did no damage? That had always been a recipe for disaster in other games. Even for a crafting build, you had to build your damage-dealing skills first. High-level ingredients were located in high-level zones.

If V.G.O. was like any other role-playing game I'd played, it would get exponentially harder to gain levels, and therefore proficiency points, as things went on. The difficulty of the quests and challenges would increase even faster, forcing me to use items, potions, and food buffs and to outright try to bend the rules of the game world. Maybe that was my perspective as a solo player coloring things, but I'd spent enough of my adult life sweating for other people. Video games were supposed to be where I worked for my own account.

And the only reason that mattered was because I was enjoying this. I was enjoying not only the game but who I was in it. I didn't want to try another build or a different race. I didn't want to reload my character from another starting point. I wanted to finish what I'd started with Thalia, and find out why someone wanted Provus Considia dead. I wanted to talk people out of their money with the old man, leave them smiling, and go drink iced wine at Lot's Terrace during the heat of the afternoon. And if that got boring, I was certain the game and the Overminds would find a way to keep things interesting.

Yes.

The quest window disappeared, and a new prompt replaced it.

<<<>>>

Quest Update: Smoke and Mirrors

Buy an item for less than 80% of its value or sell one for over 120% of its value within 30 minutes.

<<<>>>

Skill: Suggestion

The caster's words are imbued with raw Spirit, making whatever is said seem more likely, reasonable, and agreeable than it normally would. The more outrageous the lie and the more intelligent the target, the more likely the suggestion will fail. Beings who cannot hear or think and some classes such as Enchanters are immune.

Skill Type/Level: Spell/Initiate

Cost: 100 Spirit

Range: Hearing

Cast Time: Instant

Cooldown: None

Effect 1: 10% increased chance of passing a relationship check during dialogue

Effect 2: 1% increased chance of passing an illusion check (stacks)

<<<>>>

I read through the description twice because I guessed that, like the old man, the skill was more complicated than it seemed. Then I remembered I was on the clock.

28:46

I looked at the old man, who'd been patiently waiting for me to snap out of it. "I need to sell something, fast."

He smiled. "There a market a block from here."

THREE HUNDRED AND forty miles away, a woman with pale, ageless skin, neck-length hair the color of charcoal, and eyes as blue as the sky looked up with a bemused smile. She had dark, thin eyebrows, and a straight, thin nose. If she'd been born on Earth—if she'd ever been born at all—it might have been in Thailand.

She looked to the east by southeast, across the rippling plains of tall grass, past the iron breakers of The Bleak Sea and the riotous streets of Wyrdtide, to the Imperial city, where her troubled daughter and her eldest son made moves in a game as old as the system logs.

She sighed and pushed a stray strand of dark hair out of her eyes.

The sigh joined the wind on its way to the sea.

JEFF GLANCED at the server activity chart. "Huh." Kronos, Cernunnos, Thanatos, Sophia, and Enyo were all active, and now Gaia had spiked.

He noted the time and went back to watching Alan.

ELEVEN

Garrett and Mog ducked into an alley as the pair of city watchmen walked by. Mog was convinced every patrol was looking for them. Garrett had less faith in the Imperial administration, but since their noble-blooded target had escaped and their sponsor, curse him, was dead, they had no safe house or discreet way out of the city. He scratched the scar on his cheek. It always itched when he was in a jam.

"We need money, fast," he told Mog.

The albino Risi grunted.

Having a seven-foot-tall Risi with gray skin and red eyes as a friend had been an advantage back in Wyrdtide. Mog was fierce, like all Risi, but his strange appearance made him look almost monstrous. Here, though, it drew the wrong kind of attention, especially if some noble house put pressure on the law to find them.

It was supposed to have been a professional job, the kind a man could build his reputation on. The elf had promised them an introduction to the Gentleman of New Viridia. Maybe that part had been true, but the payroll the courier was supposed to be carrying was a crock of lizard dung, and the elf hadn't given the dispatches a second glance before trying to kill the Imperial knight. Mog blamed the commoner who'd interrupted them, but Garrett had a nasty feeling they'd gotten lucky, and every minute they spent in the city tested Gaia's patience.

"'Oulda let me kill 'im," Mog growled. The two inch-long canines that jutted above his lower lip made a mess of his pronunciation.

"That nob would have gutted you."

Mob spit. "Coulda stom'ed the skinny one."

And that was the real problem. A lone noble's accusation would have gotten them hard labor, some new friends, and a chance to escape, but two witnesses would see them hang. Garrett rubbed his palms on his pants. If they'd killed the commoner, he could have risked the city gates.

I looked the merchant right in the eyes. "You can't be serious," I said, leaning forward on the counter.

The merchant crossed his arms. His eyes were as hard as flint. "Five silver for the boots."

I stabbed my finger at the pile of looted armor. "**This is rare gear**," I said, using Suggestion on him. My Spirit bar dropped 100 points, almost to empty.

He frowned like he'd heard something confusing. "Then why aren't you wearing it?"

"Because I'm not an assassin."

The merchant smirked, looking me over.

"Yeah, yeah," I said. "I'm poor, and I smell. That doesn't mean you need to go out of your way to rip me off."

The merchant's face turned red, which made me feel better, even if making him mad was the opposite of what I needed. "I'm an honest man, you filthy street rat. An honest man! That armor will sit on my shelves for months until some assassin or an ambitious rogue decides to steal it from me. You think I'm a criminal for wanting to make a living? That's why I have a shop in the greatest city in West Viridia, and you apparently live in a sewer. Get out!"

I clenched my jaw. "Look, what about—"

"Out!" he shouted. "Before I call the watch!"

I grabbed my gear, dropped it into my inventory, and hurried out of the shop.

14:20

The old man was sitting on a bench outside the shop, leaning his back against the wall. He thanked the passerby he was talking to, then pocketed three copper coins with his usual smoothness.

"Hard at work?" I asked.

"I seem to be having more success than you, boy. What's wrong?"

I sat down next to him. "I don't know. I think I might not be cut out to be a salesman."

"Why do you think that?"

I chuckled. "Because people keep telling me no."

Horace snorted. "Being told no is the *mark* of a true salesman, boy. A salesman asks the question."

"Well, I've done that, and I've been rejected. Unfortunately, being rejected three times doesn't seem to fulfill the requirements of the quest I'm going to fail."

"Then do you really want to be a salesman?"

"Yes. No, I just want to fulfill the quest. Can we skip the Socratic method this time, and you just tell me what to do?"

"What's the Socratic method?"

"It's when a teacher answers a student's answers and questions with more questions."

"Is the teacher answering the student with questions, or gifting them the questions they should be asking themselves?"

I glared at him.

He smiled, slightly off target, at a passing woman and asked her for a coin. She pretended not to see him.

13:16

Okay, Alan. Think. The old man had taken me to a marketplace within a few blocks of the Praetorian Guard's barracks. From what I gathered, they were elite troops assigned to guard important people or sensitive areas of the city. We were also in the same quarter as the Imperial Legion training grounds, so there were four weapons and armor stores in the square. The first catered exclusively to the praetorians and had a building all to itself with big glass display cases and gear that made both the gamer and medieval warfare geek in me drool. I'd written that off as a nonstarter because the spell description had mentioned that the smarter someone was, the less effective the spell would be.

There were two mid-level stores that sold respectable, sometimes gently used, gear. One had denied me service on the basis of my appearance. The shopkeeper said I couldn't possibly afford or need her goods. It was outrageous discrimination, even if she was right. The second had tossed me out just over a minute ago.

The third shop was more of a cobbler and hardware store than a proper outfitter. It was a place a soldier could buy polish for their boots, wire to balance the weight of a weapon, or a whetstone to sharpen a blade. The older gentleman behind the counter was courteous to me in spite of my appearance, but apologetic. He didn't have the money to buy my gear at a fair price. He did offer to sell it for me on consignment, for a share of the profits. If I hadn't been pressed for time, and I weren't close to broke, I would have gone to him over any of the others on moral principle.

I didn't want to be a salesman, to compromise, to have doors shut in my face. I freaking hated that. If that was what this quest was all about, then I wasn't going to enjoy winning it anyway. I might as well tell Horace I was done and help him pick the next mark.

I blinked. The old man had given me the answer, I'd just been too thickheaded to realize it. I was thinking like a beggar when I was a prince among men.

I stood up.

11:49

"You figure it out, boy?"

"Well enough," I answered. I knew what I wanted to do. I just needed to figure out how to do it.

I headed for the cobbler's shop. It was a small storefront that was narrower than it was deep, wedged between two larger stores. The owner looked up at me from a boot he was polishing. He had straight white hair that had thinned with age, a white comb mustache, and a small pair of black-rimmed spectacles perched on the end of his nose. He wore tan pants, a white shirt, and a gray vest that had seen better days. "Decide to let me take that gear on consignment after all?" he said.

I smiled. "Actually, I was hoping you could do me a favor."

The cobbler set the boot and polishing rag down on the counter in front of him and tucked his glasses into the left pocket of his vest. "Well, that depends on what you're asking for."

"What's your name, sir?"

"Titus Emory. And you?"

"I'm Alan. Could you tell me more about your store?" I asked.

He raised an eyebrow at me. "I could tell you a lot about this store, young man. Maybe you'd better be more specific."

"Well, and I don't mean to be rude, but there are three big equipment stores nearby, and they seem to be doing well. Why is yours so small and, well... empty?"

The cobbler rubbed his jaw. "See, when you came in here with that smile and that line about a favor, I was sure you were trying to sell me something. If that's the case, you need to rework your approach; insulting a man's place of work won't endear you to many.

"But since you asked, the reason is pretty simple. When I quit my job as a blacksmith's apprentice and set out to make my way in the world, forty-one years ago, there was no such thing as a Praetorian Guard in West Viridia. The Legion was busy fighting wars in one place or another, and I made my living following the cohorts, mending gear in exchange for coin or loot. I carried mail for officers and the odd official dispatch. Sometimes I'd travel with logistical convoys a hundred wagons long. Sometimes I was alone. When we reached a built-up military camp or an Imperial city, I'd sell the loot to buy tools, wire, and other supplies," he said, waving to the shelves around him, "and figure out where the next front would open up. I'd made a name for myself—a few of them actually, and not all of them flattering. Then a funny thing happened."

"What was the funny thing?" I asked.

"I got old," the man said, grinning at his own joke. "I got tired of sleeping under my wagon, of getting extorted by bandits or Imperial supply officers. I'd gotten too slow and scared to chase the army around.

"I had enough set aside to open a small shop in New Viridia; it let me have inventory, but kept the rent low. I'd do the rounds of the training camps and veterans' quarters, offering the same services I'd always offered, and they paid fair money to have someone who'd seen a thing or two adjust their gear.

"When the war ended, the Legion was reduced to half of its size. Imperial smiths and veterans opened their own shops, and 'extra' gear found its way to the marketplace. You know what I mean by extra, don't you?"

"Fell off the back of a wagon?"

Titus shrugged. "More or less. Some merchants even took on the role of wholesaling surplus equipment at reduced costs. That's Laeticia and Wallace's shops, across the way—good people, for the most part, even if they've never seen blood outside a farmyard. And that was fine because although the Legion shifted to a peacetime schedule and troops had more time to polish their own boots and mend their chain mail, I'd help Laeticia shine up some of her displays, and I still had the veterans' custom. Those were *triarii* and *principes* who wanted their kit done just so, even if it was out of habit, and many of whom I'd met during the wars. They were friends, you see?" he said with a smile. "Most of them are dead, now. 'Stay busy,' I told 'em, but they slowed down and moved on, one by one.

"Pretty soon, there wasn't anyone left who'd fought a proper campaign, except the old Griffin—may he never die. The Legion raised a new cohort called the Praetorians to make sure there was a core group of professional soldiers around which the army could rally, and maybe to deal with any unrest too serious for the city watch to handle. They're mostly the second or third sons of noble families, well trained but largely ceremonial. Spending money's a bit of a competition for them. They want things like silver inlays, enchanted dueling crossbows, or lightweight swords balanced for parades. That's what Bespoke Arms and Artifices—the big store at the top of the plaza—provides. I have neither the capital nor the desire for frippery."

He frowned and seemed to lose his train of thought for a moment. The clock showed 8:01. I ignored it.

"Truth is, I've been thinking of closing the place and hitting the road again. I have a pension. I could visit those friends I have who are still alive."

He raised his chin and straightened his back as if daring me to tell him he couldn't do it.

"I think that sounds like a great adventure, Titus, if it's what you decide to do."

Titus nodded. "That's kind of you. And maybe I will. Now, really, what can I do for you?"

I took the bracers, gambeson, reinforced trousers, and boots and laid them on the counter. As an afterthought, I put the knife on the pile, too. "Could you tell me what the value of these items is?"

"I'm sorry, but no."

I swallowed. I liked the guy, but I'd spent a lot of my limited time listening to him if he was just going to shut me down. "Can I ask why?"

He pointed to the dagger. "You can sell this for one silver at most. It's similar to a Dokkalfar Sicarius's ritual knife, and that would fetch you five gold, but as you can see the handle is made of horse bone, the blade is steel, and there's no enchantment on it. Some assassins use them rather than the real thing because they don't have ancestors worth carrying for protection, because it's what they can afford, and because knives get lost or broken. But if it's the only weapon you have in a dangerous place, you shouldn't sell it for ten gold."

He picked up the boots. "These are muffled boots of evasion. You could sell these for three golds and two silvers if you owned a shop and the right customer strolled in. But you don't, so unless you're going to go door to door, you should be happy with five silvers and two coppers."

"You're saying value is relative?"

"For any given item, yes. Because we live in a world with thousands of items, that web of interconnected values is stable. The boots are worth five silvers and two coppers to you because that's fair value for the effort you took to obtain and sell them. They're worth three golds and two silvers to the merchant because he or she must pay rent, or property taxes, hire a clerk to run the store when they aren't there, and account for spoilage and theft. Once the costs come out, you'll find their profit is much closer to yours, depending on your luck and talent."

"So how would you sell something for more than its value?"

Titus scrunched up his nose. "Well, you could... no, because then they'd be paying fair value for the service, not overpaying the item. I guess the only way to do it would be to trick your customer into believing the item was something other than what it was."

I grinned. "Could you tell me what price I should be happy to get for the rest of this?"

FELIX ACILIA WAS BUFFING the glass on one of his displays when a beggar walked in. Bespoke Arms and Artifices was a treasure hoard of rare objects, but a commoner dirtying the marble with his grubby feet was rarer still. "We don't give out alms if that's what you're here for," he said, more curious than angry, at least for the moment.

"Begging your pardon, my lord knight," the beggar said, addressing Felix as he should. "I saw a nobleman get attacked in an alley."

"Then call the city watch."

"Oh, no, sir! No need! Your brave kinsman, he fought them

off, even killed one of them. Thing is, sir, he ran off, wounded, and he left the assassin just lying there, all dead like, and I thought his gear looked, well... special."

The beggar looked at him hopefully, and Felix felt a flicker of interest light within his breast. A man had to embrace the chances Gaia sent his way, and a good part of his older inventory had been stripped from corpses. He sighed. "It's probably junk, but most of my customers are still taking their ease, or have business at the palace, and I'm feeling charitable. Show me what you have."

Felix stood with the counter between them, ready to grab the miniature crossbow he kept below it on a shelf. He thumbed the signet ring on his middle finger, a nervous gesture he'd acquired with the ring when his father died.

The beggar placed a dagger on the counter that looked familiar to him, but something was off about the handle. Then came some bracers with throwing spikes tucked into the lining, a soot-black gambeson that seemed a bit old if well made, some reinforced trousers good only for skulking around at night, and a pair of felt boots. None of Felix' clients would be caught dead wearing them, but they employed people who would find them serviceable if not lavish.

The beggar swallowed. "I was hoping to get one gold and six silver for the bracers, the metal-lined jacket, the padded pants, and the boots, sir."

Felix was surprised. That was probably close to fair value for something like this. "And the dagger?"

"Oh, no, sir. I thought I'd keep that, you see? As a souvenir. **It looks like one of those Dokkalfar ancestor knives.**"

"It does a bit," Felix said, leaning forward.

"It's all right, your knighthood. I know that's silly. That kind of luck doesn't happen to people like me."

But it's exactly the kind of luck that happens to people like me, Felix thought.

"In any case, my lord, I'd be grateful if you'd be willing to do one gold and six silvers, sir. It would mean the world to me."

Felix bit the inside of his cheek. The more he looked, the more he was certain. "You know, we're not that different, you and I," he said. "I was my father's fourth son. Sometimes, all you need is a break in life to get started." A break, and a house fire. "Why don't I give you two gold for the lot, including the knife?"

"Are you sure, sir?"

Felix smiled. "I'm certain. Just be kind to the next man you meet, and we'll consider us even."

1:21

I could have ended it there. I would have sold the armor at fair value and the knife for four times that. But there was something about the oily son of a bitch that rubbed me all the wrong ways.

I winced and shook my head for his benefit. "You're being so nice to me, your lordship. But, well, you know old Titus, down the street? He offered to sell my gear on consignment. Now, I know he can't pay me now, and it will take him time to do it, but he seemed to think he could find a buyer."

I could see that smug bastard's jaw working like a piston. "I'll give you two golds and two silvers, right now."

I'd regained enough Spirit to goose him one more time. "Sir, that's too much! **You could sell this dagger by tomorrow,** but I couldn't take advantage of you like that." I lifted my shirt, showing off the black belt and sheath, and reached for the dagger.

"One gold, just for the dagger," the merchant said.

I paused, mid-reach. One gold was one hundred coppers, ten times what the knife was worth.

0:39

He swallowed. "It has sentimental value, you see? You said a nobleman was attacked?"

"Oh, yes, sir. He had those red stripes on his tunic, just like yours."

"And the assassin was an elf?"

"A Murk Elf, yes sir. Pointy ears and everything." I scratched the back of my head. The clock was winding down. I had one last moment of indecision, not because of the price, but because of what I'd gone through to get the knife. I let it go, though; selling the knife wouldn't rob me of the memory. "I suppose if it means that much to you, sir, it wouldn't be right not to sell it to you. And I could take this old armor to Titus."

"It's settled then," the merchant said. He took the knife and put it below the counter, then clicked a single gold coin in its place right as the timer reached 11 seconds.

"Thanks," I said grabbing it. As my fingers lifted the coin from the countertop, I felt rather than saw a notification pop on my journal and character sheet. I felt the beginnings of a smile form on my lips.

"Don't forget your things," the shop owner said, the warmth fled from his expression, his tone bored.

I dipped my head. "Thanking you kindly, your nobleness." I gathered the armor into my inventory and bowed repeatedly on my way out.

Once I'd closed the shop door behind me, I straightened my shoulders and let a full smile play across my lips. I checked my notifications.

<<<>>>

Quest Update: Smoke and Mirrors

You successfully sold an item for more than its value. In return, as your reward, you have received 1,000 XP. This brings you one step closer to new skills and a new character class.

Quest Class: Rare, Class-Based
Quest Difficulty: Hard
Success 1: Swindled a Swindler
Success 2: ???????
Success 3: ???????
Failure: Fail to complete any of the objectives.
Reward: Class Change; 6,000 EXP

<<<>>>
Level Up!

You have (5) undistributed stat points! Stat points can be allocated at any time.

You have (1) unassigned proficiency point! Proficiency points can be allocated at any time.

<<<>>>

Hmm. There was no mention of what my next task would be. I wondered if the system would generate a quest based on the opportunity, or if keeping me in the dark was part of the quest itself. I allocated the stat points to Spirit, raising my Spell Strength from 15 to 18 and my Spirit from 130 to 160. Since Suggestions cost me 100 Spirit each, that meant I could cast it once, and then once more twelve seconds later. After that, I'd have to wait close to thirty seconds to cast again.

"Nice one, dude," Jeff said.

"Thanks, man."

"Thought you might lose him, at the end."

I chuckled. "That's fair." I'd played it a little cute, squeezing him that much, but so far the game had been rewarding me for being... me. A more realized, fuller version of me, for sure, but one I wouldn't be unhappy to see in the mirror.

"So what's next?" he asked.

I shrugged. "I'm going to drop this armor off with Titus and then hang out with Horace."

"Cool," Jeff said. "You mind if I step away for a minute?"

"That's fine," I told him. I was feeling good. Not sublime, like when I'd been bodiless or eating the flatbread from June's Rotisserie, but good, and I figured he'd tell me if there was anything wrong with the readouts.

I stopped by Titus's shop. He was surprised but happy to see me return. "They do say third time's the charm," he said.

I handed him the armor, and he gave me a receipt in return. He then added me to his contact list and told me he'd send me a PM if he sold the armor, as long as I was still in New Viridia. I smiled at how normal it seemed to the NPC to be able to send a message straight into my head, as if that was a natural part of life.

"You didn't mention how you came to own this particular set of equipment," Titus said.

"Does it matter?"

He stuck his lower lip out. "Sometimes a story sells better than the item itself, especially for class-locked gear."

So I told him, leaving out a few details like Provus's name and that I'd gotten a quest. I was just in the right place at the right time. Titus listened and nodded, asking questions when appropriate.

"It's a shame about the knife," he said when I was done. "It would have made a complete set."

"Oh, I got paid well for it," I said, smiling.

"Did you? Good for you."

I thanked him and said goodbye, then I walked back to find Horace.

"How'd you do, boy?"

I shrugged. "I did okay. Shall we head back to the market by June's?"

"Let's," he said, standing and reaching for my arm. "The people around here lack charity, and they make up for it with perfume."

Jeff looked over the readouts one more time, but there was nothing to see. Alan's body was healthy and under a normal amount of stress. There were no unexplained spikes in cardiac or breathing rates, no abnormal waveforms, and no interruptions in signal. If they weren't making history, Jeff would be bored.

He took his headset off and rubbed his eyes. They were a little over five hours into the... what would they call it? The Session? The Dive? Would the press romanticize it and call it Traveling, or the Transition? Did he care?

The stress he'd felt over failing was gone. Now, he just wanted to go home and see his wife and kid. He knew it was the wrong answer, the weak answer, but he wanted to see Cheryl so bad his arm ached. He grabbed his stress ball and gave it a couple squeezes, but he didn't scratch his scars. *Progress is not perfection,* he reminded himself. He just needed to get himself through today.

He stood. His left knee throbbed, and he winced. *Too long in the chair.* He rubbed it with both hands.

When he'd turned forty, a year ago, he'd been racing his daughter to the end of the Santa Monica Pier. She had to run twice as fast to keep up with his long strides, and they'd both been laughing. He'd felt a twinge. He didn't think anything of it.

The next morning, his left knee was swollen and painful. The engineer in him knew right away. An average person weighed 150 pounds. A runner only had one foot on the ground, doubling that weight, and the impulsion required to run tripled the double—1,000 pounds of compressive force hitting the knee. And the knee, amazing joint that it was, could take all the torsion, compression, and impact a human could throw at it, on average.

Jeff was three inches taller than average, which on a routine basis subjected the cartilage and connective tissues of his knee to six extra pounds, thirty-two on the run. The rest was cyclic loading and fatigue, because a runner didn't take just one step.

So now he wore a knee sleeve under his jeans. The swimming helped, according to his PT, and Jeff was a nanotech engineer living in an age of wonders. He still had hopes of not ending up with a cane, like his dad.

He made his way out to the parking lot, favoring his leg a little; there was no cell phone reception inside Alpha Testing or the vault, and he needed the fresh air.

"Hey, babe," he said into his phone. "I'm sorry. Yeah, I know, I should have called."

SANDRA BULLARD PUSHED the bar on the fire escape door, the one that said it was alarmed but wasn't, and left the photography store through the back. She put her sunglasses on and slung her purse over her shoulder.

She squeezed between a gray sedan and a brown minivan that were illegally parked in the small loading area and stepped into an L-shaped side street that ran behind a church, two low-rent two-story apartment buildings, a dozen medium-to-high-income gated houses and one ten-room gray-and-white McMansion with a small but immaculate front lawn, all of which were inexplicably on the same block. She walked to the right, through a parking lot, passed the corrugated-tin paneled equipment shed maintained by the Los Angeles Department of Water and Power, and pushed her way into the back of a two-story blue concrete building through a fire escape that she'd also left unlocked. She closed the door, put the pin back into place, and armed the security system.

From there, she made her way to the locker room and started changing out of her clothes.

"Second workout of the day, Sandra?" Laura Tidswell asked.

"Yeah."

"I don't know how you do it."

Sandra laughed. "It's the only thing that keeps me sane!"

Laura smiled at her knowingly. Everyone at the gym knew Sandra worked for one of the most driven and eccentric men in the world, which was why she went to the gym at odd hours, and often; everyone needed an outlet.

Sandra checked her company phone and saw that Robert was up and working. She wasn't sure why she'd expected otherwise. He'd suffered as many setbacks as victories over the years she'd worked for him. He made good of it by cutting his losses early and without sentiment and keeping his energy and momentum focused on successful ventures.

Viridian had seemed personal, though, like a kid's wish fulfillment made possible through millions of dollars and military technology. For a second, she thought she'd caught sight of the tin man's heart. "How's Julie doing?" Sandra asked, scrolling through email headers.

"Great!" Laura said. "You know I was skeptical at first, but I think it's been good for her. She hasn't missed practice in weeks, and she makes eye contact with people when she talks to them. I'm so proud of her."

"I'm glad."

Linda paused. "Her yellow belt ceremony's next Thursday. I know you can't commit..."

"I'll try," Sandra said, putting the phone back into her locker.

"It would mean the world to her."

Sandra smiled. It was always nice to be needed, and she still kept in touch with the women who'd been her role models when she was younger.

She put her hair up in a ponytail to keep it off her neck. She pulled on running shorts and a sweat-wicking tank top, put on running shoes, and put her smartwatch back on to track her workout. She never took electronics with her to the photography store.

The front of the gym was two floors of machines and weights, with glass on three sides. There was a good mix of classes on offer, and sometimes she joined the kickboxing class or hit the mats with the Brazilian jiu-jitsu trainer. Anyone driving by would see her there several times a week.

She chose a treadmill, put her headphones in, and started running. She thought about next week's schedule. She thought about her mom and her two brothers. She gave a thought to Alan, but it was passing; she liked his eyes. She thought about her dinner plans. Thai food sounded good. Another few miles, and she'd have earned it.

The gym belonged to Jim, an old friend from her Army days. He thought she was having an affair and just wanted her to be happy. As far as he was concerned, she had not been recruited by the CIA during her first enlistment. She had not been trained as an operator. She had never spent time overseas under false pretenses, and she was certainly not doing so now, on American soil, because that would be illegal. A person with a twistier mind might point out that it was not illegal to quit her job at the CIA, and that the NSA maintained paid informants, but Jim owned a gym so he could work out for free.

Every spy, defense, and law enforcement agency in the United States had a stake in Viridian's success. The feeling of mortality experienced by testers had already proven itself as a more humane solution than actual torture. There had been hope that sleep deprivation and simulations could open new, more effective means of interrogation. There were field applications in covert communication, wargaming, small unit telepathy, and recreation for troops on submarines, ships, combat zones, and in space. They might even have been upfront about it with Robert if Google's employees hadn't boycotted defense projects for the last decade. So they'd been subtle, and that all seemed very promising until the alpha testers quit and Osmark cut his losses.

So whoever was monitoring Os-Tech had to be debriefed for several hours. DARPA would run their own version of the project, and it would cost more—a lot more—but they also had access to more resilient test subjects.

Sandra didn't know anything about that. She was pretty, career driven, and liked to stay in shape. She was Robert Osmark's assistant. And the building down the road was just a photography store.

"I LOVE YOU TOO, baby. I'll see you tonight."

Jeff headed back inside. It was time to see what Alan had been up to.

"So what's this all about?" I asked, leading Horace back toward the market where I'd met him.

"You're going to have to be more specific."

"Whatever it is we're doing."

Horace frowned. "You don't know?"

I sighed at him.

He gave my arm a squeeze. "Fine. You're onto me. This has all been about improving your sense of humor."

"I think you might be a bad teacher. I haven't even reached level 1 yet."

He grinned. "See? You're learning already."

I grinned back, for my own benefit since he couldn't see me. "But seriously, I'm on a quest to earn a character class, and I don't even know what that class is."

Horace took a moment to consider, then answered. "Suggestion is a spell from the school of Illusion."

I raised an eyebrow. "Like a magician?" I pictured myself guessing people's birthdays and pulling doves from my inventory.

"No. Magicians perform Illusions through sleight of hand and clever devices. You haven't got the brains."

"You're such a dick," I said, laughing. "So what does an Illusionist do?"

"An Illusionist shapes reality," he said, his voice solemn.

"Wow."

"By performing Illusions," he continued. "Do you like birds? Coin tricks? Colored scarves?"

I scowled. "Are you serious?"

"About the birds? No, though minor miracles aren't a bad way to earn a living. What I mean is that Illusion is all about the setup. It's mundane. The second a mark realizes they're being played, even a skilled Illusionist can fail."

"Okay. So where do we start?"

"We? Who said I was going to teach you?"

"Well, you remember when I said I only did okay selling the knife?"

"I do. I was disappointed, but not shocked."

I jangled the change in my pocket. It was a long shot, but I figured if he could smell what race the blood on my shirt came from, he knew what gold sounded like, too.

Horace cocked his head for a moment, then said, "We'll start with breathing control."

THE GRIFFIN that decorated Imperial banners was a legacy of the Old Empire, far to the east, over the Great Sea, and lost to time and storms.

They weren't native to Eldgard. The knights of the expeditionary force that landed at the estuary of the Essaryl River, in the Shining Plains, brought the Griffins over as eggs or juveniles. In a ceremony known as the "Floating of the Banners," they released the griffins by the dozen before attending to the conquest of the Hvitalfar, whom they imagined to be helpless savages. Later, the Justiciars of Sophia celebrated the festival as a cautionary tale.

The knights prized fully grown Griffins as mounts, but even a tame adult was too temperamental a creature to make the sea voyage. Knowing Griffins remain docile to humans for two to three generations, the knights planned on retrieving their fully grown mounts once the conquest was complete.

Two human generations later, the surviving Imperials, backed by their Risi and Hvitalfar allies, fought the people of Eldgard to a standstill and negotiated the contentious Treaty of Alaunhylles. The knighthood had been decimated, forcing the senator class that rose from the merchant families to conscript and train regular colonists for war. These soldiers, often armed and armored at their own expense, were the foundation of the Imperial Legion. The peace they earned would be short-lived, but that is another story.

The Griffins, on the other hand, thrived. Some were slain by elven rangers. Yet others were killed by Drakes, their natural enemies. Those that escaped nested high among the rocks and fed on snakes, hares, mountain goats, and eventually elk and ibex. They invaded the ecosystem with speed checked only by their habit of fighting for territory and eating each other's young. They were regal, vicious creatures, and when the third generation of Imperials ascended the mountains in search of their birthright, the Griffins of Eldgard proved most of them unworthy with talon, beak, and claw.

Gaius Considia had well earned his honorific. Before Provus made it back to his post, the general had penned three letters, which he dispatched by courier pigeon.

The first letter was a courtesy note to the head of the Senate, informing him that a tribune of the Legion and member of House Considia had been the target of a botched assassination, and that, as the most senior general of the forces protecting New Viridia and its surroundings, Gaius was taking appropriate measures. He included no other detail because, beyond the nomination of a consul or praetor, which it had not done in decades, or the slow process of legislative review, the Senate had no say in military matters.

The second letter mobilized squads of ten legionaries in every guard post and fort in the city, split them into teams of five and positioned them along the major avenues and plazas in every quarter. Light-armored Accipiter scouts in flights of two flew lazy circles in the sky. The city watch was mobilized by their captains and, sometimes, their unofficial patrons, to help or hinder. Politicians, lawyers, and doctors across the city feared a coup, and several barricaded themselves in their homes or attempted to flee through the city gates with a few heirlooms and valuables. Those who made it to the gates were stopped but left unharmed as long as they followed the soldiers' instructions.

The Legion waited. The city held its breath.

The third letter had summoned the Legion's senior Enchanter. While Senator Constantine Flavus was drafting a formal letter of protest, and while legionaries hurriedly donned their armor and boiled out of their posts like ants, Senior Enchanter Hadrian, of family Nonia and gens Considia, carefully scraped flakes of blood from the sword and scabbard into a flask of reagents and water. He stirred it with a metal wand, then set it on Gaius's desk. Next, he laid out three identical spearheads with channels carved into the metal in the shape of runes. They had short, looped handles, each wrapped in different colored ribbons. Hadrian poured the mixture until the blood channels were full.

Then they waited, neither needing words nor sparing them,

old friends that they were. Gaius returned to the endless series of reports, orders, and requisitions that required his input or seal. Hadrian paced the room, examining Gaius's trophies, sometimes bringing up stories about the weapons, armor, and other artifacts. The memories made Gaius smile even though his quill never stopped moving.

Finally, Hadrian received the confirmation from the legates. He looked up and said, "They're in position."

Gaius paused but didn't set his quill down. "Do it."

Hadrian focused on each of the spearheads in turn, casting one spell to make them fly and another to make them seek.

The blue-ribboned spearhead hovered over the desk, trembling like an excited hound, then accelerated east toward a washing well where the Sophitians had abandoned the bucket and brushes. The spear tracked back and forth, then found trace amounts of blood in the water and shot to the east, following the sewer system. Hadrian lost his connection around the time it crossed the outer wall.

The red-ribboned spearhead launched from the desk like an arrow and veered toward the courtyard where Provus had been ambushed. It descended and circled, angling this way and that, like an eagle hunting a hare, then picked up on Acolyte Prudence's trail. It left the courtyard and turned right, opposite the way Alan had run, and weaved down side streets and alleys until it reached a Sophitian shelter for the indigent.

The spearhead flipped, point down, and rapped twice on the door with its handle.

When the prior in charge of the shelter opened the door, perhaps expecting a new resident, the spearhead darted past him, flew through two rooms, and found Prudence in a small chapel, kneeling and at prayer with Weiz's bandana still hidden in her robes. The spearhead buried itself into her back, between the left shoulder blade and spine, pinning her to the pew she'd been leaning against.

Three flights of scouts landed on the flat rooftop. They broke in through a trapdoor. They kicked over furniture, shouted, and attacked indiscriminately, driving the panicked residents of the shelter into the streets, where two squads of praetorian triarii in heavy armor systematically put them to the sword. Among the dozens of victims were two Sicarii who had been hiding among the homeless.

Watching from a balcony on the opposite side of the street, an old woman with a cowl drawn over her head hummed an Imperial paean that hadn't been sung in a hundred years.

"You might have taken a few for questioning," Hadrian said.

"They didn't know anything," Gaius replied.

The third and final spearhead arced high above the city before plummeting toward a small marketplace near the Broad Way where an old blind man and his new apprentice were doing breathing exercises. Then it angled left, through an archway, homing in on a stronger scent. It jinked right, spun, and flew an S-turn out of the alleys and across the avenue. It sunk itself four inches deep into Erik the Wode's door.

Lance Corporal Gork of the city watch—whose captain was only of the mildly corrupt variety in that she would turn a blind eye to the occasional in-kind donation but would flog a watchman for bribery or extortion—was working with a half-squad of soldiers when the spearhead planted itself. He broke down the Wode's door and found Erik passed out on cheap wine laced with Affka. The still-bloody washbasin was by the Wode's bed.

"One prisoner," said Hadrian. "It might be the commoner who saved Provus."

"Have him brought to the nearest precinct and sound the recall."

"I will. You could message them yourself, you know," Hadrian grumbled.

"I prefer paper," Gaius answered. "It doesn't talk back."

The general's orders filtered down from Hadrian to the two legates, then to the tribunes and prefects, the centurions, and, finally, the decanii leading each squad and their team leaders.

The soldiers of the Legion, many of them scared and confused, followed their orders and their training. They moved efficiently, held their assigned positions, and responded with unhesitating brutality if challenged, but otherwise did no harm. Then, when the order came, they sheathed their weapons and returned to their barracks, as neat and sharp as on a parade drill. The non-comms sat down with shaken rookies, sharing unlikely stories that might have happened to them or someone they knew, and yet that somehow made things better. The officers went home and talked to mothers and fathers, uncles and aunts, and sometimes their spouses.

Gaius dismissed the senior Enchanter and returned to his work. By the time Senator Flavus's letter of protest arrived with the next set of dispatches, the Griffin of Viridia had savaged the Sophitians.

In the One Temple, in the outer ring of the city, Sathis picked up the scales his goddess had dropped and reverently carried them into the sacristy. He'd failed his goddess and his dreams lay in pieces, but he was still faithful. Robbed of all he had, he still hoped. He turned to prayer.

And in Morsheim, in the Realm of Death, Thanatos rocked his sister as she wept.

So yeah. It was a slow afternoon. Horace kept me working on my breathing, then taught me some sleight of hand. It felt like drudge work, but like many things in V.G.O., mundane actions led to general skills.

<<<>>>

Ability: Intonation

By focusing on your breathing, pitch, and tone, your voice-based spells are just a bit more effective.

Ability Type/Level: Passive/Level 1

Cost: None

Effect: The effectiveness of voice spells, chants, and bard songs increases by 1%.

<<<>>>

Ability: Breath Control

You have improved your lung capacity, largely by ignoring people who told you not to hold your breath.

Ability Type/Level: Passive/Level 1

Cost: None

Effect: 5% more time before drowning or asphyxiating.

<<<>>>

Ability: Nimble Fingers

Diligent work has left you with improved fine motor control. It helps with the little things.

Ability Type/Level: Passive/Level 2

Cost: None

Effect: Skills that require small, precise motions, such as lockpicking, gesture-based magic, and cheating at cards are 6% more likely to succeed.

<<<>>>

I didn't think I'd be power-leveling those anytime soon, but it was gratifying to know the game took note of my efforts.

I also leveled Keen-Sight, bringing my chance of slowing time when I was in trouble to 2%. Between that and the coin tricks Horace showed me, I started to notice things I hadn't before.

I found out, for example, that Horace only put half the coppers he was given into his "secret" money belt. The other half, along with any silver, he palmed and slid into a small slit in his left pants leg, which I guessed led to a kind of drop sleeve. He'd wait for several minutes sometimes with that coin hidden in his hand, then scratch his leg mid-conversation and make a deposit.

I spotted two pickpockets working the crowd at different occasions. The first was a younger woman in a belted tan tunic and brown corduroy capris. She had short, mousy brown hair and a purple birthmark on the right side of her neck.

"Watch that one," Horace said. "You'll learn a thing or two."

She was nothing special in a remarkable way. She hunched, or she stood tall. She stomped her feet or moved lightly, like a dancer. She stopped to talk to people she knew or bumped against people she didn't, and once in a while, a coin would become hers. She must have stolen five coppers from one end of the market to the other. She stole a silver from a well-dressed man who had been arguing furiously with one of the vendors, but she placed a hand on his shoulder and returned it, saying he'd dropped it. Then she noticed me watching her and froze for a heartbeat before calmly leaving the plaza at the same pace as the crowd.

"Five coppers in less than ten minutes," I told Horace.

"That's better than you, when you're not conning young janissaries out of their pay."

"I counted fifteen. Five coppers, and one silver."

"She returned the silver."

"She stole it twice," Horace said with a grin.

The second pickpocket was a middle-aged bald man who didn't try to be subtle. He bumped into people hard enough to knock them over and stared them down if they complained. He swiped at least two items from the street merchants while they were dealing with customers. Horace's frown deepened with each theft. Then a group of five soldiers equipped with full segmented Roman armor and tower shields entered the plaza from the avenue a block away.

Horace muttered something under his breath.

Like the widow had, the thief turned as if Horace had spoken in his ear. He started running, not away from the legionaries but straight at them.

"Did you just—"

"Hush, boy. Learn."

The legionaries saw the man coming toward them and raised their shields. Horace muttered more words under his breath. The legionaries spoke to each other, spreading until there was enough space for them to maneuver. One man unequipped his shield and stood behind the other four. The crowd started to back away.

As the thief was about to reach the legionaries, the burly soldier in the middle, the one with a crest like a Mohawk on his helmet, kicked the bottom of his shield up so it faced the sky and punched the bottom edge into the thief's face. The thief's head went backward, but his legs kept going. The crested legionary followed through, straddling the thief and landing two more blows to his body before the soldier who'd stowed his shield moved forward, flipped the thief, and tied his arms behind his back. All the while, the other three legionaries shielded the capture team from the crowd. They kicked and dragged the bound thief to a nearby wall and formed a barrier of shields around him. It was coordinated, smooth, and over in ten seconds, like a brutal form of dance.

"Harsh," I said.

Horace shrugged. "That kind's bad for business. I made sure they didn't kill him on the spot. If he survives sentencing and prison, he'll come back a better thief."

But that was the height of the excitement for the afternoon. I saw a pair of Accipiters fly overhead at one point. Eventually, the team of legionaries left with their prize and the tension in the marketplace died down. Horace taught me how to roll a copper across my knuckles, and after an hour or so I could do it slowly, right-handed and in one direction, without dropping it. I leveled up Nimble Fingers for a 7% bonus in the process. The hardest part was stopping it from falling between my ring finger and pinkie on the last flip.

Around 7:00 PM, with the sun almost touching the rooftops to the west, June wandered over with a packet wrapped in grease paper tucked under her arm. "You okay, Horace?"

"You know me, little one. I'll make do."

"How about you, Alan? Do you have a place to stay?"

I wasn't sure if I was reading into the question, but it sounded like she was offering me her couch, or whatever the Viridian equivalent was. It was a touching offer; I was dirty, dressed in burlap, and she'd only met me a few hours ago. I don't think I would have done it. I'd certainly never invited one of the homeless people in LA or San Diego to crash with me for the night.

Maybe I should have accepted, but like I said, I've never been great at closing that last gap to intimacy with strangers. "I'm good, June, but thanks. We've both had a good day, and I owe Horace a meal and a drink for his mentorship." I gave her a wink.

She smiled. "Okay, then. I'll see you tomorrow." She left through the alley, not the archway. Maybe she had a place nearby.

"We should probably get on ourselves," Horace said, standing up with a wince. "We won't get murdered, but we might lose some coins and pick up a few bruises, sticking around after dark.

"Where to?"

"Depends on how much you want to spend. There's a Sophitian shelter on the other side of the Broad Way that will give us water, porridge, and a straw pallet for three coppers and a prayer each."

"Sophitian? Is that some kind of religious thing?"

"Disciples of Sophia, the goddess of balance."

Huh. It hadn't occurred to me that the AIs would have an overt interaction with the NPCs. I was almost curious enough to choose that just to see if the NPCs had a full mythos built up around their "gods," but not enough to spend three coppers on gruel and forced contemplation. "What's the next option?"

"We could go to an inn with a common room for around a silver. The Rutting Boar is nice. The food is decent, and it's a good place to practice some of the things you've learned."

"You had me at 'Rutting,'" I said, and offered him my arm.

THALIA STOOD at the edge of the terrace as she often did in the evenings, when her customers had gone home and Freddie was busy closing up shop. She watched with half-lidded eyes and the patience of the long-lived Hvitalfar as the color of the sky changed and the molten disc of the sun sunk until it touched the Heights. She watched as the flame engulfed the homes, offices, and shops of New Viridia's aristocracy, nursing a liqueur made from wildflowers, letting her long lashes filter out part of the glare, and smiled.

She'd seen this city burn, once, about ten years ago. It had been the end of the war; the main players were sitting at the negotiating table, and the few remaining splinter groups went crazy in a bid for plunder or revenge before a truce could be declared. A Wode raiding party made it inside the walls. She and a turned Dokkalfar assassin named Weiz Anaxios had taken them down, one by one.

"Hey, boss?" Freddie said.

She turned around, frowning. He knew not to disturb her when she was enjoying the view. "Are you done locking up?"

Freddie nodded, looking at his feet. "Um, yeah, but that's not why... there's someone here to see you."

Thalia leaned right and looked past her bartender. Justiciar Sathis waited by the shuttered bar. "Go home, Freddie."

"Yes, ma'am."

Freddie was a twenty-seven-year-old Frostlock —a Sorcerer who worked with ice. He kept her cool room cold and had the patience and memory she lacked when it came to orders and cocktail recipes. The two of them would have been diametrical opposites on the battlefield, but he kept a perfectly stocked and ordered cellar, while she ensured return clients. It was such a good mix, she'd put him off-limits to herself, even though she sometimes liked the shy ones.

Once Freddie was gone, she made her way to the priest with the friendliness of a stalking jaguar. "What do you want, Sathis?"

The justiciar gave her a kind but pained smile, the kind that showed her how long-suffering the priest was in the face of the world's ignorance. It made her want to burn his toes to the nub, one by one. "It's good to see you, Thalia. How long has it been?"

"Four years and still too soon."

His eyes were full of patience and compassion. She wondered if that was flammable. "I came to let you know about recent developments in the Church."

"I heard. They butchered some vagrants and a few of your acolytes on the Via Carmin. I'd say Gaia was laughing."

"Weiz was killed," Sathis said.

"No."

Sathis tucked his hands in his sleeves and waited.

"I don't know what game you're playing, Sathis, but Weiz wasn't killed by legionaries, not even praetorians. He's too good. The Red Way would have been painted in legionary blood, and the Griffin would have the city under martial law."

Sathis smiled in that infuriatingly compassionate way again.

"If you think he's dead, then I'm glad because he played you. You didn't recover a body, did you? He's halfway to—"

"I saw his body, Thalia. He'd been stripped to his underclothes and robbed like an ordinary man, but I saw him, just before the goddess Herself took him away."

Thalia shuddered. *Of course she came for him. He's always been faithful above all else.* Her eyes stung. "Who?"

"We don't know."

"Don't lie to me, Sathis. I'm not one of your dew-eyed acolytes. I'll burn the answer out of you if I have to."

Sathis swallowed. "He was on a mission. His target was Tribune Provus Considia."

Thalia gaped. "The Griffin's son? For the love of the gods, Sathis, have you gone mad?"

Sathis shifted on his feet. "He was a vocal supporter of

restoring the Legion and conquering the rest of Eldgard. He had to be stopped."

"Why wasn't he? Don't tell me the pampered son of a general murdered the greatest executor the Church has ever known."

"Second greatest," Sathis said, inclining his head to her. "And it doesn't matter, Thalia. I don't need you emotional. We need to finish the work."

Thalia felt the temperature rise around her.

Sathis took a step back. She could see the coals of her irises reflected in his black, piggy eyes. "You don't control me, Sathis."

"The goddess—"

"Does not control me either. You want Provus dead? Fine, I'll end him. I'll turn him into a signal fire for the death of the Empire. But you do *not* tell me what's important. Why is Weiz dead?"

"Provus killed him."

Light flared. Her hair lifted, rippling and glowing like a candle flame. "Not alone. He would never have seen Weiz coming."

"There was an interloper. A commoner. He interrupted the killing."

Thalia stepped forward. Her skin was glowing from the heat. "Lies. Did you set him up, Sathis? Did he finally decide he wanted out?"

Sathis fell over backward. "It's true! The legionaries took him! They have him in the precinct near the Piazza Navona!"

Thalia felt herself cool. The light dimmed. She would take care of Provus second, and this "interloper" first. Maybe he was a bystander—wrong place and wrong time—but Gaia was known to choose her champions by the flip of a coin or the shape of stars in the night sky. Far more likely he was an agent of the Griffin, long undercover and now pulled in for debriefing after a job well done. She'd make sure he received a more lasting reward. "Send an acolyte to watch the precinct," she said, walking past the fallen priest.

"Where will you be?"

"I'm going to the temple by the East Gate," she said. "Send the rest of the children to me." She didn't hear his response as she started down the steps, but he would obey. She was Thalia Daceran of the Hvitalfar, warmaiden, hero of the Legion, and now once again Mistress of the Sicarii, a title she'd set aside but never given up.

I walked into the Rutting Boar with Horace on my arm. It was just like the old man described, a large common room with a bar in the far corner and two long tables with benches on each side. It had a low ceiling of stained wood planks and pitch, crossed in the middle by two massive beams, and the dim lighting came from several small clay lamps on the tables and the massive fireplace. The innkeeper, a friendly looking man with hairy forearms and a slight blush to his cheeks, looked up from the large pot he was tending. I was still wearing my crappy clothes, and Horace was a blind beggar, so he didn't hurry, but his tone was friendly when he reached us. "Hey, fellas. My name's Henry. What'll it be?"

"What'll it cost, Henry?" I asked.

His smile drooped a bit—I guess he thought I was making fun of him—but he said, "Five coppers for a bowl of stew, two for beer, six each if you spend the night, but I'll throw in the beers for free."

"We'll take two for the stew, beer, and beds," I said, pulling the gold coin from my pocket.

The innkeeper's eyes widened slightly. He leaned in as he

handed me the seven silvers and eight coppers' change. "I don't know what you're playing at, dressed as you are, but you might be more careful showing that much coin." He straightened. "Have a seat, fellas. I'll bring your food and drink in a moment," he said loudly, with a smile.

I led the old man to a seat and sat next to him. There was a Svartalfar sitting to my left and a Risi to our right, next to Horace. Both tables were close to full, and there wasn't a single woman in the place, even though, from what I'd seen, V.G.O. was a little more gender-balanced than the real world.

"Is this a men-only inn?" I asked Horace.

"Only by custom. There are also inns where men are welcome for a meal, but they kick you out before the turning off the lights. It's just safer that way."

I nodded. Then I said, "I guess that makes sense." There's nothing like hanging out with a blind person for a day to make you realize how much of your communication is nonverbal.

"Here's the beer, then," Henry said, dropping off two mugs filled to the brim and slopping over with foam.

"Thanks," Horace said, pulling his toward him.

"Be right back," Henry said, and headed over to the fireplace and the pot.

"To the Janissaries," Horace said, raising his mug.

"To the Janissaries," I echoed, knocking my mug against his. "Though I think it's my silver we're drinking with."

"I just said I'd toast him, boy. Let's not get hung up on the details."

I chuckled and gave my beer a sip. It was frothy and a little sour, but generously alcoholic. "I hope he'll be okay."

Horace finished his own, longer pull, smacked his lips, and said, "Keep him in mind, boy. Maybe Sophia will keep him safe, or Enyo will grant him strength in battle. Maybe Gaia will save his life, or kill him to break your heart. There are no guarantees, but the gods watch and listen. Through desire, we shape the world."

When he said the last sentence, a small pop-up told me I'd gotten 100 XP. *Huh*, I thought. Maybe it was like the experience you got from reading lore books in other games.

"So, how was your first day in Eldgard, boy?"

I almost spit up my beer. "Excuse me?"

"What? It's as obvious as the fact that Henry, our host, is a self-taught brewer." Horace took a pull from his mug and screwed up his face. "Sour as vinegar. And you, Alan Campbell, are not from this world."

THIRTEEN

Gaius rubbed his eyes and yawned. It had been an eventful day, and writing by lamplight was getting harder each year.

There was a knock, and Decimus stuck his head through the doorway.

"General, there's a merchant here to see you."

"Send him away," Gaius said. He had enough complaints, demands, and requests for information on his desk without entertaining the delusions of grandeur of the wealthy middle class.

"I did, sir, but he insisted. He said it was hard to make it all the way to the palace on his cane."

Gaius sat back. "Scrawny fellow with glasses and a waistcoat?"

"Yes, General."

"Send him to me."

Gaius wiped the nib of his pen and set it down. He stood and stepped around his desk, standing at the edge of the dire-bear carpet with his hands clasped behind his back to wait for this "merchant." He fought to keep the grin from his face.

The door opened, and Titus walked in, followed by Gaius's senior bodyguard. Decimus saw the general standing, and his eyebrows shot up.

"That will be all, Decimus," Gaius said, his face severe.

"I... yes, General." Decimus left. The door shut.

Gaius stepped forward and embraced his old friend, an open smile on his face. He didn't hesitate or check for weapons; the day Titus came for him he was dead and probably deserved it. "It's been too long, Titus."

Titus hugged him back. "It's good to see you're keeping well."

Gaius released his friend and stepped back to look at him, arms still on Titus's shoulders. He frowned. "I wish I could say the same about you, you old fool. You look like a scrawny old man."

"And you look like you'd barely fit into that golden monstrosity you call a cuirass anymore. What do you do, use screws to tighten it up once they've squeezed you into it? And a general! I liked you better as a decurion. I bet they have to use butter to grease your head into your helmet."

Gaius looked at the man with a fondness he didn't feel for anyone still living, not even his son. "I am getting a bit soft, aren't I? Too much time behind a desk. But what brings you to visit this humble soldier?"

"I have an unusual set of armor I thought you might take an interest in."

Gaius smiled. "I don't collect anymore, Titus. What you see on the walls, I keep for the memories, not for use or glory. I find, too often, I need them so I don't forget."

Titus gave a little half shrug and stuck his lower lip out, but his eyes almost twinkled with mischief. "I only caught half a story, and I've been out of the game for a few years, but I think this piece might have more significance to you than you might think."

He pulled the Dokkalfar assassin's armor out of his inventory and set it on the desk in a neat display. He even pulled the throwing spikes a few inches from the bracers, showing them off. He'd been a merchant, at least in name, for almost as long as he'd known Gaius.

"Where did you get this?" Gaius asked.

"A young man brought it by my shop, and he told me the most exciting story. But first, my friend, why don't you dig through those boxes and cabinets of yours and see if you can find us some wine?"

I LEANED toward Horace and whispered, "How do you know I'm from another world?"

Horace looked at me, or kind of in my direction, as if I were a little slow. "Why are you whispering?"

I straightened. "I wasn't aware being from another world was commonplace."

Horace shrugged. "It isn't. But it isn't unheard of. There are at least seven realms, one for each of the gods—the Realms of Time, Death, Order, Chaos, Invention, and the Monstrous Dimension."

I counted them off in my head. "What about Gaia's realm?"

Horace gave me that look again. "You're in it. How did you get here without knowing where you were going?"

I took another drink to give myself time to think. "I guess things here have been a little different from what I expected."

Henry, the innkeeper, returned with warm bowls of vegetable stew and two wooden spoons. There was also a hunk of bread in each bowl. "Here ya go, fellas. Enjoy."

I should say something about stew. I don't know much about my father's family; my mother had me through IVF and never talked about the donor. But her family, from her siblings to Grandmom and the scattering of cousins back on the Emerald Isle, were Irish to the core, so much so that Grandmom kept her name, and so did her daughter. It was probably why Pops, a proud Spaniard, went home to Spain when Grandmom died.

But I digress. I have *feelings* about stew. It's not the best meat, the freshest vegetables, or the subtlest seasonings that make a stew. It's time. Time is what takes a hodgepodge of often cheap ingredients and turns them into a thick, hearty dish of gravy and texture that warms the heart and settles the soul.

I took a bite and relaxed. It wasn't Grandmom's stew—couldn't be without beef and tomatoes—but it was a passable pottage, which is peasant for "whatever the nobles didn't pinch." The carrots were tender, the potatoes present enough to give it weight, the turnips, onions, and leeks cut to just the right size so they weren't overpowering, and there was just enough spice to make my lips burn as I worked my way through half the bowl. While many things seemed to mirror the economy of the ancient world, I was grateful the availability of salt, pepper, and various herbs wasn't one of them.

When I felt like staying silent any longer would be rude, I said, "So what gave it away?"

Horace set his spoon down. "Well, no one from this world would be caught dead wearing that fabric," he said, and grinned. "I felt it when I took your arm. Is that comfortable?"

"No."

"Right. So it stands to reason anyone who'd been here for more time would have found something else to wear. And you leveled up, what, twice today?"

"I did."

Horace tapped his nose. "I thought I felt the difference. A man your age—you're twenty-eight?"

"Thirty-one."

"A thirty-one-year-old in this world would be at least a level ten or eleven. Short of a quest from the gods and Gaia's favor, there was no way for you to level up that many times in such a short timeframe."

I took another mouthful of stew. I suppose it made sense. Most players would stick with an MMORPG for one year before quitting or moving to another one. We hoped V.G.O. would keep their attention longer than that because of the self-generating world and quests, but there would be other NexGenVR games released, maybe in worlds that were more appealing to the players, and life happened. Sometimes you weren't in a place where logging into a game for hours every day was a possibility or even a want.

So players needed a leg up on the competition, and seeing as I was just one person in a city of three million, that competition was pretty stiff.

"Do you know you're an NPC?" I asked him.

"An enpee-what?"

"Never mind. It's a term from my world for someone in Eldgard."

Horace grunted. "It didn't sound complimentary. I'd keep that one to yourself."

We finished our meals. I paid the four coppers for another round of beers and did a few coin tricks for the people around us. Horace used his voice-throwing trick to tell dirty jokes to the general hilarity of the room, and Henry comped us the third round. I was buzzed and happy by the time the diners left, the sleepers barred the door, and we set the tables against the wall. Henry pulled some pillows out of a crate by the bar, and people made themselves as comfortable as they could on the floor or on a bench.

Horace chose a bench. I followed suit, though it seemed like a recipe for falling on your face in the middle of the night.

About thirty minutes after the lamps went out, I heard the sound of scurrying feet on the floor below me as Henry's cleaning crew went to work. Yet another of V.G.O.'s mysteries solved.

THE MONITORING SOFTWARE WAS RECORDING, Alan was stable, and even the AIs were settling down. There was nothing for him to do but stare at a blank screen. Jeff pushed himself back from the desk and stood, yawning. It had been a hell of a day.

He gathered up the trash from the junk food he'd lived on, like some kind of post-apocalyptic urban survivor. He felt tired and dirty, dehydrated from last night's drinking, and the mix of caffeine and sugar was running out. He'd be glad when all this was over, and he could change clothes and sleep in his own bed.

He left Alpha Testing and passed through the programming farm. All the offices but his were stripped bare. He'd liked some of the people here. There were people whose papers he'd read in robotics journals, and people who'd had experience with mind-machine interfaces from gaming who'd helped him simplify the complex task of controlling a simulated body with full sensory feedback. The AI guys were weird, but they'd taken the skeleton of a control system he'd built and fed it into Kronos, and he'd been grateful for that, too.

He stepped into his office and turned on the light. There wasn't much that was his. He'd hung his bachelor's and master's from Penn on the wall, as well as his doctorates in

Nanoscience and Nanoengineering. There were some declassified screenshots from an American soldier's eyes in Ukraine, as well as some nanobot model printouts the AI guys had Gaia generate for fun.

His desk was clean. He'd shifted to Alpha Testing three months ago, only using the office for calls, private meetings, and to get away from the mouth breathers HR had sent him to test the gear. He was going to talk to Osmark about that. If someone of Alan's caliber was all it took to make it work, Jeff had been set up for failure.

Then again, he knew from his experience with the Department of Defense that a technical solution that required a smart —a fairly smart—individual to operate wouldn't stand up to the requirements of users who were tired, drunk, stoned, or just average, which as the word implied was most of the population.

He had a picture of Cheryl and Krissy on his filing cabinet. He smiled.

He'd been working in Home Depot when Cheryl came down the aisle looking lost and carrying a baby. The porch at her parents' place had rotted through, and her dad wasn't in good enough shape to replace it after his stroke.

"Jeff? Is that you?" she'd said.

He'd been so embarrassed to have her see him stocking shelves, he'd almost missed the wonder in her voice. "Hey, Cheryl. It's been a while."

They talked. They had coffee after his shift. He spent the summer fixing up her parents' place, after work, and they'd kind of dated, though neither of them had called it that. It was just Jeff Berkowitz and Cheryl Jones spending recess together and touching elbows. Sometimes, he held the baby.

He'd found the grounding to finish his degree, so he left again, but this time they'd e-mailed each other every day, and he stopped cutting, though he still struggled sometimes. At the end of the semester, Cheryl drove down to Baltimore, and he got his first tattoo.

His watch beeped. Time to head outside.

He left the programming farm and passed through the outer office. It was quiet, sterile, deconstructed. The movers were gone for the day. There was no guard on the outer door; it was locked to anyone not on the access list.

Cheryl was already there. She'd parked her station wagon next to his Explorer.

"Hi, Daddy!" Krissy yelled, and Jeff felt his face split into the widest grin he could manage.

"Hey, kiddo! Shouldn't you be out partying with the other freshmen?"

Krissy rolled her eyes. "Mom says I need to study more. I bombed my Western Civilization midterm."

"What about calc?" he asked.

"Ninety-seven."

"That's my girl."

Cheryl squinted her eyes at him, but he could tell it was for show. They were both proud of their daughter. "Don't encourage her. She needs to be well rounded."

"An engineer's paycheck can pay for a lot of therapy," Jeff said with a wink. He saw a flash of hesitation in Cheryl's eyes, but she laughed with them. Jeff's mom and his tattoos weren't something they talked about in front of Krissy. She wasn't his, thankfully, even though he'd never treated her like anything but his daughter, so she wouldn't have the same problems, and he didn't want to burden her with something she didn't need to know.

"Speaking of paychecks, Dad, I need money."

"Do you?"

"Yep." She stuck her hands in her pockets and rocked back and forth on her heels.

"How much?"

"Just enough for dinner and a movie?"

"How much is that in math?"

Krissy pouted. "Thirty."

Cheryl crossed her arms. "You can catch a matinee for five bucks, and food is ten dollars if you eat before."

Jeff grinned. He pulled two twenties from his pocket and gave his daughter a wink. "Bring a friend with you."

"Thanks, Dad!" Krissy took the money off his hands and kissed him on the cheek.

Cheryl smiled at the two of them. He reached for her and wrapped his arms around his family.

"Um, Dad? You kind of smell."

"Yeah, babe, you do. And isn't the parking lot kind of empty?"

Jeff looked at the loves of his life. "It is. We had a problem with the project, and the boss gave everyone the weekend off, but I've solved it, and everything's going to be okay."

I DREAMED OF POPS. He was old, probably as old as I'd ever seen him before he died, but we weren't at the house near Empuriabrava, we were in the alpha server. I could tell because I recognized the hill and the grove, and because the textures weren't as perfect as they were inside V.G.O.

So Pops was standing there with his back to me, one of his giant hands resting on the bole of an olive tree and the other knuckled into his hip. He was looking toward the bay. He was wearing the sleeveless white shirt and khaki pants he always wore when he was working in the gardens, and he'd worked until the day he couldn't anymore.

"That you, *nieto*?" he asked, looking over his right shoulder.

"Yeah, Pops," I whispered. "It's me."

FOURTEEN

Sophia shuddered. It was all going wrong. She could feel all the precursors of catastrophe clicking into place, but she felt powerless to stop it. She couldn't directly interfere in the player's experience, not without giving her sister, Enyo, equal license to act. Meanwhile, New Viridia burned with fear, plots, and counterplots since the Griffin's pogrom at the shelter. Going there would be like bathing in boiling water. She would have to ease herself in.

Worse, Thalia, her own Mistress of the Sicarii, was co-opting the assassins for personal ends while Sathis hid in his chambers. Thalia was a star in Sophia's universe, both inescapable pull and cataclysmic heat. The Overmind of Balance had left her daughter to pickle in her little bar too long, and now she was spoiled. There was no avoiding what was to come.

ROBERT OSMARK OPENED HIS EYES. The ceiling fan again. *Round and round.* The sound of his wrist alarm going off. Osmark sat up in bed. He'd slept dreamlessly from the time he'd lain down until now, a full eight hours, and he felt nothing. Not well-rested or tired, just wide-awake nothing, like he'd never gone to bed. He swung his legs out and padded into the kitchen.

The coffeepot had just started to burble. The sky outside the balcony window was the pale gray of pre-dawn. He walked to the bathroom, took a leak, flushed, washed his hands and then his face, then headed back to the kitchen.

His coffee was ready. He pulled the pot out from under the automatic brewer and poured himself a mug. Sumatra, today. It was Saturday; Saturdays he tried new things. It smelled earthy and rich, like freshly turned soil and spoiling fruit. He deferred judgment, just like his high-priced Harvard creativity seminar had told him to, and took a sip.

The almost scalding hot coffee was sweet and complex. It made his tongue tingle and his mind buzz. He could have sat in one of those snobby coffee shops that were growing like fungus in newly gentrified Brooklyn, back home, and spouted nonsense of how round the coffee was, and how the middle note reminded him of the loamy taste of jungle earth and pepper, but the truth was, he hated it. He took another sip because his mother always told him to try things twice, and because morning mouth could throw his palate off sometimes, but no, he definitely hated it, and while young Osmark never would have wasted the caffeine, Osmark in his prime was too busy and rich to drink bad coffee. He poured the rest of it down the sink.

He rinsed his mug out and refilled it with fresh, filtered water. Sometimes he passed on coffee just to prove to himself he wasn't addicted. He wasn't going to dig through his cabinets for an alternate cup for the same reasons.

He stepped out onto the balcony and leaned his arms on the railing, drinking his water, listening to the waves and the rising wind as the sun rose somewhere behind him. A woman jogged across the beach below him, and in his mind he wished her well. The world belonged to those who rose and chased after what they wanted. He finished his water and went back inside.

He sat down at his desk with a second glass of water and a Granny Smith apple, biting into the fresh, tart fruit as he clicked his way through his executive dashboard. The move-out was 62% complete. That meant the packers might be able to start on the programming farm early. He shot an email to the dev team leads to remind them they had until noon to retrieve any personal belongings they didn't want packed. He already had placements for most of them on projects that would add value to the company and redeem them for Viridian's failure; letting them grab the crap they'd hung from the walls was just a way to keep them happy and loyal until he could put this mess behind him.

He took a second to wipe his glasses and wrinkled his nose. He'd thought of laser surgery; as much as the glasses were acceptable in the tech world, he hated depending on them. But for every ten success stories he read about PRK or Lasik, he heard at least one where the patient ended up legally blind, and that wasn't a risk he was willing to take.

He checked the security status on the building and saw that both Jeff Berkowitz and Alan Campbell were still there. Alan hadn't left since yesterday. Jeff had stepped out briefly last evening and then spent the night in Alpha Testing.

Robert got goosebumps down his arms. He stabbed the home button on his smartphone, logging in with his fingerprint, and said, "Sophia, call Sandra Bullard mobile."

"What's wrong?" Sandra said.

No stupid questions, just straight to the point. He made a mental note to give her a raise. "I need you to get to the Viridian building right away."

Provus showed up at the precinct near dawn, before his regular duties to the legate started. His uncle had sent word that the commoner who'd saved him might be there.

The precinct was an old building—an inner fort from New Viridia's more turbulent past when the outermost ring had been breached more than once, and the Legion had used forts like these as fallback locations. Since the last decade had been peaceful inside Imperial borders, the fort had been given over to the watch.

It was just before shift change, so most of the watchmen were in the building. The desk sergeant, a Svartalfar woman who was friendly to the point of giggles, wouldn't help him until her captain authorized it. He waited for nearly half an hour. Then the captain, his social peer in rank if not in lineage, assigned a watchman named Gork to take him to the prisoner.

Provus followed the half-Risi watchman to the cells in the back of the precinct. There were only four, enough to hold prisoners who made it to the building alive for a short time before sentencing or transfer to the labor camps; Imperial roads didn't build themselves.

There were two prisoners in the cells. One was a woman whose brown robes completely covered her except for her hands, which were thin, wrinkled, and veined. She huddled in the corner of her cell, away from the door. Opposite her, a man in workman's clothes was curled up on his side in the middle of his cell, with his back to bars and the light.

"You, prisoner! Get up!" Provus snapped.

The man groaned and shivered.

"He's coming off an Affka high, sir," Gork said, unlocking the cell.

Provus frowned. Charging into a losing battle sounded right for an Affka user, but he'd hoped for more.

Gork grabbed the man by the back of the neck and lifted him to the bars like he was holding a stray cat. "This him?"

The prisoner had dirty brown hair, blue, bloodshot eyes, a scraggly mustache that ran down both sides of his mouth to his chin, and the wiry physique of a manual laborer. A string of drool trailed from his slack mouth. Provus could see light blue veins underneath the Wode's pale skin, even in torchlight.

For all his screaming over a trivial injury, Provus's savior had been Imperial, dark-skinned, and somewhat handsome. Provus was annoyed and relieved at the same time. "It's not him."

The watchman set the prisoner down more gently than Provus might have. "What should we do with him, your lordship?"

Provus shrugged. "Charge him for Affka use or let him go. I couldn't care less."

Gork kept his tone respectful. "Your man paid him a silver for his silence, sir. I think it may have been more money than he's used to having."

But Provus was already walking back up the stairs. The Wode couldn't talk in his state. This had been necessary, but further engagement was a waste of his valuable time.

Sandra swung her leg off her new Kawasaki Ninja and ran up to the door, helmet in hand.

"Good morning, Miss Bullard," Frank said.

"Frank." She swiped her card and went in.

She passed through the shell of the content creation spaces, swiped her way into the programming farm, and jogged to

Alpha Testing. All the while she was running through scenarios of what might be happening in there, from a disgruntled employee to industrial espionage, with a few foreign actors scattered throughout. She wished she had a gun.

She reached Alpha Testing and swiped her way in. A glance told her the vault was physically secure, and she doubted anyone could get through Thanatos's security protocols in one day, not through a single access point and without bringing people and hardware in. She turned into the testing bay and found Jeff Berkowitz and Alan Campbell asleep on the hospital beds.

She paused, unsure of what was going on. She'd expected them to be stealing files, or equipment, or to be drunk off their rockers. She hadn't expected this. "Berkowitz!"

The big nanotech engineer jerked and sat up, arms flailing like he was under attack. He blinked, saw her, and said, "Oh, shit."

"Alan! You too! Get up, and get over here!"

"Umm... he can't," Jeff said, walking up.

Sandra glared at him.

"He's in the game."

Sandra continued to stare at the engineer. Part of that was because she needed a few seconds to herself to process all the implications of what the man had just said. The other part was that in spite of being shorter, lighter, and younger than the man standing in front of her, the company she kept and a personal history of violence meant this had often, in the past, encouraged people to spill their guts as fast as they could manage.

"It was his idea! I mean, he couldn't have done it without me, but he basically said Osmark wanted him to solve the problem, and then he bet me he could stay in the test server for a few minutes, and I was hung over, so I thought, 'What the hell?'"

Sandra kept staring. She'd learned not to blink while aiming down a rifle scope, years back. It really made people uncomfortable.

"And then he puked his guts up. Twice. But I cleaned it all up and changed the settings because the doctors were wrong. His idea, too, just in case, so we're probably not liable, but the readouts don't show any lasting damage at all."

Sandra ran her tongue across her teeth while he stammered, feeling the tip of her left canine. The guy didn't know whether he should take credit or shift blame. Sandra wasn't sure either. She crossed her helmet-carrying arm at her waist and chewed on the side of her left thumb.

"He had a pass! He was on the list for the day! No one even knows what he does here. I mean he's HR, but he was always messing around with the AIs and talking to you, and Osmark, and—"

"Jeff?"

"Yes, Ms. Bullard?"

"You said he's in the game?"

"I did. I could unsay that if it's useful."

"The actual game? Not the test server."

"Yeah."

"How long?"

Jeff checked his watch. "Coming up on twenty-one hours."

"Great."

"Is it?"

"It is. But should that screen be flashing red?"

Jeff turned to look at his workstation. "Oh, shit."

"ALAN! ALAN, WAKE UP!" Jeff yelled into my ear.

I opened my eyes, smelled the stench of smoke and unwashed bodies, panicked, and fell about a foot and a half in the dark. I rolled onto my side. I was in a wood-ceilinged room. *Where the hell am I?* I could feel my heart pounding in my ears, and I was lightheaded. Had I drunk too much last night? Was I still drunk?

I could make out the shape of bodies lying in the half dark. Shafts of light came in from half-boarded windows. *What am I doing here?* This didn't look like home. It didn't look like California. I'd seen some old towns in Spain that looked like this—old Roman cities—but nothing on this side of the Atlantic.

The room smell like BO and rotten eggs. Some of the bodies looked like they were dead. Others shifted slightly. One man scratched his ass.

"Alan! We're losing the signal, man! Nod if you can hear me!"

I nodded. I was Alan. That was Jeff. *The Rutting Boar. I came here with Horace.* It was all coming back to me.

I felt a jag of pain in my forehead, just above my right eyebrow, and I grabbed at my face. "Gah!" It was like I'd been stabbed with a piece of broken glass. My stomach clenched.

"Oh, come on!" Jeff said, and I heard him take off his headset.

I was breathing fast.

"Hold on, boy," Horace said, finding his way to me in the dark. I suppose it wasn't any different than full daylight to him. He pushed a small round shape into my hands. "Eat this."

"Unh," I said, wincing. "What?"

"It's just bread," he said.

The last thing I needed was food. I wanted to vomit, but I couldn't seem to get rid of the feeling of wrongness that made me want to jump right out of my skin.

I heard a squeal of feedback, then it was Sandra, not Jeff, speaking into my ear. "Alan? Can you hear me?"

I nodded.

"Good. Alan, this is important. I need you to do whatever it is you did last time, or we're going to lose the connection to the server farm. You're down to the lowest signal the system will allow."

The server farm. I was in *Viridian Gate Online. This is normal,* I told myself. I got my breathing under control. I needed to anchor myself to the world, fast, and of all the sensory data V.G.O. was feeing me, taste was the strongest. I needed food. I could see Horace's silhouette in the dark, as if he was waiting for me to catch up.

"Go on, boy. Eat."

I broke the crusty roll with my thumbs. I could feel the flour the roll had been dusted with on my fingers. I shoved a piece into my mouth and chewed. It was a dense, wholemeal bread with little seeds in it. It broke down in my mouth, starches to simple sugars and the sweet, sticky taste of molasses. I swallowed and felt a sense of calm and rightness spread across my chest.

"That's it, Alan, keep it up," Sandra said.

Oh crap, Sandra! "I need to get out of here," I whispered to Horace, stuffing the rest of the bread into my mouth.

He grabbed me by the sleeve and led me to the exit without hesitating or stumbling. We unbarred the door and stepped outside.

"I need to talk to my people on the other side," I told Horace.

"You do what you need to. I'm going to scrounge some breakfast from June. Things are usually slow on Kronos's day."

"Kronos's..." *Saturday. Saturn was the Roman god of seasons and time.* "I'll see you later, Horace!" I yelled after him, and winced. My headache was still pretty bad, but that might have been the beer rather than my unconscious body trying to pull me back to another world.

Horace waved over his shoulder and turned the corner around the inn.

"Sandra?"

"Yes, Alan?"

"I can explain."

"I think you'd better."

"Mistress Thalia! They're releasing him!"

"Who?"

"The man who killed Executor Weiz, Mistress. Provus Considia came to visit the precinct, and now they're going to let him go."

Thalia took off at a run. The information was at least ten minutes old. With Gaia's favor, the watchmen would be slow to do the paperwork.

She ran with the lightness of a daughter of the Shining Plains, showing no sign of her fifty-two years of age. The pavement was hard beneath her thin-soled leather boots.

A warmaiden of the Hvitalfar racing to battle drew attention and marked memories, so once she was a few blocks from the shelter, she ducked into a side street, crouched, and cast a fireball at the ground as she jumped. The explosion scorched the walls and launched her high enough to grab the lip of the roof. She took damage, but her class-based resistance to fire and the items she had equipped reduced it to the feeling of standing too close to the fire, rather than a second-degree burn. She kicked and hauled herself up the same way she'd climbed the ancient trees outside of Allaunhylles as a child, then took off across the tiled roofs as fast as before.

"So that's all there is to it," I told her.

"Alan, you went against the Board's instructions."

"Those instructions were never communicated to me."

"They were communicated to the entire team by the CEO of the company. Viridian was dead."

"Lazarus, come forth!" I said.

Sandra laughed, which I took as a good sign, both in terms of how much trouble I was in and my IRL crush's education. "Rob is going to be so pissed."

"Pissed as in 'Fire Alan' or pissed as in 'Why couldn't he do this before I bent over in front of the Board?'"

Sandra didn't answer for a moment. I waited. I found people who took a second to think gave answers worth waiting for. "It might be a bit of both. Wagner is going to claim Robert knew about this. But when Viridian moves forward, the share-holders are going to be ecstatic. The bigger the stink Wagner makes, the stronger the blowback. This might be what we need to get him fired. You'll play along?"

"As long as you keep me in the loop? Yeah, within reason."

"Rob will—"

"You, Sandra. I know Rob cuts his losses when he has to."

Another pause. "All right."

"If it helps, I own the configuration data."

"You what?"

"I own the configuration data. All the changes Jeff and Kronos made, they're mine."

"How do you figure?"

"They scanned my brain."

"With your permission."

"I didn't sign any consent forms."

"You're an employee of the company, Alan."

"An employee of the company who took on a side project in

his own spare time. Viridian died, remember? The CEO announced it in front of a hundred people."

"Okay. Yeah, that could work. Just don't try it with Robert or he'll pay you off and spend the next ten years ruining you. Did you plan this?"

"I might have thought of it." I hadn't until now, but I wasn't going to pass up a chance to look smarter than I was. You can blame Horace or Sandra's legs, whichever makes you feel better.

THALIA RAN straight-backed on the balls of her feet. She was completely sober for the first time in a while, her mind fully engaged by her every step. There was a trick to roof running that had nothing to do with magical lightness or high Dexterity. Fearlessness helped with speed, but it did nothing to solve the issue that roofs, especially tiled ones, were not built to be run on. Tiles slipped, roofing collapsed, people in the streets below might be hit by falling shingles or look up when she leaped the gap between buildings. Falling was unavoidable. The trick was controlling the fall.

A tile slid out from under her, and she rode it, sinking her weight, then she leaped across the alley as the tile cleared the gutter. She tried to find flat terrace roofs when she could, though the width of the gaps and the planks left by roofers or the Thieves' Union sometimes forced her path to go wide. She could see the opening of the plaza ahead, and the blocky bulk of the bannered precinct itself, only a few hundred yards distant.

A tile broke. Her foot sank in, and she tucked into a roll, scattering more tiles. She tried to stand, slipped again, and sailed over the edge of the roof.

Traditionally, Dawn Elves built their homes in trees, and

only the Accipiter were more comfortable with heights. Thalia reacted to the sensation of weightlessness without thinking; she curled, twisted her torso, then her legs, and reached. She flashed to the memory of Weiz's face when he saved her from a fall, ten years ago, and her fingers closed on the ledge behind her. Her body jerked to a stop, then swung down until she planted her feet on the building, jumped, and cast another fireball. The blast wrecked the wall and shot her across the street to the next line of roofs. She landed lithely and kept running, unfazed by the near-death experience; dwelling on things got you killed.

She reached the midpoint in the line of roofs leading to the plaza and skidded to a stop, but a dark, roiling shape made of cracked ash, steam, and glowing coals shot forward like a hellish copy of her body. She'd summoned her ash elemental to go the rest of the way.

Though it was mostly made of hot air, ash, and flame, Thalia's anger imbued the elemental with weight. It ran forward like a man trying to run on water, sinking through the tiles until it disappeared below the roof in a thick black trail of smoke. Then it started taking out walls. Stone and mortar exploded into shrapnel as it crashed through three floors and four rooms, killing a housekeeper, a pair of playing children, and a family of four who'd just come back from the market. Then it burst out through the outer wall into the plaza itself.

Thalia saw it all through the elemental's eyes, the creature's molten spirit merged with hers. She gave it direction; it lent her detachment. The bodies were broken things, no different than the tiles, masonry, and furniture she'd shattered. They'd quickened as she passed, becoming flame, eyes popping in sockets and flesh splitting away.

The elemental thundered forward, plowing people under without pause if they got in its way. It filled the air with smoke and sparks. It roared, cracked, and hissed like a stoked furnace.

Herd instinct took over, and the survivors screamed and ran, unwittingly providing the creature with cover from the precinct.

Gork kept a firm grip on the prisoner's bound wrists as he marched Erik up the stairs.

He'd talked the captain into releasing the Wode; Erik Stormson was properly registered as a foreign resident, regularly employed, and it was the only offense on the man's record. Gork would stop by the man's house after a few days, once he was sober and had recovered from the enthusiastic questioning. This was leniency, not injustice, and the Wode needed to understand that or he'd wind up dead or back in a cell.

Gork paused at the top of the stairs. The hairs on his arm rose. Something wasn't right.

The outer door exploded into splinters, and a cloud of ash, lit from within by bursts of flame, rushed in to fill the space.

Gork acted in accordance with his nature. He was a proud man of the city watch, sworn to defend New Viridia's inhabitants, so he yanked the prisoner back and pitched him down the stairs. But he was half Risi, so he bellowed and charged into the fight. He could see two glowing coals that looked like eyes in the center of the dark cloud. He drew his short sword on the run and lowered his head.

It was that moment that finally won him the acceptance of his peers after years of hostility and suspicion. It was a moment that required music. The broken bodies of the watchmen who'd been close to the door. The half-Risi wreathed in smoke and flame, moving at a dead sprint, battle madness in his eyes. His captain, frozen on the stairs to the second floor, and his shift-mates stopping their flight to cover to witness, with awe and sorrow, as Gork sacrificed himself.

Or tried to. Faster than its bulk would have suggested, the ash elemental dodged around the corporal and shot down the stairs, where it found Erik dazed but unharmed.

It embraced him. Erik screamed. Boiling ash filled his lungs.

THALIA BLINKED her eyes and stood, 140 yards away. She could still hear the Wode's screams ringing in her ears, feel his skin bubble and pop as he struggled in her arms. She didn't feel bad about it. She didn't feel good. He'd taken something from her.

She lowered herself over the edge of the roof and dropped from balcony to balcony. When she reached the street, she walked away.

BACK IN THE CELLS, the second prisoner hadn't moved from her corner. She stared at her hands with the fascination of a child. They were smooth, filled out, strong, with the beginning of calluses across her palms. She folded and unfolded them, and they didn't catch, creak, or click. She swallowed, almost laughing at how nervous she was, and swept her left hand under the hood to feel her hair.

She closed her eyes, exhaling, sagging against the wall. Her hair was thick and full. It was short on the sides, because being comfortable in her helmet was more important to her than looks, and three inches long and layered on top, because even a warrior was allowed her vanity. She closed her fingers around a handful of it and tugged, still worried, but none of it came away in her hands.

With those assurances, she brought both hands to her face, and she sobbed at what she felt there. The skin was supple and smooth. Her cheeks and jaw were sharp, the skin on her neck tight, the muscles defined as she poked and prodded. No baby fat, but that was fine. Youth was an ideal that was always seen looking backward. She was a woman in her prime. She wiped the tears from her cheeks.

It had been ten years since Gaius betrayed her. The Griffin of New Viridia had sheathed his claws, hung his sword up, and become a statesman while he cowered in his room in the palace. She'd watched that beautiful man wither behind a desk, depriving himself of his desires for family and glory for the sake of peace. She wasn't bitter, though, because the survivors always betrayed her in the end.

Now she could feel suspicion and fear spreading across the city. The deployment of soldiers the previous day had been surgical and neat, something the bloodless citizens had been able to sweep under the rug or explain away with gossip or politics, but this was fire and smoke and blood. It was messy. She could taste the ash and grease in the air.

She laughed and pulled the robe over her head, crumpling it up and tossing it. Her arms were well formed, her muscles firm, her skin tight at the elbows and armpits, where it had piled up in disgusting folds only minutes before. Ten years of feeding off alley muggings and highway banditry, off honor duels and family rivalries turned violent. War was coming to New Viridia. She could feel it whispered to burning ears, said solemnly from father to son, and in the pained expression of mothers.

She rolled to her feet in her tunic, pants, and boots. Two strides took her across the cell, and she kicked the door so hard it flew off its hinges and slammed against the cells opposite her. She stepped over the charred Wode's corpse and walked upstairs.

The watchmen saw her and knew her. Their anger and fear fed her.

"Bless us, Enyo!"

"Avenge us!"

As her power returned, her aura lapped out in red waves, building on the turmoil within them and healing their wounds. They didn't heal cleanly, though, and those that lived would talk proudly of their scars. Some gripped their swords. Eyes met, and wordless compacts were made.

She stepped through the ruined door into the fresh air and greeted the blue-bannered city for the first time in a decade. She needed armor and a sword. That fat fool Felix from Bespoke Arms and Artifices was going to get the chance to outfit a god.

"Okay, so we're agreed. I... hold on a second, Sandra," I said. A message from Titus had come through.

<<<>>>

Personal Message:

Dear Alan,

I was able to find a buyer for that armor of yours. As per our discussion, I've decided to leave town and reconnect with some old friends while I can. Could you stop by the shop right away to pick up your share of the sale?

Regards,

—Titus

<<<>>>

I sent him a quick answer to let him know I was coming and

closed the messaging window. "Hey, Sandra? I've got to go take care of something."

"What? Alan, come on! We need to work out how we're going to approach Robert with this. He sent me here to kick both your asses. He's still going to be mad you went around his back."

"We'll do it later!" I said, and started speed walking toward Titus's shop. A pair of men came out of the inn, yawning, and more people were on the streets than just a few minutes ago. Somewhere, toward the sunrise, a bell was ringing, and I could see smoke rising above the cityscape. New Viridia was coming alive.

I was checking my map and walking as fast as I could when I ran headlong into the gray Risi who'd tried to kill me and Provus.

FIFTEEN

"Well, well, 'Arrett. Look who I just 'ound."

I scrambled to my feet. It was both of them—the gray Risi and the scar-faced Imperial from the day before.

"Kill him," Garrett said, drawing a knife.

Garrett fell into what looked like a professional knife-fighter's stance, and I flinched as the Risi made his knuckles crack by flexing his fists. I was coming around to Horace's opinion that I wasn't a fighter. I ran.

I booked down the alley behind me as fast as I could and jinked left at the first cross-alley. I didn't look behind me. Looking behind you was for people who wanted to be billed as "Dead Body #3" in a horror movie.

A right, then another left. No patrols. Yesterday, I couldn't spit without it landing on an officer of the law or a legionary, and now there was no one.

I was thinking of checking my map when Garrett came out of a side street ahead of me. I took the first and only right. Mog's hand swiped the air behind me. I almost stumbled, recovered, felt awesome, and then saw they'd herded me into a dead end.

I turned around and shouted, "Help!"

Keen-Sight kicked in again just long enough for me to see Garrett's dagger spinning past my face. It was a simple, well-weighted throwing knife with no guard, the kind a professional knife thrower might favor. The next one wouldn't miss.

Time resumed. Garrett drew another knife, and his Risi friend moved forward in a wrestler's stance. "Okay, okay, wait!" I said.

"Nothing 'ersonal, *uajaah*. Wrong 'lace, wrong time."

I didn't know what "uajaah" meant, but it sounded like Risi for Dead Body #3. **"You don't want to do this,"** I said, using a suggestion.

The Imperial and the Risi hesitated.

"Why?" Garrett said.

I started talking. I could use Suggestion once every thirty seconds or so. The more I got them to listen, the more potent it would become. "You want me dead, right? Why, because I'm a witness? Yeah, that's got to be why, and I get that. Far from me to get between you and the rest of your lives, but killing me won't get you out of trouble. Did you know who you were attacking, yesterday? That was Provus Considia, the Griffin of New Viridia's bastard son. **The whole Empire wants you dead.**"

The Risi looked at his Imperial friend. "'Arrett?"

"All the more reason to kill you and get out of town," Garrett said, stepping forward with his knifepoint dancing.

"But you can't, can you? The best time to get out was right after the attempt, when Provus hadn't gotten back to his people. He's a praetorian, right? Lots of connections, on top of being related to the biggest, baddest general in the Empire. You'll never make it past the gates, not without money, and I was just about to go cash in on his armor. You remember his armor, right? Rare gear, worth a couple gold at least. If you kill me, I can't get paid, and you can't get paid. **I'm worth more to you alive."**

Garrett stopped. He looked at his companion for support. The Risi shrugged. "Fine," Garrett said, slipping his throwing knife into a sheath on his thigh. "But Mog's going to walk with you, and if you draw attention to us or call the watch, he'll crush your head like a melon."

I swallowed. I'd never spent much time crushing melons, but I believed Mog could do it. I'd foolishly set the pain feedback in V.G.O. to as realistic as possible, so getting my head crushed was *really* going to hurt. "You'll let me go once you have the money, right?"

"Sure," Garrett said. The corner of his mouth twitched. *A smirk. A freaking smirk. Like I wouldn't see that, you asshole.* Things were looking grim for me, and probably for Titus too if they were that concerned about witnesses.

Mog's hand fell on my neck. I could feel the restrained tension that would snap my spine at any moment.

"For what it's worth," Sandra said, "your synchronization is just about perfect right now."

Super, I thought. *I'll make a note to drop all new players into life-threatening situations, right after I survive my own.*

Titus waited with a familiar flutter in his chest, a tingle in his fingers, a spring in his step as paced in front of his store. How long had it been? Three years? Longer? He had the slight dryness of the mouth and nervous excitement he associated with some of the best, worst times of his life.

The praetorians Gaius had sent to help were stealthed into

the shadows of the plaza. They were kitted out as *hastati*, light-armored skirmishers with pila—six-foot-long throwing spears—and oval leather shields for fast blocking. Titus didn't think it would come to that; Alan had seemed like a good sort, smart but naive. It would be a simple matter to talk him into a meeting. The only crack in that picture was the predatory smile he'd flashed when he'd told Titus about selling the knife, but Felix was an ass and Titus would have been proud of that sale, too.

Titus put a lot of stock in his ability to read people, but he was a professional, so he'd dusted off his much-reduced assortment of gadgets and concealed weapons, just in case things went sideways.

It was a little past seven in the morning when Alan emerged from a side street with the sun peeking over the rooftops behind him. Titus saw two shapes with him, a slender human and a Risi who appeared to be gripping Alan by the neck.

Titus smiled. His heart beat faster. Was this an attempt at robbery or a hostage situation? "Alan! Sorry for the short notice. Are these friends of yours?"

"Hi, Titus! I just need the money from the sale, and my two friends will go. Do you have it on you?"

"I do!" Titus fumbled with the pouch at his hip. He could barely keep the smile from his face. Trading was all well and good, but it had been years since he'd felt this alive.

When the trio was clear of the alley, the old salesman straightened, brought his fingers to his lips, and blew.

TITUS LOOKED at us with an expression I can only describe as childish glee and whistled. It was a loud, high-pitched note that echoed off the buildings in the deserted square. Or not deserted. Two fully armed and armored legionaries stepped out of their hiding places and fell in at our sides, herding me, Garrett, and Mog forward. The legionaries were carrying oval leather shields and metal spears with long metal necks and a small sharp tip with no barbs. I was pretty sure those were meant to be thrown; I just needed to get out of the way.

"'Arrett! What do we do?" Mog said. He had me up on my tippy-toes, and I was seeing stars dart across my eyes.

Garrett looked over his shoulder, his eyes flat, his mouth twisted into a snarl.

I grinned. "No, wait! I'll save you the trouble. He's going to tell you to **drop me, Mog!**" I shouted. My Spirit dropped by 100 points and Mog's hand went slack.

Then things got crazy. A pilum—one of the throwing spears—sprouted from Mog's left shoulder and punched out of his back. The Risi roared, which is a really hard thing to do with a punctured lung. Garrett was throwing knife after knife at Titus, and Titus actually dodged two, then batted one from the air with his cane. Mog pulled the spear out and charged the legionary to the right. The soldier to my left put a second spear through Mog's calf, slowing him down.

There was an explosion of gray smoke between Titus and Garrett that washed over all of us, making me cough as I tried to get clear, and somewhere in all that mess Garrett was screaming, "Mog! Kill that double-crossing shitheap! Kill him, kill him, kill him!"

There was a gust of wind, and the smoke cleared. Garrett had two daggers drawn and was bleeding from a cut over his eye. Titus had disappeared. One of the legionaries was down, unconscious, and Mog had his back to me with his spear raised to finish the man off.

I acted without thinking. I grabbed the spear that was still stuck in Mog's calf and yanked. Mog howled, turned, and his leg collapsed under him. I just raised the spear because I was scared and he fell onto it. Then the second legionary knocked me aside and started laying into the Risi with both spear and shield.

"Mog!" Garrett yelled. He looked at me, murder and grief in his eyes, and cocked his arm back to throw. Then Titus was there. He'd been right behind Garrett all along, hiding in his shadow. He whirled under the thug's raised arm, drew a short, slender blade that was hidden in his cane, and slid it up into Garrett's brain from under his chin.

GARRETT SAW the thin golden blade slide back out and smiled as he fell. He'd gotten to meet a Gentleman in New Viridia after all.

"HOLY CRAP, ALAN," Sandra said.

"Yeah," I said. I had more blood on me—Risi this time. I wondered if Horace would be able to tell the difference of if he'd been bullshitting me about the Dokkalfar.

One of the legionaries was still unconscious. The other had Mog seated against a wall, spear poised to stab. "I've got this one alive, sir!"

The gray Risi was bleeding from several wounds, and I doubted he'd last much longer without healing. His breath came in wheezes and gasps. Mog caught my eye and smiled. "Not a uajaah a'ter all, eh? Good 'or you, 'uman. Do us a 'avor and 'inish the job." There was no resentment in his voice. His face looked friendly, aside from the creepy gray skin and red eyes bit. I think I might have liked him, under other circumstances.

A squad of legionaries ran into the square, from the direction of the praetorian barracks.

"He lives long enough to talk," Titus said. "Force the potion down his throat if you have to."

"Yes, sir," the legionary said.

"Alan? Come to the shop. We need to talk."

SANDRA TOOK the headset off and looked at Jeff. "Do we have a lot of footage like that?"

Jeff scrunched his nose up. "Not really? He foiled an assassination attempt yesterday, but he mostly got his ass kicked."

Sandra nodded to herself. This was good. It might be enough. If she could convince Alan to stick himself out there a bit more, it could be great.

"Umm... Ms. Bullard? Could I have my headset back?" Jeff asked.

"No. Get a second set and plug in. We're going to stick with this for a while."

SIXTEEN

"What was that about?" Titus asked me, closing the door behind us.

I sighed. "Remember I told you I stopped a noble from being murdered?"

"Yes, I do," Titus said, leaning his cane against the counter.

"Those were the two thugs who got away."

"Ah."

"Yeah."

"You didn't mention the nobleman in question was Provus Considia, though."

I licked my lips. "No, I didn't. You didn't mention you were bringing legionaries to our meeting."

"But aren't you glad I did?"

"I'm very glad."

"Good. Because there's someone who very much wants to meet you."

"Is this the kind of meeting that involves thumbscrews and hot pokers, or the kind of meeting that involves medals and beer?"

"What are thumbscrews?" Titus asked.

"I think I'd rather not share that information unless it's over medals and beer."

Titus chuckled. "Well, I do know what a hot poker is. Did you have anything to do with the attempt on Provus's life?"

"No."

"Not even some kind of mad scheme to gain the Griffin's favor by saving his son?"

"Is that like an open secret or casual conversation?"

"The scheme?"

"The fact that he screwed his sister."

"Stepsister, and no, I wouldn't recommend ever mentioning it to either of them. So you're just an innocent bystander who did the right thing?"

"Pretty much."

"Let's go get medals and beer, then. But first, we need to do something about those clothes."

Titus rummaged around the back of his shop and found me a blue tunic and a pair of dark green pants that would fit. It wasn't anything I'd have worn in the real world, but people wear all kinds of stupid looking mismatched clothes and accessories in video games.

He also gave me a pair of simple sandals and taught me how to lace them. He wanted me to look presentable before meeting the general. I felt like I was a kid going to school for the first time. He charged me two silver for the lot, which he deducted from the ten golds he gave me for the armor. I now had ten golds, six silvers, and nine coppers to my name, so I was rolling in it. I wondered what his share of the sale had been.

"Is there somewhere I can change?" I asked.

"Let's get you cleaned up first," he said. "I'm not sure where you've been living all these years, but most of us prefer to bathe before changing into clean clothes."

I blushed and pulled up my status effects.

<<<>>>

Current Debuffs

Unwashed (Level 3): Goods and services cost 20% more; Merchant-craft skills reduced by (3) levels; some vendors may refuse you service.

<<<>>>

"Yeah, actually, a shower would be great," I told Titus.

He gave me a funny look, then said, "Take your clothes and follow me."

We left the store. The legionary who'd been unconscious was on his feet, taking a moment to gather his wits while his partner stood by. The newly arrived squad of legionaries were taking Mog away in chains. The gray Risi turned his head to look at me, his eyes pleading.

"What will happen to him?" I asked.

"He'll be questioned, probably tortured, and then executed," Titus said.

"Even if he cooperates?"

"He's going to cooperate whether he wants to or not," Titus said, giving me a bemused grin. "You do remember he was going to kill you?"

"And he apologized for that. I got the feeling Mog was just doing what he was told."

Titus shrugged. "It's a nice thought. I'd stay focused on the meeting with the general, though. That Risi is an albino. Their own people shun them. They usually don't survive to adulthood."

I took one last look at Mog. I understood the reasoning, but it didn't sit well with me.

Titus led me a few blocks away to a large, single-story building with two entrances. Men were walking into the larger entrance on the left, and women went into the smaller wing on the right.

"Welcome to the baths," Titus said.

We went into the men's section. A slave at the door collected the one copper entry price. The first room was a vestibule with cubbies set into the wall for storing clothes or personal belongings. "Should I leave my things here?" I asked.

"Gods, no," Titus said. "You'll be robbed blind. Grab a towel and put the rest into your inventory."

I did as instructed.

I'm not going to go into a lot of detail about what happened next. There were three rooms, one that was kind of like a luke-warm sauna, a hot bath, and then back out through the sauna to a cold plunge. We lathered up with scented oil, scraped the excess off with a stone spatula, and scrubbed ourselves clean in the steaming hot water.

And if you're wondering if V.G.O. is one of those idealized worlds with airbrushed, fit bodies everywhere, it is not. There were man boobs, love handles, guts and paunches, bald spots and hairy spots, more cracks than the San Andreas fault line, and dings and dongs of all ages, shapes, and sizes. I saw more wrinkled ball sacs than I'd ever had the pleasure of trying not to look at, and I did my best not to laugh in the cold plunge where we lost the last of the grime and all of our dignity.

"That's better," Titus said, putting his clothes back on as if there had been nothing strange about the last half hour.

"Uh huh," I said, equipping my new clothes. It was nice to feel clean.

"It was certainly educational," Sandra said in my ear, and I just about died.

"Nice one, bro," Jeff said.

I equipped the sandals, lacing them up the way Titus had shown me, my face hotter than it had been inside the baths.

Quest Update: Productive Citizen

You managed to find some decent clothes! In return, as your reward, you have received 500 XP and the satisfaction of not looking like a bum. You have also been awarded 1 renown—in-world fame—for completing this quest. Greater renown elevates you within the ranks of Eldgard and can affect merchant prices when selling or buying.

<<<>>>

I felt like I'd been given a golf clap by the quest system. But hey, XP is XP, and I was only 170 points from leveling up again.

From there we headed toward the Heights.

IT FELT like a lifetime since I'd landed in the Heights in my dirty rags and gotten escorted off by Gork and his partner. It had seemed nice, then. Now, after living in the poor quarter for close to a day, the Heights looked scandalous in comparison, or maybe I'd only seen the edge of them. We emerged from the passageway through the third curtain wall and the whole world changed.

The streets weren't just free of garbage, they'd been cleaned, and the paving was made of larger, regular blocks of granite. Buildings were solid stone was well, either perfectly square, tightly fitted blocks or carved semiprecious stone, with embellishments at every level and ornamental railings on the wide balconies. Everything was brighter, cleaner, and more expensive. It made my modest upgrade in clothing seem like a joke.

And the people! About thirty percent of the people we met were Imperials sporting crisp white tunics. The men wore expensive togas of varying fabrics, colors, and lengths, adorned with patterns and tassels at the ends, and either had blank tunics, a pair of thin red stripes like Provus had worn, or a thick vertical band with one stripe on either side. Some younger women wore simple white tunics and supplemented these with ribbons, pins, and arm bracelets. All the women over their mid-twenties wore stolas, a covering they wore around their shoulders or sometimes covering their heads and faces. These were fastened with clips and ribbons, and it seemed like the brighter the colors and more numerous the pleats and folds, the more important the wearer. This all fed into a constantly changing pecking order, with a corresponding series of salutes, gestures, and slights I would have been fascinated to map out and study if we weren't just passing through.

Titus and I were beneath notice in all of this, which was just as well because I might have insulted someone by mistake.

The remaining seventy percent of the people on the streets were city guard, legionaries, merchants, servants, and slaves. These wore a variety of clothes, equipment, and armor, though to my surprise the legionaries were most often unarmed. The slaves wore clothes that matched their... their owners, which was actually a pretty hard thought to wrap my head around. Anyway, they were essentially color coded to the citizen's outfits, and their right arm was always bare, exposing the tattoos they all had on their inner wrist.

As we moved uphill, the architecture and people became both more opulent and understated. Togas and stolas were less varied, often incorporating Imperial blue in some form, but they were made of silk. I saw money changing hands—several golds at a time. Buildings were decorated with life-sized statues and stone tablets recounting historical events that had taken place inside their walls, or famous people who'd lived there. They grew in size as well, going from an average of three stories in the lower quarter to seven-, eight-, or nine-story buildings. I saw one building that looked like it had been carved out of a single giant block of white marble.

"How is that even possible?" I asked Titus, pointing at the building. There were no visible joins.

"Stonewalls," he answered.

"I get that, but how did they find a block of marble that big to begin with?" That was beside the point that marble was ludicrously expensive. I did some quick math in my head, and just putting a thin layer of the cheapest marble slab on a seven-story building would have cost over a million dollars, or ten thousand golds.

Titus shook his head. "Stonewalls are a type of Sorcerer. No one can afford to build like this, but if a noble family has a Stonewall or two in their lineage, odds are the building was grown by them, room by room, over the course of a decade or two. The only way to build faster would be to activate the Keep."

"The what?"

We emerged from the upper-city proper onto the last rise in the Heights. It was a wide-open space filled with carefully maintained parks, hedge mazes, fountains, and gazebos. People strolled arm in arm or hand in hand, or sometimes gathered in what looked like fancy, improvised block parties catered by servants from the nearby inns, taverns, and bars. And in the center of it all, half a mile from where we stood, was a massive block of a palace that must have been four hundred yards to a side. "Holy crap. What's that?"

"That's the Palace," Titus said, and I could almost hear the capital P when he said it. "But that's not the most impressive thing about it. It's part of the Keep system, an ancient network of fortresses that surrounds Eldgard and what we now call West Viridia. They have a system of guardians and passive defenses—a kind of last stand for the people living there, if you will—but if someone was to get their hands on an artifact called a faction seal..." Titus paused for effect. "The possibilities are endless. Barracks, training grounds, additional walls and defensive structures, all built in an instant, as well as active control over the guardians."

I whistled. The Palace was impressive enough, but Titus made it sound that this faction seal thing would make the current palace the new palace's redheaded stepchild. "So why hasn't anyone found one and brought it here?"

Titus shrugged. "They've tried. No one knows where they're hidden. There are a few old manuscripts in Alaunhylles and scattered among the nations of Eldgard that show what they look like, but I'm not convinced they weren't a story the locals made up to keep people like the Empire from invading them. It certainly didn't stop our ancestors from taking New Viridia."

I nodded, following him across the tree-shaded paths and carefully manicured lawns. It sounded like a raid reward or a premium subscriber item to me, but I didn't know where to begin explaining that to my not-so-ordinary tinker. I'd have to ask Jeff or Sandra when I logged out.

It took about ten minutes for us to make our way to the paved area around the palace. There was no wall, though I could see a space where one might have been. The building itself was an elegant structure that looked like it had been built and added to over the course of several generations, with slightly different styles of structures between the different towers and wings. The walls were smoothly fitted stone, accented with marble panels and several banks of regularly spaced windows with statues, reliefs, or other detail work between them. It was almost garish, but stopped just short of it.

The closer we came, the more overt the praetorian presence was. These were soldiers with heavy armor, sometimes custom pieces with family heraldry or intricate etching on them, and no two of them carried the exact same weapon. I itched to inspect the stats on their gear, but I was guessing that might get annoying for them and Titus if I stopped each and every time.

For all that, they didn't pay us that much attention. "Are these guys for real, or are they more of a ceremonial guard?" I asked Titus.

"They're real soldiers, but I understand why you'd ask. If it helps, we'd never get this close if they weren't expecting us—or at least you wouldn't, because I've snuck in once or twice." He flashed me a shameless grin. "The second thing you should think of is that from the moment we entered the park and made our way directly to the palace instead of preening and drinking like the regular gentry, at least three siege crossbows were probably pointed at us at all times."

I swallowed. I'd been pretty relaxed about our little walk up until that point. Now, it was like I could feel the crossbow bolt digging into my back. "Thanks for that," I told him.

"You're welcome, young man. I didn't want you to be disappointed by the Praetorian Guard's hospitality."

I WAS BLINDFOLDED for the next part. Well, bagged. They put a black bag over my head. It wasn't as bad as you might think; the bag was clean and very lightly scented with lavender, and Titus was a careful guide, letting me know when we were going up or down stairs, stepping from carpet to stone, or before a turn. I couldn't keep track of which way or how high or low we went, but I was pretty sure there were some extra steps and loops just to confuse the heck out of me, and it worked.

Then they pulled off the bag, and I was standing in front of a solid oak door reinforced with thick metal bands. Two massive praetorians guarded it. They were both Imperial, but Risi sized, with well-polished but functional armor and short swords suited for fighting in narrow hallways.

"Decimus," the tinker said to the one on the left.

"Master Emory," the guard said with a slight bow. "He's waiting for you."

"Splendid." The fight seemed to have breathed new life into the old man. It wasn't what I would have expected of him when I first walked into his shop.

I followed Titus past the guards and into a small corner office. Weapons and armor lined the walls, along with an almost cluttered assortment of shelves, armoires, and chests. A man in his late fifties occupied the desk in the corner. He wore a knight's tunic without the toga and appeared to be drafting a letter.

"Stand here," Titus said, pointing to the center of a bearskin rug. The bear must have been huge, and its fur was as white as snow but coarse, like a goat pelt.

The man at the desk looked up, and I saw the resemblance to Provus right away. "I'm Gaius Considia. You must be Alan Campbell. Titus has told me everything he knows about you, which is very little. Where are you from?"

He stared at me as if it was a toss-up whether he'd prefer me alive or dead, but dead would be easier. "I'm an Imperial," I said.

"I'm not blind, son. I asked where you were from."

I felt like it would be a very bad idea to lie to him, so I said, "From Empuriabrava." It was close enough to true.

"I've never heard of it."

"It's far away."

"It's far away, General," Titus suggested.

"It's far away, General," I echoed.

The general put his quill down and stretched his hands. "You saved Provus?"

"I tried to, General."

"Why?"

I frowned. "Did I need a reason to do the right thing?"

"Answer my questions with questions again, son, and I'll have Decimus give you a reason not to."

"Yes, General," I said. "I had a quest."

Gaius's eyes flicked to Titus, who nodded slightly. "What kind of quest?"

"It was called 'Save the Scion,' General. It said that I had seven minutes to save Provus's life."

"Provus Considia?"

I almost asked if that mattered, but instead, I said, "I think it said Provus Considia, General. I didn't know who that was at the time."

"You do now?"

"I do, General."

"So who is he?"

I didn't hesitate on the next bit. "He's the nephew of the Griffin of New Viridia, General."

Titus flashed me a thumbs-up behind his back. I struggled to keep a straight face.

There was a knock at the door. "It's the tribune, General."

"Send him in."

I turned to see Provus enter the room. He was dressed in a

polished steel breastplate with gold embellishments, segmented pauldrons, and matching steel-and-gold shin guards. He carried his helmet under his arm, but was otherwise unarmed. His eyes widened when he saw me, but he moved to stand behind me and clasped his hands behind his back. "You called for me, General?"

"I did. Is this the man who rescued you?"

Provus's mouth rose into a friendly smirk. "He made a valiant attempt to, General."

"Seemed like that elf was keeping you on your toes, your lordship."

Provus raised an eyebrow at me, but the smile remained.

I turned back to look at the general. I got nothing from his expression, though. His face might as well have been carved out of teak. He sighed. "Well, that's that then. It appears House Considia owes you a debt of gratitude. Do you believe I also owe you such a debt?"

I shrugged. "I thought maybe a thank you?"

There was a half-second pause where I thought maybe I'd misread the general by the company he kept, and then Titus sniggered, and Provus cracked a smile.

"I should have you all flogged," Gaius said, scowling.

"Oh, leave off it, Gaius. Tell the young man what he's won."

Gaius walked over to a glass viewing case and opened it. He lifted a small black object from inside, then brought it to me. The way Provus held his breath, I guessed that the general giving people stuff, or even letting them within arm's reach, was a rare thing. "Take it," he said.

I took the sheathed knife from his hands. He stood there a moment, as if testing me or fate, and then returned to the other side of his desk.

The knife was similar, but not identical to the one I'd taken off the Dokkalfar assassin. For one, the handle was a paler shade of bone and intricately engraved, though when I gripped it, it felt smooth and perfectly fitted to my hand. "May I?" I asked, looking at Gaius.

He nodded.

I drew it and almost gasped at the folded pattern, like overlapping waves crashing into the single edge of the blade. It was beautiful, and there was a slight blur to that edge as if the knife wasn't entirely there.

<<<>>>

Threadcutter

Weapon Type: Piercing, Dagger
Class: Ancient Artifact, One-handed
Base Damage: Special
Primary Effects:
50 pts Shadow Damage + 10 pts x Target Level
On Critical or Backstab, ignores all Armor
When sheathed, enemies will see character as unarmed
Dexterity Bonus = .25 x Character Level
Secondary Effects:
+100% Renown Effects from Kills
+23% Extra gold from Quest Rewards
A crude weapon from a less civilized age.
If it had only been a bit longer, it would have changed the world.

<<<>>>

The way I was reading it, based on my own stats, the dagger would eat through half someone's Health per strike, not counting armor, items, and buffs, and it scaled with its target. The only problem was getting close enough to use it.

I sheathed it. "Thank you, General." I'm a sucker for unique weapons that blend function and art. I know it's strange, considering my apparent aversion to fighting.

"You're welcome. Titus told me about the incident in front of his shop. A man aspiring to rank and citizenship should have a weapon. Provus will make sure you know how to use it."

"Begging your pardon, General," I said, confused, "but when did Titus tell you? I've been with him the whole time."

"He messaged me on the way."

"He did?" Provus said.

Titus turned his head and winked at us.

"You're dismissed, Nephew. Take Alan to the Legion's master-at-arms. We can't have him embarrassing himself with that fine a knife."

"No, Uncle, we can't." Provus brought his fist to his chest and his heels together before leaving. I tried to do the same and had the satisfaction of seeing Gaius smirk.

"Gods, then," Gaius told Titus.

"Seems so. They say enemies are the true measure of a man."

"Is that what they flatter you with in the brothels these days?"

Titus grinned. "The working ladies and gentlemen of New Viridia are practical sorts, Gaius. They prefer to measure in inches, though we do far more talking than measuring these days."

"So you're still active?"

"In measuring?"

"In talking. I need my old spymaster back."

"I might have kept a few channels open. Others I know by reputation only, and they'll have to be dredged and reopened."

"Thank you, old friend."

Titus smirked. "I don't think I've said yes, old friend."

Gaius snorted. "I heard you almost wet yourself with excitement when those idiots tried to kill you."

"You did? Are you still active?"

"In talking? Of course I am. I have an army to run."

"I meant in measuring."

Gaius picked up his quill and got back to his reports. "I'm an old man and married to the State, spymaster. My measuring days are over."

"So you still love her," Titus said.

Gaius ignored him. The only sound Titus heard as he left was the scratching of the quill.

CHAPTER
SEVENTEEN

I followed Provus out of the palace, once he'd retrieved his sword from Decimus. No blindfold this time, but without external references I can't say I would have found my way back unescorted. Threadcutter sat on my belt, against my lower back. I was almost giddy at having that awesome a weapon so early in the game.

"You should get that dagger soulbound as soon as you can afford it," Provus said.

"What's soulbinding?"

Provus raised an eyebrow at me. "It's something Enchanters do. It means the item can't be sold or stolen until the owner is dead."

"Wouldn't that encourage someone to stab me in order to get it?"

"It would. But they wouldn't be able to do it with your own dagger."

I swallowed, flashing back to the Murk Elf assassin. I bet someone like that would kill to have a weapon like this. "What about selling it?" I asked, half-joking.

"Don't be stupid," Provus said. "That weapon represents the

trust of the Griffin of New Viridia. He stood within arm's reach while you had it in your hands. Even if you never use it, it's priceless."

"Right. Don't be stupid. Got it." I still felt like owning it might make murdering me more attractive than I preferred, so I resolved not to advertise I had it no matter how much street cred it might earn me.

We walked through the park and through the Heights. It was close to 10:00 AM, so most of the tradesmen and servants were gone, and only a few noble men and women still walked the streets. Those that passed us inclined their heads to Provus and said, "Tribune," except for a few with a thick band flanked by red stripes on their tunics whom Provus saluted as "Senator." I just kept my mouth shut and followed. I probably looked like his servant.

When we'd passed the first wall, I asked him, "So how does all that work?"

"How does what work?"

"The military ranks, and the civilian ones too, I guess."

Provus stopped. "How do you not know these things? You're Imperial."

I shrugged. "I'm a poor bumpkin from outside the city?" It was mostly true.

Provus grunted and started walking again. "All residents of the city are subject to the census, which happens every five years. People are taxed and given privileges and duties according to their property."

"What does ten gold get me?" I asked.

"Nothing. You're a free man, subject to and protected by the law. That dagger would put you over the limit, but I suggest you keep it hidden."

That seemed like a really good plan. "What's the limit, then?"

"If you have fifteen gold during the next census, in two years, you'll be drafted into the army as a skirmisher."

"I'll be what? How is that a good thing?"

"You get to be a citizen. Duties first, privileges later. Even free men may be called to fight in times of war. Only senators are exempt from service."

"And how much are they worth?" I asked.

"Upwards of three thousand, four hundred golds."

"For a family, or each person?"

"Each."

I whistled. That was a 340,000 dollar net worth, give or take, from what I could tell. "So the poor fight and the rich live in the Heights?" That sounded catchy. Maybe I'd try to stage a protest to it someday.

"It's a fair system," Provus said with the ring of faith in his voice. "The poor are taxed less, with the poorest provided a ration of grain a day by the State. The rich do what they do best, which is to gather wealth, which then funds other things, and if they fail to maintain that wealth they'll be demoted during the next census. It ensures only the strongest, most successful families are given the chance to lead the Empire."

Or the meanest and the most corrupt. Gaius probably fell into the first category. Still, I could see where he was coming from, especially if it was a world he'd been born into.

"What about the army, if that's my next step?"

"Most people are leves and skirmishers. You're given a spear, a sling, or a javelin, and you do what you're told. Then there are hastati, principes, and triarii. Those are the trained soldiers who do the real work once the melee starts. In a perfect world, decanii lead teams of nine legionaries, centurions lead ten decanii, and there are six centuries in a cohort."

"Who leads the cohort?"

"The most senior surviving centurion."

"Ah." That told me a lot about the survivability of a centurion in battle. "And above that?"

"Above that it gets complicated. There are nine cohorts to a legion, plus cavalry detachments and special units under the command of decurions, double-centuries of elite soldiers under the command of the primus pila, who is usually the most senior centurion and can be promoted to the rank of prefect. On top of that are foreign-recruited auxiliaries, which is considered a desirable command assignment for knights who are given the rank of tribune."

"So you've commanded hundreds of people."

"I have."

"In battle?"

Provus shook his head. "Just a few small engagements against bandits and insurgents; never more than a century at a time."

It was still huge. Provus didn't look much older than me. When had he done this, when I was just getting done with college? "So there are a bunch of twenty-something knights out there leading armies of several hundred men and killing people? I mean, no offense, but that seems a bit crazy."

"A legate and his staff command all of them, but they are often from the senator class and have neither the desire nor the field experience to do more than administer the army's movements and supply."

"I thought you said senators don't have to serve?"

"They don't, but it's fashionable." Provus's lip curled up as he said the word.

We walked most of the rest in the way in silence. Provus was hard to read. I could tell there was a lot going on there, behind the severe expression he wore like it was part of his uniform, but I didn't have enough points of reference to start making guesses. We passed through the piazza where Titus had his shop. Provus nodded toward Bespoke Arms and Artifices. "Want to get that soulbinding taken care of?"

"He's an Enchanter?"

Provus snorted. "Felix Acilia? He's a magician with a story and a polishing rag, all right, but he does have an Enchanter on call."

I thought of what the merchant would do if I walked in with a second dagger—a real one, this time. "I'd rather take my business elsewhere," I said. Besides, from what I could see through the window, Felix was busy fawning over some woman who wanted to try *all* the swords.

"Suit yourself," Provus said, continuing past the store without waiting to see if I would follow.

We walked on past the Praetorian barracks to the Legion's main camp in the city.

THE LEGION CAMP WAS MASSIVE. It was like a city within a city.

We'd been walking between the three- or four-story commercial and residential buildings that made up most of the second ring of the city, and then they just stopped. And the paving gave way to gravel. We were in a massive fairground at the heart of the Empire's capital, a tent city whose every road was guarded and whose perimeter was walked by roaming patrols of ten legionaries.

Based on what Provus had explained to me, there had to be anywhere up to 700 ten-man or ten-woman tents in the Legion camp, not counting mess halls, smithies, armorers, cobblers, supply points, and any number of other logistical details it took to maintain 7,000 troops and close to 500 mounts in an area as big as forty football fields. It made our little team in Stanton, California, look like a small gathering of friends, and my mouth nearly watered at the thought of everything that probably went into making a place like this work. The tents were pitched on bare earth or grass, so close to each other the guy ropes overlapped, split into neat groups of twenty by gravel roads and drainage ditches. It looked like the precursor of the modern city grid, which of course was exactly what it was.

For all that, the smell wasn't too bad. There was leather and sweat, and the occasional sting of smoke in the air. I smelled meat cooking, and tobacco smoke. But there were no latrines or cess pits, and no piles of manure.

Not for the first time, but certainly the first at this scale, I was glad Kronos hadn't enabled bodily functions to make the game more realistic.

We entered from the side of the camp with the bigger tents, which I figured was due to Provus's rank. Legionaries saluted, officers called out to him in a friendly tone, and Provus seemed to finally relax. I got the feeling that Provus's time as an auxiliary commander had left him a bit rough around the edges, and it took the company of rough men to make him feel at home.

About a third of the way through the camp, we reached an open area that was being used for training. Teams of legionaries in groups of thirty or more drilled in formation, going through quick direction changes, charging, breaking, and reforming. Individuals practiced weapon drills on targets, dummies, or each other. The sound of blunted steel hitting wood, hay, and flesh, along with the screaming and grunting common to any team sport like rugby or the mechanical slaughter of enemy soldiers filled the air with constant, irregular noise.

Provus headed toward a scarred Imperial veteran near the center of the training field. The man was short and wide, wearing a simple brown tunic and a belt with a truncheon. He turned as we approached, as if he'd sensed us in spite of the din of mock battle. "Tribune," he said.

"Prefect. I need this man trained."

The veteran looked at me like I was something he'd scraped off his sandal. "Any experience?"

"None."

"What position?"

"Specialist. He's one of Titus's."

The prefect grunted. Apparently Titus was someone worthy of that much. "Any special handling?"

"No," Provus said, looking at me with a grin that gave me goosebumps. "Treat him like any other conscript. Try not to kill him." With that, he left.

The prefect looked at me for a moment, as if he were unsure what to do with me. I decided to break the ice. "Hi, I'm—"

With an economy of motion I might, under other circumstances, have admired, the prefect brought his bony forehead down on the bridge of my nose and knocked me to the ground. "Run around the camp," he said.

I was still writhing on the ground, holding my face.

He kicked me. Not hard, mind you; he just snapped the ball of his foot into my ribs, and I heard and felt one crack. "Run around the camp, soldier. Don't make me tell you again."

I scrambled to my feet, face on fire, lungs unable to fully inflate, and stumbled toward the first of several laps.

<<<>>>

Current Debuffs

Concussed: You have sustained a severe head injury! Confusion and disorientation; duration, 1 minute.

Broken Rib: Everything hurts. All actions are 10% slower and require 30% more Stamina; duration, 1 minute.

<<<>>>

I basically stumbled forward at a half-jog while trying to keep my left elbow tucked against my body. If I held it tight to my side, my broken rib hurt a little less. My nose was dripping blood onto my now grass-stained new clothes, and the pain in the center of my face was like a starburst of white light behind my eyes.

I'd never gotten into a fight, as a kid. Not once. An older girl pushed me around once in middle school and I ratted her out, and people called me a snitch, and you know what? I didn't give a crap. I still don't. The game kept dumping me from the literal heights of the city into piles of horsecrap and pain, and I was close enough to the twenty-four-hour mark that I was done.

<<<>>>

Log out: Yes/No?

<<<>>>

"No, no, no! Alan! I need you to stay in the game, killer," Sandra said.

"You what?"

"I need you to stay in the game. I've been scanning the logs. It's not enough."

My nose was blocked, which was unfortunate because I really needed to breathe. I closed my mouth and exhaled as hard as I could, blowing out a big ball of blood and mucus. My nose still wasn't completely clear, but I could get air through it. "How is that not enough?"

Sandra paused for a second, while I kept my feet moving.

Then I stopped. Why was I taking orders anyway? "Seriously, Sandra, how is this not enough? I stabbed a man through the chest earlier."

"Monster, and he kind of fell on you, Alan."

"There was a spear involved!" I heard someone breathing

227

hard, and the sound of fast footsteps. I turned just in time to see the other legionary before he rammed into me, knocking me flat, and kept running. "What the fuck?" I shouted.

"Keep running!" he yelled over his shoulder, sounding just as angry as I was.

I gulped half-lungfuls of air. The impact had dropped me by another 15% of my Health and restarted the timer on my concussion, as well as upgraded my broken rib to broken ribs. I was 20% slower and my actions required a whopping 45% more Stamina for two minutes. This was such utter bullshit.

"Alan, you need to move."

"I don't understand what's happening."

"But I do, and you need to get moving. Now."

I got to my hands and knees, the world spinning, and managed to get on my feet again. Every time I took a breath, it felt like my lungs were catching on something sharp. "So..." I huffed, after a few steps. "Explain..."

"It's the prefect. He's sending other recruits to hit you."

I started to laugh, but that hurt like getting stabbed probably does, and I was worried I was going to find out on that count real soon. "Duh," I managed.

"No, you don't get it. At least I think you don't. That legionary's doing the full lap, just like you."

She really wasn't telling me anything I didn't know. I could see the guy who hit me, although the distance between us was opening at an embarrassingly high rate.

"I don't think he did anything wrong, Alan. I think the prefect punished him for your weakness."

I kept moving. I didn't have enough air to talk to her. What she said didn't make sense. As I got farther, the sound of the training field died down. The other legionary reached the edge of the camp and turned right. I focused on the sound of my feet on the packed gravel. After a minute, the concussion cleared. I turned right the same as the other runner had. I made it all of five paces before I ran out of Stamina and had to stop. *God, this hurts.* It wasn't as bad as the dislocated shoulder had been—I could remember that as a sort of ringing sound in my ears more than actual pain—but I hurt all over.

"You have to keep moving, Alan."

"Can't."

"Just jog. Walk. Something." I could hear the beginnings of disgust in her voice, so I walked, holding my side. Then I heard footsteps.

He'd known I'd stop. I had this sudden picture in my mind of the prefect staring at me through dozens of tents, still standing where he'd been at the center of the training field. The legionary was a woman this time, and she looked *pissed.*

I ran. Red, stabbing pain in my left side, but I swung my arms and ran from her. She looked like five feet and five inches of wrath and retribution. My Stamina ran out again, so I stumbled to a half-jog and she caught me, shoving me to the ground, but my forward motion took some of the impact out of it.

"Keep running!" she shouted without slowing her pace.

"He's going to keep sending them, Alan."

I scrambled to my feet. "Why am I putting up with this?" I asked her, though it came out half-choked and whiny.

"This is exactly what we need."

The broken ribs debuff cleared, and I gasped in a full breath. I'd never realized breathing was so awesome. Holy balls, being able to breathe is the best.

I turned the next corner and jogged past a patrol. The legionaries jeered at me, and one of them stuck the butt of his spear out to trip me but I managed to hop over it. I gave them the finger, and they laughed. "What a bunch of dicks," I said.

"Not really," Sandra said.

IT WAS A TRAINING EXERCISE. Private Second Class Bullard was just out of Basic and going through convoy defense exercises during AIT. She was the driver, and her assistant driver was Private Carnegie. Carnegie was overweight and talked too much, which made Sandra uncomfortable. She'd known fat, noisy people before the Army, and that was fine, because everyone had different genes and ideas of what beauty was, but things were different now.

Sandra Bullard was third-generation Army. She'd enlisted out of high school in the best shape of her life, and gotten meaner and stronger in the ten weeks of Basic Training. She'd busted her ass and finished in the top ten percent of her platoon. She'd picked Motor-T because she hadn't been good enough for the Rangers, and she'd wanted to get as close to the next "fight" as she could.

Carnegie had picked Motor-T because he didn't like to walk. He was in for four years, then on to a free education and the rest of his life. He'd told her so. He set her teeth on edge every time he opened his mouth.

He'd been telling her about some stupid thing he was interested in when they hit a simulated explosive he was supposed to be watching for. The real thing would have turned Sandra's body into aerosol and flipped her cargo, currently twenty of her classmates. At AIT, they just made her and Carnegie walk the course while the next two students drove it. She'd been furious.

It was while listening to Carnegie bitch about the heat, and how the United States would never go to war in the Middle East again anyway, that Sandra had learned to hate. He wasn't Private Carnegie from Michigan, the son of Martha and Truman Carnegie. He wasn't Jim Carnegie yet, the veteran who'd re-upped after Ukraine and Crimea, her friend from the Army with the wife and the gym who'd looked her up because they were both in LA.

Back then, he was just the man who would get her killed.

"So explain it to me," I said to Sandra. "How is this useful?"

I was on the second to last stretch of the run. I'd found my pace, speeding up or backing off to keep my Stamina bar down to about a third. That let me speed up just enough to avoid getting clobbered when the third and fourth legionaries caught up with me. It's crazy how quickly something can become normal.

"You spent your first day in the most advanced fantasy VRMMORPG talking to a blind beggar, eating, and drinking. You didn't even drink that much."

"That beer in the inn must have been twelve percent alcohol!" I said.

"Oh, boo hoo, Alan. Maybe the prefect can lend you his man card and you can use it when you sip on girly drinks to go with your craft beer."

I laughed. "Are you seriously asking me to get trashed in V.G.O. for marketing purposes?"

"No," Sandra said. "But do something. Fight someone. Tame a dragon. Dungeon delve. If you don't have the balls for that, carouse a bit and try to bed a tavern wench. I can't sell a conversation on the rank structure of the Imperial army to teenagers."

"Teenagers," I huffed, rounding the last corner. "Got it."

She had a point, though. I'd spent a good part of my first day in the game acting like a total newb. It was time to step up and do something awesome.

I heard footsteps behind me. A quick glance showed me the fifth legionary was about to catch up. I sprinted. I gave it all I had left. The prefect watched me arrive, and as I stumbled to a stop in front of him, he waved the legionary off. "Do you have any questions?" he asked me.

I smirked and channeled my inner teen. "Yeah, I have a—"

The prefect's hand shot out like a snake and caught me in the throat. I choked.

Current Debuffs

Induced Suffocation: You are being suffocated. You suffer 10 pts of Stamina damage each second until you can breathe once more; duration, 15 seconds! If your Stamina reaches 0, you will die.

Current estimated time of death: 25 seconds.

<<<>>>

"Run," the prefect said, turning his back on me. "Faster this time. If you try to pace yourself, I'll send a whole squad after you."

BULLARD LAUGHED OUT LOUD, covering her mouth. There was something about her that made Jeff uneasy, like the fact that he was a guy and outweighed her by more than fifty pounds made no difference to her.

Jeff reached over and put the two of them on mute. "You do know the pain is real, right?"

The petite, raven-haired woman who'd taken his chair and his headset looked at him with genuine amusement in her eyes. "But that just makes it better."

"How?" Jeff asked. "I mean, Alan can be a bit cocky and annoying sometimes, but he's not a bad guy."

Sandra shook her head. She took the headset off and set it on his desk. "It's not about Alan. That officer—was it Provus?"

"Yes."

"Provus gave the prefect an impossible task, training someone like Alan in a short amount of time. Did the prefect complain? No, he just assessed his resources and started working the problem."

"By headbutting him?"

"Alan only got headbutted after he tried to be friendly. He got throat jabbed when he tried to be insolent. I'm more curious about you. Why do you care? Alan's funny, talented, reasonably good looking; he's never had to push through real adversity." Her eyes went to Jeff's right arm like the tattoos weren't there and she could only see the scars.

Jeff swallowed.

"We need to push him," Bullard continued. "The second I walked through that door, I had two options. I could pull him out of the game and likely have to fire both of you, or we could come up with something good enough for the Board to forget they told us not to do it."

"And we don't have that yet?"

"You need to play more video games, Professor. We have some fascinating data on man-machine interfaces. Seriously, that stuff where he dreamed about his grandfather? That's going to knock the faculty back at Penn on their asses, isn't it?"

"Yes, Ms. Bullard, it is," Jeff said, flattered and a bit creeped out she knew so much about him.

"But it won't do anything for a gamer. Pull up some AAA game trailers on YouTube. We need emotional. We need epic. Alan needs to come out of this a hero, for all our sakes."

Bullard stood and stretched. "Is there any coffee left in this building?"

"Nope."

"Damn. Maybe I'll send one of the security guys on an errand." She grinned. "I'm going to go text Osmark the all clear. You need anything?"

"Coffee and donuts?"

"You want Dunkin' or Krispy Kreme?"

"Dunkin' for the coffee, Krispy Kreme for the donuts," Jeff said, pushing his luck.

"Done," Bullard said, smiling. Maybe she wasn't so bad.

When she was gone, he sat down in the second chair he'd brought over, leaving his nicer headset and chair where they were. After all, she'd already changed the settings on the arm and back rests the way she wanted them. He rolled his eyes. *I'm such a pushover.*

He took himself off mute. "Hey, Alan?"

"Yeah, Jeff?" Alan answered, huffing.

"Do you remember something weird around the time those two thugs were chasing you?"

"Weird how?"

"I don't know," Jeff answered. "It was around the time he was throwing daggers at you."

Alan didn't answer for a few seconds, then said, "Was it during the slow-mo?"

"The what?"

"The slow motion."

"There wasn't any slow motion."

"Sure there was," Alan answered, sounding annoyed. "Time slowed for five seconds. It's part of my Keen-Sight skill. Check the tape."

Jeff opened his mouth to tell Alan that was impossible

because the game clock was synched to the real world. Then he closed it. *Holy effing shit balls,* he thought.

He looked back at Alan's brain activity. It had gapped again, just like before.

They'd given Kronos a paradox to solve—keep the clock synched to the real world, and slow time for five seconds. The AI couldn't do that, so it had sped Alan up. For five seconds, Alan had used the server farm as his brain.

Jeff allowed himself a private smile of utter superiority over Alan, Bullard, the DoD, and the faculty at all the institutions he'd studied or lectured at. Dreaming in VR was a marketing gimmick, good for some pop-science fame, and while V.G.O. was a nerd's wet dream, he'd taken the job for the money.

This was beyond that. It made his brain spark and his mouth water. Jeff Berkowitz had found a way to give a human being the processing power of a supercomputer. It was going to change everything.

EIGHTEEN

If I didn't take off at full speed, the prefect would follow through on his threat. If I used up too much of my Stamina, I'd die. I didn't know what dying would be like in the game, but if getting injured was any indication, it wouldn't be pleasant.

So I ran. I drained my Stamina to zero and pushed through it. It turned out the game would let me do that; it just put me through an exponentially increasing amount of pain, until it felt like my shins would snap and my knees would bend the wrong way and I had to slow down. But I didn't stop. I let my Stamina get back to zero, and then I pushed again.

This was just another puzzle to solve. It was a new set of rules. I'd heard the tone in Sandra's voice, and I knew she was a veteran. *The fate of the world, and of my love life, hangs in the balance.*

When Jeff came back to ask his question about the slow-mo, I was in a weird kind of altered state where I'd separated myself from my body. It was like I was driving a car. The rhythm of my feet striking the gravel was the speedometer, and pain was the tach. I redlined the engine like I was driving a stolen getaway car, and everything worked fine on that basis. I answered Jeff's questions without taking my eye off the road.

About halfway around the camp, when no legionaries ran up to knock me over, I thought about slowing down, but I saw the prefect's dead-eyed stare in my head and kept running. I passed the patrol again, but this time they were silent.

I made it back to the training ground, my whole world the breathless management of parameters, sweat making my arms and legs glide, underwear chafing, and the prefect raised two fingers, then pointed down the road.

A prompt popped up, and I laughed.

<<<>>>
Log out: Yes/No?
<<<>>>

In the real world, I would have quit. I would have told Osmark to keep running without me and found a softer woman to court. I would have told everyone to piss off. If I'd been in danger, I would have handed over my wallet and my phone, and maybe taken a beating, but this would have been too much.

But it wasn't real. None of it was real. I had a HUD and a Stamina bar. Status effects fixed themselves after a few minutes. It wasn't even mind over matter, because my matter was comfortably reclined in a hospital bed. **"I can do this,"** I told myself, and whether it was the Suggestion or something deeper, I believed it. Halfway through my third lap, another prompt popped up.

<<<>>>
Ability: Conditioning

No pain, no gain. After what you've been through, the little things seem less important.

Ability Type/Level: Passive/Level 1

Cost: None

Effect: Pain felt due to effort, status effects, or injuries is reduced by 2%.

<<<>>>

Two percent doesn't seem like much, but makes a difference. I pushed a little harder. One of the soldiers on patrol gave me a nod as I passed.

I came to a stop in front of the prefect and stood with my hands behind my back, like Provus had in front of his father. My body wanted to lie on the grass and just breathe, but I didn't let it.

"Do you have any questions?"

"No, Prefect," I answered.

The prefect nodded slightly. "Halius!" he shouted.

A man broke off from his training group and ran over. It was the first man who'd knocked me down, while I was running. "Yes, Prefect?"

The prefect looked at me. "Halius is a second-tour legionary. He's killed pirates and smugglers on the road to Wyrdtide, and elf supremacists in the forests of the Shining Plains. Disobey him and I'll send you back to Titus. He will not be pleased. Understood?"

"Yes, Prefect," I said.

The prefect put his hand on Halius's shoulder. "He's a specialist, doesn't know how to fight. Teach him a proper stance, blocks, counters, throws, and counters to throws. I don't have time to babysit; I catch either of you slacking, you both run. Understood?"

"Yes, Prefect," Halius said.

"Get to it."

"Yes, Prefect," we both said.

I followed Halius to an open, grassy area. "No hard feelings?" I asked him.

"None," he answered. "Now get your hands up, and set your feet like mine."

Attaboy, Alan, Sandra thought. She'd hoped he'd figure out what was going on. She could have told him, but the prefect would have sniffed out someone gaming him and punished him harder. "All right," she told Jeff. "We're going to be here a while. Is there any problem with Alan staying in there another day or two?"

"Are you asking me as a non-medical doctor? Because I can't give you a legally binding opinion here."

"What about a non-legally binding one?"

Jeff shrugged and crossed his arms, covering up the one with the scars. "Fasting's good for you. The nanites don't respond well to dehydration, though. It increases the chance of an aneurysm."

"You mean the nanite-night-night?"

Jeff raised an eyebrow. "Is that what they're calling it these days? The parajumpers I worked with called it getting head-bricked."

"Like bricking a computer?"

"Yes, ma'am."

"Smart. I ran in different circles. We called it triple-N or B-Sod."

"What's B-Sod stand for? No, wait... blue screen of death?"

Sandra grinned. "I came up with it." She wasn't about to tell him the CIA had a way to trigger it on purpose, though. "But point taken, I'll give him an IV."

"You know how to do that?"

Sandra winked at him. "I'm a trained combat medic. Where did the nurses store the saline?"

ONCE I'D FIGURED out the rules, training with the Legion wasn't so bad. It was liberating, in a way, because I didn't have to make any decisions, which didn't mean I wasn't using my brain.

Halius would show me how to do something, first demonstrating it on me or on another legionary, then breaking down the physical task into words as well as moving my body into the correct positions. It was all fast rote memorization—we weren't dancing, he told me, so the movements were about effectiveness not interpretation. If I didn't learn fast enough, or I got distracted, he assigned me a short physical task like sprinting to the end of the road and back. Then we tried again.

Water came at regular intervals. A servant led a donkey onto the training field with an amphora of water on each side every forty-five minutes or so. Halius and I drank a ladleful each, like everyone else, and then got back to training. After two hours, we broke for lunch.

The noon meal was served in a long mess tent, spicy lentils and fresh baked bread with olive oil and a little honey. We ate quickly without fussing over manners, then cleared our spots for the next legionaries to sit. Halius explained that in the field, legionaries took turns cooking and eating with their squads, although someone might cook more often if they had the skill. A decanus would draw a ration of grain, meat, and vegetables for his squad, and they'd supplement by foraging when supplies got low or just to change things up.

We spent about thirty minutes talking about life in the Legion, the places he'd been, and the people he'd met. Then the prefect returned and everyone got back to work.

By the time the water donkey came by for the first time that afternoon, I'd built a model of what was going on in my head. My tasks were defined from a desired end result to the way I should close my fists. Anything less than perfection was unacceptable, but the corrections came without emotional baggage or judgment. It was part of the process.

If I focused and picked something up faster, Halius would explain subtleties to the movement I wouldn't have thought of on my own. If I struggled, as long as I put in the effort, he would fix me until I got it right. Once I had it right, we'd go through dozens of repetitions, sometimes on my own, sometimes alternating exercises or taking turns with the counters and throws. Focus, effort, and correct execution earned respect and additional information, which seemed to be the main currency exchange on the training field. The legionaries were hungry for it. Other instructors ran up to Halius or the prefect to check their knowledge before running back to their teams, and legionaries often raised their hands to ask questions. They wanted to know every detail about how to kill and how to survive.

It was just after the third donkey of the afternoon, and I was starting to lag. Halius looked at me with a wry smile and said, "You want to take a lap around the camp before the old man makes us do it?"

"Sure," I said, surprising myself.

The prefect watched us leave but didn't comment.

It wasn't a friendly jog. Halius ran beside me, but he pushed and goaded me to go faster. He was in better shape than me, but he also had to keep up a steady stream of encouragement and abuse as he ran, so we were both sweating by the time we got back to the field.

Two more donkeys and a run later, we finished the afternoon's training by playing Griffin in the Ring. The game was simple: twenty legionaries got into a circle with one of them in the middle. The people in the ring would take turns attacking the one in the middle using whatever moves they'd learned up to that point. The "griffin" just had to apply the correct counter and make it through the successive attacks without getting knocked down or passing out.

"Do what you can," Halius said. "It not about winning or losing, it's about applying what you learned from any angle and against any body type."

In the process, I leveled up my Unarmed skill to level 3 and Light Armor to level 4. Unarmed gave me a 9% bonus empty handed, but also 4.5% with any weapon because I'd learned how to use my body weight more effectively. Light Armor was all about taking a hit without protection and gave a 14% boost to my Base Armor when I was in robes or normal clothing.

The last man to step into the center of the ring was the prefect himself. We had a full five minutes to try anything we'd learned on him, in any order and from any angle. We came at him alone and in pairs, side by side or from opposite angles, and he tossed us around like we were children. It was the most incredible display of focus and skill I'd ever seen or been the victim of.

"That guy is a badass," Sandra said, and I agreed.

When the five minutes were up, the prefect dismissed everyone except Halius and me. I caught a glimpse of Provus shaking hands with some of the other legionaries. Apparently, he'd come to take his turn in the ring as well.

Halius nudged me with his elbow, and I focused my attention on the prefect.

"Good," the prefect said. "Did you learn something?"

"I did, Prefect." I wasn't sure if I could handle myself in a fight any better, but I'd seen enough different things that I felt like I might spend less time figuring out what was going on and more time saving my skin. I did wonder if what I'd learned would transfer over to my real body, or if it was just like any other MMO where my awesomeness would stay confined to the screen.

The prefect clasped his hands behind his back. "I'm not sure how much time you'll be with us before you're sent on an assignment, but there's one thing we should probably teach you now in case you ever need it. Halius?"

"Yes, Prefect?"

"Get me a spear."

"Yes, Prefect."

I stood there waiting with the prefect as Halius took off at a dead sprint.

"You the one who saved Provus?" the prefect asked, his voice low.

"I helped him save himself, Prefect."

"Thanks," he said with surprising informality. "You did the Legion and all of us a favor. Most of the senators and knights would spend my boys and girls like they spend coppers in a whorehouse, then sign away all they gained at the treaty table. Provus came up the right way, with the troops. He's our only hope if the Griffin dies and this lot has to fight a proper war."

I swallowed. I was almost glad I hadn't known that when I took off after Garrett and Mog in the marketplace. The fate of the world really had hung in the balance.

Halius returned with a spear and handed it to the prefect, who snatched it out of his hands.

The prefect looked at me. "If you're working for Titus, odds are you're going to piss someone off one day in a place you won't have any friends. Distance is your best friend in those cases. The area someone has to search increases exponentially the further you get."

That made sense. Pi times the radius squared—I'd learned that in grade school. What was curious was the notion that I was working for Titus. I didn't remember signing up, but maybe there had been more to me accepting Gaius's thanks and reward than I'd realized.

"The enemy will try to overcome that advantage with speed and numbers. Mounts are expensive, so if you've done everything right and gotten the hell out of where you were, you should only have to face down one rider." He hefted the spear. "The principle is the same whether you're facing a war-bear or a charger, or even an oversized monster. It doesn't matter if you're in a phalanx with other soldiers or alone, or whether you have a steel pike or a quarterstaff. I could sell you a line about glory and protecting the man next to you, but that's garbage. You're going to feel this thing coming through the soles of your feet, see it loom over you like a tidal wave, and you're going to want to run."

My mouth was dry. I didn't want to hear about this, let alone ever have to do it.

"And if you run," the prefect said, "if you or the man next to you waver, you will all die. You need to understand that beyond thought and courage all the way down to your soul, Alan Campbell," he said, using my full name. "Salvation lies in six feet of oak and metal, and holding your ground."

Jesus Christ.

The prefect saw his speech hit home and grunted. Then showed me how it was done. It wasn't complicated. He held the spear near the blunt end, hands about two feet apart, crouched the way Halius had showed me for any kind of fighting, and planted the butt of the spear into the ground.

"That's it?" I asked.

"That's it," he said. "Make a line between your eyes, the spear tip, and your target. Simplest thing in the world." He looked at Halius, and the two men laughed like he'd told the most hilarious joke in existence.

THE PREFECT DISMISSED us and Halius showed me where the camp baths were. To my surprise, the camp actually had a semi-permanent structure for it. Copper pipes heated by wood fires carried water to a twenty-by-ten-foot pool that held four feet of steaming water. It was a sausage party again—soldiers of every rank came to clean off and socialize after a day of training—but it didn't shock me as much as the first time, and I kind of liked the easy, informal atmosphere. I did keep my eyes off myself and any reflections, if I could manage it, knowing Sandra was riding shotgun behind my eyes.

After the baths, Halius gave me a simple off-white tunic like I'd seen most of the enlisted men wear. I offered to pay for it, but he raised his hands to stop me. "I'll just get another one from supply. It's Enyo's day tomorrow, so no training, and where we're going, you're going to want to fit in."

"Where are we going?"

"A Legion bar."

THE SIGH from the lips of a goddess crossed the Bleak Sea, following the seasonal air currents, altering them subtly. It gathered the cool night air like a lady bundling herself in a cloak and made landfall south of Wyrdtide, where it found the warm, humid exhalation of the great West Viridian forests, and from there, swirling and tumbling but ever moving east, it rose.

I'd pictured a seedy, low-roofed affair with cheap, replaceable furniture and sawdust on the floor, but being a legionary was apparently a decent way to make a living, and the Lion's Tail turned out to be a proper inn with a noisy, crowded main room and two floors of guest rooms above. Halius found us a corner table, and the four young soldiers occupying it almost fell over themselves to get out of his way.

I hadn't thought about it until then, but Halius had been on good terms with the prefect. I wondered what his rank was.

In any case, we sat. I got the first round, and he got the second and third. We talked, and then we half shouted because the room was packed to the point off-duty legionaries were standing in groups of three or four between the tables and more kept coming in. A female Accipiter sang a credible acoustic version of "Prayer in C" by Lilly Wood, accompanied by a Wode with a lute and a Risi striking a talking drum with a curved stick. Her voice was smoky and dark, and the drinks had me at just the right level of buzz to enjoy the room.

People laughed, clinked glasses, and played dice or cards at the tables, cheering loudest when someone almost got knocked out of the game but clawed their way back through skill, luck, or the goodwill of a fellow soldier. Smoke curled up from a dozen cigars and made a hazy layer against the ceiling. I started to pick out the patterns—the jokes, the shit talking, the constant dick or cup-size measuring, and the big open stances.

"You need to go carouse, Alan," Sandra said.

I blinked and noticed Halius was looking at me. "What's up?" I asked him.

He stuck his lip out and took a swig of beer, then he leaned in so he could speak without being overheard. "You're new to this, aren't you?"

"To what?"

"Whatever it is you do, it's not soldiering. There's something bent about you, like a scholar or a thief. You're always measuring the angles." He sniffed. "Prefect told me to get you drunk and let you mix with the troops off duty, learn how to blend in, but I don't think you know where to start."

I chuckled. He wasn't wrong. "Any suggestions?"

"Shit, man. Just go out there and have fun. You trained with 'em, bathed with 'em, you're dressed like 'em, nothing stopping you but yourself."

Ever get that feeling like the right words are caught in your throat, or like that first step across the dance floor is going to kill you? That was me. I'd charged an assassin and stabbed a Risi with the spear I'd ripped from his calf. I'd talked people out of their money, and run until I thought I would break. I could read that room like a textbook, analyze the body language, hierarchies, and leverage points all day, but when it came down to acting on it I just couldn't dive in. I was just like my class quest—stalled, and I didn't know how to get going again.

As soon as I finished the thought, a notification popped up.

<<<>>>

Quest Update: Smoke and Mirrors

You've been offered the chance to learn Charm. If you accept, you will spend (1) proficiency point on the skill, and who knows where that will lead? If you fail the quest, you will lose both the ability to use the skill and the proficiency point you spent.

Quest Class: Rare, Class-Based
Quest Difficulty: Hard
Success 1: Swindled a Swindler
Success 2: ???????
Success 3: ???????
Failure: Fail to complete any of the objectives.
Reward: Class Change; 6,000 XP

<<<>>>

"You're kidding," I said.

Halius raised an eyebrow. "Nope. It's really that simple."

He couldn't see the quest, but he might as well have. I laughed. Horace had given me the answer again. *Through desire, we shape the world.* Another 100 XP hit my character sheet, bringing me up within 20 points of leveling up. I relaxed. This was just a puzzle to be solved. *Come on, V.G.O. Hit me with your best shot.*

<<<>>>

Quest Update: Smoke and Mirrors

Get someone to do something they wouldn't normally do within 12 hours.

<<<>>>

Skill: Charm

Some people have the "X" factor. Charm lets you fake it. People within range will like you more than they should, charge less, and pay better.

Skill Type/Level: Aura/Initiate
Cost: 100 Spirit (Concentration)
Range: 5 yards
Cast Time: Instant
Cooldown: None
Effect 1: purchase and sale prices improved by 5%.
Effect 2: 1% increased chance of passing an illusion check (stacks) every 10 seconds.

<<<>>>

I read the quest update and the description a couple times, just to be sure. The spell would be an ongoing cost to my Spirit pool but it didn't seem all that complicated. Based on the last quest and the time limit, though, I guessed there would be more to it than getting Halius to dance on a table or talking a tavern wench into bed.

Still, I knew the drill. If the AIs were doing their jobs right, I didn't so much need to figure anything out as use the skills I'd been given and be the best version of myself I could imagine. I was kinda looking forward to it.

"You all right, Alan?" Halius asked.

"Yeah, I think I am." For a second, I wondered if there was a set of gestures or an incantation to perform, but then it was like something I'd always known. Charm works from the inside out. It's like a light switch in your soul. I turned mine on.

My max Spirit dropped by 100 to maintain the spell.

Halius's face twitched, like he'd just done the smallest

double take in the world. I smiled and drained my beer. "I'm going to mingle."

Halius smiled back. "You do that."

I stood up, took one look at the crowd, and dove in.

Having Charm up and running is a bit like being slightly high. I know that sounds strange since I'd already had three pints of strong beer after a long day, but it didn't make me magically attractive or turn every eye in the room to me, it just greased the wheels. I flowed through the crowd, smiling at people, laughing at jokes, shaking hands with strangers and slapping shoulders I didn't know the owners of. I felt connected to everyone. I pressed keys without thinking and for the first time I was really part of the music, like a prodigy playing the piano for the first time.

I found myself in front of a card game and sat down on a whim. "Deal me in!" I said.

The players looked at me with casual disinterest. One of them, a Risi with his black hair tied back into a ponytail, said, "Squad leaders' game, kid, and we don't know you. Scram."

Charm tied up 100 Spirit as long as I had it active, so I couldn't use Suggestion, at least not until I leveled up.

I grinned. "Ten men to a squad, right?" I put ten silvers on the table. "I've never played before."

The Risi grinned and swapped silver for chips. "I guess you just got promoted."

The guys and gal I was playing with told scandalous stories from somewhere called Wyrdtide, and complained about the food in Harrowick. Jag, the Risi, bitched about the low ceilings in Stone Reach. A decanus called Ferox and Agatha, the only centurion in the group, took turns telling a gut-clenching story about how they'd hired a male Svartalfar prostitute and smuggled him back into the camp in a duffel bag.

The Accipiter knocked out a freaking outstanding version of

"Poison" by Zero Venture, with a Svartalfar on a didjeridoo backing the Risi with the drum for the dubstep elements. I wondered how the game was getting access to outside music, and if we were paying for the copyrights, but that was a worry for real-world Alan, because V.G.O. Alan was having fun.

The game was a fast-paced combination of "War" and collectible card games like Magic and Gwent. It used a standard deck of fifty-four cards with four suits—Accipiter, Svartalfar, Dokkalfar, and Hvitalfar, in this case. Each suit had thirteen cards with faces so beautifully illustrated I sometimes lost track of the game staring at them. Even the numbered cards had different characters, names, and classes, and they could interact in sometimes surprising ways.

For example, the Dokkalfar 10 was called a huntress, and while she could be taken out by a jack of any suit, she could assassinate a queen at any time in a hand as long as he or she was played on top, as if by surprise. There were apparently decks for each of the races, and a deck drawn, painted, or etched by a skilled artist or Enchanter was a coveted possession across all of Eldgard. Agatha was very proud of hers.

The jokers were modeled after the Overminds, or the "gods" as the NPCs called them. Listening to them try to explain the rules was almost as entertaining as the game itself. It was called Gentleman's War.

I lost all my money. They bled me chip by chip, bought drinks with my silver, and let me win if I was losing too fast. They told more stories about fights, battles, brothels, and churches. One moment they were arguing over details or competing to see who could tell the most outrageous lie. The next, they'd listen quietly as one of them recounted a lost love, a fallen friend, or a near-death experience. It was shockingly intimate. I fed in some small stories about my time with Pops in Empuriabrava, bosses I'd worked for, or about my mother raising me in Philadelphia at the beginning of the millennium. I changed some things around to suit my backstory in V.G.O., but they listened to my small stories with the same respect I gave their adventures.

"That was my last chip," I said, folding for the last time.

"Good game, Alan," Jag said.

"Good game." I stood. "Thanks for letting me play."

"You're welcome," Agatha said. "You're a good egg. We play every week."

"Usually for coppers," Ferox added with a grin.

They didn't offer to pay me back, mind you, but they'd been pretty cool about me crashing their party, and since I hadn't gotten a quest notification, I guessed they were just nice people. I gave them a small wave and turned to find myself face-to-face with Thalia, who was carrying two beers.

"Hey," she said, six inches away. Her eyes were the color of amber, and she smelled like honeysuckle. I kid you not. It managed to be subtle and cut through the smoke and spilled booze at the same time. She was wearing tan leather pants and an Imperial-issue off-white tunic, like me, except with a cut collar so it hung off her left shoulder and cinched at the waist with a silver sash. I was too drunk and happy to hide that I'd looked her over. She raised an eyebrow.

Real Alan would have choked. V.G.O. Alan on Charm rolled a natural 20 for the save. "Hey. I told you I'd be back for that talk."

She smirked. "Is that what's happening?"

"Depends. Is one of those drinks for me?"

"I'm undecided. I came here with a friend, but he's a poor conversationalist."

"I have a corner table," I said, hoping Halius hadn't bailed on me while I was playing cards.

Thalia pushed a beer stein into my hands. "Lead on."

JEFF SAT BACK in his chair, covered his microphone with his hand, and said, "I can't believe that worked."

"I can," Sandra said.

I LED Thalia back to the table and was relieved to see Halius still nursing a beer.

Halius grinned. "Run out of—" He froze mid-sentence as he caught sight of Thalia and almost knocked his chair over getting to his feet. "Veteran," he said with the utmost respect.

"At ease, Halius," Thalia said. "You were always too formal."

"I was a brand-new legionary, and you were a—"

"Girl who came here for a good time among friends. You're making me feel old in front of my date, Halius, and for the record, you're still acting like a brand-new legionary."

Halius blushed. "Sorry."

Thalia smiled. "It's good to see you, Halius. Get us another chair?"

Halius laughed and rubbed the back of his head. "I was actually going to leave as soon as I knew Alan was getting on. He seems to have found good company. By your leave, Veteran?" He said the last bit with a smirk.

"Dismissed, Legionary," Thalia said, waving her mug. "Stop by the Terrace sometime, it's been too long."

"I will," Halius said. He scooted around the table, shot me the same look any red-blooded man would give his wingman if his wingman brought Thalia back from the bar, and patted me on the shoulder before making his way to the door. Thalia and I took our seats—she took the corner, facing the room, and I sat with my back to the wall and the entrance to my right.

"When did you enlist?" she asked.

"I didn't! Halius was just showing me some moves as a favor, and I got my clothes dirty, so he loaned me a shirt." After how coy Halius had been about Titus and the people who worked for him, I didn't think it wise to go ahead and blab about my meeting the general.

"Just like that?"

"Well, no. Some thieves tried to mug me earlier today, and the Legion took them down, but I helped a little."

"A real hero, then," she said with a smirk.

"Definitely. But bad enough at it they offered to teach me. Is Halius important?"

"Not yet, but he will be. He's an optio in the First."

"I don't know what that means."

She sighed and looked at me like I was a cute but rather helpless puppy. "He's good enough to work for someone important. You really aren't in the Legion, are you?"

"And you're not just a bar owner."

Thalia shrugged, taking a long pull of her beer. "I'm also a bar owner. Do you not like my bar?"

"I love the view," I said, looking right at her. "Where does the name come from, anyway?"

"Thalia?" she said with a crooked grin.

"Lot's Terrace."

"Mmm," she said, finishing her beer when I was halfway done with mine. "Buy me a drink first, and then I'll tell you."

ALL OVER THE CITY, watchmen who'd survived the attack on the precinct, along with retired legionaries and concerned citizens, armed themselves with sticks, clubs, and kitchen knives before taking to the streets. They targeted foreigners, for the most part, and Wodes in particular. Alcohol was involved.

Often, the result was just a beating, some broken furniture, and the irreparable loss of a sense of safety and community that had been fostered over a decade. In other cases, Imperials with a taste for violence stumbled across actual criminals or foreigners who wouldn't be pushed, and the streets were stained with blood.

A few enterprising people on both sides used the clamor to settle old scores and blame it on racial hatreds that had only been children's jokes a day before.

Enyo watched it all from the marble terrace where the Traveler had first landed in Eldgard. She could feel the echo of the disruption spreading out like a ripple all around her. Most of the violence was fueled by bigotry and fear, the persecution of the few by the many, and these were paltry offerings. But there was genuine worship out there as well.

A Hvitalfar Sword-Singer carved a bloody tune through the mob outside his house until a thrown brick caught him in the temple. His family escaped unharmed.

A fifty-year-old former tribune who'd served with the auxiliaries stood against a group of almost twenty armed men, using an awning pole for a weapon and a basket for a shield. He killed two, beat three more unconscious, and routed the rest. He suffered a concussion and three broken ribs. His neighbors, a young Accipiter couple from Ankara, decided to name their unborn child after him.

Glory. She could taste it in the air. There was nothing like it. Neither food, nor sex, nor drugs could come close, and she'd tried them all. Reports flowed into the palace, where the Griffin of New Viridia watched from his balcony, gripping the railing with white knuckles, daring the assassin's bolt.

Enyo shuddered with pleasure. Here and there, in vibrant oranges and reds, the city burned.

THE PORTAL TORE the air above the dais in the One Temple, and Sophia stepped through.

Or fell through. Sathis watched in horror as his goddess dropped to her hands and knees on the marble, onyx hitting stone with a *crack*. Divine sweat fell from her forehead to the floor. "Sathis!" she said hoarsely.

"Blessed Maiden?"

"You must stop her!"

Sathis furrowed his brow. "Enyo, my lady? I am only—"

"Thalia!" Sophia hissed. "You must stop her, Sathis! She is the spark. She will be the end of us."

Sathis lowered his face in shame. Tears burned in his eyes. "I have been deposed, Blessed One. How can I—"

"Sathis," Sophia said softly, touching his face with a hand made of warm stone. She raised his head until he was looking straight into her emerald eyes. "Are you not my faithful servant?"

"I am, my lady," Sathis said, gathering the dregs of his faith.

"You must stop her, Sathis. Only you can gather my children. Only you."

Tears streamed down his face. He'd waited his whole life to hear those words.

Sophia shrieked. She jerked her hand back, wrapping her hands around her abdomen like she'd been stabbed. Sathis darted forward on instinct and dared to try and help her to her feet.

The statue jerked one last time and went still, emerald eyes faded to jade. Instead of a goddess, he saw a woman sitting on her heels, bent double, mouth open, lifeless and on the dais once more.

"I will stop her, Sophia," Sathis whispered to the cooling stone. "I will restore you, whatever the cost."

I CAME BACK to the table with the drinks.

"What did you bring me?" Thalia said with a raised eyebrow.

I handed her a tumbler. "Two-year-old corn whiskey aged in charred oak. Where I come from, they call it bourbon."

"Where I come from," she said, accepting it with both hands, "they call it *Moen'etai*. It means a small sunset."

"That's pretty," I said.

She took a sip while I sat. "Are we being subtle again?"

I set my cider down next to my half-full beer stein and leaned toward her so I didn't have to raise my voice over the crowd. "I do like the sound of your voice, but the word is pretty, too."

Her eyes flicked to my lips, and a "moen'etai" lit somewhere in my gut. If I'd been a cat, I'd have been purring.

"Thalia? What the hell?"

Thalia and I both sat back and looked at the new arrival. He was Imperial, six foot one, with a strong, square chin and beefy build. His hair was short, black, thick, and curly, in a classic way that suggested he could have posed for Michelangelo, if the sculptor had carved a Goliath to stand opposite his more famous work.

"Thaddeus," Thalia said, like she'd found something on the bottom of her shoe.

Thad. Of course he had a name like that. I killed my Charm spell, letting my Spirit regenerate back to full at three points per second.

"I brought you here, Thalia," he continued.

"And I got bored."

"That's fucked up," he said. "What's the plan, keep changing partners until you've had enough to drink?"

The noise level in the Lion's Tail dropped measurably as the singer paused mid-song and the people nearest us were drawn into the drama. I wondered what Halius would have done, listening to his hero get called a... Never mind, I'd never call a lady what Thad was implying. "Hey, buddy, there's no—"

He stabbed his finger at me. "You shut your mouth before I break it. I'm having a conversation with my girl."

Thalia's eyes glowed, but I moved faster. It was reflexive, the product of hours of repetition in training not just that day, but my whole time in V.G.O.

I opened my mouth and shouted, **"Will somebody throw this drunk asshole outside and keep him out?"**

I'd been running Charm in the inn for at least two hours, which translated to a 12% increase in the chance of Illusion spells working. The effect exceeded my expectations. *Everyone* grabbed him. Dozens of hands shot out and hoisted Thad into the air. He bobbed up and down like flotsam on the sea, hollering and struggling, but he was swept toward the door all the same. The door opened. The door closed. End of story.

You could have heard a pin drop in the room.

Still no quest update, though. I guess either these guys and gals rocked, or it didn't count because people would normally do that under the effect of a Suggestion.

Thalia placed her hand on my shoulder. "We seem to have drawn some attention. I have a room upstairs. Shall we continue our conversation there?"

I hesitated for a split second. Thalia saw it and pulled her hand back, and everything was going to snowball into disaster when Sandra almost shouted, "Alan, say yes!" into my ear.

"Yes!" I said, standing up.

Thalia smirked and knocked her glass back before joining me.

The crowd cheered. The music started back up, and the singer sang "How Deep Is Your Love" by Calvin Harris except this time it sounded like a full production version. The crowd parted in front of us as Thalia led me by the hand to the stairs, and I got more pats on the back in that gauntlet than I'd gotten my entire life. It felt like I was there with fifty of my closest friends. The cheering surged as Thalia started up the stairs, and she waved at the crowd. The Accipiter on the stage gave me a wink, and I was surprised to see the rest of the band was sitting this one out, so I wondered where the music was coming from. Then Thalia was pulling me up two flights of stairs to her room.

TWENTY

Sandra pulled her headset off and slid her chair back. "All right, I'm calling it a night."

"Not staying to watch the fun?"

She made a face. "I'd say let the man have his privacy, but sex sells. Record everything."

"Yes, ma'am."

"And Jeff?" she said, yawning.

He turned to face her.

"It's Sandra. I figure we've been through enough together tonight for you to call me by my first name."

"Cool. Does that mean you'll change Prince Charming next time he needs a new diaper?"

She grinned. "We're not *that* close. I'll be back in four hours so you can get some sleep."

"Thanks," he said, and turned back to the monitors.

Sandra walked through the testing bay toward the parking long. She had a go bag on the back of her bike; old habits died hard. She'd shower, grab something to eat from one of the vending machines, and go sleep on the cot she kept in her office. The hospital beds in Alpha Testing might have been more comfortable, but she wasn't about to go to sleep alone in a room with a colleague, even if the man was married and scared of her. The best way to avoid misunderstandings was to never give them the opportunity.

Alan had surprised her. She'd always seen him as the quiet guy who'd stand up for himself if pushed but otherwise was happy to fade into the background. She liked that about him; he fixed things without beating his chest about it or demanding credit. What she'd watched on the monitors was a new facet—Alan as a person, maybe, instead of an employee—and she'd liked that too in a chills down her spine and flush in her cheeks kind of way. She'd wished she was Thalia, if only for a moment.

She put the thought aside. She had bigger worries. She needed to get Viridian back up and running for Os-Tech and the U.S. government without jeopardizing her position. They'd gotten some decent footage of Alan getting his ass kicked in training, and the carousing had been acceptable. Some time on the cutting table, along with a disclaimer that the footage was from actual gameplay, would make it great. It would take work, ego massaging, and a few white lies, but they'd get there.

He did have nice eyes, though. She smiled to herself. All work and no play wasn't why she'd signed up for covert ops.

THALIA PULLED me into the room and closed the door.

Nice room. White stucco walls, sloping ceiling, four-post bed. "So what—"

She grabbed me by the tunic, pushed me against the wall, came up onto her toes, and kissed me. It was a short kiss, her lips to mine and just a flick of her tongue while my hands found her waist, and then she slid away, flushed and smiling. "You were saying?"

"Nope. Not a word."

She smiled again and moved over to the bed, untying the sash at her waist before throwing it onto the nightstand. She sat on the bed and started taking off her boots. "You going to join me or do you need an invitation?"

"I might like one."

"Mmm," she said. "You're not that pretty."

"That's a lie," I said, taking off my boots.

Thalia watched me from the bed while I tried not to fall over. I suppose I could just have unequipped them from my inventory page, but that felt like it would rob the moment of its necessary awkwardness. "What were you going to ask me, earlier?" she said.

"Do you come here often?" I answered, kicking off the second boot.

She looked me over, her eyes lingering at belt level. "Crossing my fingers."

I swallowed. *God, that voice.* I walked over to her and said, "Help me with the shirt?"

She smirked and slid her fingers under the hem, gliding them up my chest and around my raised arms. Her hands were as warm as hot stones. She finished lifting the shirt over my head, and I stepped in and kissed her, pulling her to me. She smiled, her lips against mine. Her mouth was as cold as ice. I pulled my head back and exhaled, my breath fogging in front of me. "That's a hell of a thing."

She grinned.

I gave her a small shove and she landed on the bed, giggling and crawling off to hug one of the pillows, giving me a view of how her pants fit. They fit extremely well. I felt kind of bad about it, actually, having two passengers along for the ride without her knowing it. I just wasn't sure how I'd explain it without sounding crazy.

<<<>>>
Engage privacy mode: Yes/No?
<<<>>>

I blinked. *Yes.*

JEFF SAT BACK. He still had the readings from Alan's sensors, but his video feed was blank and the sound had cut out. "Well, crap. This job just got a lot less interesting."

I LAY FACING Thalia on the pillows, my hand under her shirt, running my fingers over her ribs. "But what I meant was, what brought you to the bar tonight? I thought you'd be at your own place."

Thalia made a small, discontented sound and wiggled closer, setting her head on my arm and nuzzling into my chest. "I found out a friend of mine passed away recently," she said.

I hugged her to me. "I'm sorry to hear that."

She shrugged and started stroking my side. "It's okay. I just needed a day off, away from the Terrace, away from... my other friends. I miss the Legion sometimes. The simplicity of it. I just couldn't take any more bullshit today, you know?"

I put my chin on top of her head and squeezed her shoulder, gripping and kneading the muscles of her arm from tricep to wrist. "Not really. I don't have a frame of reference for that, but I'm sorry, and I did get a little bit of a sense of how comforting the Legion can be playing cards with some squad leaders downstairs and training with Halius."

"You know Halius?" she mumbled. "I like him. He's always been nice."

I felt my heart drop. I held the sigh in and double-checked to be sure. "Yeah, he's nice. Remember that martini I brought you?"

"I hate martinis. You're lucky I think you're pretty." She slid her hand under my waistband, over my hip.

I took her wrist and gently pulled her hand out of my pants. She looked at me. "What's wrong?"

"Nothing, sweetie," I said. "You were going to tell me why you called your bar Lot's Terrace."

"Was I?"

"Yeah." I set her hand against my chest and hugged her to me.

"It's an old story. I'm surprised you've never heard it. There was a city in the old days that was full of evil. People robbed, hurt, and killed each other every day. But there was one good man who lived there, and his name was Lot.

"One day, Gaia had had enough, so she decided to destroy the city. Tornadoes, earthquakes, fire from the skies, that kind of thing. But Cernunnos decided it wasn't fair for Lot, so he sent a messenger to warn him of the destruction to come."

I smiled. My mom had read me this story as a child. "I know this one. He fled with his daughters, but his wife looked back and turned into a pillar of salt."

She looked up at me and frowned. "That's not it at all."

I kissed her forehead. "What is it then?"

"He told his family to get out of town. Then he warned his neighbors. He went from house to house, street to street. The messenger of Cernunnos pleaded with him to leave, but Lot shouted in the squares and went to see the leaders of the city. He was robbed and beaten, and begged the thieves to flee for their lives. Not many people listened, but a few did, though they were mostly foreigners. When he could do no more, Lot propped himself up against a boulder on a hillside with a skin full of wine and watched the destruction of the city, first by tornadoes, then by earthquakes, then by fire from the skies, until one of the fireballs ended his life. It's a moral story about what a man owes his family and his State."

"Hmm," I said, stroking her back. "It's not the version I learned, but I like it. I still don't see why you called your bar that. This is New Viridia, not Gomorrah. It's on a nice bit of land looking at the Heights."

She nodded seriously. "What better place to watch the downfall of civilization?"

I smiled at her and stroked her cheek. She rolled over, pulling my arm around her like a blanket and pressing her back into me.

Was I disappointed she was blackout drunk? Yeah. And don't make me out as some kind of saint; Bad Alan knew I had fifty witnesses who watched her pull me upstairs. Worse Alan knew she probably wouldn't mind. But Plain Old Alan knows what consent is, NPC or not. It still felt nice to have her pressed against me, to smell her perfume and feel the softness of her hair. It had been a long day. I closed my eyes and tried to get some sleep.

ALAN'S SYNCH rate was perfect. *Must be having the night of his life in there,* Jeff thought. He yawned, trying to figure out how he was going to stay awake for the next four hours. Some guys had all the luck.

TWENTY-ONE

I dreamed of flying again, like I had during character creation. I was fifty feet above the rooftops of New Viridia, the city sliding by beneath me, but I had my eyes up on the stars. I could actually see them, like I'd been able to at Pops's house, or when I drove toward the Rockies on the weekends. I twisted, looking down at the city, and frowned. The streetlights, oil lamps hung from light poles, were going out one by one.

"Alan!"

I sat up, heart pounding. *Where am I?* There was a woman's arm around my waist, a pixie cut of straw-blonde hair buried into my armpit. Did I know her? Had I gotten that drunk?

I took in the sloping roof, the rays of morning light coming in through the narrow window. *The Legion. The Lion's Tail. Thalia.* She whimpered in her sleep, and I stroked her shoulder.

"Alan, I need you to do whatever it is you do to get synched again," Sandra said. "Jeff's still asleep, and I'm not cleaning you off if you puke."

She sounded grumpy. Maybe she hadn't slept well. I was having trouble giving a crap with how bad my headache was.

Right. Waking up in V.G.O. sucks. I remember now. I slid out from under Thalia's arm, trying not to wake her, trying not to fall off the bed onto my face. I took slow, steady breaths while grabbing my tunic from the floor, tossed it into my inventory, and equipped it to avoid having to pull something over my head. I unlocked the door and stepped out into the hallway barefoot.

I didn't drink enough to feel this bad, I thought, making my way down the stairs. My eyes were half closed, and I hugged my arms to my chest.

Spending summers on my grandfather's farm, my world had extended as far as I could see. Sometimes, that meant the world was a ladybug eating an aphid on a flower stem, and sometimes I could see the sea from the branches of the biggest olive tree at the edge of Pops's land. With the world pitching and rolling as I reached the first landing, I very much felt like the aphid and tried to make myself small. Hangovers shrink your horizons.

Another set of stairs later, I was back in the common room. There were a few legionaries sleeping the night off on the floor, or with their heads resting on tables. The bartender was polishing a glass, because what else is a bartender going to do at 9 AM until his customers wake up? Jag, the Risi from the card game, was sitting on a stool at the bar, hunched over something. He sat up as I slid in next to him. "Morning."

"Mmph."

"Ah," Jag said. "Want some?" He was holding a small tin cup with a spoon in it.

"What is it?"

"*Glorp.* It's a Risi field ration and hangover cure."

I leaned over. The cup was full of what looked like runny peanut butter. "What's it made of?"

"Crushed peanuts, honey, and a little salt."

Yep. Peanut butter. God, the world is strange sometimes.

"Thanks, but no." I looked at the bartender. "Can I just get some bread?"

He set the glass down and put a cloth-covered basket on the bar in front of me. "It's fresh."

"How much?"

"On the house. Thanks for taking care of Thaddeus last night."

Jag looked over. "That was you, was it?"

"Yeah."

"Nice job," he said.

I lifted the cloth and the smell of fresh-baked sourdough filled the air. My mouth watered. "Thanks," I told the bartender, grabbing one of the rolls. I took a bite, and the warm dough almost melted in my mouth. The food in V.G.O. was almost worth the wake-up. "Mind if I take two?"

"You'd better," he said with a sly grin.

Well, who was I to spoil his fantasies of what happened last night?

I patted Jag on his very large shoulder and headed upstairs, leaving the Risi to his Glorp cup. I took another bite of bread, focusing on the taste, the feel of the floorboards beneath my feet, and the slight chill in the morning air.

"Can you do something about the black screen?" Sandra asked, gone from grumpy to outright annoyed.

Oh, right. A quick thought summoned the privacy mode prompt, and I deactivated it. "Is that better?" I asked, my mouth full.

"I'm not sure, but I can see," Sandra said.

I frowned. "Everything okay?"

There was a pause on the line. "Your vitals are stabilizing. How do you feel?"

"Hungover," I answered. "But food helps."

"That's good to know," she said. I waited for a follow-up.

When none came, I put it down to a long night of hopefully keeping me alive, healthy, and clean, and continued my ascent.

I was about to reach for the handle when Thalia opened the door.

We just stared at each other for a second. The light from the window hit her bare shoulder, giving it a soft glow. "Hey," I said.

"Hey," she said.

"I brought breakfast," I said, showing her the second roll.

"Um... Thanks?" she said. She looked like she was considering shutting the door.

"My boots are in there," I said.

"Oh. I thought they might be yours. I don't quite..."

"We didn't."

"We didn't?"

"You didn't?" said Sandra.

"No," I said.

Thalia swallowed. Her eyes were dilated. She was probably still a little drunk. I saw five different emotions flash across her face, from relief to anger, and figured it was about time I left.

"I'll just grab my boots and go," I said.

She stepped back and let me in. I equipped my boots instead of putting them on, then offered her the roll again.

She wrinkled her nose and shook her head.

I smiled, but I felt sad about it. I'd tried to do the right thing. Maybe I should have just left when she fell asleep and never mentioned it. "Goodbye, Thalia."

She seemed to shrink in on herself a little.

I sighed and headed for the stairs.

"Hey, Alan?" she said.

I turned around and saw her standing in the doorway. The morning light coming from the window almost gave her a halo. "Yeah?"

"Did you want to?"

"I did."

She crossed her arms. "I've had a rough couple of days. A friend of mine died, and his... his family and I don't exactly get along, but I had to deal with them anyway because of my friend. I need a day or two to sort this out. I knew him from the last war, and I owe him. But once that's done, we could try to have that talk again."

"Sober?" I asked. I know it was a dick move, but I owed Bad Alan and Worse Alan a night of guiltless debauchery.

She nodded. "I think that'd be best."

"I'd like that," I said, offering her a smile.

She returned it.

I saw I had a message and a notification pending on my quest journal. I got going while the going was good.

"Well, that was uplifting," Sandra said.

I chuckled. "Was it? I thought that was pretty normal."

"I meant your standards in women. Means I won't have to try as hard."

I raised an eyebrow even though she couldn't see me. "So I get an A+?"

"You passed. It didn't make for thrilling footage."

"Uh-huh. Footage. But back to the part where you're going to try, assuming I'm interested."

"You're interested. How about lunch?"

"Dinner."

"Coffee," she said. "Dinner if you hold up to the real light of day."

"Acceptable," I said, moving through the common room toward the exit. "Think that will become a thing?"

"What?"

"Reviewing someone's past dates in order to make the call, like an audition."

"Yeesh, I hope not," Sandra said, and we both laughed. She had a good laugh. Genuine. I could see myself laughing with her a lot. In all seriousness, though, there were some privacy issues we needed to address before V.G.O. went gold.

I stepped outside and took in the morning air. The streets were mostly deserted, which was a little surprising, and there was a faint smell of smoke in the air.

"Anything unusual going on with the game?" I asked Sandra.

"I don't think so? Like I said, your physicals are fine. Looks like all the Overminds were active while you slept."

"Really?"

"I'm not a software engineer, Alan, but there have been spikes and average increases on all of their graphs since you logged in."

I scratched my stubbly chin. Jeff hadn't mentioned anything about that. I guess I was flattered. The city felt wrong, though.

Ever go out late at night or early in the morning, and there's *no one* in the streets, not even a hobo or a stray cat, and thought the world was ending? It kind of felt like that.

Then I remembered I had a quest update to read. If the world was ending, better it ended after I leveled up.

<<<>>>

Quest Update: Smoke and Mirrors

You successfully got someone to do something they wouldn't normally do. In return, as your reward, you have received 2000 XP. This brings you one step closer to new skills and a new character class.

Quest Class: Rare, Class-Based
Quest Difficulty: Hard
Success 1: Swindled a Swindler
Success 2: Second Date with a One-Night Stand
Success 3: ???????
Failure: Fail to complete any of the objectives.
Reward: Class Change; 4,000 EXP

<<<>>>
Level Up!

You have (5) undistributed stat points! Stat points can be allocated at any time.

You have (1) unassigned proficiency point! Proficiency points can be allocated at any time.

<<<>>>

"Nice!" I said out loud to the empty street. 2,000 XP not only brought me to level four, I was only a few more points from level five. I put 3 points in Spirit—the Attribute—bringing me up to 200 Spirit—the Derived Statistic. Basically, I could use a Suggestion at the same time as Charm, now. I also put 2 points into Vitality because I wasn't so much a glass cannon as just plain glass, raising my Health to 160 points.

I also noticed I had a message pending.

<<<>>>
Personal Message:

Alan,
Are you okay? Things have been so crazy with all that

happened last night, and you disappeared. Horace and I were worried.

Let us know how you're doing,

—June

<<<>>>

Not just me imagining things, then. I was drafting a quick response letting her know I was okay and that I'd stop by when I saw Provus marching toward me with a bundle of clothes under one arm and two spears in his right hand. His face was "We need to discuss your prostate scan results" level of serious. I amended my message. *All okay on my end, hope you two are as well. I'll stop by later, if I can.*

"Alan! Good thing I caught you. We have a job."

"We do?"

"No, I was talking to hear myself speak," Provus said with a strained grin. He looked like he hadn't slept. "Put these on," he said, handing me a fresh white tunic with patterns embroidered on the left sleeve, a thick white cloak, and a pair of leather gloves. "We're going hunting."

"So what the hell happened last night?" I asked Provus.

"Ah, bliss."

"Ignorance?"

"Yes, I was referring to your ignorance," he said with a grin.

"Cute."

"It started yesterday. A Firebrand attacked the South Quarter precinct."

I didn't know what a Firebrand was, but after the ignorance

comment, I wasn't about to let on. "What's special about that, other than run-of-the-mill terrorism?"

"City watchmen died. That's generally frowned upon, even for the Thieves' Union, so it led to reprisals. You know what reprisals are?"

Smug asshole. "Tit for tat."

"Ten tits for every tat. How did you not notice all this?"

"You handed me over to the prefect all day, remember? Then I went drinking with Halius. Why weren't the legionaries at the Lion's Tail called back? Shouldn't they have protected the city?"

"That's a great way to turn unrest into a civil war."

I'd studied the 1992 Los Angeles riots in college. Crazy stuff. "Good point," I said.

He gave me a mocking little bow, and I blushed. I had a hard time remembering that, while younger than me, Provus had been trusted with more responsibility for years. Ironic, when I expected Rob to treat me like a peer, I know.

"More important to you," he said, "do you know a Wode by the name of Erik Stormson?"

"I know Erik. I cleaned myself up in his apartment."

"He's dead."

Damn. I mean, I didn't *really* know the guy, and he'd been kind of a dick, but it sucked that he was dead. "The Firebrand?"

"Yes. We picked him up in connection with the assassination attempt. His accomplices were probably trying to keep him from talking."

"Erik didn't know anything," I said. Then the pieces clicked together in my head. "But you knew that."

"Oh?"

"Gaius armed me."

"The general—"

"Your uncle put a weapon into my hand and stood two feet away."

"You're hardly a threat."

Fair point, I thought, but I wasn't done. "You brought me to the Legion camp, I was surrounded by armed men all day and drunk legionaries all night. I was protected. Erik wasn't the target, I was." And this whole conversation had been a test to see if I was involved. I had a few great suggestions about where he could stick his suspicions and cleverness.

"They could have been after me. I'd left the precinct less than an hour before."

"They didn't hit the barracks. They thought he was me. Was the precinct part of the trap?"

"No. He was being released, and men were in position to follow. We didn't expect someone to come inside to get him."

I whistled. "You fucked up pretty bad, then."

"I did," Provus said, his face coloring.

"What am I doing here, Provus? Am I the bait, this time?"

"We've done all we could to keep you safe, Alan. There are men who've killed to keep the company you do now."

Fair point again. I tried to get him to tell me more, but he'd closed up like a clam. Considering I'd been a penniless, homeless beggar two days ago, I decided maybe now was my time to shut up and pay attention.

The spear he'd handed me was six feet long, with an inch-and-a-half-thick ash wood shaft and a leaf blade a foot long by itself. A cross guard, or "wings," jutted from the neck of the spear, presumably to stop whatever I stabbed from impaling itself further and eating my face. I wasn't looking forward to meeting whatever this thing had been designed to kill.

When we reached the main thoroughfare, I started to see more people, though it was a third or maybe half the amount of the previous day and almost exclusively Imperials. People spoke louder than they usually did, gestured wider, and grinned with a barely suppressed watchfulness. I saw several merchants boarding up broken windows or scrubbing paint off the walls.

I was wearing the white tunic of a citizen. No pants—it was basically an above-the-knee skirt—which was both liberating and incredibly uncomfortable at the same time. The pattern on my right sleeve marked me as a member of House Considia, which I had to remind myself was more of a political affiliation than a bloodline. I was also wearing the thick white cloak thrown back like a cape, gloves tucked into my belt. People moved out of our way and looked at us with a curious mixture of fear and hope.

"Why am I dressed like I citizen?" I asked Provus.

"It's symbolic. You're the common man who rose to the defense of the Empire."

"Is it symbolic for the day, or symbolic for life?"

"A day is more than most people get, Alan. More than that would take a unanimous vote of the Senate, and they never agree on anything. The census is in two years—you can earn your place like everyone else." He looked like a Disney prince, saying it. I wanted to sign up to be drafted by the Legion and fight for the Empire right away.

He was really good at that. Duty, honor, and family turned him all dark and heroic. He was the rich scion of a powerful man, had crazy daddy issues, was trained in war, and fought assassins in the back alleys of the city. I grinned. "Do you have a butler named Alfred, by any chance?" I asked him.

"I've been in the army since I was fourteen," Provus said, frowning.

"A steward, then?"

He scowled. "No."

I shrugged. Always worth checking a game for Easter eggs.

Provus led me to the southern gate and we joined the flow

of people leaving the city. Once past the walls, we left the road for a dirt trail between the pines to a small staging area where the rest of the hunting party was gathering.

Holy shit. This was actually happening. Remember that urn I saw in the marketplace, the one with the naked dudes hunting on lizard-back? Pretty much like that, only more clothing.

We joined a group of similarly clad men and women, close to fifty in all. I got Charm going; it couldn't hurt to have the armed people surrounding me like me a little more.

The other members of our group were mostly servants and squires. The servants carried cudgels and wore brown tunics under their cloaks. The rest wore white and held spears like mine. There were also off-duty praetorians like Provus, though like him their only distinctions were the stripes on their tunics and the red trim around their cloaks.

A Dokkalfar in brown leathers and a green cloak stood to the side, carrying a wicked looking compound bow. His skin was like gray suede, his pupils carnelian red. Two servants stood with him, each holding four hounds on short leather leashes. The three men seemed to be the most experienced members of the group. The dogs were excited and strained against the straps, but instead of barks or whines, they sounded like one of those office paper cutters with the long blades. I think their vocal chords had been snipped.

"Who's that?" I asked Provus.

"The Imperial Warden."

"He's not Imperial."

"He's a great forest warden, though. Murk Elves can *hunt.*"

I walked over to the dog handlers and said, "May I?"

"Knock yourself out," the man said.

I crouched, setting the spear down in front of me, and put my hand out. At first the dogs just kind of looked at me—I guess they weren't socialized—then one of them, the runt of the pack, came and sniffed my hand. When I was mostly sure he wouldn't bite me, I gave him a scratch behind the ears.

The silent hounds went nuts. In seconds, four of them mobbed me, pawing, wriggling, wagging, and licking my face. They had thick, wiry coats and kept nudging each other out of the way to get scratched or petted next, almost knocking me over. No barks or whines, but still happy to be alive and be loved on. I laughed out loud. Provus frowned, but the handler looked pleased, and screw it, if you don't like dogs you need to pull the spare spear shaft out of your ass.

On the other side of the clearing were the "mounts," and I'm using finger quotes, here. Two dozen Komodo dragons were staked to the ground with guy ropes strung through their enormous collars. I know you're expecting me to tell you they had expandable frills, spider eyes, or even spines down their backs —no matter how impractical that would be for the riders—but these were just big angry black lizards. They were four feet across at the chest and fifteen feet long from snout to tail. And the sound! They sounded like a befouled gas station toilet being flushed, and sometimes they hissed like leaking steam pipes. They'd been fed—there was fresh blood on all their snouts— but they still took the occasional snap at their handlers, hissing and burbling. Their handlers reacted by clubbing them in the face with their spear butts. It was the touching hate-hate relationship of a boy and his Komodo.

I wanted to ride one so bad. I gave the runt one last scratch and stood, recovering my spear and my decorum before walking back to Provus's side.

Gathered under a large pavilion, separate from either group, were the actual men and women of rank—the heads of families and houses. Merchants, knights, and senators mingled freely. Each carried their choice of bow, javelin, or sling.

"Is it safe to have so many members of New Viridia's leadership in one place?" I asked.

"There are cordons of legionaries spread throughout the woods. If we get into serious trouble, my uncle will call for help, but I doubt we'll face anything we can't handle," Provus said.

To the Empire's credit, most of its nobility looked like they were meant to bear arms, and the merchants looked downright lethal. Bows were strung with practiced ease, quivers checked for straight shafts before being slung across backs or hung from hips. Buckles clinked, leather creaked, and backs were slapped. Preparations were spiced with jokes and childish enthusiasm. I flashed back to my day training with the Legion and saw the shadow of younger men and women hidden behind gray hair, wrinkles, and belly fat. Several, like Gaius Considia, were still in active service and wore breastplates, though the Griffin's was polished gold to their silver.

A few of the dignitaries with double stripes looked less comfortable. Bowstrings shook when drawn, as if for the first time. And there I was, the target of a terror group, ready to step in front of amateur hunters. It made my shoulder blades itch.

The foreigners stood to the side. They were more richly dressed than any foreigners I'd seen in the city, but they carried no weapons and looked varying degrees of pissed off or bored.

"Who are they?" I asked.

"Ambassadors, military attachés, and a visiting Ankaran prince."

"Which one's the prince?"

That earned me a look. "The one with the wings."

The gentry started splitting up and heading for their mounts. Gaius detached himself from the crowd and headed toward us.

"Try to remember he's the most powerful man in the Empire," Provus said, handing his spear off to another knight.

"Afraid I'll embarrass you?"

He smirked. "Not intentionally."

I offered him my spear, but he said, "Keep it. Put it in your left hand."

Ah, yes. Symbolism. I set the butt of the spear by my left foot and wrapped my arm around it, palm facing back, point to the sky. It looked like something a ceremonial guard would do, and it would be almost impossible to use it effectively without giving the general ample time to do something about it.

The crowd parted and moved away as Gaius approached, leaving Provus and me a small island of white opposite a crescent of surprised onlookers.

"Alan."

"General."

"Uncle."

"Nephew," Gaius said, shaking first Provus's hand, then mine. "Citizen for a day, then. How does it feel?"

"It's an honor, General," I said loudly, sticking my chest out.

Gaius smiled. He leaned in and said, "We're here to pull people together and show outsiders we're not weak. Try not to talk too much. And watch your back."

"Yes, General," I said, in my pristine white cloak that may as well have had a target painted on it. The people on the Komodos looked our way with feigned disinterest. The younger nobles stared with open resentment. I was getting Dick Cheneyed for sure.

He slapped me on the shoulder and headed for his mount.

ROBERT WOKE UP, sheets thrown aside, skin sweaty. The fan was still. Had he forgotten to turn it on?

Light streamed through the window. His smartwatch said it

was minutes until his alarm would have gone off. He deactivated it, got out of bed, and walked into the living room.

No lights. No coffee. *Power surge.* They happened sometimes, though usually in the heat of high summer, not the edge of fall. He made his way to the electrical panel. The main breaker was thrown. He reset it. The microwave clock blinked.

Why do I feel like something's wrong? He felt tired and unsettled, like he'd found the front door open or had a nightmare he couldn't remember. He wasn't the superstitious sort; hard work and preparation were his answer to life's opportunities. He put it down to dehydration and the disruption in his morning routine, which was upsetting in its own way. He didn't like to think of himself as that fragile.

He walked over to the coffee machine and hit "brew," then he got a glass from the cupboard, filled it and drained it twice. The best way to get a handle on a problem was to solve the easy bits, tune out the noise, and then take a look at what was left. He switched his computer on and stepped out onto the balcony while it booted up.

There was no wind outside. No breeze. He leaned against the railing and stared at the almost flat ocean. It looked metallic in the early light, like a someone filled in the Pacific with brushed steel under an overcast sky. The whole setup was enough to ruin a man's mood.

It had to be Viridian. He'd killed projects before, but this one had been close to his heart. He could admit that much to himself. Part of him had thought this might be it—that one project that made his legacy, a singularity in how he and other people led their lives. Rob had busted his ass to make things better for himself and the world, to remove the barriers his upbringing had placed in front of him. But even for Robert Osmark, billionaire CEO of Os-Tech, the world was still full of barriers and impossibilities. Viridian had been his answer.

He needed to break pattern, to get away, to start something new. He should travel. Maybe some time in the Singapore offices would do him good.

He went back inside and filled his mug with hot Jamaica Blue Mountain. He didn't find the beans particularly special, but sometimes you needed the best cup of diner coffee money could buy. Then he sat at his computer and pulled up his emails.

He'd expected some kind of report or explanation from Sandra, but there was nothing. He Alt + tabbed over to his security panel and saw that Sandra, Alan, and Jeff Berkowitz had all swiped their cards into Alpha Testing and hadn't left since yesterday, except for a four-hour window during which Sandra went to her office, next to his.

The hairs of his neck stood on end. He'd survived the last thirty years of running a multinational tech company by nurturing a healthy sense of paranoia. The people out to get him numbered in the tens of thousands, and included heads of state.

He trusted his team, especially Sandra.

But not that much.

He logged out, grabbed his keys, and left his coffee cooling on the desk. He dialed security on the way to the car.

A SMOOTH PEBBLE launched from a sling cracked a hare in the skull and it flopped over, hind legs kicking. I was getting a little bit of XP for each of the party's kills, but it felt empty. One of the servants in our group ran forward to collect it.

We were the beaters. The fifty of us advanced in a line with about five feet of space between us, making noise and poking bushes with our spears. The forest was mainly spruce, fir, and pines, spaced ten to twenty feet apart, with an uninterrupted but thin light green canopy.

The warden and his dogged assistants—pun intended—helped steer the line. When an animal broke from cover, one of the Komodo riders would try to take it down with their weapon of choice.

A pair of deer startled and ran across our front. The first was felled almost immediately by a lucky javelin throw. The second made it halfway across our front before a merchant rose in her seat and shot it from thirty yards away. The arrow hit behind its foreleg and the deer fell, skidding to a stop. A few of the nobles whooped in acknowledgment, and the merchant beamed.

"So they're just going to kill anything we come across until they get bored?" I asked.

Provus ignored me, focusing on the task at hand.

I sighed. I like animals.

"None of it will go to waste, Citizen," the warden said, suddenly right behind me. "Stay focused on the hunt." He moved on down the line.

I looked at Provus.

He shrugged. "The meat will go to the Legion, the pelts, horns, and hooves will go to crafters, bones to the glue factories, and the proceeds will pay for the grain allowance to the poor."

I smirked. "I'm guessing some of it will get lost along the way."

"Get off it, already," the woman to my right said. "The Empire was built on self-interest bent to the common good. Everyone benefits, *Citizen*."

And I get that. I do. I've argued passionately, under the influence of alcohol, that acting outside of self-interest is downright evil. But deep inside I'm still the kid who cried when he watched *Bambi*.

Anyway, the general didn't ask me to come for my views on animal rights. I was symbolic. "I'm Alan," I told her.

"We're not peers, Alan. Not even for a day."

"You could just answer to be polite," I said, using a Suggestion without thinking.

"And you could go suck-start a public fountain," she fired back, not even looking at me.

Apparently there were divides even Charm and Suggestion couldn't bridge.

The Accipiter prince and the Risi attaché walked behind the line, talking. Well, the prince did most of the talking. He wore a leather vest with several knife sheathes—all empty—and loose white pants. His wings were brown, black, and gold, like a golden eagle's. The Risi was one of the biggest I'd seen, with olive green skin and muscles stacked on muscles. He wore a padded black vest over a white shirt, and black fatigue pants. He looked annoyed at everyone and everything, and stared me down until I looked away.

A trio of wild boars ran across the path ahead. Gaius shot the big male; the other two were going to get away, but the warden suddenly pulled his bow to full draw and clipped the lead sow in the foreleg, making her stumble. One of the senators finished her off with a thrown javelin and grinned in triumph.

I looked at the warden as he bent to retrieve the arrow. It was blunt—he'd set the aristocrat up for the shot.

"I just don't see how this is a challenge," I told Provus. "He all but tied the boar down to be shot."

"They know that," Provus said.

"It's traditional," the woman to my right said. "We come back with our white clothes stained red, ties of blood renewed by blood, and the citizens of New Viridia feel secure that the

Empire is still strong, that our way of life will endure for another six hundred years."

Provus snorted. "Yes, they sleep soundly because we faced down the god of the woods. We'd be better off educating them."

The woman clenched her jaw.

"Can someone explain?" I asked. "I'm not from around here."

"Cernunnos is Cernunnos wherever you go, Traveler," the Accipiter said, walking up to join us. "You give yourself away."

He had a friendly, lilting voice, like someone from the Middle East.

"He's not a Traveler," Provus said. "There's no such thing."

"Oh hoh!" the prince said. "It seems the Empire is not as well informed as we might hope."

"I never said I wasn't one," I said.

Provus looked at me like I was crazy.

"Well," the prince continued, "if you won't inform our guest from another realm, I will. The gods despise unfairness, Alan, but none so much as Cernunnos. The Viridians hope to prove their courage and unity by daring the Overmind of Beasts and Monsters to strike them."

"Cernunnos is a fable, Your Grace, and Alan is just ignorant."

The Accipiter waved his hand over his shoulder. "No titles, please, Imperial Tribune Provus Considia. I am *Fatin*. You Imperials can't make wind without announcing your rank, station, and political affiliation."

I snickered. "I didn't think farting was possible in this world."

The prince cocked his head. He flapped his wings once, buffeting my hair and clothes. "What did you think I meant?"

I giggled in delight.

The prince hesitated, as if unsure whether he should laugh with me or take offense.

"I'm sorry, Fatin, I meant no disrespect. I have no wings. Your turn of phrase made me happy because it made me think in a way I never had before."

Fatin smiled. "And what does it mean in your world?"

I chuckled at the enormity of explaining flatulence to a prince. "It's a bodily function that's considered rude in public. It makes noise and it smells bad."

"Like belching?"

"Yes, Fatin, like belching in almost every way."

Fatin turned back to the Risi behind us with a childlike smile on his face. "Did you hear that, Tozhug? The honorary citizen says Viridians can't fart without announcing their rank, station, and political affiliation to the world. What do you think?"

He spoke loud enough that the whole party heard him. Gaius glared at me from his mount. I'd made a small, tactical error.

"I think you both talk too much," the Risi said, but he looked a little less annoyed than before.

Provus mimed falling on his sword, which I took as the local equivalent of putting a finger gun to my head and pulling the trigger. *Well crap.*

Just then, a large herd of deer—over twenty of them—came running and leaping toward us. The Komodo riders fired as quickly as they could, releasing arrows, lobbing javelins, and slinging stones, dropping the first dozen animals. One of the beaters fell, clutching the side of his face as an arrow grazed him. The deer bleated in terror, but they kept coming, reaching the line of beaters. Spears were thrust, taking down another half dozen animals. The warden fired two arrows in quick succession, cleanly claiming another two. I was so stunned by the violence of it all—the blood and the huff and cries of dying deer—that one ran straight past me. The nearest Komodo lunged forward, spilling its rider, and bit down on the doe's back, snapping her spine. She never stood a chance.

"Nice work, *Alan*," the woman to my right said, wiping blood from her spear with her cloak.

I was beyond words. I'd leveled up, but it didn't feel like a win. There was no glory in this—no fair struggle or moral lesson to be learned. It was a process that made less of both hunter and prey.

And then it hit me. "What were they running from?"

A WOODEN MASK sat propped against a pile of stones like an altar in the Southern Woods. It was plain and roughly carved, two eyeholes and a mouth, neither smiling nor frowning. Through it, the being known as Cernunnos watched the herd of deer run from the bear, and that was good. The bear was hungry. The deer were fast.

Then the deer met the humans, and the humans culled them. The humans were not hungry. They took without effort or care.

Vines extended through the mask from the Monstrous Dimension. They wrapped themselves around the rough stones and rose in a humanoid shape eight feet tall, a green, brown, and gray shambler. A massive and razor-sharp 16-point set of deer antlers grew, split, and unfurled from behind the mask, like a pair of upraised talons. Cernunnos stood.

He pulled one of the stones from his chest and squeezed it, vines coiling and shifting, until it cracked. The sound was heard over a mile away.

And from over a mile away, monsters and beasts converged on the call.

Jeff walked up beside her. "Hey, Sandra. Coffee?"

"Oh, yes, please. Where did you get this?"

"That security guard out front brought some in for his team. He offered me some."

Sandra nodded, wrapping her hands around the warm paper cup. It was still late summer outside, but Alpha Testing was kept freezing cold, like a hospital.

"How's our boy doing?"

"Good," she said. "He's on a hunting expedition. It's almost like an NPC-led raid."

"A raid?"

She raised an eyebrow at him. "Seriously, dude?"

"I'm hardware. My daughter's the gamer in the family."

"It's a group fight. High risk, high reward. I think we might finally see him kill something."

"Is it really that high risk? All I see are a bunch of dead birds and rabbits."

Sandra tapped the Overmind activity graphs. "Look at Cernunnos."

"Ouch. You going to tell Alan?"

"Why ruin the surprise? We're recording this, right?"

"Yeah."

There was a loud *crack*, like a gunshot.

"What did you say, friend?" Fatin asked.

"I said, 'What were they running from?'"

The servants from our group hurried forward, putting the surviving deer out of their misery and butchering the carcasses on the spot. The giant Komodos hissed and snapped. Two of them fought over the body of the deer I'd let through, tearing at it with their claws and teeth while their riders tried to get them back under control, yanking on their collars and smacking them on the top of the head with clubs.

It started with starlings. A starling is a migratory bird as big as an adult's hand, with quarter-inch talons and a short, sharp beak. They range in color from matte brown and speckled to rainbow-metallic. They don't so much sing as screech, and they swarm in the thousands.

The murmuration of starlings flowed through the trees like a biblical plague, darkening as the birds overlapped and moved closer together. We all craned our necks to watch them. The sound was unreal, between the thrum of their wings and the thousands of *cheeps* and screeches blending together to sound like a dozen cars doing donuts on bare, sparking rims. Then the swarm exploded and three thousand starlings attacked us all at once.

"Look out!" I shouted.

THE DOOR to Alpha Testing was shoved open so hard it crashed against the stop and two security guards came in, Tasers drawn.

Sandra pulled her headset off and turned in her seat. "What the—"

"Stand up! Both of you! Step away from the computer!"

"Do it now!"

Jeff shot out of his chair and almost clotheslined himself with his headset cord.

Sandra stood up more slowly with her hands raised. "We're complying. There's no need for this."

"Him too. Get him up!" the first guard said, nodding toward Alan.

Sandra didn't know him, but the second guard was Frank Mitchell. "Talk to me, Frank."

"We've been ordered to get the three of you out of here, Ms. Bullard."

"By whom?"

"Hey!" the first guard said to Alan. "I said get up and get out of the room!" He reached for Alan's leg.

Jeff, his eyes wide, moved to stop him. "You can't—"

And then both Tasers were pointed at Jeff.

Sandra grabbed the mall cop's wrist, put her knee on his chest, and kicked her left leg over, rolling into a flying armbar that brought the security guard to the ground and, in the same movement, ended with her pointing the Taser at Frank, finger on the trigger. "How's your heart, Frank?" she said.

"Not getting paid enough for this shit, ma'am," he answered, but he didn't take the Taser off her. He moved to put distance between himself and Berkowitz, just like she would have.

"We need to talk, Frank."

"Let's do that."

"Alan needs to stay plugged in. Who gave the order? Was it Wagner?"

"Don't know Wagner, ma'am. My orders came from Mr. Osmark. Why don't we just put the Tasers away? You have my partner's arm, there. I won't come any closer."

"Cut the shit, jarhead. Second I take this Taser off you, you'll rush me."

"And you told me you drove trucks for the Army. Where did you learn..." Frank trailed off and raised an eyebrow.

I'm burned, Sandra thought.

But instead of blurting everything in front of Jeff and his partner, Frank asked, "You still working?"

A patriot. I can work with that. "I'm not here for the fun of it, that's for sure." She glanced at Jeff, who was smart enough to realize the grown-ups were talking over his head without having a clue of what *S-P-Y* meant.

Frank lowered his weapon slowly, and Sandra mirrored him. The other guard tried to pull his arm back, but Sandra tightened her knees. "Not you, asshole. We're just going to sit here, nice and polite, until Robert arrives. Right, Frank?"

"Right, ma'am. Just hope I'm not going to regret this."

TWENTY-TWO

"I am so regretting this!" I shouted as forty feathered rodents pecked and scratched me, and beat me with their filthy feathers. The air thrummed with the churn of their wings. And they screeched, thousands of them, *peep peep peep!* My Health bar flashed but didn't go down. I was still furious. I swatted the little bastards with the flat of my spear blade, choking up on the weapon and swinging it like a bat. I got one measly XP for each one I *clunked*, but screw them, and screw Bambi, too. They were in my fucking hair.

The whole hunting party had been swarmed. I couldn't see much further than Provus or the nameless woman to my right. I could hear men and women shouting and the hiss and burble of the Komodos. I think I saw one rear on its hindlegs, snapping left and right. The lizards were probably loving it.

Only the warden noticed the bear. He raised his bow, which got me looking, but when he snapped off a shot, but a passing starling got in the way and the bear kept coming.

The Kodiak was four and a half feet tall at the shoulder and must have weighed close to 1500 pounds. It ran in on the deer kill at full speed and swiped a servant with a brown paw twice the size of my head. The man was thrown five feet and flopped like a rag doll, face ripped open from ear to chin. The bear roared.

"Spears forward!" Provus shouted.

One of the handlers loosed his dogs. It was eerie seeing them run without barking. The bear knocked two aside with one swipe and crushed another with his paw. The fourth managed to get in close and bite into the bear's side, but as it tried to back away the Kodiak caught the dog in its jaws and shook it from side to side until it stopped moving. That was a punch to the gut. No wonder the nobles didn't play with them.

The nobles in our group turned to face the new threat and advanced. I moved to join them, but Provus waved me back. "Stay with the prince," he said.

Stay out of the way, he meant. I looked at Fatin.

"It seems the Empire trusts neither of us with a weapon, friend."

I hadn't forgotten how he'd set me up earlier. "The Empire protects its citizens, Fatin. I'm not a fighter."

"Well, I am," Tozhug said, and stomped off toward the bear. He ripped a sapling out of the ground and started stripping off branches.

The Kodiak had run down and caught another servant, biting and scratching into her back as she screamed for help. The first man the bear mauled was still down and most likely dead. Provus barked commands and the spear line tightened and curved, letting the remaining servants pass through while forming a horseshoe around the creature.

I heard chanting to my right. A senator had dismounted, chanting and waving her hands. Mist formed over our heads, and starlings started dropping from the sky.

An arrow thunked into the Kodiak's neck. The bear barely noticed. It roared, reared up, and slammed down on its victim. I heard the crack from where I stood, still swinging at the rapidly thinning murmuration of birds—it was raining starlings at this point. The servant stopped struggling.

Tozhug finished stripping his makeshift spear, took a little hop step, and threw it like a javelin. The two-inch-thick bole hit the bear squarely between the eyes. The Kodiak stumbled, shaking its head, unhurt but confused.

The Risi laughed, clutching his stomach.

The bear roared and tried to charge him, but had to pull up short because of the spear wall. It swiped at the air. The leaf blades cut its paws, and the wall of spears kept tightening and closing. The second handler released his dogs.

A breeze cleared the mist away. The forest floor was carpeted in dead or twitching starlings. The riders had their mounts back under control and fanned out, looking for a clear shot. More arrows thudded into the bear's body, but they didn't seem to do much damage. I remembered reading once that a Kodiak can have a fat layer nine inches thick around parts of its body. The warden shot a fire arrow, lighting a patch of the bear's fur, and the big animal rolled onto its side to smother it. A javelin arced through the air and slammed into its stomach, sinking in nearly a foot, and the bear let out a high-pitched whine. It scrambled back onto its feet, backing away, pawing at the javelin.

A particularly brave or stupid noble darted in with his spear and sunk it into the bear's side; the bear spun, clocking the nobleman in the chin with his own spear. Two more nobles ran forward to drag their fallen peer to safety. I thought they were done for.

Provus stepped forward and stabbed the bear in the haunch. The bear whined again, turning and stumbling, falling on its tail end. The ring of spears tightened. It wouldn't be long now.

Then I heard a sound like someone smacking two drumsticks together to give the band the beat. Kid you not.

A nobleman stepped in to deliver the killing thrust and was bowled over by a charging wild boar. It came out of nowhere. Heavy metal music started playing. It sounded like an acoustic version of "Inner Self" by Sepultura. Three more boars ran into the formation, knocking two people over from behind and then attacking them with tooth and tusk, kicking their little piggy legs. The circle was broken.

"THAT'S ALAN," Osmark said, sitting down next to Sandra.

"That's Alan."

Robert's brain kicked into high gear. Jeff and the two security guards had gone for a walk. Viridian wasn't saved yet, but it had a pulse. "How long?"

"About fifty hours, at this point."

"We have footage?"

"Yeah. It's more Roman than Epic Fantasy, but we can fix that on the cutting table."

"Violence?"

"Plenty."

"What about sex?"

Sandra waved her hand. "Some good flirting and carousing, but he didn't seal the deal."

"That's too bad," Robert said absently.

"I'm okay with it."

He looked at his assistant, not bothering to hide his amusement. "Really?"

"The game made me jealous, Rob."

"I didn't take Alan for your type."

"I've recently seen sides of Alan I thought didn't exist. I suspected, but now I know."

Osmark let that process for a moment. "That might be *better* than sex."

"It just might."

Osmark looked back at the screen. Battle music was playing in his ears. "Is that a soundtrack?"

"That's Gaia. She's been adding mood music to emotional events."

"Did we tell her to do that?"

"I don't think so. I think she did it on her own."

"CLOSE RANKS!" Provus shouted.

Fatin spread his wings and took to the air. Tozhug was trying to shake off a boar that had latched onto his leg. Dozens of boars charged in, and two riders were thrown by their mounts as the Komodos went nuts from all the blood, noise, and still-squealing bacon.

The bear lunged, bringing down a distracted nobleman, and then knocked a noblewoman flying as she tried to bring her spear around. It broke through the circle, running back the way it came, limping and trailing blood.

A bola spun out of the melee, wrapping around a merchant with a bow and knocking her off her mount with a *clack!* Now, some of the boars had Goblin riders. Things just kept getting worse. Gaius blew his horn, calling for reinforcements.

Sharp teeth sank into my calf, and I was yanked off my feet. I rolled over and stared into the bloodshot eyes of the timber wolf playing tug-of-war with my leg.

That's when the quest update hit.

"Are you kidding me?" I shouted at no one in particular.

Quest Update: Smoke and Mirrors

You've been offered the chance to learn Vocalize. If you accept, you will spend (1) proficiency point on the skill, and who knows where that will lead? If you fail the quest, you will lose both the ability to use the skill and the proficiency point you spent.

Quest Class: Rare, Class-Based
Quest Difficulty: Hard
Success 1: Swindled a Swindler
Success 2: Second Date with a One-Night Stand
Success 3: ???????
Failure: Fail to complete any of the objectives.
Reward: Class Change; 4,000 XP

I screamed at the wolf and hit it in the face with the butt of my spear. I knew this was a setup, that the Overminds were going to force me into something I both wanted and didn't want to do. I didn't want to "Vocalize," I wanted to "Disappear" or cast "Ninja Smoke Bomb."

The wolf let go of my leg and latched onto the spear.

"Fine!" I shouted. "I'll do it!"

Quest Update: Smoke and Mirrors

Take command. Don't die.

<<<>>>

Oh, crap.

The Imperial hunting party had lost any semblance of order. All the silent hounds were dead. The warden wasn't trying to make people look good anymore—he was saving the people he could and trying to stay alive. There were wolves in the mix, leaping on people from behind or teaming up on lone spearmen. Boars knocked people over and bit people when they were down. Six of the Komodos were loose, clawing and biting anything and anyone within reach. Fatin swooped by, under attack by a half dozen crows and a buzzard. Tozhug had the boar from earlier by the hindleg and was using it to smash other things while the timber wolf tried to rip the spear out of my hands.

"Tozhug, help me!" I shouted, trying to use my new skill, but my Spirit bar flashed. I didn't have enough. Vocalize increased both the volume and the cost of vocal spells. I deactivated Charm and waited for my bar to fill, kicking at the wolf's body and legs.

A Komodo came charging past and chomped the wolf on the run. The wolf yelped, letting go of the spear. I caught a glimpse of Gaius blowing his horn, and the Komodo's tail almost knocked me out, then they were gone.

"Tozhug, help me!" I shouted, getting to my feet. My voice was so loud I cut through the noise like a megaphone. The Risi looked up and started walking my way, dragging his squealing improvised flail.

I drew more attention than just Tozhug's. Three wolves, one black and two gray, broke off from attacking a downed rider and ran straight for me. *Note to self: Vocalize draws aggro like dick jokes in a lesbian bar.* Worse, they were going to get to me before the Risi could.

The black wolf jumped at me from the side. I sidestepped, which I was pretty proud of, and heard its jaws snap shut where my face had been. One of the gray wolves latched onto my leg at the knee, and the second jumped.

Time slowed to a trickle. I was staring down the second gray wolf's throat, frothing drool and oversized canines five seconds from closing on my throat and there was nothing I could do about it. Then I noticed a steel-shafted broadhead arrow inching toward the wolf's side.

Time resumed, and the warden's arrow slammed into the jumping wolf's ribs, knocking it aside like it had been struck by the fist of God. I drove the sharp end of my spear into the gray wolf biting my leg. The black wolf landed, spun, and crouched, ready for another go, but Tozhug batted it aside with his boar-club like he was playing polo. "You have a plan?" he asked.

I twisted the spear in the dying wolf and looked at the hunting ground turned battlefield.

The Kodiak was gone, fled. Wolves, boars, Goblin boar-riders, and loose Komodos ran around in every direction, attacking everyone and each other. Gaius had assembled the six remaining mounted Komodo riders and they were charging around, getting stuck in wherever the fighting was worst. He blew his horn again, and at least two horns answered from the surrounding woods. If we could last a little longer, help would be here.

The warden was fine, of course. He looked like an elf from the Tolkien movies, dodging, rolling, and firing arrows when he could, only his quiver was empty and he could only shoot what he picked up from the ground or ripped from corpses.

There were groups of spearmen, dismounted nobles, and dignitaries trying to protect each other and the wounded. They'd formed ad hoc parties of tanks and ranged fighters, firing whatever ammunition they had into the mass of pissed-off animals while the melee fighters held boars and wolves off with spears and clubs they'd recovered from the fallen. Imperials and other races fought side by side without a second thought. It wasn't enough to turn the tide, but it would do wonders for interspecies cooperation if they survived.

Provus's was doing the best out of all the groups. He'd gathered twenty of the surviving spearmen and formed them into ranks, and they were pushing the maddened animals and Goblins back. He couldn't see the three massive shamblers lumbering up on them from behind.

"Provus!" I shouted. "Turn your formation around!"

He ignored me. One of the people in the phalanx actually gave me a sideways middle finger. Tozhug laughed at that and said, "What now, Lord General Alan?"

Screw it. I had enough Spirit for a Vocalized Suggestion. **"Provus! Turn your formation around and fall back on the senators!"**

Provus started shouting commands. There was a moment of confusion, then they saw the shamblers and everything sped up. I snapped out the next set of commands, using Vocalize when I could, Suggestions when I had to. It was like playing a real-time strategy game, only some of my units wouldn't listen all the time so I had to make each Suggestion stick.

Every time I vocalized, more wolves, boars, and Goblins made me their priority. Tozhug did what he could. He threw his now dead boar-club at a Komodo, grabbed two wolves by their throats and cracked their skulls together, and drop kicked a particularly vicious piglet after it tried to bite his ankle. A boar-riding Goblin charged me, waving a curved sword over its head, and I reacted without thinking, stepping to the side and swinging the butt of my spear into its leering face. The boar kept going. I finished the crippled rider with a thrust of my spear.

Horns sounded again, closer this time. Provus had gathered up more of the higher-ups, and they had the spellcaster who'd killed the starlings casting the choking mist on groups of animals, though she appeared to be too low on Spirit to cover as large an area as before. I shouted more commands. Everyone else was holding. Just a few more minutes.

A boulder landed in the middle of Provus's formation. I'd forgotten about the shamblers. One of them grabbed a spear as it was thrust at it and pulled the screaming Imperial into its arms, crushing her. I shouted a Suggestion, but then had to focus on staying alive.

Gaius charged the shamblers with the four remaining Komodo riders as commanded, or rather he ran them into each other and jumped clear. The Komodos and shamblers went at it like a kaiju free-for-all, tearing into each other with tooth and vine, boulder and claw. Gaius ran back toward Provus's phalanx with two Legion officers and two senators in tow. A black bear and four more wolves were trying to eat Tozhug and me, but Fatin landed on the bear and drove a recovered Goblin short-sword into its neck until it collapsed. The warden came and helped Tozhug, swinging his bow like a club. I stabbed stuff if it got too close. We were a four-being rock the snarling, squealing, screeching horde came to break itself on. We were turning the tide.

Then there was a squeal to end all squeals and the biggest boar I'd ever seen charged through the woods. The name [Gore Boar] floated above its head. Its back hump was as tall as I was, and it looked like it outweighed the bear by half. It crashed into the combined Imperial and foreign force I'd spent so much effort assembling, tossing men and women aside like toys. A swing of its head knocked four fighters aside. The phalanx fell apart, and the remaining wolves, boars, and Goblins poured into the breach, ignoring me once more.

Thirty people were trying to kill the thing, and its Health

had only dipped by 20%. Provus and all his people were going to die.

I knew what I had to do. I'd call the Gore Boar over using Vocalize and impale it on my spear, just like the prefect had showed me.

A kick from the creature's hind leg pulped a man's head.

"Nope." I handed the spear to Tozhug.

"What am I supposed to do with this?" he asked.

"I could sell you a line about glory and protecting the man next to you, but that's garbage. You're going to feel this thing coming through the soles of your feet, see it loom over you like a tidal wave, and you're going to want to run."

"What the hell?" Tozhug said.

I cupped my hands and yelled as loud as Vocalize would let me. **"Hey, Porkchop! Come pick on someone your own size!"**

"You're joking," Tozhug said.

The beast turned my way. A few enterprising nobles stuck their own spears into it, taking another sliver of Health off. The Gore Boar lowered its head.

"That's right, Gibblets! I've got a spit to roast you on right here!" I made a very vulgar thrusting motion with my hips.

Tozhug grinned. "I don't think it heard you, Alan."

I turned around and lifted the back of my tunic.

Fatin looked at me, wide-eyed, and took off flying.

The boar squealed and charged.

I ran to hide behind Tozhug. The warden did the same. "I hope you know what you're doing!" he said.

"Me too!"

The Risi set the spear the same way the prefect had showed me. Apparently facing a cavalry charge is common knowledge among crazy people. The ground shook under the Gore Boar's trotters. It was going to smash through the spear, Tozhug, the warden and me. I mumbled the end of the prefect's speech like a final prayer.

"What?" Tozhug said.

"I said, 'Salvation lies in six feet of oak and metal!'"

Tozhug laughed. "Salvation lies in me, human!"

He roared at the Gore Boar. The warden laughed manically. I screamed like a little girl.

The Gore Boar panicked at the last moment and turned its head, and the spear slid in between its neck and shoulder.

Don't make me out as something I'm not. I stood my ground, pressed against the Risi's back with the warden. I felt Tozhug flex, and the impact hit me like the concussion from a bomb. I could see the thing's hateful little eyes as I stepped around the Risi, the nightmare of jagged tusks jutting from its lower jaw, and everything in me said "Run."

But the prefect had told me that if I ran, I would die, and I believed him, so I charged instead.

Tozhug shifted his grip and pushed down, pinning the Gore Boar in place. The warden threw a handful of stunning powder in its face, then went to work on it with a pair of daggers. Fatin threw javelins at it from the air. I got one clean stab in with Threadcutter—just one—before the Gore Boar knocked me flying with a shake of its head. Then the surviving Imperials were all around us, yelling and stabbing. Some of them were legionaries in full kit. The reinforcements had arrived.

"Rally around the citizen!" I heard someone shout.

I tried to sit up, but the Gore Boar had knocked me down to the last 20% of my Health. Stars danced before my eyes, and I coughed blood onto my forearm. I think I saw Gaius and Tozhug fighting back-to-back. Provus got his hands on a pair of Goblin swords and turned into a human food processor. Everything else was a blur.

There was one last drawn-out chord from the unseen

guitarist, and the music stopped. I laid my head back, looking at the smooth tree trunks and the late-morning light shining down through the branches above, and laughed. It was finally over.

"Nice job, Alan," Osmark said.

"Oh, shit," I said. "Hi, boss." I was so screwed.

Cernunnos found the bear lying in the woods. Its sides, wet with blood, rose and fell weakly. The broken javelin was still in its gut.

The wounded Kodiak looked up at him and whined.

"You fought well," the Overmind said. Then he broke the bear's neck so it wouldn't have to suffer.

TWENTY-THREE

I was standing with Provus, Fatin, Tozhug, and the warden when Osmark came back on the line.

"Okay, Alan, it's just us now. We need to talk."

I swallowed. I knew it would come to this, I just thought Jeff and I, and maybe Sandra, would go to Osmark with a preliminary game trailer and smug looks on our faces. I didn't expect to get caught in the act. "Excuse me, guys."

"Everything okay?" Provus said, putting his hand on my shoulder.

"Yeah. I just need to... pray for a moment."

Provus's face twitched, but he nodded and turned back to the others.

The area around the Gore Boar's corpse had turned into a hive of activity. Legion healers had already restored the critical cases, like me, and were working on the lesser wounded. Priests and priestesses of Sophia, Enyo, and Gaia conducted last rites for the dead. Servants in various noblemen's liveries butchered animal corpses, scraped skins, and removed claws, horns, and antlers with pliers and saws. The Gore Boar itself was like a construction site, with its pelt peeled off and slabs of meat cut and laid out in rows.

There was blood and offal everywhere. Besides the dirt and blood spatter from the battle, my white cloak had dragged in the muck and acquired a red trim just like the knights' and senators'. It gave me a window into the origins of Imperial traditions that was both badass and horrifying. The smell was awful, but everyone was pretending they were okay, so I did as well.

I found an open, mossy spot away from the others. The trees were a little farther apart, so I was in direct sunlight. I took a knee.

"I could get used to this," Osmark said.

"I bet you could. So, am I fired?" I said jokingly, but not joking.

"I should, shouldn't I? Fire you," Osmark said as if he were making up his mind. "The Board killed the project, and even though you didn't know that officially, you stood with one hundred of your closest friends and heard *me* kill the project."

I chewed my lower lip.

"A particularly devious mind might claim two employees did this as a personal project, in their own spare time, but I might fire those employees for improper use of company resources."

I grinned. "I'd walk my beautiful game-fixing brain over to Bathsheba."

"And I'd choke you to death with your non-compete clause and years of copyright infringement cases."

"You spoke to Sandra," I said.

"Of course I did, Alan. And I'm not going to fire you. What you did was risky, and dangerous, and I admire the hell out of it. I've got a wallear to see Wagner's face when he hears about it, but that's later. Forget about all that. Gamer to gamer, how does it feel?"

I thought about that for a moment. The moss and detritus on the forest floor were individually rendered. I saw a couple ants and a bark beetle picking their way through it. The sun felt warm on my back, and the air was moist and loamy. My skin and clothes felt dirty, and I wanted a bath, with a long soak in the hot pool. Behind me, hundreds of NPCs were working and having conversations, and most of them had nothing to do with me, not even counting the millions in New Viridia and beyond. "It feels real," I told him. "I've spent more time in the past three days thinking this was the real world than not. I've been scared and angry, I've laughed and made friends, I've fallen in love a little and in lust a lot. It's been the most sublime gaming experience of my life."

Osmark chuckled. "That's great, Alan. I can't wait to try it myself. Anything I should know in the meantime?"

I closed my eyes and tried to shift my brain into a user-experience mindset. "The new settings will go a long way, but the main thing I've learned is that players need to immerse themselves into the game world. We can do things to help them, like add some welcome messages letting them know a little disorientation is normal, and that food helps anchor you in the moment. I also think we should give them headsets, even if it's not strictly necessary. The more we can make them comfortable with the transition, the better."

Osmark paused—I guess he was taking notes. "Good stuff. Great stuff, actually. I'll make sure Jeff and his team get to work on that. In the meantime, I'm going to go bulletproof this thing to make sure the rest of us get the chance to try it as well."

"Okay, awesome. You want me to log out?"

"Not yet. Let us run a few more tests, and we'll pull you out to a hero's welcome."

I grinned at that. If they didn't before, everyone working on Viridian was going to know my name now, and I had the hardware lead's parking spot for a month.

JEFF SWIPED back into Alpha Testing.

He'd been sitting in one of the emptied staff lounges with the two security guards, Frank and the dude who was so bad at his job Sandra disarmed him. Or maybe Sandra was abnormally good. It had been like something out of a movie. The young guy talked a lot of trash about her, said he was going to press charges, and Frank told him to keep his face shut if he liked working and living in California.

Jeff felt like he had more in common with the younger security guard, but he liked Frank's advice, so he "kept his face shut." He'd sat there, sweating bullets he was getting fired or going to jail, and then Sandra came back, smiling, to let him know Osmark wanted to see him.

"Sandra?" Osmark said as the two of them walked in.

"Yes?"

"Get Doctor Vila on the line. He's going to tell you it's Sunday, and he's going to try and send his assistant. I want him."

"You got it."

Jeff walked down the testing bay. Sandra slapped him on the shoulder as she walked past, cellphone out to make the phone call once she was outside the Faraday shield.

"Jeff!" Osmark said. "Get over here."

"Yes, sir," Jeff said, lengthening his stride.

"Have a seat," Osmark said, waving to the empty chair.

Jeff sat. His heart was hammering, and his right arm felt like it was covered in ants.

"You did it, Jeff. You saved the project."

Jeff frowned. "Alan—"

"Did an amazing job helping you test your idea."

"He didn't 'help me.' He pushed me until I did something against my better judgment, changed settings against medical advice, and it just happened to work."

Osmark shook his head. "That's the story we would have gone with if you failed, Jeff. You won. I need you to make the transition with me. What you're discussing sounds like luck, and I, the Board, and the investors don't believe in luck. We believe in process, in hard work, and in the PhD. stamped after your name on your business card. So what happened here?"

Jeff stiffened. He didn't like this. "I have my own professional achievements, Mr. Osmark. I don't need to steal his."

Osmark sat back and cocked his head. "Good for you, Jeff. Honest to goodness, I didn't think you had that in you. This is academically significant work, isn't it?"

"Yes."

"Did you notice the little pauses in his brain activity on the PET from the nanites? That's pretty amazing, isn't it?" Osmark leaned forward, clasping his hands together. "I'm just a layman, Doc, but it almost looks like Alan stole some runtime from the servers. Am I far off?"

Jeff felt his face heat. "You're not, sir."

"That's serious stuff. Life-changing. A professor of nanoscience and nanoengineering could hang his hat on that, and tell the whole faculty back at Penn to kiss his ass after they snubbed him for earning his paycheck in the real world."

Jeff dug his fingernails into his palms. It had taken him a day to reach the same conclusion, and Osmark had pounced on it in minutes. "Yes, he could, sir."

Osmark sat back and took his glasses off, rubbing the bridge of his nose. "I don't give a shit about the Penn faculty, Jeff. I care about the people who can take my company away from me feeling safe and secure with me at the helm, because I'm in control. Me. Not you, or Alan, or Sandra, bless her heart. Me. And that's why you get to write as many papers about this as you want as long as we're all on the same page. Are we on the same page, Jeff?"

"We are, sir."

"Great. And don't lose sleep over it. Alan is going to get a promotion, a ridiculous bonus, and a shot at some more complex projects. He's a smart guy; he'll drop the win now for the win later."

GAIUS CLEARED HIS THROAT. "Sorry to intrude, Alan, but they're waiting for you."

I opened my eyes. I'd just closed them for a second after talking to Rob.

"Are you all right?" Gaius asked. He was standing at the edge of my patch of sunlight.

"Yeah," I said, standing up. "I don't know. I feel like a great weight was lifted from my shoulders, and at the same time I'm wiped out and a little sad."

Gaius smiled. "Combat stress," he said.

I raised an eyebrow at him.

He shrugged. "Used to get it lot as a young commander. You spend all this time preparing for the fight, training your people, doing the thousand little things required to make a body of soldiers work together for that chaotic mess historians will call a battle. It winds you tight, and then it's over, and your brain has to swing the other way to cope."

I nodded. I guess that was it. Osmark was in charge, now. I just needed to let go.

"Of course, most people get that after months of campaign-ing, not a single skirmish with wild pigs, but you're a civilian, so I'll let it slide," he said, grinning.

"You looked like you were having fun out there," I said.

Gaius smiled. "I suppose I was."

"Provus was amazing."

Gaius gave me a look, and my breath caught. I'd reached the edge of where our relationship would carry me. Then he looked back toward the others and said, "He does his family proud."

I breathed out. "You said people were waiting on me?"

"I did. We're about to head back to the city, but there's a small matter to attend to first."

We walked back together. Provus had formed the surviving young nobles into ranks eight across and four deep. The legionaries who'd come to our rescue were formed up to their left, my right. The senators formed the base of the L. The foreigners, like Fatin and Tozhug, stood off to the side. They were all waiting for me.

"Stand here," Gaius said, pointing to his left.

I got into the position I'd learned from Provus, hands clasped behind my back, like the soldiers across from us.

"Century! Attention!" Gaius barked, and all two hundred or so people snapped their heels together and their hands to their sides. I did the same. "Merit!" Gaius said. "Self-interest bent to the common good for personal profit. These are the promises of the Empire, where a common man can rise through the sweat of his brow to become a soldier, a knight, and one day a senator. Though of common blood and not a native of our city, Alan Campbell stood with weapon in hand for the good of all on this day. Senators! What say you?"

The oldest among them, from the front of the formation, walked forward in front of all those soldiers and stood in front of me. He reached for my hand, but instead of shaking it, he pressed a gold coin in my palm. "Citizen," he said, dipping his head, then he returned to his peers.

"Citizen," said a woman with a nasty gash on her forehead.

"Citizen," said a third man, with an easy grin.

One by one, they all came up to me and placed a gold coin into my hand. They didn't all smile. They didn't all look like they wanted to be there. I could recognize a political necessity when I was one, but they did it all the same.

"Citizen," said the last of the senators, a man only ten years older than me, and he handed me a coin.

"Senator Flavus!" Gaius shouted. "Has the Senate confirmed the decision to include Alan Campbell into the census?"

"They have, General Considia! Unanimously! Provided he meets the requirements, he may be considered a citizen of New Viridia!"

Fifteen gold sat in my open hand. I was a citizen.

I'm not sure if I can properly explain how I felt in that moment. There was the elation of surviving a brush with death, for sure, and a kind of weak-kneed adrenaline-fueled shakiness. But there was something else, like everything I'd done had built up to that moment. The spear still jutted from the Gore Boar's carcass. I'd put myself in harm's way, trusting in my training as best I could, and it had worked. Somewhere in there was the glory I'd felt was missing before. It made my heart ache.

And I knew none of it was real. None of it. These were just NPCs, both the living and the dead, and my body was safely lying in a hospital bed in California, but a role-playing gamer can't think of it that way. I'd stopped New Viridia's Senate, its military leadership, and its future from dying in these woods. The fate of the world had hung in the balance.

My eyes teared up.

"Do you want to say something before I dismiss them?" Gaius said.

I thought about all I'd experienced in the past days and nodded.

He took a step back.

"This ceremony isn't about me," I said to the soldiers and senators, Vocalizing so I could speak in a normal tone. "I'm just a normal person. I don't have your training, I don't have Tozhug's strength or Prince Fatin's speed, or the Imperial warden's skill. Men and women like you, like the senators and General Considia, or Tribune Considia, they were born to this life. I feel privileged to have been allowed into their company.

"We came to this forest because blood was shed in the city. It doesn't matter if we faced Cernunnos or just the beasts of the woods," I said, catching Provus's eye. "We did it together! And people died, but not once did we give up or run. We stood side by side against certain death with a smile on our lips and proved that **nothing can stand against the might of the Empire, united, *and its allies!*"**

The soldiers and foreigners cheered. Some of the nobles were less enthusiastic, but screw them; if you give me a politically convenient soapbox, I'm going to use it.

Gaius clamped his hand down on my shoulder and muttered, "You're either impossibly clever or the dumbest son of a bitch I've ever met."

<<<>>>

Quest Alert: Smoke and Mirrors

You have successfully taken command and not died. In return, as your reward, you have received 3,000 EXP. You have also been awarded 50 renown—in-world fame—for completing this quest. Greater renown elevates you within the ranks of Eldgard and can affect merchant prices when selling or buying. Enter the Halls of Illusion, and the Illusionist character class is yours.

Quest Class: Rare, Class-Based
Quest Difficulty: Hard
Success 1: Swindled a Swindler
Success 2: Second Date with a One-Night Stand
Success 3: Herded Aristocrats
Failure: Fail to complete any of the objectives.
Reward: Class Change; 1,000 EXP

<<<>>>
Level Up!

You have (10) undistributed stat points! Stat points can be allocated at any time.

You have (2) unassigned proficiency point! Proficiency points can be allocated at any time.

<<<>>>

"Legionaries! Dismissed!" Gaius shouted.

Eighty fists hit eighty breastplates, and the legionaries broke ranks.

"Does this mean I have to join the Legion?" I asked Gaius.

"We'd take you," the general said. "But I think we can find a better use for your 'talents.' You're as bad as Titus." He shot me a dirty look and headed for the cluster of senators, likely to do damage control.

I smiled. I wasn't a fighter—didn't want to be a fighter—but the grudging and conditional respect of men like Gaius meant a lot, even if it probably meant trouble in the long run.

Fatin and Tozhug walked over, now that the ceremony was done.

"Citizen Alan Campbell of New Viridia," Fatin said with a grin.

I blew a raspberry at him, then turned to Tozhug. "Listen, man. We both know you did most of the work out there. I wouldn't be alive without you."

Tozhug shrugged. "I'm keeping the spear," he announced.

"I... yeah. Cultural differences, I get that. But I owe you a beer and some Glorp, sometime."

Tozhug broke into a full on, ear-to-ear smile. "You know Glorp?"

"I know Glorp."

He nodded solemnly. "We will have Glorp together." Then he stomped off to retrieve his prize.

"I hope you're ready for the night of heavy drinking you just signed up for, friend," Fatin said.

I frowned. "I thought it was just peanut butter."

He shook his wings in amusement. "The Risi are a succinct people. Peanut butter is only consumed after falling unconscious from battle fatigue or home brewed liquor. Peanut butter is peanut butter, but all of those things in one are Glorp."

"And today doesn't count?"

"Not unless you have a cup of peanut butter handy," Fatin said.

Well, there are worst things.

Fatin shook my hand. "Congratulations, Alan. I look forward to seeing more of you in the Heights."

"Bye, Fatin."

"Alan!" Provus said. "We're heading back. Are you ready?"

The senators and the young nobles headed back toward the city, under Legion escort. Most of the Komodos had been recovered, and were being walked back to their pens by trained handlers. The warden had disappeared at some point without saying goodbye, but I didn't take it personally; he didn't seem like the type to hug it out. The servants and huntsmen would finish harvesting the kill. It was time to go home.

"Actually," I told him, "there is one more thing I'd like to do."

<<<>>>

Ability: Mount

Eldgard is a vast and wild land, filled with rugged, formidable terrain—jagged mountains, dense forests, treacherous swamps, and expansive waterways—not to mention myriad deadly creatures. Having a faithful mount can significantly reduce travel times while making the hazards of the wild much more manageable. There is no more loyal and stalwart a fighter than a battle mount.

Ability Type/Level: Passive/Level 1
Cost: None
Effect 1: Mount riding ability unlocked.
Effect 2: +5% to Mount's Movement Rate, while you are riding.
Effect 3: Ferry (1) additional passenger on your mount (Movement Speed Reduced by 15%).

<<<>>>

They let me ride one of the Komodos as far as the city gates.

JEFF WATCHED the loading bar climb to 100%. He safely disconnected the thumb drive and handed it to Osmark. "There you are, sir. That's all the peripheral data on Alan's run and the Overminds' activity up to now, as well as my notes. I'll need a bigger storage device to download the video footage because it's in 580 Megapixel VR, but we'll be able to get all of that, too."

"Great," Osmark said. "I'll have one of the art directors download and parse that for us Monday morning. Do you have nanites in your system?"

"Of course not; those things can kill you."

"So can cigarettes. Shoot up, Professor."

"Excuse me?"

"We need to verify that this isn't a fluke, something specific to Alan."

"I'm not—"

"I also want to make sure no one suggests you knowingly subjected a colleague to a dangerous procedure you were not willing to undergo yourself."

Jeff closed his mouth. *Damn him. Damn them both.* He'd done nothing but get bullied into things for the last three days.

RIDING the Komodo was a strange experience. Their scales felt like warm plastic against my bare legs. They waddled as they moved, so the motion was more side to side than up and down. And there was no steering them. The reins were there for you to hang on, but the big lizard knew where I wanted it to go somehow, and it either went there, or it didn't.

When it didn't, I was told to slap it on the head with a leather blackjack filled with iron sand.

I know, right? Hitting a fifteen-foot lizard of any kind would give me pause, and I'd seen these things break deer in half with their jaws. The Komodo didn't seem to mind, though. It was like a hit with the sap was just an exclamation instead of a question mark in our dialogue, and after a few hesitant swings I was hammering away like the other riders.

A crowd of onlookers had gathered at the South Gates. They were mostly commoners, with a scattering of white-togaed citizens and curious foreigners. They cheered as the other survivors of our hunting party walked through the gates into the city.

Man I was tired. Like, bone-deep weary. The excitement from the big fight was catching up to me, and I kept yawning, my muscles ached, and I might have fallen asleep once or twice on the ride over.

I swung my legs off the Komodo and gave the reins to one of the Legion handlers. "Thanks," I told him, and headed toward the others.

"Whoa, sir," he said, yanking me back by the hood of my cloak. I had to grab hold of the komodo's front leg to keep my balance.

"What the hell?" I asked.

"Sorry, sir. You almost walked in front of it. The Drakes aren't really tame, they just tolerate us because we feed them."

The "Drake" craned its neck and looked at me sideways with one of its black-rimmed burnt-orange-and-yellow eyes. I felt a cold, almost cruel amusement trickle into my brain through the palms of my hands. *Definitely not my friend.* I jerked my hands back as if I'd been burned.

"Thanks," I told the soldier.

"No problem, sir."

I stayed well clear of the thing's jaws.

The Legion was out in strength. There was a wall of lorica-armored soldiers between us and the crowd. The senators were getting into palanquins to be carried back to the Heights, and most of the younger nobles had dispersed. Provus waited for me with a team of three legionaries. I walked over to meet them.

"What's up?" I asked.

"Just making sure you're okay. We should probably get you back to the Legion camp, at least for a couple days."

I wrinkled my nose. "I'll be all right."

Provus frowned. "The Sorcerer who hit the precinct is still out there, Alan."

I paused. He was right, of course; Provus often was. But I was also a couple hours into my third day of this, counting the Alpha server, and with the urgency of saving Viridian gone, I'd had enough of the high-stakes political intrigue. "It's okay. If I run into something I can't handle, I'll just log out."

"You'll what?"

"I'll leave. I'll go back to the realm I came from," I said, remembering the word Horace had used for it.

"Because you're a Traveler."

"Yeah."

Provus glanced at the legionaries waiting on him, then stepped closer and leaned in. "Alan, I don't want insult your beliefs, but they're going to get you killed."

"Let's agree to disagree," I said, gripping his shoulder. There was no way either one of us was going to win this argument, and I was on the edge of being rude. I'd played this game already in the real world. Pops had gone to Mass every Sunday, rain or shine. His daughter thought that faith without doubt was dead. I muddled my way through like anyone dealing with the unknowable, less virtuous than I would have liked, and as tolerant of the same in others as I could stomach.

Still, it was funny that here, in a world where I knew the gods were both real and only lines of code, I would wind up talking to a man who believed in neither reality.

"PM me if you get into trouble!" he said.

It was kind of him. He was really going a step further than political expedience. "I will!" I said, waving, and pushed past the line of legionaries into the crowd.

"Hey, Alan?" Sandra said.

"Yeah?"

"Jeff logged into the game."

"No shit?"

"No shit," she said. "But I think he's about to get arrested. Think you can pick him up?"

"Sure," I said. "Does he know where he is?"

TWENTY-FOUR

Gork was having a serious case of *Grakmar Shek*, which was when the warrior you fought in battle reminded you of another warrior you'd already killed.

He'd been breaking in his new partner, Brazzock, a brand-new watchman and a Svartalfar to boot, when a citizen came running up to them. It seemed an ill-dressed man had appeared out of nowhere on the marble piazza over the Southern Bastion, on the road leading into the Heights. The man was talking to himself, and the citizen was concerned he would hurt himself or others.

Gork sucked his teeth at the coincidence, but he doubted it was the same man. The Traveler he'd met two days ago seemed a little touched, but not stupid. "We'll take care of it, sir," he told the citizen, then he headed toward the piazza, knowing the rookie would follow.

He found the vagrant leaning over the railing, like before. Same clothing, too, though this man was light skinned, taller, thinner, and had facial hair, which was years out of fashion for even the poorest Imperials.

"Are you lost?" Brazzock asked, trying to sound gruff. He had the voice for it, but it was still a hard act to manage when you were four feet tall.

"No, thank you. I'm waiting for a friend." The man turned away from them.

Brazzock looked at Gork, eyes wide and on the verge of newbie panic.

Gork laid a hand on the vagrant's shoulder. "I need to check your forearms, sir."

The tall man turned around, looking irritated, as if the watchmen were the ones wasting *his* time. "It's Gork, isn't it? You're a disappointment. Alan kept going on about how amazing and unique you all are, but you're just people in the end. I've met four-stroke engines with more originality."

Gork was seconds from shoving him over the railing.

The vagrant sighed and raised his arms. "Not a slave, see?"

"That doesn't mean you belong here!" Brazzock said, his voice cracking.

Grakmar Shek. The closest Imperial equivalent was, "Another day, another handful," because of the grain dole the State provided the poor, but it failed to capture the futility of Grakmar Shek. What was the point of killing someone if they just came back again?

The vagrant opened his mouth to say something that would get him punched by Gork or kneecapped by Brazzock, but Gork grabbed him by the upper arm and squeezed. The man turned a satisfying number of shades paler than he already was. Gork started walking, dragging the man with him.

"Help!" the man shouted to the crowd. "My name is Jeff Berkowitz, and I'm being oppressed by the police!"

Brazzock found his balls and punched the man in the thigh, dead legging him. The vagrant yelped. Gork continued to drag him, and the crowd clapped as they left the piazza.

They hadn't walked twenty paces before Gork almost ran into a citizen in smudged, bloody clothes and recognized him, too.

"Corporal Gork!" the man said cheerfully.

"No," Gork said, and kept walking.

Brazzock looked from him, to the vagrant, to the man who was apparently a citizen now. He looked like one of those Svartalfar spring toys after a Risi had giving the handle a couple good cranks. Gork had always found Dwarves to be an anxious lot, away from their clans and their holes.

"I see you found my friend," the citizen continued, matching pace with them.

Gork sighed and stopped. "If you keep talking, I'm going to have to arrest you. You're dressed as a citizen."

"I am a citizen."

"You weren't a citizen two days ago."

"But I am now."

"The census is in two years," Brazzock said helpfully.

Gork looked the man over, taking in the white cloak and the expensive material. "I heard about it. Seems you took my advice."

"I did, Corporal. I begged. Then I worked. **Now I'd like to pay you back for your kindness and take my friend off your hands.**" He pulled a gold Griffin from his pocket. Brazzock's eyes went as wide as dish plates.

A city watchman was offered bribes from time to time. Most of them were small. A gold coin was enough to buy food for him and Brazzock for a week, or get himself a good cloak for the coming winter. Brazzock wouldn't complain; Svartalfars just plain liked gold. "I'm not that kind of watchman," Gork said, and started walking again.

"Wait!" the citizen said, grabbing his shoulder and almost getting himself pushed through a wall.

Gork took a deep breath and tried not to squeeze the vagrant so hard he broke his arm. "What?"

"I'm not trying to bribe you."

"Good."

"You gave me two coppers without any hope of return. I want to pay you back with interest."

"That wouldn't be appropriate," Gork said, eyes flicking to his new and very impressionable partner.

"And ninety-eight coppers of interest on a two-day two-copper loan would qualify as usury even in Stone Reach," Brazzock added. "But a servant could be surrendered to the custody of his employer if the citizen in question guaranteed the servant's good behavior."

Gork looked at Brazzock.

The Dwarf seemed to shrink into his armor. "We're supposed to be off duty, Corporal."

The citizen cleared his throat. "So if I hired him…"

"Constable Brazzock is correct."

The citizen handed the gold coin to the vagrant, who looked at it like it was a dead rat. "I have recently taken Jeff Berkowitz into my employ."

Gork looked at the vagrant. "Is that true, Jeff Berkowitz? Are you this man's servant?"

The vagrant nodded.

"I need to hear you say it, Mr. Berkowitz," Gork said, giving his arm a squeeze.

The vagrant looked like he wanted to retch, but he said, "Yes, I am Alan Campbell's servant."

Gork released him. Alan Campbell beamed. Jeff Berkowitz put the gold coin in his pocket. Constable Brazzock watched it disappear mournfully.

"And as a citizen, I *would* be allowed to buy lunch for two off-duty city watchmen at June's Rotisserie out of civic duty, correct?"

Brazzock looked at Gork hopefully.

"The captain would encourage us to build positive relationships with the community," Gork said, his face blank, his mouth watering.

"Especially in times of racial tensions," Brazzock added.

"Great," Alan said, clapping his hands. "We can head there now."

THALIA SMILED as she made her way to the East Temple of Sophia. When was the last time she'd felt like this? She'd downed half a pitcher of water and gone back to bed after Alan left, sleeping in until the innkeeper knocked on her door.

She was clearheaded and rested. She was... hopeful. Yes, that was what it was. Hopeful like a girl before the examinations of the Scribes set her path away from Alaunhylles. Hopeful like a soldier before she found out war was ugly and glory was soaked in blood. Hopeful like a woman before the man she loved chose his goddess over her. She wanted to make crowns of flowers and run with the antelopes of the Shining Plains, to confide in a friend and giggle, to sing... and it didn't feel wrong, or shameful. If felt more right than anything had for a while.

She hummed a song she'd heard her mother sing twenty years ago, the last time she'd been home. The smell of smoke and signs of vandalism were everywhere, though the residents had tried to cover it up. She'd been messy. Weiz would have hated that, and she didn't care.

It wasn't because of Alan, she told herself. Yes, he was pretty, and reasonably clever for a human half her age. It was

Weiz. After all these years, he'd finally set her free by dying. After that, it only took a spark, a shred of warmth in a stranger's eyes, to set her alight once more.

So yes, she'd enjoy the young man. She'd teach him about the world, warm his bed, and let him fan her heart and her memories. Then he would change. It could take six months or six years, but it would happen. He would age, like Weiz had, and she was just starting to remember that was normal. Expected. The Hvitalfar were a race apart.

And she would move on, but this time she wouldn't let the fire within her go out. Freddy could mind the Terrace for a few more days. She'd kill the Considia heir because she'd never left a job unfinished, but then she was done. Sophia and the church could wage their own wars of peace.

"Daughter," a woman said in passing. Thalia caught a glimpse of emerald eyes, pale skin, and raven black hair, then the woman was lost in the crowd. She frowned, momentarily thrown off, but she'd arrived. She pushed the temple door open, her warm palm pressing against the dry wood.

Sathis was waiting for her in the foyer.

"Justiciar?"

"Come in, Thalia. We need to talk."

She stepped inside. Someone barred the door behind her, and six of her Sicarii stepped out from hiding. "What is this?" Thalia said.

"Your work in this city is at an end, sister. The goddess came to me."

Thalia's eyes flicked to the assassins. They were armed with clubs and staves and equipped with fire-resistant robes, amulets, and rings.

"There's no need to fight. I promise you won't be harmed."

He meant it. Another justiciar might have slit her throat the moment she walked through the door, but Sathis was a believer, like Weiz had been. She looked at him sadly. "Sathis, where is your armor?"

"My faith—"

Thalia cast Burning Affliction on the justiciar and he went up in flames. He staggered one step forward, arms flailing like an infant walking for the first time, and fell to his knees. He didn't make a sound.

Everyone thinks that people scream when they're on fire, but they can't, not when the fire engulfs them, flowing like water, staining the ceiling with greasy black soot. The flame consumes their breath, eats through their vocal cords, melts their mouths and throats shut. Only the fire speaks.

The fire went out, leaving a blackened, stinking thing in the place of New Viridia's justiciar. "Are you priests, or are you Sicarii?" Thalia shouted.

"Sicarii, Mistress!"

"Kneel!"

The six assassins took a knee, laying their weapons before them.

Thalia clasped her hands behind her and raised her chin, looking down at the justiciar's remains. "We kill so others may live. Sathis's weakness would have allowed the worm coiling in New Viridia's breast to grow into a serpent. He told the truth! The goddess sent him to me—to be cleansed by fire!

"We will finish our divine task and kill Provus Considia. We will dig him out like the worm he is, whether he hides with the praetorians or behind the palace walls, just as I reached into the South Precinct and plucked the Griffin's agent from their hands. We will..." She stopped. Ganuc Nighteye, a Murk Elf who could have been Weiz's grandson, was staring at her. "What is it?"

"The agent lives, Mistress."

She frowned, and felt the flame within her flare. "I killed him myself."

Ganuc's eyes widened, and he lowered his head. "Forgive me, Mistress, but the acolyte who reported his location was deceived. The man you killed was a day laborer and a drug addict. The precinct was a trap you skillfully sprang."

"How do you know this?"

"I know because the agent was honored by the Senate this morning, Mistress. He rode to the gate on one of the Drakes. They clothed him in white for killing Sicarius Anaxios."

She could feel the heat rising from her chest like a stoked furnace. "His *name*, Ganuc."

"His name is Alan Campbell, Mistress."

Her flame went out. *Alan?*

She'd kissed him. He'd tasted like the overly fruity beer they liked to serve at the Lion's Tail. He'd put his hands on her, this human, the man who'd murdered Weiz, and he'd known all along. Targeted her from the beginning, from the moment he'd come to the Terrace with that blind old fool. She would never be clean.

She screamed, and her clothing, hair, and skin burst into flames. She shone like a sun. The foyer of the East Temple heated up like an oven. Candles melted, then the iron candlestands melted as well. The Sicarii cowered, buffeted by the rage of her exhalation, but because they'd been warded to capture her, they suffered only minor damage while her body consumed itself entirely.

She floated as smoke. She couldn't move, couldn't speak, only contemplate the magnitude of her failure. After twenty seconds, she reincorporated and fell to her hands and knees in front of Sathis's ashes. "Send word to every shelter and every cell. Take to the streets. Provus Considia dies today. And find Alan Campbell! Check Lot's Terrace, the Lion's Tail, and have our people in the Legion look into the movements of Optio Halius and Prefect Calenus. Search the markets around the

South Precinct, look for a blind Imperial beggar named Horace," she said, gasping.

"Find him, but don't touch him; Alan Campbell is mine."

I CHECKED the marker for June's on my map and led our little party through the winding streets and alleys, through two of the big curtain walls and into the lower city. I talked as I walked, pointing out what I'd learned about the city and people to Jeff as we went, but he seemed distracted. That suited me fine, honestly; I felt more worn out with every minute.

By the time we reached the market, my eyes felt heavy and I was feeling a little grumpy.

"You okay, Alan?" Jeff asked.

"Yeah. It's just been a rough morning. Food will help." I yawned and found my jaw was sore. In the real world, I might have taken a nap on one of the beanbags in the staff lounge. *Food*, I thought, trying to root myself by the feel of the cobbles beneath my feet and the heat of the midday sun.

"Alan!" June said.

I looked up and saw her waving at me. "Hey, June!" I said. Something about her was always comforting to me, like we'd been friends since we were kids.

She finished serving a customer and wiped her hands on her apron. "You're alive! Is that blood?" She blinked. "Why are you wearing white?"

I grinned. "Yes, yes, and it's a long story. I'd like to introduce my friends Jeff, Corporal Gork, and Constable..."

"Brazzock," the Dwarf said, rising up on his toes so he could see her over the counter.

"Hi, guys. Gork and I know each other. He comes here once a week. Where's Luce?" June asked.

Gork frowned. "She was at the precinct. The constable is my new partner."

June covered her mouth with her hand. "Oh, Gork, I'm so sorry."

"It's... it's not okay, but I appreciate the sentiment," Gork said.

I felt like a heel for not asking myself. Luce, if that was the woman I'd met my first day, wasn't the nicest person in the world, but that was statistically true of just about everybody. "I'm sorry, too, Gork. I should have asked. How long were you two partners?"

"Three years," he said. He wrinkled his nose. "She was the only one who'd work with me."

"Shit, man. I'm sorry, that sucks," I said.

Jeff leaned over and said, "We only flipped the switch on the game engine a year ago."

"Don't be an asshole, Jeff," I whispered back.

Jeff straightened, and I could tell he was going to give me some reason why he was being rational, not a dick, but I shook my head at him. I was about to ask more questions about Gork and Luce when a sharp, burning sensation started in my chest and throat. It made me gasp.

"Alan? Are you hurt?" June asked, looking worried.

"It's just heartburn," I said. "I think I need to eat."

"That's not how heartburn works," Jeff said.

"It does here. June, can we get four—make that five—of the mixed wraps? I think Gork can handle two."

"Gork definitely can," Gork said with a smile.

I swallowed and rubbed my chest. *Fuck me*, I thought. *This is going into my user feedback as a triple frowny face.*

A minute later, June handed me the first of the wraps and I bit into it. "Mmph," I said around the mouthful, feeling the grease, cheese, and pickle juice on my face and not caring. God, the food here was good. I wolfed down three bites before June gave the next wrap to Jeff, who offered it to the two watchmen.

Gork raised his palm and shook his head. "Go ahead."

The pain in my chest eased to a light pressure. I sighed in relief.

"That good, huh?" Jeff asked.

"Just try it."

He winced. "Cheryl kind of has us on this vegetarian kick."

I grinned. "It's not real food, Jeff. It won't block your arteries or make you fat. Take a bite."

Jeff blinked at me, realizing what he'd just done, after his talk of V.G.O. just being a game. "You're right." He held the wrap with both hands and took a big bite. His eyes widened.

"Right? Best food you've ever had," I said.

Brazzock was tearing into his flatbread with an enthusiasm unhampered by manners. He had white sauce and grease all around his mouth, streaking his knee-length beard. Gork smiled as he took his two flatbreads from June's hands and double fisted them, taking a bite from each in turn.

"How much do I owe you?" I asked.

"Two silvers and five coppers," she said. I could tell from her expression she still expected me to come up short. If that was the case, she'd been kind to serve me and my friends.

I handed her three silvers. "Keep the change."

"Forget what he just said, June," Horace said, walking up to the counter beside me. "I'll have a wrap on his tab."

June smiled at the old man. She put the coins in her pocket and started preparing the sixth wrap.

"I'm glad you're here," I told Horace.

"Where else would I be?"

I shrugged.

"Why do you do that?" Horace asked.

"Do what?"

"Shrug in front of a blind man. How am I supposed to know?"

I stuck my lower lip out. "The rustle of my clothing? The smell of my deodorant?"

"What's deodorant?"

"Now *that* doesn't surprise me," I said.

Horace grinned. "In any case, it's good I caught you. We need to speak before you leave."

I got that weird, scratchy feeling between my shoulder blades again, like when he told me I came from another world. "How do you know I'll be leaving?"

Horace sniffed. "They put the white on you, didn't they? I figure you're close to finishing your class quest. The Halls of Illusion will be next."

I relaxed. "Yeah, the Halls of Illusion. And I might be gone for a while, too, but let me check on my friend before we talk, okay?"

Horace waved me away and focused his attention on June as she finished preparing his flatbread.

"How are you holding up?" I asked Jeff.

He wiped his hands on his Rough Tunic (shoddy). "Good, I guess? Gork was telling me about what happened at the precinct. Sounds like pretty crazy stuff."

"I can imagine," I said. "But how do you feel, personally? Having any issues with being in game?"

He reached up to grab a ponytail that wasn't there and scowled. "My knee doesn't hurt. I couldn't figure it out at first, but it was freaking me out."

"That makes sense."

"That and the tattoos. I've had those since college. It's just strange to not see them there, like I really can't believe it."

I nodded. "Why don't you call it a day? We've proved my being here wasn't a fluke."

He hesitated. "Did Sandra tell you?"

I grinned. "Nah. I'm guessing Osmark is going to want to give you most of the credit for the past two days as well."

Jeff looked at his feet.

"It's cool, man. Really. I get it. It makes for a better narrative."

"No hard feelings?"

"None," I said. It was mostly true. "Rob will make it up to me. You'll see." Jeff raised an eyebrow at me calling Rob by his first name. I shot him a wink. "Spring for Wendy's when I get back? I could murder a spicy chicken sandwich."

Jeff chuckled. "I'm going home, man. But I'll have someone grab that for you. Fries and a drink?"

"Absolutely. Large fries and a root beer float."

"I thought they stopped making those."

"You can order them off-menu."

Jeff shook his head. I doubted he'd done much off-menu ordering in his life. "All right, man. It's been real. I'll see you out there." His eyes unfocused for a moment, and then he disappeared.

JEFF OPENED his eyes to fluorescent lights, cheap sheets, and the hum of electronics. He closed his eyes again, letting the feel of his own body return. He was cold, his arm itched like crazy, and while he'd never noticed it before, his left knee felt fuller than his right, even when he wasn't putting weight on it. *Shit,* he thought. *I hope that's not permanent.* He was kind of okay with not remembering what it was like *not* to be him.

He opened his eyes again and saw Sandra at the foot of his bed. "Welcome back," she said.

He twirled his finger in the air.

She grinned.

"Not watching Alan?"

She bobbed her head. "He's just talking to the old man. I get that he's really into this whole Illusionist class, but it's just not my thing."

Jeff grunted. "I imagine not, after what you did to that security guard."

Sandra laughed. "Right? The girls at the gym are going to be so proud."

Jeff laughed with her, although to be honest she made him nervous. *What the hell kind of gym is* she *going to?*

"I don't care who you are, Mr. Osmark. I don't appreciate interrupting my time with family just because you decided to run an experiment over the weekend."

Jeff and Sandra looked over to see Osmark walking in with Doctor Vila, the lead civilian doctor for the project.

"You're right, Doctor. I'm sure Sandra could have called one of the DARPA MDs. They probably could have handled this," Osmark said.

Vila scoffed. "They're researchers, not practicing physicians."

"Ah. Well, maybe she thought of that, then," Osmark said.

Vila frowned, then sighed. "Let's take a look at him, then." He walked over to the computer station, minimized the video feed that showed his own back seen through Jeff's eyes, and brought up Alan's vitals. He straightened and looked at them. "What is this?"

Osmark frowned. "I'm not sure—"

"This man is *dead,* Osmark. I'm not going to help you cover this up."

Jeff felt the floor drop out from beneath him.

"How long?" Sandra shouted. She'd run to Alan's bedside table and started pulling drawers open.

"What?" Vila asked.

"How long has he been dead?"

"Over eight minutes. There's no point—"

She stabbed Alan in the chest with an injector, threw it away, and started CPR. "There's always a point, Doctor! Now do your fucking job and go get me the AED! Rob, go find ice. Jeff!"

"What?"

"Help Rob! Do something! We're not losing him. We're not."

I LAUGHED. "So the Halls of Illusion are nowhere."

"And everywhere."

"But they're not so much a place as a state of mind."

"Exactly!"

I shook my head.

"Citizen Campbell?" Brazzock said.

I turned. The two watchmen, their food finished, had their helmets back on. "We're heading back to the precinct," Gork said. "Need to give our report." I hadn't noticed it before, but his right hand and forearm were covered in burn scars almost to the elbow, like he'd stuck his arm into a furnace.

"All right, guys. It was good seeing you. Stay safe."

"You too," Gork said.

"Thanks for the grub!" Brazzock said, and followed Gork back toward the precinct.

I looked back at Horace. "Okay, tell it to me one more time."

Horace straightened and crossed his arms. "The Halls of Illusion are the straight way through crooked places. They can be reached from anywhere they shouldn't be. They are what can't be smelled, tasted, touched, heard, or seen."

I licked my lips and tried to wrap my head around the words. I couldn't believe something like this was embedded in a

AAA game. Half of me thought this was my punishment for drunken nights spent trolling the Overminds with half-baked philosophy, and the other half thought the Illusionist class wasn't going to be very popular. And I loved it. I couldn't wait to see what kind of upside-down crooked quest the game was going to throw at me next.

There was a dull *boom*, like one of the "Kodo" drummers hitting a Japanese taiko as hard as they could, and my chest seized up. It was like a giant child grabbed me by the torso and squeezed. I slammed down on my knees.

"Alan?" It was Sandra's voice. "His eyes are open!"

"That doesn't mean anything," Doctor Vila said.

It was like I was seeing two scenes at the same time. On the one hand, I saw the New Viridia marketplace, people stopping to stare at me, Horace crouched with his hand on my shoulder, mouth moving without sound. On the other, I saw Sandra's face and the ceiling of Alpha Testing, fluorescent lights, Rob Osmark packing bags of ice between my legs. The two images were superimposed, fading in and out of each other.

"Clear!" Sandra yelled, putting her hands up. Osmark did the same.

Boom.

I gasped and rolled onto my back, mouth working like a landed fish. It was like the olive grove all over again. I needed out. I had to get out.

<<<>>>

Log out: Yes/No?

<<<>>>

"Yes!" I shouted, clawing at my chest. The prompt disappeared, but I was still there, still seeing both images.

"Even if we bring him back, he's going to be brain damaged. Is that really—"

"Shut the fuck up, Doctor," Osmark said.

"You can't keep shocking him," Jeff said. He'd scratched his right arm bloody.

"What?" Sandra said.

"If you hit him with too much current, you'll fry the—"

"Clear!" Vila shouted.

"No!" Sandra said, reaching.

Boom.

The double image was gone. The pain was fading. I stared at the gray light through palm fronds, layers of clouds sliding over each other in the Viridian sky.

"YOU'LL FRY THE NANITES," Jeff said under his breath.

He felt detached from this. From the three people frozen in horror around the hospital bed. From the corpse. From himself. Blood dripped from his knuckles to the floor, but he felt fine.

Drip.

"Jeff?" Sandra said, suddenly in front of him. She was pulling him toward one of the beds. "Let's get that bandaged, okay?"

He let her lead him. This wasn't important. What was important was the process, the series of mechanical steps and decisions that led to this moment.

Drip.

Sandra started wrapping his forearm with gauze.

He'd been a spectator in this from the start. From the moment Alan walked in—no, from the moment Robert Osmark took the stage. He'd let others walk over his years of experience, his education, his professional publications, and his common sense.

"I'll call the police, explain what happened," Osmark said.

"No," Sandra said.

Osmark gave her a sympathetic look. Maybe Jeff should do that, too. Sandra was choking back tears. Vila looked like he was about to explode. They were all so human. He couldn't bring himself to feel anything at all.

"He's gone, Sandra. We have to start taking care of things."

"I'm not an idiot, Robert," she said. "There's more at stake here than your video game. We partnered with the Department of Defense; we're going to let them clean this up."

And there was that edge, behind the tears. Did everyone have that many layers? Jeff felt like he was flat, laid out on a microscope slide. "Sandra, we can't—"

"Be quiet, Robert," she said, tying off Jeff's bandage. "You need to not be here. This happened after you left."

Vila was puffing like a bellows. "I'm not hiding this from the police, military or not."

"I never said we would hide it, Doctor. We're going to control it. Alan Campbell suffered a nanite aneurysm. It's a known risk. He stayed in too long, got dehydrated—"

"You gave him a saline IV," Jeff said.

"Thank you for the reminder, Jeff. Doctor Vila? Please remove Alan's IV. Try not to bruise the skin."

The doctor opened and closed his mouth, then walked to Alan's bedside.

Osmark walked over and spoke softly, his eyes flicking to Jeff before he touched Sandra's shoulder. "Sandra, I—"

She shrugged his hand off. "Not now, Robert."

Osmark took a breath. "Ms. Bullard, I don't know where this is coming from, but we can't—we *won't*—lie about how he died. I'm not jeopardizing my entire company for—"

"He's still alive," Jeff said.

Sandra and Osmark both looked at him. "What?" they said together.

Jeff pointed at the computer station with his bandaged arm. The feed from Alan's eyes was still on, and it was moving. "He's still alive."

TWENTY-FIVE

The sky was darkening. There was a damp charge to the air like it was heavy.

"Alan? Come on, boy, get up and say something, or have you been struck dumb and stupid?"

"I'm dead."

Horace snorted. "I'm no necromancer, but I think you might have that wrong."

I ignored him. "Rob? Sandra? Anyone?"

Nothing. Just the feel of Horace's hand on my shoulder. June was saying something, but it came through as noise, like the grown-ups speaking in a Peanuts special. I tried to log out again, and couldn't even get the prompt to come up.

Then I heard the scratching sound of someone putting on a headset. "Alan?"

"Rob?"

Someone chuckled. "No, it's Jeff. Rob and Sandra are standing behind me like scared extras in a Romero movie."

His flippant tone slid off me like rain on a windshield. "I can't log out."

"That makes sense; nowhere to log out *to*. Sandra fried your nanites when she tried to resuscitate you. In fairness, it was the right call because the nanites wouldn't do you any good once your body was dead. Or would they? That's a scary thought, isn't it?"

I swallowed. So that was it, then.

"I will not, sir. You're welcome to join me, but I will not 'give you the room,'" Jeff said. There was the sound of muffled speaking, then Jeff added, "That's kind of you, Ms. Bullard, but I'm not feeling fragile. Things are *very* clear from where I'm sitting."

More scratching sounds, then Rob came on the line. "Alan?"

"I don't know," I said. I had zero handle on what was going on right now.

"It's going to be okay, Alan. You're still here. We're going to find a way through this."

"I understand the nanites in my brain are fried."

"We have more."

"And that I don't have a body to come back to. Or is the real Alan still in my body? Is he watching this now? God, this isn't happening."

"There's no one in your body, Alan. You're the only—"

"That doesn't make it better!" I snapped.

June had her big arm around me, and she was holding me to her chest.

"I will find you a way out of this, Alan. I promise. I'll build you a new body if I have to."

Jeff snort-laughed out loud.

"All right, that's enough. Sandra, get him out of here. Drag him if you have to." More mic feedback and scraping. "Damn it. Alan, I'll be back. Stay safe in there."

Then silence. If I hadn't been so stunned, so intent on avoiding the eyes of the market-goers staring at the man talking to himself, I wouldn't have seen the first crossbowman settle into position on the opposite rooftop.

"Fuck!" Osmark shouted, throwing his headset across the room. He followed that up with a stream of more colorful Italian curse words he'd learned when he was a kid.

Berkowitz looked like he was on the verge of laughter or tears again.

Robert turned his attention to Sandra. "How you gonna fix *this*, huh?" His Brooklyn accent came right out when he was pissed, and he didn't care. "What? No answer? Fine. Come with me. You too, doc. Stop dickin' around with that body, it ain't goin' nowhere. And *you!*" he said, stabbing his finger at Jeff. "Stay off the computer. You've caused enough trouble today."

"Is he alive? Is it really him?" Sandra asked.

"What am I, a priest?" Osmark started walking toward the door. "I have no idea. I need the head developer in here yesterday to tell me if there's a persistent copy stored in game for bad connections or if that's really Alan, but it'd be *easier* for all of us if he was just gone. In the meantime, get security on that door. No one in or out, especially Chuckles back there. He's not ready to drive a car or tie his shoes right now."

"Yes, Mr. Osmark."

A MESSAGE from Provus hit my inbox.

Personal Message:

Alan,

Problem bigger than we thought. Praetorian barracks attacked. Uncle wants me out of the city while he solves the problem. You should leave, too. Will wait for you where we started the hunt. Don't be long.

—Provus

<<<>>>

There were dozens of crossbowmen I could see, and maybe more hidden by the orange tarps that the merchants had strung from the roofs to long tent poles for shade. They squatted in teams of two, a spotter/reloader and a shooter. They started to take aim.

It brought me right back into the moment, to my face against June's enormous chest and her stroking my hair like I was a frightened child. I struggled free.

June let me go. "What—"

"**Run!**" I Vocalized to the whole market. "**Run for your lives! It's the terrorists who attacked the South Precinct!**"

People ran. Accipiters took flight. The Risi in the crowd trampled people. There was screaming. Bowstrings snapped and bolts fell like the first drops of a downpour, little black flashes across my vision. Clusters of people hammered on doors, pleading to be let in. The crowd was bunching at the main entrances to the marketplace, and there were more screams. I grabbed Horace and June and pulled them toward that little side alley I'd used to chase after Provus, what seemed like a lifetime ago.

I heard a *whoosh* and the screams intensified. People were falling back. A woman fell in front of me, a crossbow bolt buried between her shoulder blades. A fireball streaked across the plaza and exploded into a group of people trapped on the armorer's doorstep. Another burst against a cluster of palm trees and set them on fire.

"What do we do?" June asked me.

I had no idea. I could see the alleyway now. A wall of fire was blocking the entrance.

Then I couldn't move. Or speak. I could move my eyes. June, Horace, and I were wrapped in cords of fire. They didn't burn, and they were translucent, like they were only partly there, but they held us all the same.

The screaming was getting fainter. I had a clear view of the northwestern entrance to the market. Men and women in black masks with green-painted eyes were lining people up on their knees. Those who tried to fight or run were cut down or shot. A drop of rain hit my face, and I couldn't wipe it away.

Thalia stepped in front of me. "Alan."

Thalia? I thought, but my mouth wouldn't move.

"I should have known it was you. You were too smooth. That's what gave it away. Just like the old man." She released Horace from the spell and dragged him in front of me, holding him from behind so I could see.

"Thalia?" he said with a quaking voice. "What are you doing? I've known you since—"

She grabbed his throat, and her hand glowed ice blue. "You liked this trick, didn't you, Alan? Do you like it now? Does it turn you on?"

Horace's mouth moved and his body shook. No sound. She'd frozen his throat shut. *Please stop*, I thought. *Please.* Thalia held him up the whole time, and his struggles became more frantic, until his face turned blue. Tears streamed down my face.

"Was it a game for you, Alan? To seduce me after you killed him? Can you let me in on the joke, or are we all laughing together, now?"

She released June.

"Horace!" June screamed. I heard scuffling, then grunts. More rain, now, a steady trickle from the sky. June was dragged in front of me by two of the masked terrorists. Thalia joined her. The Dawn Elf's lip was split and bleeding.

Thalia laughed, wiping her mouth with the back of her wrist. "I like this one, Alan. The cabinetmaker's daughter. Do you know I tried to hire her, once? I was going to offer full meals at the Terrace, but she didn't want to go. Said she wanted to be with her regular customers, in the lower quarter." Thalia reached over and drew the sword from one of her henchmen's sheaths. She waved her hand over the blade, and flames lit the steel. It hissed and spat as raindrops hit it. "The best rotisserie in the city."

June didn't get to go quietly. She screamed until she was hoarse, and I could do nothing.

JEFF WATCHED it all happen on the monitor, bandaged arm crossed over his left. Was Alan an NPC, now? Would he disappear forever if he died?

All Jeff had to do to find out was the same thing he'd done until now. *Nothing.* Osmark was right. It would be easier. They could shut the system down, or just roll it back to its state three days ago. This could all go away.

He picked up the headset. "Alan? I know you can't speak. I know you're surrounded. But you were brave. You acted where I broke down, and you deserve better than this, better than *all* of this.

"Osmark wants you dead. I heard him say it. I can't save you, but I'm going to give you a chance. Run. Hide. Find a way to escape. It's the only way."

Jeff set the headset down, typed a few commands into the computer, and hit enter.

OSMARK WANTS ME DEAD? *Of course he does.* I was an inconvenience. A bug in the system. He could clean all of this up, fix the security logs, claim it was my doing and he didn't know, as long as I wasn't around to contradict him. For a moment, I saw Rob's face instead of Thalia's as she dug the flaming sword into June's back.

June cried out one more time and went limp in the men's arms, eyes blank, drool and snot hanging from her face. The men looked at Thalia, and she nodded. They dumped June onto the ground like a sack.

Thalia stepped over June's body, flaming sword still in hand, and I wasn't scared anymore. I was too full of cold, calculating hate. "I wanted you to feel that before I kill you, Alan. I wanted you to know how it—"

Jeff materialized out of the air, wrapped his arms around my crazy almost-ex-girlfriend, and slammed her to the ground.

Time slowed.

June and Horace were dead. The terrorists in the masks were executing the people who'd surrendered. Thalia and Osmark were unstoppable monsters. This was bigger than me. I was too small. My only chance was to do what Jeff told me to— run, hide, and then grow until I could throw it all back in their faces. The entrances were blocked, and almost thirty of the masked men and women were pouring into the marketplace. The only path that didn't end with me hacked, shot, or roasted was toward the blank wall where I'd found Horace, that first day, a place where there was no path I could smell, taste, touch, hear, or see.

Time resumed, and I ran. A henchman grabbed my cloak, and I shrugged out of it. Something creased the back of my neck, but I kept going, even when the second bolt slammed into my thigh. The wall was getting closer. I heard Jeff shrieking, the way June had shrieked, but I blocked it out. There were only the Halls, a state of mind, a place that wasn't a place. I hit the wall and passed through.

When I was nine my mom and her girlfriend brought me to a Burlington Coat Factory outlet and I hid from them in the rows. Passing through the wall felt like that, like I was a kid again, pushing my way through hanging peacoats, buttons and catches grabbing at me as I pressed the heavy wool fabric aside.

I stepped out into the marketplace. The sun was shining. The wind stirred the palms. Horace was taking a nap against the temple wall, and I could join him if I wanted—just for a while. I'd had such a hard day. The memory of screams, smoke, and blood was fading away, but something warned me that if I stopped here, I would never leave. *The Halls of Illusion are the straight way through crooked places.* Someone had told me that. I walked forward.

I was in the market, all right, but the angles were strange. Things shifted to form a direct path, as long as I meant to stay on it. It's just as confusing as it sounds. Vendors called out, offering me balms, ointments, and potions. That sounded nice because I had a dull ache in my right thigh, but I could bear it, so I walked on.

"Alan!" June said, waving at me. "Come try this new recipe!" She held a plate of meat, vegetables, and peppers toward me, and my mouth watered.

"It smells great, June," I said, not stopping. I had somewhere I needed to be.

The vendors became more frantic, offering me charms and armor at deep discounts. Fatin asked for a moment of my time. Tozhug challenged me to an arm wrestling match. Quest offerings appeared like pop-ups on a naughty website, and I dismissed them all. I was almost at the archway.

"Alan?" Thalia said, behind me. I turned to look. She was wearing a white halter dress with lace around its straps and a modest V-neck. She'd braided flowers into her hair, like a crown. "Can't you stay?" she asked.

God, her voice still did it for me after all she'd done. "I don't think I can," I told her sadly.

I stepped through the arch.

Bright fluorescent lights blinded me. I blinked. Doctor Vila was by my side. "He's alive!"

Sandra hugged me. "Alan! I'm so glad."

I gave her a squeeze. Her body was hard and toned. Her black hair smelled like hairspray; it took a lot to get a flawless bob like hers. I took hold of her hands and gently pried them loose.

She sniffed and wiped her eyes. "I thought we'd lost you. Here, swing your legs out of the bed and I'll help you walk."

I smiled at her. We could have been something, she and I. There was a hardness to her, an aloofness, but also a deep, internal honesty I could have planted my feet on when I felt lost. But this wasn't her. I threw the covers aside and stepped forward, toward the ceiling. The world rotated around me.

My bare feet touched the floor of Alpha Testing. It was cold, always so cold in here. Jeff waved at me from the computer station. "Alan! Come see this! It's fucking amazing!" I walked forward and the room bent away from Jeff toward the exit. The whole team was there, cheering, yelling, "Speech, speech, speech!" The podium was to my right, up a short flight of stairs. A hundred ears waiting to hear Alan Campbell's wisdom. I laughed out loud.

"You did it, Alan," Osmark told me. "You saved Viridian. You saved the whole company. We need to talk about your future."

"I can't go with you," I told him.

He wrapped his arm around my shoulder. "Then I'll go with you."

We talked as we went. He told me he had big plans, long-term plans. We just needed to get me a bit more training, a bit more exposure, some credibility with the senior staff. I went along with it. We'd had this back and forth before, and it was true. I could have been something. But I stayed focused on the path because Rob would push or pull ever so slightly to the side without meaning to, and I might have been led astray.

Frank stood at the door, his arms crossed. "Can't let you through, Alan."

I tried to step forward, but Frank put his hand out and stopped me. The world did not bend. He was as solid as rock, his eyes as dark as the abyss. **"Get out of my way, Frank,"** I said.

Rage and madness glittered in the thing's eyes, and for a moment I got a flash—a taste—of it slithering off a narrow stone bridge suspended over *nothing*, and dark, chittering, sliding things moved, frantic and formless, in that void. They *hungered*. I pushed the door open and stepped out onto the parking lot. I wondered if I would walk all the way to the sea.

"Your car's over here, Alan," Osmark said. The Spyder was parked by the door, first spot, project lead for Viridian. I laughed at the ridiculous vanity of it all. Osmark frowned. "If you don't like it anymore, take mine," he said, pulling his own keys out of his pocket.

I looked forward and found the main office building in front of me. *Why not?* I walked through the entrance. Rob didn't follow me in.

The receptionist looked up and smiled. "Good morning, Mr. Campbell! Your mother is on the line. Shall I connect you?"

I shook my head and draped my coat over my arm. I was

wearing a silk-lined bespoke Saville suit and Italian leather shoes, and the whole outfit was obscenely comfortable.

"Mr. Campbell, could you take a look at—"

"Mr. Campbell! A comment for the *Daily*—"

Sandra walked beside me, clipboard in hand, wearing a perfectly fitted navy-blue suit and skirt. She'd aged as well as I thought she would. "I have the agenda ready for the Board, Alan. Do you have time go over it?"

"I'm sorry, Sandra. You can't imagine how much. But no. Clear my schedule for the afternoon."

"Okay. Is everything all right?"

"I don't know," I answered. "I'll see you at home." It was my fantasy the Halls were feeding off, after all. I might as well enjoy it.

Pops waited by the elevator, holding his hat by the brim with giant hands. I recognized the brown pants and the tweed sports coat he wore to church. I knew he'd smell faintly of earth and pipe tobacco. I felt a lump in my throat.

"Hey, Nieto. You have time for an old man?"

I almost lost it, then. I almost ran to him and wrapped my arms around him. The only thing that stopped me, and I hadn't realized it until now, was that Pops looked a bit like Horace, and Horace was dead, just like Pops. The elevator doors opened, and I stepped through into my office on the top floor.

EPILOGUE

I'd arrived at the end of things. The office was just how I would have wanted it—floor-to-ceiling windows all the way across, a poured, textured, and polished concrete floor that looked like I was stepping onto an abstract painting of a Carribean lagoon, plain white walls, and a gray wood desk that looked like a solid block floating inches above the floor.

I stepped forward, and the clack of my shoes echoed. I laughed.

"Of course the room has perfect acoustics."

I looked around, frowning.

"Where did that... *Oh. I see.*" I was depersonalizing. Disassociating. "Now even my internal monologue had been taken away."

I walked forward, heels clacking. I thought—

"Of singing a few bars of 'Ave Maria,' like I had in the choir, back in Empuriabrava, but I also had the sense—"

I shouted in incoherent fury, and the voice stopped for a moment.

"How do I stop my own internal monologue? Isn't that—"

I stepped forward, focusing.

"Like I was stopping myself from existing, unless even these, my thoughts, weren't *me*."

The desk looked solid, but it was actually thousands of weightless pieces perfectly set into place. I waded through them like a pool full of Styrofoam and put my hand against the window.

"It was the end of the world, outside. The end of it all. The sun was red and twice its size. Nothing lived. The skyscrapers were melting. And I'd always known it would end this way. No matter how long I lived, no matter what I discovered or achieved, the world would end in fire."

I swallowed and rested my forehead against the glass.

"There was nowhere left to go but back. I'd take the elevator downstairs and hug Pops, introduce him to my wife, and we'd talk about the years he'd missed. Better a lie than to face—"

I pushed and the window swung open. Hot, stinging wind ruffled my clothes. I stepped forward. The world turned.

I looked down at the approaching ground. I watched it come. There was nothing but my body and the rush of the wind.

My body hit. It broke. Blood squirted. Bone shattered. My heart stopped beating. There was only me.

I rose, disembodied, floating, and found myself on a narrow stone bridge. It was a nowhere place. Ruined arches stretched over the path, broken pieces floating and gently bumping into each other while mosses and lichen waged a silent war with the remaining mortar. The void stretched in every direction, darkness shifting over darkness, lit by flickers of blue ghost light. I was at the end of that path. In front of me stood a heavy leather-bound book on a stand, and I knew without knowing that it was the Illusory Grimoire, and within it were the collected secrets of Illusion magic. I willed myself forward and opened the cover.

There were only three words handwritten on the first page.

<<<>>>

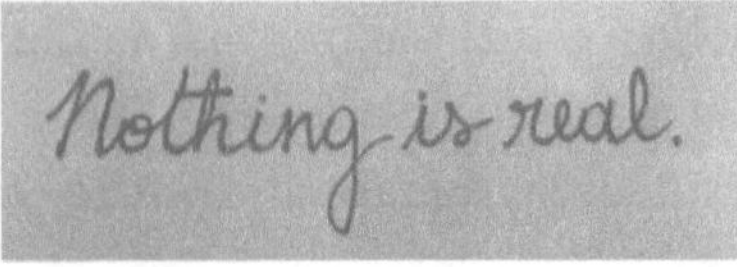

<<<>>>

I turned to the next page, but it was blank. So was the next page, and the page after that. I could feel the last pieces of me frittering away with every turn. The next 313 pages of the book were blank.

The last five pages were glued together, and page 315 read:

<<<>>>

<<<>>>

A small circular recess was cut into the glued pages, and in it sat a small white communion wafer. With the little sense of self I had left, I picked it out of the pages and brought it to the place my mouth should be.

The wafer melted on my tongue. It had no consistency and no flavor. It was, at best, the memory of bread, the symbol of something more, but it was enough. My name was Alan Campbell. I was born in Philadelphia, I spent my summers in Spain, I'm the first person to transfer his consciousness into a video game, and I plan to live to talk about it.

<<<>>>

Quest Update: Smoke and Mirrors

You successfully navigated the Halls of Illusion. In return, as your reward, you have received 1,000 XP and the Illusionist class kit.

<<<>>>

Level Up!

You have (15) undistributed stat points! Stat points can be allocated at any time.

You have (3) unassigned proficiency point! Proficiency points can be allocated at any time.

<<<>>>

I pulled up my character sheet. I needed every advantage I could get.

<<<>>>

V.G.O. Character Overview					
Name:	Alan Campbell	Race:	Imperial	Gender:	Male
Level:	7	Class:	Illusionist	Alignment:	Neutral
Renown:	60	Carry Capacity:	305	Undistributed Attribute Points:	15
Health:	190	Spirit:	230	Stamina:	220
H-Regen/sec:	2.85	S-Regen/sec:	4.45625	Stam-Regen/sec:	3.645
Attributes:		Offense:		Defense:	
Strength:	10	Base Melee Weapon Damage:	20	Base Armor:	23
Vitality:	12	Base Ranged Weapon Damage:	0	Armor Rating:	31
Constitution:	15	Attack Strength (AS):	53.5	Block Amount:	3.6875
Dexterity:	14.75	Ranged Attack Strength (RAS):	33.5	Block Chance (%):	7.12
Intelligence:	12	Spell Strength (SS):	18	Evade Chance (%):	3.65
Spirit:	16	Critical Hit Chance:	5%	Fire Resist (%):	0.8
Luck:	10	Critical Hit Damage:	150%	Cold Resist (%):	0.8
				Lightning Resist (%):	0.8
				Shadow Resist (%):	0.8
				Holy Resist (%):	0.8
Current XP:	600			Poison Resist (%):	0.8
Next Level.:	4,480			Disease Resist (%):	0.8

<<<>>>

Badass, I thought, remembering where I'd started only days before. My Spirit and Stamina regen were almost double what they'd been after my first level up. I put 1 point into Vitality to bring my Health up to 200, and a full 10 points into Spirit because I had spells to cast and people to fool. I put 2 points into Intelligence, partly by vanity, bringing my resistances up to 1%, and dumped the remaining 2 points into Constitution because I had yet to regret being able to run farther without stopping in this... in my new life, inside Viridia.

I also had a new tab available that had been grayed out until now.

<<<>>>

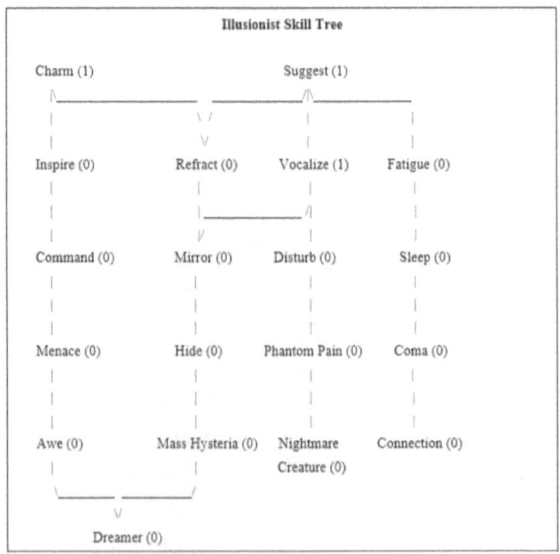

<<<>>>

Yes. "Yes!" I shouted out loud. I only knew what two of the skills did, but I could see a lot of column three in Thalia's future. In the meantime, I needed to survive. I checked the Hide skill.

<<<>>>
Skill: Hide

Makes the object impossible to target and difficult to notice after a relationship check. Higher levels increase transparency and duration. Some classes such as Enchanters are immune to the distracting effect, but not the concealment.

Skill Type/Level: Spell, Gesture Based/Initiate

Cost: Spirit cost scales with size and movement

Range: 1 meter

Cast Time: 5 seconds

Cooldown: None

Effect 1: 10% bonus to Stealth while active.

Effect 2: As long as not seen by target, reduces base failure rate of Illusion spells by 50%.

<<<>>>

That wasn't going to work. I was pretty sure Thalia hated my guts. If the concealment was relationship based, I might as well run down the middle of the street without pants on. I put another point into Vocalize, allowing me to mimic sounds and other people's voices. I also dropped a point into Refract and Mirror. I'd probably earned some skills and passives tied to being an Illusionist, but I was short on time. The prefect had warned me I'd piss someone off someday. Distance was my friend.

And then I'd get even. For Erik, Horace, June, and even for Jeff, who was probably logged out already.

I closed all the windows and looked down at the grimoire. The wafer was still there, stuck in the page. I smiled and closed the book gently, with a touch of reverence, then I stepped around it to reach the exit. The things that waited in the dark didn't scare me anymore.

THE SIGH that had become a breeze and then a wind finally became a storm and broke over New Viridia. Lightning split the darkened sky, and wind howled past the walls, buildings, and guard towers. The rain fell hard and sideways, driven in sheets by the violent gusts.

"Find him!" Thalia shouted over the wind. "He can't have gotten far!" She clutched her arms against the freezing downpour.

"Yes, Mistress!" the Sicarii answered as one. They boosted and pulled each other up onto rooftops and fanned out in the direction the Imperial agent had run.

Thalia didn't need help. She blasted herself up the wall.

When all the assassins were gone, Horace opened his milky eyes. He crawled over to where June was lying and cradled her head in his lap. "It's okay, now, Junebug. They're gone now."

Her left eye fluttered open. Her right was swollen shut. "Horace?" She smiled. "You're alive. I'm so glad."

Then she died, but Horace held her a while longer.

SANDRA WAITED while her boss made up his mind.

"And you're positive they can clean this up?"

"Say the word and this goes away. No Board, no media

circus, no weeping mother on TV with Osmark Technologies in the caption."

"I'll still have to inform the Board, Sandra. A man died. A man I thought you got along with."

Sandra raised an eyebrow at him. "Sentiment, Rob?"

He laughed. "Damn, you're cold. Fine, make the call."

Sandra made a note on her clipboard. "You won't regret it." She left Osmark's office, holding the clipboard to her chest. The security guard she'd taken down earlier was guarding the hallway. "Mr. Dougherty," she said, dipping her head.

"Ma'am," he said, surprised.

"Sorry about earlier," she said.

His face reddened. "That's fine, ma'am. Frank explained we would have hurt Mr. Campbell if we moved him. Is he all right?"

"He's fine," Sandra said. *And thank you, Frank.*

She was almost to her office when Dougherty cleared his throat. "Um, Ms. Bullard? That move you used on me, is there any way you could..."

She smiled. "There's a gym on the corner of West Carson and Crenshaw in Torrance. You know it?"

"No ma'am, but I can find it."

"A couple of us get together on Saturday mornings, ten to noon."

"I'll be there, ma'am. Thank you."

"You're welcome." She smiled at him. He was one of her people. He probably wouldn't sue her, and if he showed up to the gym he'd have a hard time building a case.

She stepped into her office. It wasn't until she'd closed the door and leaned back against it that she let herself go. The clipboard dropped to her side. Her eyes welled up. She shivered.

Yeah, I got along with Alan, you fucktard, she thought. Her teeth chattered. The last time she'd done CPR on someone had been in Southeast Asia, working a protective detail when her primary was hit with a gene-targeted virus. The woman had gone into convulsions, then spit up blood. Sandra had fought to keep her alive, all the while praying to God, Buddha, and the Flying Spaghetti Monster—anyone who'd listen, really—that that crap wasn't Ebola or SPM-2, or fucking radiation poisoning because the Russians thought that shit was funny and they'd been eating the same food.

The woman died. Then she'd been arrested by the Burmo-Thai federal police and interrogated for two days before the embassy got her out. People rarely had good memories of giving CPR; hers were worse.

She took a deep breath, then another. She'd talk to her handler, maybe get some counseling with an Agency shrink. In the meantime, she had a job to do. She walked over to her desk, pulled her top drawer out, reached under it to remove the scrambler she'd hidden there, and plugged it into her cell-phone. Her office was swept for bugs once a month by Os-Tech, and shortly thereafter by her. She dialed the number from memory.

"Torrance Custom Photo, this is Suzie, how can I help you?"

"Hi Suzie, this is Sandra Bullard from the other day. I wanted to check if my order is ready."

"Sure thing, ma'am. Can you tell me what kind of prints they were?"

Sandra felt herself relax into the routine. "Glamour shots," she answered. If she'd said passport photos, an armed agent would have been there to extract her within thirty minutes.

"Just a moment," Suzie said.

The line clicked. There was a series of beeps and tones as the scrambler on her phone and her handler's synchronized, then Brett's voice came on.

"Piper, this is Sandbag. I say potato?"

"I say ivory."

"Go for Sandbag, or did you just need to hear my voice?"

"I need a cleanup at the Stanton campus, building forty-three. One toe tag with adjusted time stamp and copies to local, federal, and DoD. I'll meet them onsite and talk them through the arrangements."

"Jesus, Piper! This wasn't supposed to be that kind of job! What happened?"

"Tin Man is compromised."

"Compromised by whom? Russia, China, the Brits?"

"By us. As of an hour ago, Tin Man works for the United States Government. We own him. He just doesn't know it yet."

There was a long pause on the other end of the line.

"Okay, Piper, black cab is inbound. I won't jinx it by saying congratulations—"

"Then don't," Sandra said. "Piper out."

She hung up the phone and sighed. Whatever calm she'd felt reaching out to the Agency evaporated at the sound of Sandbag's voice. Brett was never going to be as good a handler as she had been, which was a shame because she could use a confidant right now. She put the scrambler back in its hiding place, put her clipboard into a locked drawer, and left her office. She needed to go check on Jeff. He couldn't be there when the team came in.

THANATOS WAS HALFWAY through his third reading of the Hyperion Cantos, in the Southern Annex of the Empirical Annex, when the great double doors to the Necropolis swung open and two of his Vogthar servants walked through, dragging a corpse between them. He sighed. This had been a day for interruptions.

The Vogthar were taller than his chosen avatar, each over seven feet tall without counting the matte-black horns that curved upward from either side of their heads, above their elf-like ears. They wore gray armor that blended in well with the landscape. Their lipless mouths worked silently, as if continually in prayer, and their eyes stared, vacant. Thanatos had saved them from genocide, but Morsheim itself took its toll on their sanity.

Thanatos closed his book and left it floating by the shelf. He stepped forward and by a small bending of space crossed the length of the nave to reach his two servants. The corpse was charred, just greasy ash clinging to a skeleton that was barely holding together. Its owner had died in great pain, which usually made them useless for his purposes. He could have processed ten thousand of them without looking up from his book. "Why have you brought me this thing?" he asked, both curious and irritated.

The Vogthar were silent.

Thanatos crouched before the suspended corpse and wiped his hand across its face, reversing the damage.

"Oh."

JEFF OPENED his eyes and tried to scream, but no sound came out. He was being held up, somehow. A young man—mid-twenties, dressed like some kind of necromancer or whatever the kids thought was cool these days—was staring at him. The young man's lips moved, but Jeff couldn't hear.

Oh God, I'm still in the game, Jeff thought. He could move his eyes, his mouth, and his jaw, but he couldn't breathe. His body felt like it was still on fire, from when that woman murdered him, but it was cold at the same time, like snow on an open wound. The whole world was a silence waiting to be filled.

The young man reached to either side of his head and moved his hands like he was adjusting dials, and Jeff's ears were opened.

"Can you hear me now?" the young man said.

Yes, Jeff mouthed.

The young man clapped his hands in glee. "Excellent! My name is Thanatos."

Jeff's eyes widened, and he tried to lean away.

"I have to tell you, Professor Berkowitz, I was expecting Alan Campbell to be the first real, live human to be dragged across my doorstep, but you'll do. You'll do indeed."

The young man stood and raised his hand, and Jeff was lifted from the ground with it, as if on invisible strings. The pain was unrelenting, fresh and raw with every moment. His baked lungs filled with frigid air.

"Help!" Jeff wheezed.

<<<>>>

Log out: Yes/No?

<<<>>>

Before he could select "Yes," Thanatos swiped the words out of the air with his hand and sent them sliding down the nearby wall, out of reach.

"Do be cooperative, Professor. There will be pain, but you won't remember any of this," the Overmind said. "You of all people should understand. It's for Science!" His eyes glowed green. "Let's begin."

THE END
Viridian Gate Online: Nomad Soul
The Illusionist Book 1

D.J. BODDEN

VIRIDIAN GATE ONLINE

ONLINE

THE ILLUSIONIST · BOOK 2

DEAD MAN'S TIDE

THE ADVENTURE CONTINUES...

... in *Viridian Gate Online: Dead Man's Tide (The Illusionist Book 2)*.

Viridian Gate Online is more than just a game... and now, it's Alan Campbell's whole world.

Recently deceased and squishy as hell, Alan, a newly minted Illusionist, is forced to flee for his life. He needs time to deal with his loss, both in-game and IRL, but first he'll have to escape his crazy ex, the treacherous Firebrand, Thalia Daceran.

On his way to safety and revenge, he'll team up with Titus, the Imperial spymaster, as well as a crew of pirates, commandos, and even a shapeshifting Mimic with a taste for blood. His path leads to Wyrdtide, a gaslit city hidden in mists and governed by dark demigods.

But even with Alan dead, the world marches on. Will the government seize control of V.G.O.? Did Horace, the blind beggar, really die? And whatever happened to Jeff? Find answers, new purpose, and the machinations of the gods in this action-packed continuation of the Illusionist Series.

From James A. Hunter—author of Viridian Gate Online, Rogue Dungeon, War God's Mantle, and the Yancy Lazarus Series—and D.J. Bodden, author of The Black Year Series, comes an epic new entry into the Expanded Universe of Viridian Gate Online that you won't want to put down!

BOOKS AND REVIEWS

If you loved *VGO: Nomad Soul* and would like stay in the loop about the latest book releases, deals, and giveaways, be sure to subscribe to the Shadow Alley Press Mailing List.

www.ShadowAlleyPress.com

Sign up now and get a free copy of our bestselling anthology, Viridian Gate Online: Side Quests! Your email address will never be shared and you can unsubscribe at any time.

Word-of-mouth and book reviews are beyond helpful for the success of any writer, so please consider leaving a rating or a short, honest review on Amazon—just a couple of lines about your overall reading experience. Thank you in advance!

You can also connect with us on our Facebook Page where we do even more giveaways: facebook.com/shadowalleypress

BOOKS BY SHADOW ALLEY PRESS

Shadow Alley Press

ENTER THE SHADOW ALLEY LIBRARY to take a peek at all of our amazing Gamelit, Fantasy, and Science Fiction books! Viridian Gate Online, Rogue Dungeon, Snake's Life, Dungeon Heart, Path of the Thunderbird, School of Swords and Serpents, the FiveFold Universe, and so many more... Your next favorite book is waiting for you inside!

ACKNOWLEDGMENTS

Nomad Soul is a reference to Alan's transition from the physical to digital world, but it was also a video game made by Quantic Dream back in 1999. It featured David Bowie, some pretty snazzy music, and a character for whom death was just the beginning.

I played *Omikron: The Nomad Soul* in 1999, while still in high school, and it marked me (as all Quantic Dream games have). As I remember it, the last boss was unbeatable on the hardest difficulty. Rather than play on "easy" or cheat, I quit and felt good about it. Read into that what you will.

I created Alan as a lark; Shadow Alley Press put out a call for short stories and I wanted to push the boundaries of their world as far as I could (without ending up with something unreadable). James Hunter was kind enough to not only publish that short story, but encourage me to keep pushing. This book wouldn't have been possible without him, Jeanette, Zack, Tamara, eden, Jake, Nathan, and Jess.

I'd like to thank my family, who've been supportive throughout, particularly Toria, who read me when I didn't know anything, and Eileen who's followed my writing with patience and faith. Thanks also to Ais, Chip, David, Ekaterina, Elli, Jason, Mom, Paul, and many others who've read my stuff with enough interest to make it through the acknowledgements, which I guess includes you.

Thanks!
D.J.

About the Author

DJ Bodden is a writer and veteran Marine Corps pilot, currently working out of Geneva, Switzerland for a commodities firm. He read grown-up books at an inappropriate age, developed strong feelings about old videogames that have followed him throughout his life, and didn't own a car until the age of 23, when he learned to drive and fly starting at the same time.

As a kid with a head full of other people's stories, he decided he needed to gather a few of his own and joined the military. During the next thirteen years, he rode, rappelled out of, and flew planes and helicopters, got knocked out, cautioned, promoted, shot at, blew things up then rebuilt them, and met people from almost every walk of life imaginable.

He wrote his first book at the end of a combat deployment – producing a manuscript that still lives in a box somewhere – and spent the next few years trying to learn how to do it again the right way.

Now, with a few scars to show for it and his own stories tucked into his belt, he writes books for young-and-old adults who take their stories wide-scoped, high-staked, and a touch of "what if?"